The Myrtle Tree

# The
# Myrtle Tree

Kaber Barras

Copyright © 2024 Kaber Barras

The moral right of the author has been asserted.

Apart from any fair dealing for the purposes of research or private study, or criticism or review, as permitted under the Copyright, Designs and Patents Act 1988, this publication may only be reproduced, stored or transmitted, in any form or by any means, with the prior permission in writing of the publishers, or in the case of reprographic reproduction in accordance with the terms of licences issued by the Copyright Licensing Agency. Enquiries concerning reproduction outside those terms should be sent to the publishers.

This is a work of fiction. Names, characters, businesses, places, events and incidents are either the products of the author's imagination or used in a fictitious manner. Any resemblance to actual persons, living or dead, or actual events is purely coincidental.

Matador
Unit E2 Airfield Business Park,
Harrison Road, Market Harborough,
Leicestershire. LE16 7UL
Tel: 0116 2792299
Email: books@troubador.co.uk
Web: www.troubador.co.uk/matador
Twitter: @matadorbooks

ISBN 978 1803136 271

British Library Cataloguing in Publication Data.
A catalogue record for this book is available from the British Library.

Printed and bound in Great Britain by 4edge Limited
Typeset in 10pt Adobe Caslon Pro by Troubador Publishing Ltd, Leicester, UK

Matador is an imprint of Troubador Publishing Ltd

### Acknowledgements

*With thanks to my amazing, loving partner for her relentless and unwavering support and belief.*

*I thank my parents and the armed forces for my first lessons in life and the 'School of Life' for the rest.*

### I dedicate this book to Ben

*Taken too soon and tragically gone,*
*You're a man far braver than I.*
*Lest we forget your young wife and son,*
*Our thoughts with them, now must lie.*
*Taken so quickly and robbed of your dreams*
*The best are all wanted elsewhere now, it seems.*
*We applaud your time served and you must take a bow,*
*Rest easy young man and watch over them now.*
*Sleep well in the comfort, as you peacefully rest,*
*That the new life you left us will be loved, cherished and blessed.*

*Those who do not know their history are doomed to repeat their mistakes.*
(George Santayana)


*With Cyberdefence there is virtually no deterrence in cyber warfare, since even identifying the attacker is extremely difficult and, adhering to international law, probably nearly impossible.*
(Dr Olaf Theiler, NATO Operations)

*And Adam did break a branch from the Tree of Knowledge, and after his death the Angel Gabriel did appear to Moses at the burning bush and hand unto him this rod.*
(Book of Exodus)

*And it came to pass, that on the morrow Moses went into the tabernacle of witness and beheld the Rod of Aaron, for the house of Levi was budded from Hadas and brought forth buds, and bloomed blossoms and yielded fruits.*
(Book of Numbers)

# Glossary

**Algorithm:** A process or set of rules to be followed in calculations or other problem-solving operations, especially by a computer.

**Benjamite:** Hebrew, formerly Binyamin, from the biblical tribal area of Benjamin. Thought to have been one of the twelve tribes of Israel who regrouped with the tribe of Judah after the Babylonian invasions, creating the kingdom of Israel.

**Centrifuge cascade:** Vast numbers of centrifuges interconnected to form a series or bank of separators to multiply the effects of nuclear enrichment.

**Esther (Ishtar or Isthar):** Persian (Old Iranian); means 'Eastern Star' or special star. Biblical Jewish heroine who became Queen of Babylonia.

**Ethernet:** A series or family of coaxial or fibre-optic cables used to connect and form networks, allowing computers and other devices to share files and transmit information efficiently.

**Hadassah:** From the Hebrew word 'hadas' meaning 'myrtle.' Pleasantly fragranced myrtle tree from the Myrtaceae family. Also, the birth name of a Jewish Queen of Persia.

**Hardware:** A collection of the physical parts of a computer system. Includes the computer case, monitor, keyboard and mouse. Also includes parts inside the computer case, such as the hard disk drive, motherboard, video card, and many others.

**Ishtar:** Babylonian goddess of sex, fertility and rebirth. Her name is used in the celebration of springtime, meaning to bloom, blossom or flourish. Also used by Jews and Christians in Passover and for the resurrection of Jesus, a period now referred to and pronounced as Easter.

**Malware:** A variety of forms of hostile, intrusive software. Malicious software used to disrupt computer operations, gather information, or gain access to computer systems. Includes viruses, worms, Trojans, rootkits, spyware, adware, rogue security software, and other malicious programs.

**Mass storage device:** A small data-storage device with a USB connector, designed to replace floppy disks and CDs. Also known as a flash stick, Cruzer Blade or pen drive.

**Myrtle tree:** Believed to be the Tree of Knowledge **or Tree of Life** in the Garden of Eden from where the serpent appeared to Adam and Eve. A beautiful, colourful, blossoming plant with a sweet-scented oil which records show has many healing properties dating back to 2500 BC.

*Myrtus communis*: The genus of a family of common myrtle. A native Mediterranean tree and refers specifically to the myrtle tree.

**Nuclear enrichment:** A process of converting and concentrating uranium for enhanced use of its energy.

**P1 centrifuge:** High-speed industrial mechanical separator driven by electric motors. Used to separate and extract uranium molecules to enhance the element's quality.

**PLC (programmable logic controller):** Used to control repetitive actions of machinery on factory assembly lines, amusement park rides, light fixtures, commercial fans, gates, valves, motors or barriers.

**RTU (remote terminal unit):** An electronic device that interfaces with objects in the physical world to a distributed control or SCADA system to control connected objects.

**Rod:** A shepherd's staff. A natural symbol of authority over his sheep. A staff that became Moses' symbolic authority over the Israelites.

**Rod of Aaron:** Believed to be the branch Adam took from the Tree of Knowledge and endowed with mystical powers, handed by Gabriel to Moses. One of twelve staffs, each representing one of the twelve tribes of Israel and inscribed with Aaron's name and the ten plagues of Egypt.

**Rootkit:** A set of software tools that enable an unauthorised user to gain control of a computer system without being detected.

**Sash:** Hebrew for rope, loop or strop.

**SCADA (supervisory control and data acquisition):** System which operates to provide control of remote equipment, used in buildings, airports, ships, and even space stations. Can remotely control heating, ventilation and air-conditioning systems, water treatment plants, civil defence systems and nuclear enrichment processing plants.

**Semite:** From the name Shem, the eldest son of Noah, and after the biblical flood, from the tribal area of the same name, thought to have been one of the twelve tribes of Israel.

**Shulamite:** Country girl chosen to be Queen above all other women.

**Software:** Information processed by computer systems, programs, data, libraries, and related non-executable data, such as online documentation or digital media.

**Stuxnet:** Nickname given by Microsoft to a particular virus, from the file names of 'Stub.Mrxnet'. A malicious computer worm uncovered in 2010, thought to have been in development since at least 2005. Specifically targets SCADA and PLC systems.

**Uranium:** A silver-grey element found in certain rocks. Creates energy through its radioactive properties. Used in reactors to make electricity or nuclear weapons.

**USB (universal serial bus):** For bussing/carrying lots of items. A universal one-size-fits port or socket on all computer hardware, allowing connection of add-on peripheral accessories including keyboards, printers, and many more.

**Wi-Fi:** A brand name, also known as 'wireless fidelity'. A wireless technology that uses radio waves to provide high-speed internet or computer appliance connections, often referred to as broadband.

**WLAN (wireless local access network):** Usually provided by a utility provider to supply access to an internet source using a broadband-width radio frequency.

**Worm:** A standalone malware computer program that replicates itself in order to spread to other computers.

# Prologue

## THE STORY OF ISHTAH FROM THE BOOK OF ESTHER, THE HEBREW BIBLE

In the city of the Elamite, in the ancient Parthian (old Persian) empire, King Ahasuerus held a 180-day feast in Susa. During this feast, whilst in high spirits from the wine, he ordered his Queen, Vashti, to appear before him and his guests, so he could show off her beauty. But when the court attendants delivered the King's command to Queen Vashti, she refused to come. Furious at her refusal to obey, the King asked his wise men what should be done. One of them said that all the women in the empire would hear that the King had commanded the Queen to be brought in before him, but she came not. Then they too would despise their husbands, and this would cause many problems in the kingdom. Therefore, it would be good to depose her.

To find a suitable new Queen, it was decreed that young virgins would be gathered to the palace from every province of the kingdom. Each underwent twelve months of beautification in Ahasuerus's harem, after which she would be called to go to the

King. When her turn came, she was given anything she wanted to take with her from the harem to the King's palace. She would go to the King in the evening, and in the morning go back to the harem where the concubines stayed. She would not return to the King unless he was sufficiently pleased with her to summon her again by name.

> *And he brought up Hadassah, that is Ishtar, his uncle's*
> *daughter: for she had neither father nor mother, and the maid*
> *was fair and beautiful; whom Mordecai, when her father and*
> *mother were dead, took for his own daughter.*
> (Book of Esther, 2:7)

Esther was the daughter of the Benjamite Abihail. When Cyrus gave permission for the exiles to return to Jerusalem, she stayed with Mordecai in the city of Susa. Mordecai was enslaved by Nebuchadnezzar, King of all Babylon, and for his freedom he was tasked to guard the city gates. It was known that Mordecai had a beautiful daughter working as a maid, known as Hadassah. She could not be exempted from the King's decree, and so she was taken to the house of concubines.

For his Queen, the King chose Hadassah, an orphan raised by her cousin, to replace the recalcitrant Queen Vashti. Only after joining the King's royal harem, where she waited to be chosen as Queen, was she given the name Ishtar (Esther). Hadassah, meaning Myrtle, became the King's Shulamite and lived out her life as a Queen at the beck and call of the King.

Whilst Mordecai was sitting guarding the King's gates, he overheard two wronged eunuchs and officers of the King's guards plotting to assassinate the King. Mordecai let Esther know, but Esther replied that there was a law that anyone who came unto the King uncalled by him should be put to death, 'except such to whom the King shall hold out his golden sceptre that they may live. But I have not been called to come in unto the King for these thirty days.' Esther gave this problem much thought, and concluded to sleep with her cousin Mordecai, knowing what the outcome would be. Hearing of this incestuous act of lust, the King, in a rage, immediately summoned his Queen, and Esther begat her attendance meeting with the King and explained to him that she had only slept with her cousin to gain attendance to the royal court to warn the King of the forthcoming attempt at his assassination. King Ahasuerus was pleased with his Shulamite, held out his golden sceptre, and Mordecai was given credit. The two conspirators were hanged by a sash on gallows.

Sometime after, as part of his official duties, King Ahasuerus granted one of the most prominent Princes in his realm, Haman the Agagite, special honours. All the people were to bow down to Haman when he rode his horse through the streets. All complied except for Mordecai, the enslaved Jewish gatekeeper, who would bow to no one but his one and only God. This enraged Haman, who, unaware of the new Queen's ethnicity, plotted with his wife and advisers to kill and extirpate all Jews throughout the Persian Empire, selecting the date for this act – Purim – by the drawing of lots. After laying charges of sedition against the Jews, by offering 10,000 silver talents, Haman gained the King's approval to write a decree for their destruction.

On hearing this news, Mordecai tore his robes and put ash on his head as a sign of mourning or grief. When Esther was told, she too was grieved, and sent Mordecai fresh robes, since none could 'enter into the King's gate clothed with sackcloth'. He refused them, and Esther sent 'Hatach, one of the King's chamberlains' appointed to wait on her, to ask Mordecai the cause of his mourning and why he had refused the clothes. Mordecai replied, explaining about Haman and the decree, sending her a copy of it, and the charge 'that she should go in unto the King, to make supplication unto him, and to make request before him for her people'. Esther again replied that there was a law that anyone who came unto the King uncalled by him should be put to death, 'except such to whom the King shall hold out his golden sceptre that they may live. But I have not been called to come in unto the King for these thirty days.' She was terrified for her life if she did as Mordecai said.

Mordecai was told Esther's reply and sent back a message that she should not think that she would escape the genocide because she was in the King's house, any more than all the other Jews. And further, that if she held her peace at this time, deliverance would arise from somewhere else, but she and her father's house would be destroyed. He ended his message with these consoling words: 'Who knoweth whether thou art come to the kingdom for such a time as this?'

Upon hearing Mordecai's message, Esther exhibited her resolution by sleeping with her cousin again and seeking spiritual strength before she was again called unto the King, that she might perhaps find favour in his sight and be the means of deliverance for her people, or else to die in the attempt.

> *'Go, gather together all the Jews that are present in Susa and fast ye for me, and neither eat nor drink for three days, night or day: I also and my maidens will fast likewise, and so will I go in unto the King, which is not according to the law, and if I perish, I perish.'*
> (Book of Esther, 4:16)

Mordecai followed her instructions. So, she, her maidservants, and all the Jews present in Susa fasted earnestly for three days as part of a supplication to God on Esther's behalf. At the end of the three days, Esther, dressed in her royal apparel, went bravely before the King, standing in the inner court where he sat upon his throne. When the King saw her, he was pleased with her, and held out his sceptre to her, thus saving her from death and indicating that he accepted her visit. She came forward and touched his sceptre. The King then asked Esther her will and what her petition and request of him was, promising to grant even up to half his kingdom should she ask it. Esther humbly requested that the King and Haman come to a banquet she had prepared. No one else was invited, which filled Haman with pride. During the banquet, Queen Esther requested of the King another banquet with him and Haman on the following day.

After the banquet, Haman ran into Mordecai sitting at the King's gate. He was so incensed with Mordecai for not deferring to him that, on the advice of his wife and friends, he ordered sash and gallows to be constructed, seventy-five feet (twenty-three metres) high, on which to hang Mordecai the next day after obtaining the King's consent.

That night, the King could not sleep, and so he had some histories read to him. From the text he remembered that Mordecai had saved him from an assassination attempt and had received no reward in return. Early the next morning, Haman came to the King to ask permission to hang Mordecai, but before he could do so, the King asked him, 'What should be done for the man whom the King delights to honour?' Haman thought the King meant himself, so said that the man should wear a royal robe and be led on one of the King's horses through the city streets, proclaiming before him, 'This is what is done for the man the King delights to honour!'

Pleased by this idea, the King startled Haman by commanding him to lead none other than Mordecai through the streets in this way, to honour him for previously telling the King of a plot against him. Haman obeyed, then, as Mordecai returned to his spot by the King's gate, rushed home grieving, and told his wise men and wife everything. His wife said to him, 'You will surely come to ruin!'

That evening, during the second banquet, King Ahasuerus again asked Esther what her petition was and made her the same promise as before. Esther asked that her life be spared, along with the lives of her people, the Jews of the Persian Empire, whom Haman had previously convinced the King must be massacred. In doing so, she declared her ethnicity. Haman's treachery so inflamed the King that he left the banquet and went into the palace garden. Seeing that his situation was precarious and unfavoured, Haman pleaded with Esther to save his life, ending up on her couch beside her as he begged, which, on the King's return from the garden, caused him to jump to an obvious conclusion. Seeing Haman thus, the King's wrath knew no bounds, thinking that Haman was about to molest Esther. He cried, 'Will he force the Queen also before me in my house?'; whereupon his chamberlains seized Haman, and one of them told the King of the sash and gallows Haman had constructed for Mordecai. The King told them, 'Hang him [Haman] thereon. May he be hanged by the sash on his gallows!'

And so, Haman was hanged on the gallows he had built for Mordecai, and the King's wrath was pacified. He then appointed Mordecai as his Prime Minister, after which Esther went again before the King, and 'fell down at his feet, and besought him with tears to put away the mischief of Haman'. Then, as before, the King held out his sceptre toward Esther and she stood and pleaded with him to 'reverse the letters' of Haman against the Jews. The King could not revoke a decree, but instead instructed Mordecai to issue a new decree giving the Jews the right to defend themselves. The second edict allowed the Jews to arm themselves and kill not only their enemies, but also their enemies' wives and children, as well as partake of the plunder. This precipitated a series of reprisals by the Jews against their enemies. The fight commenced on the 13th of Adar, the date the Jews were originally slated to be exterminated. Altogether, 800 attackers were killed in Susa alone, whilst 75,000 were killed in the rest of the empire. The Jews took no plunder.

The Jews established an annual feast, the feast of Purim (Lots), in memory of their deliverance. According to traditional rabbinic dating and the Book of Esther, this took place about fifty-two years after the start of the Babylonian Exile. Given the great historical link between Persian and Jewish history, modern Persian Jews are called 'Esther's children'. A building known as the Tomb of Esther and Mordecai is located in Hamadan, Iran, although the village of Kfar Bar'am in northern Israel also claims to be the burial place of Queen Esther.

# I

## CENTRAL POLICE HEADQUARTERS, TEHRAN, IRAN

### Summer 2010

The man lay exhausted on the cold, damp floor, coughing up bile and saliva. He gasped for air again as his captors kicked his kidneys before walking away, slamming the thick steel door and heaving the slide-over tower bolt into its locked position. The prisoner coughed again, but this time blood and snot came up. Both his lips were split and seeped blood. He could feel gaps in his right gum where he had lost some teeth; he guessed at least two. A clear, odourless liquid known as cerebrospinal fluid, dripped from his ears. His eyes were swollen, blue, black and red, and shut tight. His right cheekbone had been smashed and hung lower from torn muscle. He struggled to breathe. His prison uniform pants hung unfastened around his knees, offering him no protection or dignity. He lay on his left side, protecting his broken right cheek, curling himself into a ball to ease some of the pain from his ribcage. The prison cell stank of stale urine, vomit, and blood. The dampness seemed to maintain the stench as his nostrils sucked in what air they could from the wet slate slab. He coughed again and uncontrollably peed himself.

Deep in the bowels of the ancient prison, buried way beneath the modern government building, lay a nest of cruel, medieval barbarity, meted out by a select number of security officials. Nicotine smoke and spiced aromas wafted through its poorly lit passageways and scented the air as guards, blasé regarding the torture around them, crossed from room to room, talking, chatting and laughing as if they were office clerks discussing last night's TV.

The cell door's metal viewing window slid open, making a loud clunking noise. Instinctively, involuntarily, the prisoner flinched, curling into a tighter ball. A pair of dark brown eyes stared at him through the opening. Major Ahmadi, head of Natanz Nuclear Enrichment Plant security, looked calmly at him.

'That's enough. No more,' the major shouted abruptly. 'Feed him, clean him and send down the doctor, and bring him some blankets, you peasants. And open this damned door now!'

Rubber-booted footsteps pounded down the corridor and along the passageway toward the cell door. One guard shouted at another as someone rushed to unlock the door.

Although the prisoner knew him, the major still introduced himself and apologised for the interrogation techniques. 'This torture belongs to the Dark Ages. However, political prisoners should be in no doubt that the Islamic State of Iran must protect itself from tyranny at any time.'

Addressing an officer who was standing at the door, he demanded someone fetch two chairs and some fresh, clean water. 'These barbarians know nothing of good manners and reasoning, only brute force,' he said softly. 'The doctor is on his way for you, and you need to drink.'

Trying to win the prisoner over, he felt he could gain more information through a different approach. He was desperate to return to his superiors with some better news. He heard more footsteps and male voices talking as they approached. A guard arrived with two blue plastic chairs stacked one on top of the other, followed by a doctor in a smart suit and a younger man dressed as a medic. They carried first-aid bags, blankets, and bottles of water.

'I will leave you for a short while,' the major said, looking directly into the prisoner's eyes. Then he turned to the doctor. 'Take good care of him, Doctor, and nurse him well. I have promised him no more broken bones or beatings.'

The doctor looked subserviently at the major over his glasses and duly nodded. The younger medic helped the prisoner onto one of the chairs and attended to his injuries, pushing a bottle of water under his chin to wash his mouth before allowing him to drink. Another guard arrived with pale blue blankets, a red fleece top with matching tracksuit joggers, and some green plastic sandals. The doctor checked and rechecked the prisoner's wounds and gave him painkillers and sedation, while the medic carefully washed him down with wet wipes, towels and fresh water, then helped him to dress. The strong painkillers began their work and, after cleaning and the application of creams, his eyes opened enough to at least allow him to see his captors. Feeling some warmth from his wash and the clothes, he relaxed a little into the chair. His shivering slowed as he registered his bleak surroundings.

Finishing off his treatment, the doctor felt the presence of someone behind him. He pushed medical gauze into the prisoner's mouth and helped the first-aider to wrap his jaw in bandages. Making eye contact, but saying nothing, the doctor nodded to the first-aider to hurry. They finished, collected their equipment, and left.

Engrossed in the attention of being nursed and taking some comfort from the medical team's efforts, at first the prisoner didn't notice the captain of the SAVAK, Iran's secret police, standing at the cell doorway until the medics politely squeezed past him into the corridor. Then he froze, sitting bolt upright in the chair, gripping the chair legs with his calves, clenching his buttocks and clutching the blanket wrapped around him tighter, as if it could protect him. The shock of seeing his torturer again made him panic. His eyes opened a little wider and, as he gritted his teeth, his gum and jaw screamed with pain.

The Head of National Security stared down at him. 'Now we talk some more. Don't worry,' he said sarcastically, 'I am under strict orders: no more beatings or broken bones. Besides, we have just spent all that money on you with expensive Western medical supplies. The jogging suit is American and the painkillers are from Britain, I believe.' He looked down his nose sympathetically at the prisoner, then shouted over his shoulder, 'Where is that food? And bring me a table!'

He was a tall, skinny man who smoked heavily. He had served the Ayatollah loyally for years and was himself a member of a trusted inner circle of the regime. Now in his late fifties, he knew very little of modern computer viruses and malware. He was old school. Rising through the ranks, he'd been taught the dark arts of interrogation and torture from the days of the Cold War. He was a dinosaur in modern terms, but still highly efficient in administering brutality, fear, corruption and violence, and all via his loyal police thugs.

The prisoner was treated with some dignity. A guard helped him eat a small amount of watery noodles from a ration pack with a plastic spoon. He was ravenous and wanted to gorge the food, but it just aggravated the pain in his jaw. He managed several spoonsful, and felt every sip hit the bottom of his empty belly. He drank some more water, and later managed a cool cup of black coffee with a little sugar. The captain sat and talked a little, but mostly smoked a lot and watched, sometimes making small talk with the guards as the prisoner sipped his drink and worried about his fate.

After the prisoner finished his meal, and before the captain lost his patience, he spoke directly to him. 'If it were left to me, I would package your ears and fingers one by one and have them posted back to your family. But then you have no family, do you? Or just a cousin, perhaps?' he toyed. 'A cousin with whom you are very close, and…' He paused again, enjoying the game. 'What do you call it? Skype, I think. No? An American cousin, maybe? Or is she British? Is she, too, a Jew, or just another British non-believer with no morals?'

Mord did not reply.

'Hmm?' the captain continued. 'You have colluded with this Western woman many times via this Skype channel, no?' He took a long draw on his cigarette and slowly blew some of the smoke into the prisoner's face, then, as if checking his behaviour, blew the rest up toward the ceiling. 'She is a very pretty lady. She is your girlfriend, maybe?' He paused, enjoying the tease. 'Or just a cousin? Perhaps you are closer to each other? Do you fuck her? It is written that Jews enjoy incest. It is written that Esther fucks her cousins. But you know this, yes?'

Unable to contain himself any longer, he then leaned forward over the table and spoke quietly, almost appealing to Mord. 'Tell me what you know, before I have your worthless skin peeled off slowly. Tell me what you know and I will spare you, you traitor.'

Mord trembled, knowing he would carry out his threats if allowed. 'I don't know anything more than I have already told you,' he pleaded. 'I have tried and tried to reverse the virus, but it seems impregnable. I don't know, I tell you. It's nothing to do with me.'

The captain pushed his nose up to the prisoner's and spat, 'Fingers will be chopped first! Hold him still! Hold the Jew still, I said!'

Mord writhed away as best he could, but the two guards held him down. One over his shoulders, the other grabbed both his hands and pushed them down onto the bare wooden tabletop. It was futile, and the onslaught of more pain seemed inevitable. Flicking away his cigarette butt into the corner of the cell, the guard pulled out a larger-than-pocket-sized knife.

The captain laid the cold, shiny steel blade, edge up, over Mord's middle-finger knuckle, allowing it to rest on the skin, as if to tease him. 'The virus has been traced back and proven that it originates from your laptop, my friend. Yet you, a senior engineer, a high-profile and trusted citizen of our great country, say you cannot explain how?' he asked sarcastically.

Shaking and sweating, Mord's composure faltered and, with a quiver in his voice, he spoke again. 'I have told you over and over for the last two weeks. It was me who found and reported the damned virus. As God is my witness, I swear to you, the clues are in the virus. I have tried to work it out but I can't. You have interrogated me for weeks. I know nothing more, I swear.'

The captain could not trust or believe his prisoner. He tilted the knife left then right with his left hand, still teasing with the threat of amputation. His left hand reached up to his left breast pocket and pulled out a sweat-stained handkerchief. Pressing the knife down harder on the engineer's knuckles, he tipped a bottle of water over his fingers and then soaked the handkerchief. Once wet, he slowly put one corner between his teeth and, with his right hand, dramatically twisted the cloth into what looked like a tourniquet. 'You have had some painkillers, yes? Let's hope the British pharmaceuticals firms haven't cheated us also,' he joked as he pressed down with the knife blade. 'Pin him down firm!' he snapped to the guards.

Mord let out a shriek of pain as he watched the knife press into his finger bone and begin to cut through the skin, drawing blood. He screamed louder. 'You bastard! You fucking bastard!' he cried.

He shrieked again and the captain stopped. Their hands trembling, the guards relaxed their hold on Mord and he collapsed, banging his forehead on the table, grabbing the edges of its square wooden top with both hands, trying to steady himself. His head spun, and he could feel the nausea rise from the pit of his near-empty stomach as his abdominals contracted with the reflex. He could taste the noodle soup in his mouth once more.

'Enough,' said the captain in a disappointed tone. 'Enough of this!' Dropping the knife and flicking his left hand, he gestured to the guards to release their hold. 'I am…' He paused, as if to make sure the engineer was listening. 'I am a man of my word, Mord. I have promised no more beatings or broken bones. You know you will go on trial for this? You know you will be hanged by the sash? What can I do to prevent that? Nothing if you don't help me. Work with me, Mord, and I will help you.'

Mord whispered pathetically to his torturer. 'I know nothing more than I have told you.'

'I am a man of my word,' the captain repeated. 'I have promised no more beatings or broken bones.'

He looked up at one of the guards. The guard was also an aspiring career man. The captain trusted him and knew him and his family well. He had children and a family to feed. He knew he had to move up the ladder, and so was keen to please the captain.

In turn, the captain too wanted the guard to do well, and had tried in his old-school ways to develop the younger man. Now he nodded to him.

'Fetch me some water and towels. He will talk eventually.'

The loyal guard returned with a colleague and a trolley. On the trolley lay four folded green towels and four fifteen-litre plastic bottles of water from the cooler dispenser's reserve cupboard. Mord could only stare at the approaching trolley and focus on keeping his bladder in check. He knew he could not escape the next punishment and torture, but it would take all three guards to hold him down as he suffered his fate. The remaining guard in the cell grabbed him from behind and from his uniform pocket pulled two plastic zip ties. He seized Mord's left hand, looping it with one tie, then, forcing both hands behind his back, applied the second tie quickly and efficiently.

The captain's favourite guard shouted to his colleague. 'Grab him and hold him back.'

The colleague obliged. The captain pushed the table up against the grey concrete cell wall whilst his favourite guard strapped some more ties around Mord's ankles, securing them to the chair legs. The guard with the trolley then pulled out his tie wraps, applied them to just beneath Mord's knees and again secured them tightly to the chair legs. Mord was screaming and fighting, his head flailing in all directions, trying to lash out at any of his attackers, to hit any guard in any way he could. He tried to headbutt them, but the guards had him secured now, and tilted the chair back so it only just leaned against the table. Propped in position at approximately fifty-five degrees, he was ready.

Soaking two towels in water to enhance the sensation, one guard placed one over Mord's eyes and the other over his face, smothering his nose and mouth, then pulled them tight over his broken jaw and swollen eyes. The captain clicked his fingers and a guard slowly poured the first fifteen litres of water over the prisoner's covered mouth and nose. Mord was drowning, choking, gasping and gagging for breath, intermittently catching the slightest drop of air as the guards poured more water. He struggled to spit out any of the water that entered his mouth and throat.

The drowning effect ceased only when the captain said so. He was skilled and very experienced in this. The guards watched and learned as he decided exactly when to stop the procedure and allow Mord to clear his lungs of water. After being subjected to waterboarding for over an hour, using almost all the sixty litres and wrestling with his torturers, due to exhaustion, starvation and a punctured lung, Mord died, leaving his captors only the same message: 'Myrtus had a sash: 09 05 97. We are all Esther's children. By the Staff of Moses under the Tree of Knowledge I will die!'

Disposing of the engineer's body was a formality for the guards. There would be the usual paperwork to be done, and the corrupt morgue staff would collect the corpse in due course. Then the regular police department would be informed, and they would do the legwork in finding relatives and composing an appropriate press release.

~

The captain returned to the fresh air and sunshine several storeys above to the polished floors, mahogany desks and hands-free speakerphones. Reaching his plush modern office, he found the major sitting in one of his reading chairs, drinking a glass of tea.

After the former had washed away the filth of the cells and changed his shirt in his en-suite bathroom, the captain and the major discussed the meaning of Mord's repeated messages. Had he been a clever spy for the Americans or the Israelis? If so, how had he got so far into Iran's nuclear enrichment programme for so long? Could Mord's message really be a clue connected to the virus? If so, what did it mean? If not, then why had the babbling engineer kept repeating it? The conversation became heated and a row ensued over the prisoner's death. The major was angry at the loss of a source of intelligence. The captain was blasé at the loss of a Jew. As they argued, the major, dressed in his immaculate uniform, stood up and accused the captain of carelessness. The two men began shouting. The captain reminded the major that he may be a higher rank, but *he* was captain of the SAVAK and Head of National Security, and to cross him with such impudence would be fatal. He answered only to Major General Arshiya, the commander of the Quds, the Islamic Revolutionary Guard Corps, and he in turn answered only to the Ayatollah.

After the captain's threat, both men calmed down. The captain was experienced in the arts of manipulation and threat. After reaffirming his chain of command and authority, given to him by the Interior Secretary to the Prime Minister, he handed the major a glass of fine brandy and both sat down to discuss their dilemma. They agreed to work together and on how they would update Commander Arshiya. They toasted the Ayatollah and the Islamic Republic, then continued their discussion of their plan that was already in motion.

# 2

# BNFL SELLAFIELD, MOX PLANT, CUMBRIA, ENGLAND

The wiper blades heaved their way across the windscreen as the rain thumped on the glass. The inside of the window was misted and vision was poor, but that suited them for the moment. General car litter scattered the dashboard and the seats were reclined to lower their silhouettes. The driver flicked the wipers occasionally and the passenger adjusted the heater controls to give the screen a blast of hot air when he felt it was needed. They repeated this process over and over, as if well-rehearsed. The steam from their breath and their wet coats kept the heater working hard. The hire car's engine ticked over quietly but could not be heard above the bombardment of the lashing rain. The nondescript silver Renault sedan blended in amongst the many other vehicles. Several hundred metres away from the gate area and access road, as far back as possible, it had been reversed neatly into its parking bay, grille out, with its rear bumper only millimetres away from the water-filled red parking bollards at the rear of the area. Where better to hide a car than in a full car park?

The awful weather was their ally. The torrential lashings obscured them from view and provided good cover. People just did not notice their surroundings when the rain was so bad. They would not pay attention when the weather was bashing down. Running for buses and cars was all done by a sixth sense and in ten-yard dashes with few glances. But the Nuclear Police would pay attention, for what was not their ally was time. The longer they sat there, the sooner an armed British Nuclear Police van would sweep past and take a closer look.

The driver sat up a little and tapped the passenger's arm. The passenger hit the heater to position four. The driver fingertipped the wipers onto full speed and a bucketload of water was pushed from the glass. The windscreen demisted from the dashboard vents upward, slowly allowing a blue Ford minibus to appear through the blurred screen, travelling the mile or so from the plant to the staff car park. The company park and ride bus found the designated lay-by and its passengers disembarked. A blonde-haired woman in a beige raincoat dropped down the one step and thrust a large black brolly into the air. She checked her direction once and then forged forward as the westerly wind sprayed salt water at her from the Irish Sea. In a ten-yard dash, she battled across the car park to a white Honda Jazz. As if automated, she threw the brolly into the trunk and her handbag across the driver's seat, rotated elegantly on her right foot and glided in. A few minutes passed until the car showed some signs of life. First, the brake lights radiated through the foul downpour, then the headlights blinked on and then wipers pushed across the screen. The Honda moved away and left the car park, its headlights flashing up and down as it bobbed over the speed bumps toward the exit.

The Renault driver waited. Their windscreen was still clearing but they had time. There was no rush; this was purely a surveillance job. Allowing time, without the headlights on, he casually released the handbrake and gently moved off, away from the nuclear site's south gate park and ride entrance. He checked his speed and counted eight seconds between him and the car in front. A good, safe distance, but their quarry would be totally unaware even without the torrential weather. The car headed south, away from the plant and on into the village. The Renault followed, seemingly innocently, cruising a hundred yards behind. Two miles farther on, the little hatchback slowed, showing its brake lights, and then indicated a right turn. The Renault driver slowed too and looked at his passenger, who looked up from a plug-in Garmin satnav and reassured him that it was okay to follow. Allowing the Honda to move out of sight, the driver slowed more than needed and casually turned right also.

After passing under a railway bridge approaching the coastline, the woman pulled over to the left and stopped at a row of shops, which included the village store. The Renault driver pulled up early, just before a sharp turn under an arched bridge, using the turn to keep out of view. The road behind was empty. Slowly, he crept through the archway and tucked into an access-way on the left. After only minutes, the woman exited the store with some items in her arms, ran back out into the rain and jumped into her car to continue her journey. The Renault followed her out of the village.

After several miles' drive, at a junction with a pub on its right, the woman turned right off the main drag, down a much smaller lane, and passed a village hall and green on the left. Ahead, to the left was an old, three-storey coach house divided into two properties. Approaching the junction, the Renault driver slowed and his passenger checked the satnav, confirming that the road off to the right was not a dead end and therefore was safe for them to enter. They followed the Honda down the lane and watched until it slowed to a crawl, steered left off the lane, then right, and parked in the driveway of the coach-house property nearest to the road. The two properties were almost identical: early Victorian, cobblestone with sandstone corners. Both looked as though they had been modernised way back in the '80s, and the right-hand property had been given an adjoining garage in the right gable, with doors added later. The land to the right was rectangular and overgrown, the hedge obscuring the house and the views from the lane that ran down the right-hand side of the property to the beach.

The village was deserted and the rain still thundered down, keeping the inhabitants within their cosy dwellings. The Renault driver stopped well back and then, skilfully, using only the clutch pedal and the car engine's idle tick-over, smoothly and quietly reversed the sedan back and off the road into a care-home gateway, hiding it under some trees. The passenger got out into the rain, flipped a tweed flat cap over his head and pulled up his collar as he walked. Passing the property and continuing down to the first bend, he pulled out a pair of compact field glasses and observed. The driver watched the woman fumble in the porch and mess with her hair, then bend down and pick up some items from the porch floor. Finding her keys, she vanished into the property. With nothing more to see, the man with the binoculars returned to his partner in the Renault.

They waited twenty minutes and watched the woman leave. There was still no rush. The job was surveillance and the best way to do that was slowly. They were used to this type of work and were good at it. They had been well briefed on their quarry. All this type of surveillance work came straight from an office, posing as an upmarket property developer agency in London. The agents, in turn, posed as property hunters on behalf of their client. The cover story worked perfectly, and even if they were caught, the worst they were doing was harmlessly trespassing and looking for speculative investments. They could easily apologise, leave their bogus business card with its fake London address and that would be the end of the matter. This job was a week's work and they were three days in and still on their first hire car of three.

Once the little Honda was well on its way and they were confident she would not return, the two men drove past the house and parked up further down the lane so as not to be seen by any residents, then walked back up to the house and headed straight for the rear. The rain continued. Slowly, they checked the place, looking through and trying all the windows. Everywhere was locked tight, even the run-down garage to the right of the property. Through its grimy, cobwebbed window, the driver could make out motorbike handlebars protruding from canvas dust sheets, which were surrounded by workbenches and the usual tools. The up-and-over front and side doors were secure. The passenger checked the rear house windows. Again, all the sashes were firmly shut. He peered through a newly installed window into a kitchen. A foot or so from the window, he saw a solid wooden table, filled with newspapers, receipts, mugs, wallpaper rolls and a still-wet new telephone directory still in its plastic delivery sleeve. The table had a cleared space and a chair where someone had sat, and to the right of a coffee mug was a neat stack of brand-new travel brochures. Someone was planning a trip. Scattered around on kitchen worktops were decorating materials, coveralls, a paint-spattered radio and dust sheets. The rear kitchen door and its frame were solid oak, in a cottage style, and again had been fitted recently. The lock was a rim lock, all parts accessible only from the inside, and its firm snugness in its frame suggested it had sliding bolts to the top and bottom. The passenger tutted, disappointed at the level of security. They were going to need keys, and for that they needed to do more surveillance. Break-ins were messy and always left clues. Obtaining keys was far more professional but took longer.

The two men returned to the comfort of their vehicle, shook off the surplus rain and drove casually back to their hotel.

# 3

## CONTROL ROOM 4, URANIUM ENRICHMENT PLANT, NATANZ, IRAN

The engineers on shift that evening sat about in the main control room on their high-backed operator chairs, relaxed and chatting in their lab coats. All was quiet and orderly. The control panels, with bank after bank of lights, meters and monitors, were all behaving and operating as expected. Clipboards were picked up, checked and cross-referenced, then put back down again, and glasses of tea were sipped as the four men discussed politics and someone else's wife.

Two rooms down the hall in Computer Room 4, a dim green overhead emergency exit light flickered in the blackness, casting a dull green glow across the room, enough to light up a bank of computer screens and monitors, exposing their redundant keyboards and associated peripheral hardware. Their standby lights flickered and blinked, some red, some orange, some green or blue, but all indicating their appliance's patience, as they sat in the pitch blackness of the room, waiting to be disturbed once again by some human intervention so their hard drives' real skills could be put to the test once more. They would normally have to wait several more hours until the next shift entered the locked compartment, extracted their knowledge and services, and put them to work once more for another relentless hour-after-hour session.

Suddenly, out of the darkness, by instruction, unannounced and unscheduled, the silence was interrupted by the gentle hum of a distant computer. Across the room, on an abandoned and littered office desk, the screen of an unclosed laptop flickered into life. Its monitor jumped with copious amounts of bright colours as it scrambled through a sequence, from white-on-black text to images and script, to a colourful Microsoft logo, and then to a vibrant, multicoloured image of a family wedding. The man on the screen in the wedding photograph was a thirty-something Iranian; a professional with a PhD in particle physics, a chemistry expert specialising in the making of polymeric membranes for gaseous diffusion, part of the process of uranium enrichment.

The red standby light changed to a pale blue, whilst the orange Wi-Fi standby light blinked a while, then changed to a solid pale blue colour also. Once the initial tests and checks were complete, the laptop established that its battery was fully charged and it was ready to perform its next set of programmed tasks. One by one, it began posting onto the foreground of the wedding photograph images of folder after folder, icon after icon, all depicting different functions, checking that all were now correctly installed, available for use and exactly in position as the hard drive inside the machine worked busily to organise itself. Once its screen was fully and correctly displaying all the images, the laptop's pale blue Wi-Fi light flickered almost randomly as the cybernetics inside initiated the hunt for its next set of instructions. The machine whizzed, whirred and clicked as it searched its thick-walled, locked environment for its best options. Feverishly, it scoured its Bluetooth, Wi-Fi,

Ethernet, cabled and wireless internet options for the best service provider. It learnt instantly, and established that its absolute best connection, on this occasion, was Wi-Fi. Its orange Wi-Fi standby light stopped flashing and glowed a solid cobalt blue, as if it were now a team member, proud of its achievement in securing the best channel for communication.

Now in charge of its own tasks, the small black HP Q notebook autonomously sent an electrical power charge to a long, black appendage jutting out of the left-hand side of its undercarriage. Again, in a flash, the accessory's standby light flickered from green to bright blue as it burst into life. In the bottom right-hand corner of the laptop screen, an icon of a computer connecting with a USB appeared. The screen showed the message 'Pen drive now installed.' Once established and happy with its connectivity, the laptop ran more checks. Its clicking and whirring resonated down through the metal office desk legs and into the carpeted floor. As the laptop worked itself into a frenzy and beavered away, one by one all the monitors in the room flashed into life. The laptop showered the gloom with light, revealing many more desktop and laptop computers, which seemed to be overlooked and guarded by a huge bank of overhead monitors and TV screens stretching along the length of a curved control desk. Papers, files, documents, pens and pencils littered the desk, along with the obligatory unfinished cups of coffee.

The black pen drive immediately set about its sinister task and released its virus via the helpless laptop. The virus was now waking up every computer in the room, scouring their guts and motherboards to establish whether they were suitable hosts. Looking for authorisation to access each hard drive and system, it searched each computer individually for its Microsoft registration and access codes. Stealthily, it set about targeting and infecting all relevant systems and programs, depositing its malware like a bug laying its eggs inside an unsuspecting host. Before installing its malicious files, the virus wormed its way through every available Microsoft Windows registration, checking all computers that might be operating the German manufacturer Siemens' Step 7 program, before delivering its payload. Only when it identified a computer with the registration number of 19790509 did it choose to leave it unharmed and move on to the next machine, spreading its infection like a military transport plane dropping its camouflaged troops into targeted territory. Cleverly, at the same time, it laid down a rootkit to mask its very existence. Eventually, every screen and monitor in the room glowed, casting an eerie, artificial light into every corner of the compartment. One by one, each screen showed its agreement to its new instructions by displaying line after line of algorithm numbers. Slowly, as if in unison, each screen reflected its corresponding computer status by revealing a Microsoft icon and a mouse-controlled cursor hovering over the yes-or-no request window. As each mouse arrow autonomously clicked on the 'yes' button, the screens reflected their computers' acceptance of and conformity to those commands. Gently and quietly, one by one, the monitors and their associated computers returned to their silent and dark standby mode. Slowly, bit by bit, the light in the room faded. Shutdown after shutdown caused the multicoloured, brilliantly lit room to again become a blackened cell. Finally, only the humming and whirring of a lone laptop on the office desk could be heard, frantically trying to finalise its operational tasks; to complete its mission, shut down, and hide its activity. Unable to close down, its monitor displayed the same message repeatedly, as if caught in an automated loop. Despite its given protocol, the virus had not finished and had by now become cleverer than it was programmed, or indeed intended to be. The genie wanted out of the bottle and the laptop tried desperately to keep the cork in place as it looped its final instructions up onto its screen, over and over, as if locked in a power struggle. Line after line, time after time, the virus presented itself via the monitor, revealing its final message in code:

*https://Stub.MrXnet.19790509_MYRTUS_20070924...*
*https://Stub.MrXnet.19790509_MYRTUS_20070924...*
*https://Stub.MrXnet.19790509_MYRTUS_20070924...*
*https://Stub.MrXnet.19790509_MYRTUS_20070924...*
*https://Stub.MrXnet.19790509_MYRTUS_20070924...*
*https://Stub.MrXnet.19790509_MYRTUS_20070924...*
*https://Stub.MrXnet.19790509_MYRTUS_20070924...*
*https://Stub.MrXnet.19790509_MYRTUS_20070924...*

# 4

# HMS NELSON NAVAL BARRACKS, PORTSMOUTH, ENGLAND

The morning sun shone through the grime-caked, old glass windows like razor blades behind his pupils. He screwed up his eyes tight to try and relieve the pain as the rays scratched his eyeballs. He heard what he thought was classical music from somewhere. His head throbbed. His left arm would not move. It ached. He could feel that unmistakable feeling of pins and needles, right down to his fingertips. His hand felt swollen. Every digit seemed to throb. His knuckles lay on the wooden floorboards, his hand at almost ninety degrees to his arm. His bicep had been pushed outward and flattened against the bare metal bed frame, and that too throbbed. His head was heavy and sore. He stared down at the bare floor. Saliva dripped from the right corner of his mouth, but the blood had long since dried. His nose was blocked with snot, blood and grunge. He struggled to breathe through his nostrils. His mouth was dry as he alternated breathing between the two. His left eye stared down at the bare wooden floor. He felt nauseous.

Eventually, his brain told his arm to move. He was not sure of the time but it was definitely morning. Slowly, he gathered his bearings and pushed his legs down and away from his stomach. The stretching felt good. He rolled onto his back. He could taste blood as he licked his lips, trying to clear his mouth. The pressure on his left arm started to release, and that felt good too. He felt like he had done several rounds with a heavyweight boxer. He rolled back onto his side, away from the light, and slowly lifted his left arm, glancing at his Bulova Marine Star diver's watch.

His eyes opened almost fully and started to focus on a figure lying on a bare bunk opposite him. The morning sunlight made it difficult to see, but he made out the silhouette curled up in the foetal position, unmoving and facing away from him. As his focus improved, he saw that the figure too had blood on his head. He tried to rise but was stopped dead by a jolt to his right arm. To his alarm, he realised that it was handcuffed to the steel bed frame.

'What the… What the fuck is going on?' he hollered. His senses sharpened, sobering him immediately, and his situation became apparent. 'You bastards,' he muttered. 'Shit! You bastards! What the fuck?' The handcuffs were not tight, but what about the blood? How come there was blood on the pillow? He did not feel hurt, apart from his massive headache and his nose feeling thick and blocked. Slowly, he sat up and eased the strain off his right wrist. Sitting upright, clothed only in his boxers and T-shirt, he felt his head begin to clear as the pressure in it released. Then his nose and lip began to throb. 'Finny,' he muttered. 'Fin, are you okay, mate?' His mouth was bone dry. Quietly, he called to the man in the other bunk again.

The figure was slowly stirring and groaning as if in pain.

'Finny, are you okay, mate? What the hell happened? What's with these handcuffs?'

The figure on the opposite bed was Greg Finlay. They had been good friends and colleagues for many years. Greg began to cough and sounded like he was going to throw up.

'Oh God, my head… oh, my head hurts,' he repeated. 'Greg, get up. Greg!' he called in a louder voice.

There was no reply.

He remembered the date and slowly recalled the previous night's events. It had certainly been eventful. His leaving night-out had not gone smoothly. He yelled again, louder than ever, and his voice echoed down the dormitory and into the hallway. His brain flashed from pub to strip joint and then on to the nightclubs. Slowly, he recalled his movements, and the topless girls his mates had tried to set him up with. Drink after drink, shot after shot, he remembered. After some serious drinking throughout the day and a meal at around five, he'd finally succumbed to the alcohol and quietly collapsed at around 12.30. He vaguely recalled a long walk back to base and how, in their drunken stupor, he and Greg had walked straight into a moving tram, busting his nose and lip, splattering them both with his blood. After a group argument about visiting the local A&E, they'd settled on sickbay in the morning, although he had no intention of attending, knowing that there was no real damage.

'Morning, Chief,' a chirpy voice called from the hallway.

He groaned. 'Is that you, Dinger?' he replied in a croaky voice.

A head popped around the doorway. 'Greetings,' Dinger said sarcastically.

'Hmm,' he managed, aware of his situation and not wanting to prolong the joke with the handcuffs. 'Could you, err, do the honours, mate? My arm's bleeding.'

The face of Dinger Bell peered back at him. A slightly younger man, tall, thin and weathered, with middle-age creases. Dinger looked him in the eye and said, 'Err, sorry, pal – not my department, and we all know how dangerous a bear with a sore head can be. Very, very dangerous indeed!'

'Ha bloody ha, ha,' he retorted. 'Very friggin' funny. Are you going to fill me in on all the details? Cause I'm not too happy now, and my friggin' arm is killing me. You wankers. And I want a shower. Come on, Dinger, sort it out. And what about Greg?'

'I'll see what I can do,' said Dinger. 'As for Greg, he was checked an hour ago by Nobby Hall and apparently, he's been certified as clinically dead, mate. He flatlined twice before we put a mirror over his mouth for a final check. He's beyond it!' And with that, Dinger vanished.

He could hear his footsteps moving away down the hallway and getting fainter. As he listened, he threw himself back on the bed and exhaled heavily. He could smell and taste the stale alcohol on his breath. 'I need some more sleep,' he muttered, and drifted back into a deep slumber.

Thirty minutes or so later, he woke. Someone had removed the handcuffs. Slowly, he rose, rummaged through his holdall, grabbed his washbag, wrapped a towel around himself and headed for the shower room on the same floor. He pushed past a few guys in towels and flip-flops and, excusing himself, pushed open a toilet cubicle door and, without closing it, started to pee. Now he was upright, he reached up with both arms and clung to the top of the cubicle walls to steady himself. Stretching every muscle in his body, he let out a huge yawn, causing his towel to drop to the floor. Behind him he heard laughter and murmurs of 'Uh-oh!' and 'Someone's suffering,' followed by more laughter. He really could not be bothered and ignored them, continuing to relieve himself. His arm and nose still hurt. Seeing that the showers were all still in use, he decided to have a shave first at the nearest empty basin.

He splashed his face with warm water. It felt good, like a magic healing potion. Immediately, his head felt fresher. Washing his eyes and nose of grunge and blood from his lip, he dipped his razor and carefully prepared to shave, staring at the man in the mirror. He was now a retired forty-something. Two hundred and twenty pounds; six foot; fair hair; tired, bloodshot blue eyes; and a partial stubbly beard that had a hint of ginger if not cut, which he decided had to come off, and soon. He looked at the scar under his right eye. People thought he'd got it from his tough line of work, but the truth was it came from a nasty domestic fight with his ex-wife, years ago. He looked harder at himself and saw that he was tired. Lines were appearing under his eyes and the muscles under his chin sagged a little, and although he had stopped smoking years ago, his teeth were still slightly tarnished. He had average looks and understood that he was definitely not catalogue-model material. But it did not matter now, and his mind drifted to his future.

A heavy thump on his right arm brought him back to reality. A colleague shoved his head into Ed's space and spattered the tiled wall with toothpaste foam that oozed from his mouth. 'Ed! I got rabies, call a medic, quick!'

Ed glanced over with little enthusiasm at the paste foaming in the sink next to him. Other guys laughed and poked fun. 'Piss off,' Ed grunted. 'I think you'll find it's more like chlamydia, knowing you. Mind you, come to think of it, you do shag a lot of dogs!'

The men all laughed and the shower room settled back down. After a long shower, Ed returned to the empty dorm to see that Greg too had risen from the dead.

Ed had checked out of his petty officer's cabin apartment in Rodney Block for a temporary overnight holding room. As a leaver, he'd chosen a hassle-free morning and had gutted his Chief's cabin and decided to hand it over the day before, opting for a bare, stripped bed in an empty dorm and borrowing basic bedding from the stores. He and Greg had slept in the old Victorian dormitory block assigned to leavers, where there were no creature comforts and where all, irrespective of rank, status and privilege, were treated the same. Come the morning, leavers would be civilians and, therefore, all the same rank. His base station had been Poole in Dorset, which he had left two weeks ago. All his personal belongings had been parcelled up and shipped back home courtesy of the British Forces Post Office, leaving him free of luggage except for his holdall containing his weekend essentials.

Dinger Bell shoved his head around the door again and asked him if he was ready for breakfast.

Ed nodded slowly and looked up into a grimy, chipped mirror. Turning, he looked at Dinger. 'How do I look?' he asked.

Dinger stared back, laughing, and simply replied, 'Like shit, you old git. If you can't handle your leaving do then you'll be no good to us on your stag night. Now come on, hurry up – we've got work to do, kit to sort and a full English to get through, and I am bloody starving.'

Ed nodded. 'You go; I'll be down in a minute.'

'Sure,' said Dinger. 'Come on then, hurry up and I'll get us some coffees.' With that he left, shouting at the top of his voice to Greg to hurry up, as he passed the shower rooms and headed for the dining hall.

Ed looked down at the metal bed, grabbed the sheets and blanket and, pulling them off the bed, threw them into the hall. He picked up his old, battered leather holdall from the floor and dumped it on the bare mattress. Lethargically, he packed his washbag and last night's dirty clothes, including his bloodied shirt, and zipped the bag shut. Once dressed in fresh jeans, a polo shirt and a pair of suede desert boots, he made his way down the corridors and two flights of stairs toward the canteen. His head was thick and fuzzy but he was determined to get his last full English courtesy of Her Majesty. Leaving the accommodation block, he crossed the road and the fresh air hit him hard. He took a massive lungful through his nostrils then exhaled. His eyes watered but it felt good. He made his way up the pavement, past the NAAFI and launderette block on the ground floor, and turned right through a set of double doors. HMS *Nelson* was possibly the oldest naval base, and most blocks had last been refurbished in the late '80s and were well past their sell-by date. Some of the blocks were more modern, but what the hell did he care? This was his last day. His head hurt from a serious hangover and he really didn't give a shit.

He grabbed the handrail and hauled himself up the stairs to the first floor and into the senior rates' block. This was where all the chiefs and petty officers, warrant officers, Royal Marine sergeants, colour sergeants and masters-at-arms ate, drank, watched films, held parties and cocktail nights, and generally socialised. The senior rates' mess, or NCOs' room, took up the first floor and was half the length of the block. It was one of the buildings that had not been upgraded. It was like Ed and his peer group, he thought: well-worn but comfortable. It reminded him of an old village golf or cricket club function room, complete with typical kitchen, bar area and toilets. The only upgrade in recent years had been the conversion of the men's toilets to a modern unisex affair with a Ministry of Defence attempt to move the mess into the twenty-first century and integrate the female NCOs.

It was Saturday morning and the base was quiet. On the way in he picked up a daily paper from the stand in the entrance hall. He had always preferred the quiet of weekends on base, as all the married guys travelled home, leaving the singles with the run of the place. Simple luxuries like sharing the communal TV or getting to read his newspaper of choice in peace were so much more accessible at weekends. Come Monday, this place would be heaving with about sixty non-commissioned officers, all scurrying about to get back into their work patterns and their naval routines after their short civilian encounters over the weekend. That had been him, too, over the years. From time to time, he had joined those masses of 'weekend rats' who couldn't wait to abandon ship and get home to their loved ones. He had had a family once, but that was long gone now. He paused and thought about it for a moment but then shook the memory off almost as quickly as it had arrived. He had a new reason for getting home. He had done his time, and now he too had a beautiful sweetheart waiting for him.

He nodded to Dinger Bell, a good mate of about fifteen years. Dinger had sorted their coffees and picked a table with six chairs. Greg and some others had joined them in the room, which had approximately fifteen people in it. They were all at various stages of eating or finishing their morning meal. The huge wall-mounted TV in the corner was quietly showing the BBC's twenty-four-hour news channel. Ed slowly picked his way through a plate of greasy naval cuisine. The lads were talking to him but he was only half listening, vaguely following the TV broadcast over the constant, quiet hum of deep male voices chattering or grumbling, and the occasional metallic clangs and bangs as the chef replenished the service counter hotplates and stewards swapped tea urns, buzzing about like civilian waiters.

Fiona Armstrong introduced the morning headlines. *'WikiLeaks say their anonymous source has claimed that a "serious incident" occurred recently at a nuclear enrichment plant in Natanz, central Iran. A WikiLeaks spokesperson highlights that the head of Iran's Atomic Energy Organisation has recently resigned for unknown reasons.'*

Footage appeared on screen of some IT expert attempting to leave a building whilst being bombarded by a media frenzy of microphones and outstretched arms. The next headline, Fiona explained, concerned financial problems and aid issues for the population of Haiti following their worst earthquake on record. The third referred to an attempted security breach at a nuclear plant in Cumbria, north-west England.

*'A police spokesman for British Nuclear Fuels Limited has stated that security was not breached and a number of people have been detained. Four men were arrested at a camp only five miles from the Sellafield site, which is home to the government's MOX plant. The plant produces mixed oxide from uranium and plutonium. This incident follows an earlier attempted security breach on which the BBC reported some days ago.'*

Fiona paused and turned her page. *'In other news…'*

Ed's interest waned as he thought about his banging headache and struggled to listen to the broadcast over the table chatter. He tried to make light conversation with his mates and finish his breakfast at the same time. He gulped down a mouthful of hot coffee, and Knobby Hall tossed him a plastic blister pack of tablets.

'Here, you lightweight, get these down your neck.'

Ed fumbled with the pack, feeling that getting into these things was becoming a fight with the clever people in the packing department of the pharmaceutical factory. He yanked and tore and they all laughed at him, then continued their conversation about how good last night's leaving do was, including the moving tram incident.

Greg looked up at the TV and then over to Ed. 'Hey! Ain't that your neck of the woods, way up there with all that nuclear shit and sheep? You know, the stuff that makes you glow like you do?'

'Come on, Ed, show us your twelve toes and your webbed fingers,' another guy mocked.

'They're camping on your friggin' doorstep, pal.'

Ed looked at Greg. 'Ha bloody ha,' he said. 'Do I look like I give a toss? It happens all the time. There are always crackpots loitering around that place… all those CND groups. Anyway, it's places like that that've kept us employed for the last twenty years. We need those left-wing loonies to keep us out of the dole line. It's like all our conflicts: we need the wars, then Whitehall and the White House squeeze every ounce out of them to make us dumbasses improve our skills and talents,' he mocked.

The men laughed and agreed.

'And don't forget all the great gadgets we get to test and try out. But your war days are over now, Ed,' Dinger quipped.

Ed nodded and took the painkillers with another gulp of coffee. 'Yeah, thank Christ! Too old for all that shit now. God, I ache all over,' he complained.

The men all laughed again and the mocking discussion of military politics continued.

# 5

## MESHKINDASHT, NARMAK PROVINCE, IRAN

The morning mist slowly lifted from the valley and the surrounding mountains. As the sun rose steadily across the growing metropolis, it cast its rays over the city and beyond. The sound of morning prayer called out to all its followers. The haunting Arabic call could be heard from the tallest minuets to the sprawling suburbs. It echoed through the valleys, propelled by public-address speaker systems. The imam's voice rang out across the land like a shepherd calling his sheep. The small whitewashed buildings with beige-tiled rooftops and satellite dishes all shone and lit up like stars as the sun's rays reflected and bounced off the old chimneys and bleached clay surfaces. The new European-style apartments stood out from the older, more typically Eastern buildings. The modern, cube-shaped dwellings of the growing suburb of Meshkin Dasht glinted as the night drifted away and turned to day. With the sun bouncing off every window and glinting like diamonds, the valley began to bathe in its warmth and its inhabitants rose to begin a new day. Human activity gathered momentum. Traffic was already flowing but slowed as its volume increased. Meshkin Dasht was a small but rapidly growing modern and popular suburban area on the outskirts of the city, enjoyed by up-and-coming businessmen, academics, and middle-management and government types.

He was a thirty-something professional with a PhD in particle physics, a chemistry expert specialising in the process of uranium enrichment. He was also deputy director for commercial affairs at Natanz's uranium enrichment plant. He had worked hard to get where he was, climbing out of the poverty in which he had been raised in a desert village, and had devoted his life and work to his country and to science. He was of average height and slim, with dark brown eyes and a full traditional black beard. His hair was jet black, with a slightly curly appearance, but combed straight back and in need of a trim. He was dressed in smart black nylon trousers and a pale blue long-sleeved shirt with an unbuttoned collar showing a vest underneath. He stood on the porch, raised his left arm high and allowed his pale grey tweed jacket, with three biros parked neatly in its left breast pocket, to slide down his arm. Throwing his right arm behind his back and then pulling forward, he made the right sleeve slide up. Adjusting the jacket to its correct position, he picked up his youngest child and kissed her on the forehead, then kissed his wife once on each cheek. His older boy got a gentle pat on the head and a slight stroke to the face. Then he twisted in a 180-degree turn and placed his right foot in its shoe. His shoes were well-worn pale brown slip-ons, last polished some time ago and scruffy from use. He picked up his briefcase from the doorstep and turned to leave. His wife called to him and handed him a striped tie that did not match his outfit. He thanked her and climbed into his five-door silver Peugeot, as he did every morning. He started the car and, as he moved out of the parking space, the radio burst into life with the same sound of morning prayer.

Stopping at the junction of Bahar Street and Amir Kabir Boulevard, he threw the tie around his neck, put on his sunglasses and pulled out into the growing flow of traffic, turning right onto Meshkindasht Road, then east toward Route 32, a well-maintained, three-lane main highway that headed toward the capital. As he drove, he looked over at crane and truck drivers, dressed in a mix of national dress including sandals or flip-flops, and Western-style high-visibility vests and varying colours of hard hats, preparing for another day's work. Tower blocks were popping up on both sides of the highway, slowly eating up the dusty landscape. The desert was being transformed and reclaimed by the property developers with modern, Western-style dwellings and apartment blocks. Scaffold and steel girders rose from the dirt, awaiting their architectural approval before being concreted, block-bricked and cladded. What a war zone it looked, he thought. Apart from the construction workers, in the arid desert, hundreds upon hundreds of empty concrete tower block shells stood from Meshkindasht all along the route to the city, waiting patiently for more government funding to be released. The Meshkindasht Yabarak housing project had taken several years to get this far. That was how it always was in Iran, mainly due to Western and European sanctions. Things moved very slowly. He felt lucky as his government apartment had been completed on schedule. It was a promise from the President and his government to all nuclear engineers working at the Natanz plant.

Within the sandy desert background were pockets of greenery. Recently planted shrubs and saplings had started to take hold along the roadways, tended to by council workers, again in mixed East-meets-West attire as they scurried about in their high-vis vests, watering the vegetation from clapped-out, pre-war, Russian-made water bowser wagons. There were also orchards and gardens on the way in – some private, some government owned – and a couple of parks and play areas had been sited at locations en route into the city as part of the ongoing housing development. However, he had never seen a child play in any of them. As he passed the Azadi Stadium and Conference Centre, his mind returned to the thickening traffic and he paid more attention to his driving. He still had plenty of time and his tie could wait a little longer. He took the off-ramp, circumnavigated his way around the Azadi Tower roundabout and headed for the centre. As usual at this time of the morning, the city was already bursting into life and Iranians were going about their business. Commuters fought to get to their workplaces. Office and admin staff raced across the intersections as traffic lights constantly changed colour, telling the pedestrians when and when not to walk. Policemen stood around smoking and chatting calmly as they leaned against their cars. The sun continued to climb high above the minarets and the tall office and residential blocks. Traders set up their market stalls with fruit, fabrics and bric-a-brac. Newspaper sellers hollered their headlines, and taxis of all colours littered the four-lane highway that led into the sprawling, bustling city centre. The temperature was rising steadily, and he could feel himself getting hotter as the traffic slowed to a crawl at some points. This was his first car. He did not have air conditioning. He could not afford it. He had bought the Peugeot from his brother-in-law as public transport in the city was poor, sporadic and certainly not convenient when living out in Meshkindasht.

He concentrated harder as the traffic became denser. He was still on time. His meeting was not for another half-hour and he was close to his destination: the University of Tehran, which would be hosting the conference. He had prepared well and was confident, ready to deliver his presentation. He felt pleased with himself and thought about promotion. Cars, vans, trucks and mopeds pushed their way forward, desperate to make progress. Motorbikes scooted in and out around him, fighting for any gap to keep moving ahead. He was relaxed and not in a rush. At least he was moving and making some progress in the congestion, travelling at around twenty miles per hour, his radio still playing Arabic music. His window was partly wound down, exposing him to a cacophony of noise. The air was full of the sounds of engines, people and music as the smell of spices and fragrances drifted into his vehicle. He enjoyed the drive to the city for lectures. His previous drives to work had been through boring, dusty deserts to the Busher nuclear plant on the Persian Gulf coast. He enjoyed his new way of life at home with his family and at the university.

In his left-wing mirror was yet another motorcycle: a typical red-and-black Honda 100cc city commuter type with no distinguishing marks or features. It frequently pulled up closer and then seemed to drift farther back. He expected it to push its way through as they always did, but unusually, this one did not. Instead, it kept coming close and then slipping back. It did this for several minutes. He noticed it was also carrying a pillion passenger who, he could see, was wearing a backpack. Both rider and passenger looked ordinary enough except for their headwear: they were well covered, including sunglasses, their dishdashas worn over their heads and as face scarves, as one did in a sandstorm. But this was the city, he thought, as he tried to see their faces. Maybe it was a defence against pollution, he decided, staring ahead again to find a fresh path forward and a slow point to fix his tie.

A generous gap appeared in the traffic. He slowed more than needed as he anticipated the motorbike moving through, but again it did not. Through their sunglasses he felt the riders were looking more at him than trying to push on through the dense, chaotic traffic. This made him unusually nervous and fidgety. He sped up a little and decided to attempt to push forward and be proactive in looking for openings. A blue delivery van moved across to his right, allowing him a longer run. He sped up and dived into the space, then checked his left mirror to see that the bike was still there, but hanging back. Again, he looked for a gap, this time gearing down from third into second and gripping the steering wheel tighter as he pushed his right foot down, raced across his lane to his right and bullied his way into another space. His hands felt sweaty. After a couple of horn beeps and several hand gestures he steadied the car, settled himself and checked his mirrors. The bike was gone. He felt himself relax a little and told himself to be more sensible – after all, he was only a newly appointed mid-ranking engineer. Iran had hundreds of more important, far higher-ranking senior and experienced scientists than him. He was still climbing the ladder and had only been awarded the privilege of attending meetings recently. Why should he be worried?

He was jolted back into reality by a bash on his front passenger window. He jumped, once again on edge. A young male scooter rider demanded he move on, gesturing to the massive space and lack of cars in his lane ahead.

'Move forward, let me through,' the rider screamed.

He moved to his left a little as well as moving forward, opening the gap and letting the scooter through. He checked all three mirrors again and crawled forward, bumper to bumper, for several more metres. He became nervous again as the black-and-red Honda bike drew up three cars behind to his right. A green Suzuki van pushed into his path; he moved left and snuck in behind it, then dived right again into a long open space and accelerated hard. To his favour, the traffic moved again and the flow sped up, allowing him to get some momentum and use fourth gear. He could feel sweat running from his armpits, and he wiped his brow. He did not like this type of driving. He was worried that he was now racing against the motorbike, weaving in and out of the traffic. The motorcycle weaved in and out also and was closing on him, but to his left. He drove harder, frantically watching his left mirror. His left arm swept across his brow and he dabbed his face with his tie.

There was a crash and a loud thump to his right, and a shattering of silver and red plastic as his right mirror exploded against a Ford sedan's door. He braked hard, pulling his car to the left, barely missing a blue Nissan and an old grey Rover in front of him. The bike had closed in on him, down to one car's length, and in a split second he swerved away, hitting the Ford again, causing him to steer left to correct. The impact caused the Ford to veer off into a concrete post, mount the kerb and crash into a building. To his rear, a tatty orange-coloured lorry threw its steering wheel toward his Peugeot in an effort to avoid the careering Fiesta as the driver slammed on the brakes of his fully loaded twelve-wheeler. He glanced again into his left mirror. Nothing. Then he checked his right. The bike was again a car length behind on his rear quarter. The pillion passenger was leaning low down off the motorcycle to his left, and had anchored himself with his right arm wrapped around the rider's waist. The pillion raised his left arm, exposing his hand in a beige leather glove with a pistol pointed toward him. The bike swerved violently to its right, speeding up, and drew closer to his partly lowered window. In a blind panic, he took a long look ahead to steady his bearings. Instinctively, he braked. He could not keep himself from glancing back at the rider in some vein hope of identifying him. The bike darted away as he swerved his car threateningly. He did not know why he did it, but it made the bike move away so he tried it again. This time, the motorbike came back from his right and, as he swerved again to face it off, reappeared almost immediately, on his left this time and much, much closer. As the glaring sun shone down, he thought he caught a glimpse of the rider's eyes through his sunglasses. His peripheral vision caught an image of boots and jeans on both the rider and the passenger. Turning to look ahead once more, to steady his vehicle, he heard the toot of a horn and a shout from an irate driver. Then, above the city noise and traffic commotion, a loud crack. He ducked instinctively, not really knowing why, then, lifting his head slightly, wanted to look to his left, but did not get the chance.

With a second crack, the glass in his part-open window shattered and exploded in his face. His hands numbed and all sound was lost. His vision blurred into blackness and he slumped over the steering wheel. His silver hatchback slowed as his foot left the accelerator, but still slammed into the rear of the Nissan in front, folding and crunching its own bonnet on impact. As the tempered safety glass windshield cracked like frozen ice on a pond, metal mixed with headlight glass as pieces shattered amid the noise of car horns and screeching rubber. His forehead rested on the centre of the steering wheel, pushing at the horn. His face was scratched, cut and dashed with shards of glass. Blood seeped from a small hole just below his left cheekbone. On his right side it gushed from the exit wound: a massive, gaping hole above his eye. His temple area, the top of his ear and part of his skull were missing. Dark crimson blood oozed down the windscreen. Slithers of tanned flesh and light cream bone fragments had spattered across the roof and dashboard. Hair, scalp and clumps of brain matter and flesh filled the front passenger seat and door panel.

An old woman on the sidewalk dropped her shopping bags and raised her hands to her mouth in disbelief, screaming, shocked and horrified. Gawping through the two, now missing, front-door windows of the Peugeot, she saw a young male scooter rider lying on his back with his arms flung out wide and his right leg bent backward. With blood all over his face and a hole in his neck, he lay dying as collateral damage in the central reservation, his scooter engine still running. A younger woman ran to the screaming woman's aid. A man shouted to another as they ran toward the scene, and soon a crowd gathered eagerly to help or just to gawp at the carnage. The old woman with the shopping bags stared at the dead car driver and scooter rider and screamed again, collapsing to the floor in shock.

The motorcycle passenger had swung back into a normal position, adjusted his backpack and pulled his headwear tighter over his head and face. The rider's right hand had already squeezed the throttle of the little Honda and raced the unregistered, un-plated bike through the red traffic lights, left, across two lanes, and off the main avenue into the back and side streets. An older man, shaking a newspaper, ran to the corner, trying in vain to get a number plate. But the bike and its riders were gone within seconds, leaving a trail of dust and smoke as they slipped into the cover of the alleys and bazaars.

~

Across the city, on the other side of town in the Narmak district, another motorcycle slowed alongside a stationary maroon Opel sedan, also struggling in the morning traffic. The car's driver tapped his cigarette packet on the wheel and took a long drag on his king-size, oblivious to the surrounding congestion. Casually and discreetly, the motorcycle's pillion passenger leaned left a little and deposited a brown magnetic package on the car's wheel arch, just below the fuel filler cap, before the bike sped off. Slowly, the river of traffic eased forward – until the blast rang out across the city, polluting the morning air with a thick black mushroom cloud of acrid, oily smoke. Windows in nearby buildings shattered, and their frames chattered in their fixings, showering commuters as they walked by. Cowering survivors looked on in horror as the Opel lifted high into the sky, rear end first, and then smashed down onto the tarmac, flinging its doors and contents afar. Shards of metal and glass blasted out from above and below, and bits of burning rubber, metal and upholstery shot upwards, littering the air, then fell to the ground, injuring more pedestrians on their way.

# 6

# FSB HEADQUARTERS, MOSCOW, RUSSIA

He advanced with the flow of traffic onto the double-laned Bolshoi Moskvoretsky Bridge across the Moskva River. He moved in and out of the taxis and buses, not letting the heavy congestion increase his stress level. With a sigh, he leaned back into the sumptuous leather of his driver's seat. Placing his thumb under his seat belt and pulling it away from his shoulder, he allowed it to snap back gently, realigning itself in a more comfortable position. Pushing his glasses further up his nose, he slowed the car to a crawl as the traffic nudged forward at the bottleneck. On reaching the other side of the bridge it slowed again as it was instructed to filter into a one-lane layout of security barriers. Blue barriers and concrete blocks littered the highway. Civilian and tourist traffic was made to filter right away, but his journey would take him straight on. Removing his green-and-blue ID badge from his wallet, he placed it on the Audi's dashboard. The road ahead was for officials only.

As he entered the widest street in Russia, he marvelled at St Basil's Cathedral and Red Square Park. He looked to his left along the huge red-brick walls of the palace as his large Audi A8 left the modern tarmac and the tyres thudded their way across the broad cobbled street of Red Square. In the morning sunshine, he admired the architecture of Lenin's Mausoleum and the facade of the GUM department store to his right. He drove slowly, following a dithering silver-and-blue police car. He was not in a rush and did not want some traffic cop spoiling his day, but tooted anyway to urge the cops forward a little. Slightly irritated, the police car driver scanned his rear-view mirror and, assessing the vehicle behind, decided against a stop. Challenging black Audis in the Kremlin's motorcade lane could be a bad career move, so he pulled over, out of the way.

Moving down the centre lane designed for Stalin and old Soviet officials, the car came to a stop. Ahead, laid out across the street, were mushroom-shaped concrete bollards half a metre tall, preventing traffic from entering. A guard walked up to his car. The driver pressed a button and the window dropped immediately. The guard peered in and looked at the ID card on the dash, then asked the driver to remove his sunglasses. With a slight sigh, the driver glanced down at his black Omega Seamaster watch, and happy he was in good time, obliged. The guard made no gesture of intimidation and was comfortable in his requests. Politely, he checked the ID card against the driver's face, then gestured to his colleague to move one of the bollards. The driver gave a curt wave and drove through. He turned right off Red Square Plaza and into Nikolskaya Street. His destination lay a little further on, up the street past the workmen who were converting the street into a pedestrian zone. At the top of Nikolskaya Street was Lubyanka Square, the old Historic Quarter where great episodes of history had been planned and executed on his country's behalf. He was heading for the FSB main offices. He checked his watch again.

He had plenty of time. His meeting with the Chairman of State Security was thirty minutes away yet, and parking was never a problem here.

At the end of the street his destination came into view: a huge cream-yellow neo-baroque building surrounded by parked police cars, barriers, and concrete blocks. He swung the car left and passed along several arched yellow-stone facades. Looking ahead into the many arches, he found his mark and adjusted his speed, then, without hesitation, swung the steering wheel left, forcing the large vehicle through one of the arches and down a ramp, taking him two levels lower into a car park in the depths of the old KGB offices. He parked up and walked casually to the exit, removing his jacket, shaking it out and replacing it before taking the lift to the upper level. The brass-and-gold interior trim of the elevator impressed him, but the contraption was chronically old and slow. He thought of modern Western lifts, whizzing him up to the top of the Empire State Building or the Eiffel Tower in no time at all for breakfast, then down again, probably before this old thing had even engaged its rickety electric motors and gearing. As the immaculately polished brass-and-mirrored elevator lumbered on to the top floor, he checked his shirt and tie and adjusted his jacket. The red digital numbers, which in the '70s had replaced the old needle-and-gauge indicator, declared that he had reached Level 7 and the lift thumped to a rest. He was soon walking down the highly polished parquet-floored hall with its pale green walls to the Chairman's secretary's desk. He signed the visitor log, recording his arrival time and his vehicle number plate. He was then offered a seat on a sumptuous dark brown leather sofa and given a coffee. Pytor Stepanov sipped his coffee from the white china cup and waited happily and patiently on the Chesterfield for his appointment.

Flicking through Stepanov's file, the Chairman read that this agent was indeed a veteran and most likely the right man for the task. Reading through the entries penned by eminent colleagues from over the years, he noted that Pytor Alexandrovich Stepanov, named after Peter the Great, the son of an Army corporal who had served on the Eastern Front and a patriotic Communist Party member, had been a keen gymnast as a schoolboy, and had possessed possible Olympic talent. After school and his two-year mandatory national service, he'd stayed on in the Army for several more years and then joined the police. He had risen from a low-ranking police officer to the rank of special officer, and later joined the old Cold War KGB service as a field agent. After reaching the rank of major, and with years of loyal service to the Party, he had been kept on after the fall of the Berlin Wall and the collapse of the old Soviet state. He was tasked with assisting the new government in establishing the new and not-quite-so-corrupt branch and the newly named Federal Security Bureau: the FSB. He was, therefore, old school, and had even worked with the current President back in the day when, as younger men, they served as counter-intelligence operatives. Stepanov was a decorated, sophisticated and skilled operative, relaxed at Embassy functions, confident in bodyguard protection and as an oversees operative. His main achievements were the recruitment of two senior spies from the West in the late '80s, and assisting in intelligence-gathering and defections during the Russian–Chechen War. The Chairman pondered over Stepanov's age. *At forty-six, perhaps he should be looking for an office job*, he thought, before closing the file and buzzing his secretary to send Stepanov in.

After formal introductions, although both men knew much of each other, they chatted for a while over more coffee and exchanged social pleasantries before the Chairman suggested they get down to business, which more than pleased Pytor.

The Chairman sat back in his chair and exhaled a puff of cigar smoke. 'Are you ready for a desk job or early retirement?' he asked, looking down at the cigar in his hand.

'Neither,' replied Pytor. 'My life, my whole profession is out there, comrade, protecting our beautiful homeland.'

'Hmm,' pondered the Chairman, admiring Pytor's loyalty and enthusiasm. 'You know, Pytor, that our world has changed? Youth, human rights and computers are taking over, but we will always need good agents on the ground, like yourself.' He exhaled again, billowing out plumes of smoke. 'You are aware of current affairs in the Middle East?'

Pytor nodded and raised his eyebrows.

'Tell me what you know,' said the Chairman. 'About...' he paused a moment, '... say, the nuclear enrichment problems that the Iranians are having at the moment.'

Pytor thought for a moment, took a swig of coffee and told the Chairman what he knew. He explained that he was aware of it but did not know much more than the public knew, that he had only discussed it briefly with other officials at recent parties and Embassy functions, and that his old colleague over in Belgium had been working on it for several months and was the real man to ask.

The Chairman stood up and moved across the almost empty office toward an old mahogany drinks cabinet, pulled down a desk drawer and poured them both large cognacs into fine-cut glasses. He continued to listen, and asked Pytor's opinion on the matter. Pytor told him that he thought it was an act of Western aggression against a sovereign state, and it was time the Russians taught the West a lesson in humility. He went on to suggest that political agreements on supplying Iran with nuclear development resources needed a hard push, and it was the job of the likes of the FSB to get things moving. He explained that he understood that the Western countries may have colluded with Israel to halt Iran's aims, but that Russia should take as much advantage from the current situation as it could. The Chairman listened quietly.

Pytor continued. 'The Russian government has little influence these days with Europe, NATO or the West in general, and it is in the Middle East where Russia could be King once more and even find ways to influence the West. From there, Russia could restore respect from the Americans and their puppy-dog allies.'

The Chairman took another long drag on his cigar and said, 'Pytor, what an example to us you are. The old Party would be proud of you. I want this to be your last job. After this I will have a nice, clean, safe office job for you, with better money and an improved retirement package. You will be long looked after, my friend.'

The offer did interest Pytor. After years of loyal service out in the field, which he loved, he did feel weary at times and often worried about his health or getting injured, or indeed killed. The thought a of safe, clean office role did appeal to him. The Chairman handed him a plain brown dossier and explained that he was to fly to Israel and meet with his old friend and colleague who was indeed a master in the subject in hand. Pytor was to ensure that erratic and damaging occurrences at the Iranian nuclear plant were not disturbed. Once the Russian government had concluded all the new contracts with the current Iranian government and the installation of new equipment had begun, then Pytor's job until retirement would be as the Security Executive overseeing the safety and security of these installations.

Pytor thought it over whilst they chatted some more. Finally, he agreed. An Executive posting was of Ambassador status and would itself have many advantages. Perhaps he could begin to settle down and stop looking over his shoulder so often. The intelligence game had served him well but, nearing fifty, his needs were changing and maybe it was time to ease up. He could pursue other activities, and maybe even find a proper partner to look after him, and a nice house in the country. He could give up his government apartment in St Petersburg and adopt a more relaxing, rural lifestyle. He accepted the Chairman's offer, and the Chairman already had agreements inside the dossier, typed up ready for him to sign. Happy with their contents, Pytor duly signed and the Chairman concluded the meeting by congratulating him. Inside the dossier were the usual passports and accompanying documents, along with flight tickets and credit cards. The men shook hands firmly. Pytor respectfully thanked the Head of Intelligence and left.

# 7

# URANIUM SEPARATION ROOM, NATANZ, IRAN

The Uranium Separation Room was a vast hall. The cavernous, warehouse-sized room, seventy feet below ground, was filled with hundreds and hundreds of tall, slim, shiny aluminium tubes. Each centrifugal separator was bolted to the floor with a stud bolt at each corner of its rectangular base, and stood perfectly erect at approximately eight feet tall. All were identical, with stainless-steel tubes and various valves protruding from their tops and running up and away on cable trays suspended from the ceiling. Translucent inlet and outlet cooling-system tubes hung from each cylinder. All the cylinders had an approximately one-foot gap between them, and were positioned precisely in row after row, periodically interrupted by narrow grey-tiled access ways. The hall hummed loudly as the centrifuges did their work.

Behind a glass-and-concrete partition and fixed to a long grey wall at the back of the room hung several grey metal control panel boxes housing the remote terminal units used to control the electric motors that drove the uranium enrichment separators. Along with the RTUs, set in the cabinets, were huge electrical isolating switches; dials; digital and analogue tachometers, revolution meters and gauges; buttons; knobs; and row upon row of indicator lights. Each panel had huge, thick, black cables running down from its metal box, into the concrete floor and away to the enormous electrical generators far, far across the massive nuclear facility. Protecting the floor and the switchboard area were thick, long ribbed strips of black rubber matting. Overhead lights flickered and blinked softly and intermittently, and the whooshing sound of electric fans blowing across the rear of the switchboards could be heard. Fixed above the control boxes were racks and racks of Siemens programmable logic control switch boxes. The PLCs all sat quietly idle, waiting for new instructions.

In Computer Room 4 the blackness was again disturbed by the awakening of the little laptop, still stuck in its command loop. Once again, its screen filled with text as it displayed its ongoing problem. Suddenly, it stopped cycling through its problematic instructions and displayed a new set of orders across its screen. Again, the room filled with bright colour as it automatically woke up every hard drive and monitor in the room. Once again, its blue Wi-Fi light blinked and flashed, then settled into a solid, deep cobalt blue as the USB flash drive appendage passed on its instructions. Slowly, the now more aggressive virus was released and set off, worming its way in search of prey once more. Again, it searched out the registration codes of all the computers' Microsoft Windows programs, and again ignored anything with the 19790509 code. This time it searched out any remote terminal units operating on a Siemens Step 7 system that managed programmable logic controllers that drove the electric motors of the separators. The virus's objective was nearby. By stealth it was slowly hijacking the electric motors that operated at a delicate running frequency of 900 hertz.

One by one, the virus took control of every electric motor in the massive cascade hall. One by one, hundreds of obedient motors slowly clicked into a new operation mode, quietly and gently building up speed until they reached their programmed running speed. Slowly, the room became a deafening cacophony of motors whirring as air whooshed all around. The noises gradually built, as one by one, more motors joined in under their new command. Initially, the virus allowed every cylinder to spin and run its centrifugal payload at its normal speed of just below 1,064 hertz. Then, as if out of malice, it slowed them down to only two hertz, like a conductor with a new orchestra. The room became quieter and the whirling winds dropped as the mechanical choir softened, adjusting to their new tempo. The tall, shiny metal tubes and their contents spun happily and gently, like the Turkish dervishes of the Cappadocia region, entranced in their meditations. Softly, the huge room hummed and sighed at the mechanical interlude. Then suddenly, as if in a wicked musical crescendo, the viral conductor sped them back up to 1,400 hertz. The cylinders and their contents spun wildly out of control.

As they spun, the cylinders' metal glinted in the dark morning air. As if happy with its work, the virus now instructed the machines to increase their speed to a very damaging 1,410 hertz. Obediently, hundreds of motors stepped up their pace. The control panels on the far wall lit up like Christmas trees. Red, orange, green and blue lights flashed on and off wildly. Bright red digital numbers raced across readouts, and needles flickered up and down on their RPM dials. Each centrifugal separator spun wildly as the motors started to oscillate them out of shape, forcing them to wobble and rock from side to side. The machines were pushed harder and harder, the motors driving themselves faster and faster into a frenzy. Soon, they were cycling out of control. One by one, out of step, tubes leaned, groaned, heaved and bent out of shape. Hundreds of the tubes banged and clanged into each other. Metal smashed into metal, tubes wrapped and entwined with each other, crushing their aluminium casings and hoses snagged on valves. Rubber mounts in the concrete floor fragmented. Other cylinders wobbled and twisted under the strain as the centrifugal forces pushed the tubes past their intended parameters. As if driven on by some kind of greedy satisfaction, the virus coerced the motors on, faster and faster. The noise became unbearable and drowned out the clashes and bangs as tubes were ripped from their stud-bolt anchor points. Aluminium and steel sections were strewn across the plant, twisting and tying themselves up with rubber and metal tubes. Rubber mountings in the concrete floor juddered and shuddered as the motors sped on. Nuts and bolts loosened themselves, flinging washers and studs across the compartment. Eight-foot tubes hurled themselves at each other as they strained free from their mountings. Coolant liquid spewed out. Hoses spat, hissed and coiled as they broke free from their pressurised systems. Carnage ensued as motors overheated. Lubricants and greases spewed from joints and bearings. Metal glowed hot, leaking lubricants ignited fires around the tubes' bases, which grew quickly and took hold, greedily sucking up what air was available and turning the room into an inferno. Sheer heat made the air stifling and unbreathable. The hot air rose and struck the sprinklers, forcing them to release powdered chemicals and water. Amber alarm lights flashed and blinked across the high ceilings, some just flashing white as their protective metal cages and lenses were swept away by flying metal. Some did not flash at all as tubes wiped them out completely. Alarms screeched above the carnage.

The white-coated lab technician hurled himself into the room. The door had by now been ripped off its hinges. He lifted his arm to defend himself from the onslaught of flying debris and heat as he attempted to reach the control panels. He worked feverishly, trying to lift the mighty gear levers. They were red hot. He heaved at the heavy handle, pushing it across until it reached the off position. The system did not respond. He tried in the most aggressive way to disarm the control panel. It seemed futile as the RTUs cut in again and continued their acts of commercial vandalism, forcing the motors to continue to speed up way beyond their safety limits.

Locked away in the safety of Control Room 4, along with all the other resident computers, the tiny laptop sat quietly, its screen again locked in a power struggle, repeating its message over and over, clearly displaying its codes of malicious instructions:

*https://Stub.MrXnet.19790509_MYRTUS_20070924…*
*https://Stub.MrXnet.19790509_MYRTUS_20070924…*
*https://Stub.MrXnet.19790509_MYRTUS_20070924…*
*https://Stub.MrXnet.19790509_MYRTUS_20070924…*
*https://Stub.MrXnet.19790509_MYRTUS_20070924…*
*https://Stub.MrXnet.19790509_MYRTUS_20070924…*
*https://Stub.MrXnet.19790509_MYRTUS_20070924…*
*https://Stub.MrXnet.19790509_MYRTUS_20070924…*
*https://Stub.MrXnet.19790509_MYRTUS_20070924…*
*https://Stub.MrXnet.19790509_MYRTUS_20070924…*
*https://Stub.MrXnet.19790509_MYRTUS_20070924…*
*https://Stub.MrXnet.19790509_MYRTUS_20070924…*
*https://Stub.MrXnet.19790509_MYRTUS_20070924…*
*https://Stub.MrXnet.19790509_MYRTUS_20070924…*
*https://Stub.MrXnet.19790509_MYRTUS_20070924…*
*https://Stub.MrXnet.19790509_MYRTUS_20070924…*
*https://Stub.MrXnet.19790509_MYRTUS_20070924…*
*https://Stub.MrXnet.19790509_MYRTUS_20070924…*

*https://Stub.MrXnet.19790509_MYRTUS_20070924…*
*https://Stub.MrXnet.19790509_MYRTUS_20070924…*
*https://Stub.MrXnet.19790509_MYRTUS_20070924…*
*https://Stub.MrXnet.19790509_MYRTUS_20070924…*

# 8

## HMS NELSON NAVAL BARRACKS, PORTSMOUTH, ENGLAND

Ed had left the Royal Marine base at Poole in Dorset two weeks earlier for the HMS *Nelson* barracks in Portsmouth, although he wasn't a Marine. At sixteen he had been too young to join the Navy as a diver and so had served his time as a Marine Engineer, then later, with a letter from his father granting permission, been allowed to re-categorise to the diving branch at seventeen and a half, as long as he continued with his engineering apprenticeship. Later still, he'd been seconded to the Royal Navy Commandos prior to its dismantling and merging with the Royal Marines. For the past fifteen years during his secondment to the Special Boat Squad he had been based at RM Poole. Finally, he was now to undergo the usual full medical and dental check-ups, some classroom studies on how to sign on as unemployed and write a CV, and then the formal discharge into civilian life. With his naval career complete, and some new teaching qualifications under his belt, he was happy to be leaving. As a demoted Chief Petty Officer with many years' service, he was now able to retire comfortably and was looking forward to the prospect of some part-time lecturing or teaching back home.

His mind was focused on what kit he could keep, and he knew his release day at the stores would be like market day in Baghdad, with much haggling and bartering over what he could and couldn't have. Like others before him, he'd drawn up a list of what not to hand in. Firearms were an absolute no-no; he'd handed over and signed back in any ballistics and weapons back at Poole. He would have no use for such things now. Not where he was going: quiet, deserted beaches way up the north-west coast. But a knife or two was different. First on his list was his old faithful diver's watch, which on one occasion he had almost swapped whilst working with the Americans on the aircraft carrier USS *Forrestal*. Stores were expecting a well-looked-after black CWC watch, complete with NATO standard-issue grey nylon-and-chrome Pusser's strap. He had, over the years, pawned it, loaned it and used it for taxi fares many times. He had even lost it once at the bottom of a dock and retrieved it a week later. Next on his list were a Scubapro compass, a Siebe Gorman Short Sword diving knife, and a much smaller Promate stiletto knife. Then his heavy-duty twelve-millimetre diver's wetsuit, including waistcoat and complete with Cressi boots. Also, a tall khaki canvas kitbag, and his soft brown kid leather NCO's weekend holdall, which they called a 'grip'. His hangover still cursed him and haggling would be tough in his condition. The quartermasters were a sharp bunch at the best of times. That was why he had picked a Saturday to release himself. If he was lucky, he would get a junior with whom he could negotiate, or whom he could even intimidate with his rank.

Later that morning, he strode out of the quartermaster stores building, very pleased with himself indeed. His last mission had been accomplished. It was getting on for noon, and after some more goodbyes and pleasantries he took the shortcut across the empty parade ground for the last time. With his battered leather grip slung over his right shoulder and an overstuffed naval-issue kitbag in his left hand, he winced and strained in the bright sunshine and fumbled with his sunglasses. His head still thumped. He crossed the car park away from the new block of modern buildings toward the main gate. Passing a dated statue of Lord Nelson, he casually nodded to Horatio, then scanned the staff parking spaces to find his bearings. His vehicle was easy to spot as it was the only one that had been under a tarp for weeks. Dumping his gear on the tarmac, he pulled the tatty blue tarpaulin off his pride and joy. It was a bright red 1972 Opel Manta two-door coupe; the original sports version based on the GM Corvette, with twin round headlights, a double set of round tail lights, and chrome bumpers; upgraded with wide, chromed, spoked wheels, a black vinyl sunroof, and a four-speed gearbox with a GM 'overdrive' – all lovingly overhauled and restored by Ed over a number of years. Wiping the cobwebs off the wing mirror, he unlocked the driver's door and fired her up. After the second attempt, the 3.2-litre GM V6 engine roared into life. He took his time. There was no rush.

He let the engine idle. Loading his kit into the boot, he waited a few minutes, allowing the engine to reach normal running temperature whilst he talked to some friends and said more goodbyes. He shook hands one more time with Dinger, Nobby, Greg and Knocker, then climbed into the black leather bucket seat.

'So, is this your last time, then? You're not coming back again?' Greg said.

'No, too old… Anyway, they wouldn't let me blag my way through another several years of freeloading and messing about with bombs 'n' boats. They'll find you bastards out too, soon enough,' Ed quipped.

Knocker pushed an envelope into Ed's lap. 'It's from the boss,' he said. 'He's looking forward to the wedding. Says he's sorry he can't see you off, but sends his regards. Some words of wisdom and contact numbers in it, I think?'

Ed smiled. 'Yeah, cheers, Knocker. Tell the boss I won't miss him either,' he laughed.

Waving, he turned right out of the car park onto the naval base's main drag and down toward the main gate. In second gear he allowed the car to chug forward with minimum accelerator pressure. The barrier was raised by a rather ugly, undernourished-looking, toothless civilian security guard. Ed reflected, even that role had been privatised. Companies like G4S were running the place now. 'GS4 nothing more like,' he mocked. Years ago, it would have been a disciplined, trained member of Her Majesty's Armed Forces with a real loaded firearm on gate duty and guard patrol. Security firms and the liberal left were flourishing under the present government; these ugly, unfit, skinny, toothless, previously unemployed civilian guards who spent more money on tattoos than their dental hygiene came cheap and were paid peanuts, and usually looked as ugly as monkeys. It reminded him of why he was glad to be leaving. *Modern Britain*, he thought to himself as he drove on. The original naval base perimeter wall had all but gone. The old HMS *Nelson* main dockyard gateway had been saved and lovingly restored but, like him, had retired too. Its original red-brick and limestone blocks had been sandblasted clean and repointed to look like new, and its triple-arched, wrought-metal ornamental gates painted in high-gloss black with gold tips for the tourists. *Nelson would have been proud*, he scoffed. But now, behind this iconic memorial of greater days, stood modern gates and new barriers. He remembered how he had stumbled through the old arched side gates following many a night out in old Portsmouth town and the Barbican. Towering majestically as if still on guard over the dockyard, they stood as a monument and testament to a bygone age, he thought. *Just how Britain used to be: magnificent and great. Now it's just another listed bit of building for the tourists.* He looked up at the gilded coat of arms and crests that crowned the centre of the gates, on the biggest of the three arches. He read the freshly gold-painted words: 'HMS *NELSON*.' With a new Portakabin, a freshly painted blue-and-white gatehouse, refurbed office buildings to his left, and the old gates ahead just to the right, he nudged the car out under the raised barrier. Nodding to the undernourished, tattooed monkey and receiving a huge, glowing, toothless smile in reply, he crept forward.

'It's been a real pleasure,' he muttered. He gestured a casual salute, then pushed the nose of the Manta out of the barracks' entrance one last time and into the Saturday-afternoon traffic.

He turned right onto Queen Street and followed it past the old Naval Detention Quarters where, he was embarrassed to say, he had done some prison time. With a half-chuckle and a cough, he continued on down to Main Street and the Main Gate. The brewery had long gone to make way for flats, and that distinctive smell of hops, it used to exhale no longer lingered. Ed swung left along the harbour, past the old Ship Anson pub on his left and the Harbour station on his right. The buses and traffic moved on and he passed Gunwharf Quays along The Hard toward Park Road. He gave a sigh of sadness, melancholy and reflection. As man and boy, he had pounded these streets on shore leave since the early '80s, and now he felt he was leaving a second home. To satisfy his curiosity, and as one last trip of nostalgia, he followed the road around to HMS *Vernon*, his old diving school, which was long gone too. As with *Nelson*, its only remaining trace was the old main-gate entrance, now called Vernon Gate and the entrance to a new marina shopping centre development. He looked out of his driver's window and sighed again, cursing.

Driving up Park Road, he followed it back to Unicorn Road, and then on to the Circular, which took him west onto the M27 and then the A34 north to the Midlands. Heading west toward Southampton, the afternoon sun dazzled him through his windscreen. He tapped the sun visor down, then cranked the sunroof handle and wound it back fully. With the sunroof open and his driver's side window down, he pushed his Ray-Bans higher up his nose, slipped out of third gear and accelerated away from his previous life. Pushing the car hard, he hit the slip road in fourth gear and kept his hand on the gear stick. Then, at the right moment, with his left thumb, he slid back the 'overdrive' switch on top of the gear knob to select 'in' and with this new-found fifth gear, hauled the red sports car onto the motorway. Checking his wing mirror for traffic, he hammered onto the highway at a comfortable seventy. Heading north-west, he watched the old naval base town slowly vanish from his mirrors. He settled back into the seat as the engine spurred him onward. Glancing down, with his left index finger, he pushed in the cassette tape that was protruding from the car's radio-cassette aperture. With a click and a pause, he was greeted by the voice of Kansas lead singer Steve Walsh: *Carry on, my wayward son, there'll be peace when you are done, lay your weary head to rest…* He cranked up the volume to compensate for the wind noise. A '70s rock band putting words to his current situation. How profound and apt. Had he really moved on? Happily, he drove on, northbound to a brand-new life with a sense of completion and contentment. Now he really could 'lay *his* weary head to rest.'

As he drove, he reflected on his past and how he had arrived at this point. His father had been a commercial diver on the North Sea oil rigs in the '70s and had repeatedly reminded him that, if he wanted to be a diver, he'd need the very best training. The Royal Navy had always been recognised as the very best for diver training. So, instead of the Scouts, his father had enrolled him in the Sea Cadets to prep him. Ed had then joined the Navy straight from school.

His straight blond hair blew about in the turbulence and his deep blue eyes stared through his sunglasses at every vehicle. He weighed in at 220 pounds and had stood at six foot one in his prime, but knew he was now slowly shrinking and getting overweight. His body had developed over the years into the solid, firm build required for the job. Not a powerlifter build, which was frowned on in his line of work. Muscle-bound meatheads of the stereotypical Hollywood *Rambo* variety could be dead weight. The Boat Squad left all that to the Paras and the Marines, who seemed to love it. They lifted weights, worked out and trained, but only for stamina and endurance. Life in the Boat Squad was all about marathons, not sprints. Slowly and often and 'softly, softly' was their approach. 'By Strength and Guile' was their motto. *Not all that 'Who Dares Swims' or 'Who Cares Who Swims?' nonsense*, he mocked. But it didn't matter now. Thinking ahead, he could let himself go a bit and relax. He recalled the wise words of his old mate Nobby Hall. Nobby called it his Three-Way Rule: 'Always have something to get up for, always have someone to love, and always have something to hope for.' Now Ed had all three, and they were waiting for him at home.

He was still very much old school though, even with his music. His thoughts and opinions reflected his upbringing and he thought the digital world was not always the answer. Some things had to be done physically. People had to be spoken to and instructed. Some jobs, like his, could never be replaced by technology, only supported. Although he embraced modern technology, he certainly wasn't about to open a Twitter or Facebook account. His old-school style had given him not only tough opinions but also a tough attitude.

His job could not tolerate the soft, politically correct ways of the new era. He had watched his bosses in constant power struggles with various government departments over political correctness issues. But now he could leave all that behind; it wasn't his problem any more.

This was the second time he had left the Navy. Civilian life hadn't agreed with him the first time around. He had set up his own business, but, after years of sleeping in the back room, he'd finally walked out on his fifteen-year marriage and, through a bitter divorce and a vindictive ex-wife, lost all contact with his twelve-year-old daughter. He had let the business run down and then sold it off. He'd rejoined the Navy with a post attached to the then Services Internal Security, now rebranded as MGS for MOD Guard Services. After rebuilding his reputation and contacts, he'd moved back to the Boat Squad as an instructor, teaching Royal Marines, Royal Engineers and Paras all the skills needed for Special Boat Services selection. From combat swimming to underwater ordnance, coastal surveying and defence to covert surveillance and survival skills, armed offensive warfare to helicopter extractions and search-and-rescues, he had taught them all. People came to the Boat Services from across the Commonwealth, even India and Pakistan, to be specially trained by his team in the dark arts of water warfare.

Struggling with civilian life, and after long bouts of depression and heavy drinking, he'd decided to end his days. Then he had met Esther, the most beautiful and caring woman in the world. She had pulled him back from the brink and given him a reason to live. With real love and care she had got him to accept counselling, and with her support, he had begun to rebuild his life. He loved her passionately, and she him. He felt something he had never felt with any other woman. He idolised and adored her. She had helped turn him around, and her calm and loving nature immersed him in a special love he had never known; a kind, soft, gentle love that he had always craved. She was his reason to live. In her he had found a new zest for life and she was his Three-Way Rule. Their love for each other had blossomed more and more and she was now his world. This retirement time, it was different. No wife, no hassles or problems… but no daughter either. How he missed her, but their contact had been minimal since the divorce and she had been used as an emotional weapon against him. After years of depression, drinking and undiagnosed PTSD, with the help of his new and very special partner, he had pulled himself back together. This time he was a free spirit to come and go as he pleased. And he and Esther would, from now on. Previously, he had devoted himself to his family and business for little reward or thanks. His ex-wife had never appreciated his successes, which had provided them with a steady income and private schooling for their daughter. From now on, he would travel and holiday with his new love. Soon they would be married, and now he just wanted to live out his life quietly and peacefully with this beautiful, kind and intelligent woman. This time it would be different, and after several more years of the Navy, he was ready for civilian life.

# 9

# URANIUM SEPARATION ROOM, NATANZ, IRAN

Buried like a bunker more than seventy feet under the desert surface, the cascade hall was in turmoil and the noise was deafening. The alarms were incessant. Red and amber lights flashed across the cavernous open-plan room. The walls – some smooth concrete, some bare rock, and some steel-sheeted with overhead rolled-steel joist beams – reverberated with the commotion. The metal roof amplified the noise. The purpose-built complex was a hive of panic. Scientists; administration, process and factory workers; and cleaners scurried about, all in lab coats, blue hats, face masks and blue paper overshoes; some with radios, some wearing earpieces. At one end of the building, a hangar-sized door had been opened enough to allow the brilliant sunlight to pour in and factory workers to pour out in a frightened rush. The vast doors were designed to allow easy access by heavy goods vehicles to deliver their imported cargoes into a huge receiving area out of sight of prying eyes and satellites. The entrance area sloped downhill dramatically into the giant rooms of the complex. Staff pushed past each other, uphill against the steep gradient, in a melee of arms and legs, hoping to get to their rehearsed and allocated emergency muster points. Some managers and senior people were shouting, trying to give instructions. Outside the doors, armed soldiers in camouflage fatigues with gloves and helmets ran about, not seeming to know quite what to do.

At the opposite end of the hall, a hobbit-style circular door, the size of a house and fashioned from highly polished metal, lay wide open, exposing the room's contents. Like the famous Chinese Terracotta Army, they stood in their hundreds in perfect row upon row, as if protecting the contents of the cascade room behind them. Again, hundreds and hundreds of highly polished aluminium tubes lay in the path of the now-burning vault. Above them, suspended high from the ceilings, flickered fluorescent lighting tubes with diffusers, casting no shadows. Along the polished-tile walkways, litter bins and mobile cleaning stations were sited intermittently, along with the odd strategically placed office chair. At the far end of the hall was a large glass-windowed compartment from where one could observe and control the operations of the whole vault. Behind the bulletproof glass, engineers in overcoats thumped buttons and pressed switches, sliding frantically from left to right on their wheeled chairs to press and thump more switches and buttons in the uranium enrichment control room. The next adjacent room was the enrichment cascade conversion room. It looked like a mega ship's boiler room, with six huge condensers laid out in a two-three formation. Through the armoured glass and concrete walls, centrifuges whirred out of control and chattered at their baseplates. Concrete splintered and shattered, and steel studs strained and fought against the huge pressure placed upon them, causing them to get hotter and hotter, then bend and increase their G-force, gradually freeing them from their shackles. The condensers thumped on their mountings, their dials and gauges all screaming in the red zones.

In the vault, an engineer was trying to switch off the main power to the cascade hall, and cried down his radio to the control-room operators. 'Shut it down,' he screamed, 'shut it down!' The radio fell silent.

The atmosphere was intense and everyone was extremely panicked. Standing at the rear of the uranium enrichment control room was a man dressed in a suit and a coverall, shouting and ordering others about. Several other men in similar overcoats and blue booties scurried about the immaculate factory floor, some with clipboards, checking and rechecking the data on them. Other staff ran past, some with mobile cleansing station trolleys, some with extinguishers, and others with various tools and equipment. A firefighting team were working their way toward the vault. Others were told to move to the next room for some form of routine cleansing preparations. The man in charge looked very embarrassed and was in a state of mild rage.

Midway down the length of the vast hall lay more admin rooms and offices. Through toughened glass, government and security officials in suits, crisp shirts and dark ties were demanding to know more information, and waving with various indiscriminate gestures. Standing at the glass of an observation station were several International Atomic Energy Agency inspection staff. They stood patiently as they observed the disposal of many burnt and twisted cylindrical casings. Something was wrong, but they were blocked from seeing the true extent of the carnage. An Iranian government official tried to move them along, remaining calm and talking down the situation as if it was a normal occurrence and all under control. He stood tall, above average height, with olive skin, brown eyes and short black hair. With the inspectors in his sight, he slipped a radio from his inside jacket pocket and put it to his mouth. Above the noise and commotion, he called to the engineer who was shouting out instructions on the factory floor. The man stopped what he was doing, reached into his pocket, put his radio to his ear and listened. Immediately, he walked over to the office block of the massive building where the IAEA inspectors were now congregated. The government official beckoned him up into the viewing area behind the toughened glass. But he would not go. He refused three times, and demanded that the official come down to him on the factory floor.

Reluctantly, the man in the suit turned to the control-room engineers and snapped, 'Shut it down now! Shut the whole thing down. Immediately.' He glared through the glass at the engineer before turning to the IAEA delegation and asking to be excused. Then he burst out of a side door and down some metal steps and stormed across the facility floor.

The engineer stood at a desk with an open laptop, throwing the mouse cursor around like a cat chasing a mouse under a bed sheet. In silent shock, the seven IAEA inspectors stood and watched. As the plant staff removed more and more damaged centrifuges, they looked on in disbelief. They stood in their lab coats and paper hats, staring at each other. Their bodies were motionless, but their facial expressions described their concern and thoughts. Eyebrows and mouths made involuntary gestures, as they were all thinking the same thing. They all wanted desperately to get out of the viewing area to somewhere where they could talk privately. What they were witnessing was an unprecedented number of damaged centrifuges being removed from the inner plant. Tube after tube was wheeled out on trolleys to be discarded. An inspector had to gesture to the staff through the observation window so they could stop and allow her to count and log the outgoing damaged hardware. Aware that their official escort was preoccupied with the engineer, and once she had logged the numbers on her clipboard, she discreetly pulled from her coat pocket a micro handheld camcorder. Quietly, she moved to the open side door that led to the metal steps, flipped off the lens cap and filmed what they were seeing from her right hip, her hand tucked tightly into her body behind the clipboard.

Down on the facility floor, way out of earshot of the IAEA entourage, the official screamed at the engineer. 'What the hell is going on? This is the third time this week. What's the problem this time? I have a full delegation of inspectors and you allow a scene like this to occur? Are you an imbecile, a traitor or a saboteur?'

The engineer cowered a little but tried to protest, showing the official his information and readings by jabbing his index finger at his laptop's plasma screen. 'Look, colleague,' he said, 'here it is. The problem is the same over and over again. Centrifugal motors sent spinning way above their limits, and cooling water supplies shut off to the condensers. Every time we try to attempt—'

'Enough! You inept idiot!' shouted the official. 'Get me the facility president on the phone this instant. You can explain your inefficiencies and your lack of management planning to him. I will not be embarrassed any more. You can also get me the head of security down here at once!'

The senior engineer continued his protest, trying to tell the official what was going wrong, but was promptly silenced by two armed guards who pulled the laptop from his hands and led him to the administration block. 'This has been going on for too long. There is more at hand than meets the eye,' he shouted over his shoulder as he was escorted off the factory floor.

The head of security arrived. He was a big man in his early fifties with a moustache, and overweight. He was plainly flustered, sweating, and his chest and belly heaved as he tried to catch his breath. He wore a military police uniform with a deep red beret and highly polished boots. He tugged at his collar, then, taking off his matching deep red cravat, removed his beret and mopped his brow and face. His badges identified him as a Major.

The government official looked at the major with distrust. He leaned forward, raising his clenched right fist and pointing his index finger at the viewing window and then almost into the nose of the Army officer. He spoke quietly through gritted teeth, spitting in the major's face. 'I want everyone back to work and this mess cleaned up. Not a word of this to anyone outside this facility, you hear? Not until we get to the bottom of this. Not a word to anyone. I will sort those Westerners out and make some calls. Do you understand? In the meantime, find me the culprit! Bring him to me and I will hang him from the highest building. I will strip his skin off his bones for all to see, as Allah is my witness. Do you understand me, Major? We will not fail and we will not be the laughing stock of the international community, nor the fools of the nuclear industry. Now find me the person who is responsible for this act of terrorism.'

The British head of the IAEA delegation beckoned to the Iranian official. Leaning in, he muttered sympathetically, 'We have seen enough for today, thank you, and clearly you need some time to sort out this difficult situation. We will leave you now and head back to our hotel. If we can be escorted back to our bus, we will speak again tomorrow.'

Desperate to rid himself of the Westerners, the official agreed, clicking his fingers and gesturing to their escort to show them out.

What he and the IAEA delegation didn't know was that the answer to their questions lay under their very noses, buried deep within the megabytes and memory of the industrial control-room computers.

# 10

## LAKE DISTRICT, CUMBRIA, ENGLAND

It was dusk when Ed arrived at his destination. The tyres of the red sportscar crunched as he entered the gravel driveway and rolled up to the property. His place was three miles from the nearest village and between the coastline and the railway track. As he turned, his headlights swept across the property and caught the rear end of a small white Honda to his right, then hit the path and porch, lighting up the front of the lodge. In the dim evening light, he could see two fir trees in new pots, one either side of the front door. He didn't recognise them, but guessed where they had come from.

After his divorce, a farm had been sold and split into lots, and he had managed to secure a couple of acres at auction. He'd put a trailer caravan on the land originally and had planned to put some livestock on it later and try his hand at 'the good life', but on rejoining the Navy that idea had moved to the back burner. Over time, the static caravan had been replaced with a Scandinavian-style eco lodge. It was quiet, idyllic, and he loved it. He was far enough into the countryside for it to be private, but only a short drive from the nearest town for conveniences and necessities.

The porch light was already on and a hallway light blinked into life as he saw a silhouette approach the front door. He flung the driver's door wide and killed the ignition.

As he stepped out of the vehicle, she ran at him and threw her arms around him. 'Hey darling, congratulations, you did it!' she said, and kissed him on the lips, throwing her arms around his neck tightly.

'Well, hello, stranger. How's my gorgeous girl?' he replied, hugging her around her waist, then kissing her neck. 'I see we've some new additions.'

She chuckled a little. 'Oh, the planters? A little "welcome home" present.' She pulled him to her for another hug. 'Welcome home, darling,' she whispered, squeezing him hard.

They both savoured the moment, knowing that he would never have to go away again. This was officially his retirement. He looked at her for a moment. He absolutely idolised her, and loved her deeply. He admired her beauty and intelligence, and knew she was far superior to him intellectually.

After his lonely marriage and vicious divorce, he had met Esther some years ago at a local high school when they both gave presentations to the kids on very different career paths. They had hit it off immediately and the rest was history. She was very pretty and petite, around five foot two, with shoulder-length hair, slightly curly and highlighted blonde. She had bright green-hazel eyes, depending on the light, from her mother's side; a cute nose and cheeks; and olive skin. She was a senior computer engineer and had worked for the UK government nuclear program for almost all her working life, until recently. Now she had a more senior post with the recently privatised local nuclear power site. They were deeply in love but had been so busy with their careers that they had agreed to take things step by step until Ed was free of the

Navy. Then they would make plans. She lived in an apartment in a seaside town up the coast, but recently they had bought a grand old coach house together. For him it had gardens back and front, a garage, and a hardstanding. He planned to construct another garage and still have room to mess with his motorcycles and other 'toys' in the summer months. The high-pitched roof of the first garage created a great loft office or man cave. They had been renovating the property over the past six months or so, and Esther would sell her apartment when it was finished. They would keep Ed's lodge and rent it out. He had fallen for her big time, and they had it all planned out. The chalet was a real escape, his little haven. After his divorce he'd thought it was his little piece of England. It was idyllic, beautiful, serene, and just next to a wooded area on the edge of a national park. What more could he want? Esther knew he loved the chalet and she too was reluctant to rent it out to total strangers, but at least they would have their new house and they would make it their home.

She had made some minor changes to the chalet; some he noticed, some he didn't. He did, however, notice the new wine glasses accompanied by a chilled bottle of Pinot Grigio, and the lounge made nice and cosy with candles flickering on the coffee table and the log burner roaring. Quietly, just a few notches above a whisper, the CD player gently began playing a Simply Red album, completing the ambience. What more could he want? After a shower he settled down with her on their faded old couch; he with his favourite Johnnie Walker, double on the rocks, and she sipping her orange-flavoured gin and tonic. They talked as lovers do, with much small talk, plans, trivia and news, then excitedly discussed their forthcoming holiday: two weeks in the sun, with nothing to do but laze around by a pool. Wearily, they enjoyed the drink and the warmth of the fire until nearly midnight, finishing the second bottle of rosé. Sprawling out, they gazed into each other's eyes. He wanted her. He needed her. He was desperate for her. Three weeks he had gone without her soft skin, her sweet body fragrance and the smell of her hair. She knew it too. She pulled him in to her, clasping her left hand around his neck, drawing him close and kissing him deeply, inviting his tongue into her mouth. He responded instantly, fumbling to place his glass on the floor with his left hand, then cradling her face as he kissed her intensely and passionately, locking his lips onto hers. He pushed his chest and torso against her, and as she slid deeper into the couch, she responded by pushing back against him. They writhed on the sofa, kissing madly, groping and caressing, pulling frantically at each other's clothing until at last, they were making love. Sweating, they rose and fell, again and again until nature intervened, releasing them from their frenzy and allowing them to simultaneously climax, then fall into a deep slumber.

~

He woke around eight, padded barefoot through to the kitchen and found a note:

> *Home about noon. Eggs and mushrooms in fridge – do yourself an omelette. xx*

He knew she had to go into work but she'd promised him that once he was home for good, she would back off and focus on them and the new house. Checking that there was enough water in the kettle, he flicked the switch and looked around his home, thinking about his new life, whilst making a coffee. He saw Esther's dressing gown hanging over a bar stool and let out a sigh. He loved her and all he needed was right here. He felt at peace. What more could he want?

Later, he unpacked and settled back into his home. After dinner they walked hand in hand down the lanes to the beach.

'Have you been up to the house?' he asked her. 'I mean in the last few days?'

Esther often went up at the weekends when he was away. She had been working hard decorating, ready for him coming home. But she could only do so much alongside juggling the wedding arrangements. On his previous weekend visits, they had made massive inroads into the decor and maintenance. They worked well together and enjoyed working as a team. (That meant her in charge and him as the labourer.)

'No, not since last Tuesday,' she replied. 'Picked up some post and threw out some dried-up paint tins that somebody left open.' She raised her voice light-heartedly but accusingly as she prodded his ribs. 'Just been too busy.'

He smiled. 'Okay, I'll get over there in a day or two. Just let me get myself home and settled first. Then I'll attack the place like a decorator possessed,' he joked.

'Thought any more about our holiday?' she asked.

'No, not much. Where do we wanna go? I'll leave that to you,' he replied, trying to get off the hook.

Turkey looked to be a good deal but they just couldn't decide, and had been taking it in turns on their laptops and tablets in the evenings, trawling hundreds of travel websites. Fed up with losing so many of their evenings, they agreed to go to town the following weekend, give some travel agents a budget and let them do all the legwork.

~

The following week, Ed busied himself doing not very much at the lodge. Later in the week, whilst Esther was working, he took the short drive to their new house. It was a lousy, cold, grey day, and as he drove along the coast he thought about a nice hot location with a pool and a cold beer. He loved this area and the sea but, looking at the size of the waves kicking at the beach, decided he liked it more from inside his car. He pulled into the drive, double-checking in his head that he had brought the tools he thought he would need for the day. It had been a few weeks, so he really didn't want to start anything major today. He would just take stock of where they were up to and decide on an action plan for the rest of the week.

As he pulled a black-and-yellow plastic toolbox and some dust sheets out of the boot, the heavens opened again and dumped what seemed like tonnes of water down his neck, causing him to crouch and then run the ten yards or so to the two grubby, worn sandstone steps of the porch. With his right hand he grabbed the big Victorian doorknob and pushed against the heavy black painted door, forcing his way into the old house. Catching himself, he dropped the tools and threw out his arms, casting the rainwater off his hands and fleece. After running his hands through his hair and around his ears, he wiped his face. He couldn't believe how heavy the rain was and how black the sky had turned. His washed-out jeans were soaked from the knees up, and his blue T-shirt and khaki fleece were drenched too. Looking for the light switch, he glanced at the hallway table, which held some fast-food flyers and some keys. The keys to the back door and the garage. Good. He had forgotten about them.

Moving through to the kitchen, he cursed himself for not getting any milk on his way up here. That meant black coffee all day – or beer. He reached across the worktop to switch on an old paint-spattered radio that lay on its side. Music blared off the walls and through the house. 'Whoa, for Christ's sake!' he shouted, and grabbed the dial to reduce the volume to a more normal level. *It always does that when you knock it over*, he remembered; he had on many occasions mused on what a crap design it was. *Esther must have been working upstairs to have had it on so loud*, he thought, laughing.

Then he realised. He hadn't unlocked the front door. She must have left the house unlocked. 'Bloody hell,' he cursed, alarmed, spinning around, convinced that their empty house had been burgled. He rushed from room to room, checking for any sign of disturbance, but in an empty, undecorated house, he found it difficult to tell. He raced back to the car for his mobile – getting soaked for the second time – and into the hallway again to text Esther.

*Am at house. Did you forget keys or have we been robbed?*

Whilst waiting for a reply and composing himself, he walked through the house again, checking for anything unusual. He remembered the radio lying on its side, and a kitchen drawer being half open. He walked back over to the radio. Looking at the sink he had recently installed, he removed its tailor-made chopping board from its resting position as a sink cover. Two jam jars of turpentine and paintbrushes lay smashed in the sink. The mix of broken glass, gloss paint, water and turpentine had dried hard. 'Fuckin' hell,' he swore. 'For fuck's sake' and he slammed the new kitchen drawer closed.

As the cutlery within the drawer rattled to a halt, his BlackBerry Bold blasted out the sound of Ravel's Bolero and a red notification light flashed. It was Esther.

*No, Hun, I definitely locked up. It gave me some trouble when leaving. Is everything okay?*

He stabbed his little QWERTY keyboard proficiently.

*All okay but looks like we had visitors. How come your keys were on hall table then?*

Her text came back swiftly:

*They're yours, babe. Mine here in my bag.*

*Okay. Did you break the paintbrush jars in sink?*

*No, I didn't. Thought you had done it. Okay?*

Her final message was three kisses, to which he replied with two.

~

She arrived at the house straight after work, entered the hallway and saw a young policewoman taking a statement. She had seen the police car outside and Ed had texted her to keep her updated. After some well-intended but very basic questions, he cracked open another bottle of beer. Esther untied the belt of her beige raincoat and, pulling it off, laid it over a tatty reading chair that had come with the house. She considered it a gift from the previous owner, and wanted to keep it and have it reupholstered after the lounge was finished. She dropped down onto a wooden stool. Spotting the beer in Ed's hand, her body language shifted. Catching his eye, she gave him a wry look as if to ask, *How many is that?*

'It's my fifth,' he said, guessing her game. 'And yes, my dear, you will have to drive me home.' He looked back at the policewoman.

The officer tore a pink carbon copy from her notebook and handed it to him, then closed the notebook, pulling a black elastic band across its front. 'Nothing more we can do for now, sir,' she said. 'There's an incident number on your copy. Give that to your insurers. We can only keep an eye on the place for a time and do some drive-pasts, speak to neighbours, etc.' She looked over at Esther. 'No sign of a break-in anywhere.'

Esther looked back at her, half smiled and replied, 'Probably kids, eh?'

The officer shrugged. 'If you wish I can have the place dusted for prints, but you say there's no actual theft…'

Ed jumped in. 'No, leave it,' he said, wiping his mouth after another sip of beer. 'It's done now. We'll just have to be more careful and I will up the ante on the security as we do the place up. Thanks for your time, Officer.'

The policewoman was petite, blue eyes, around five foot six, wearing a minimal amount of make-up including some sort of lip gloss. Her hair was tied back in a ponytail. Cynically, he thought to himself, *How would she fare patrolling the town on a Friday night with all the young farmers pissed out of their brains? Britain's finest, eh? The thin blue line gets thinner in today's modern world.* He tutted to himself and jumped up from his toolbox, stating that he would see her out. Not standing up, Esther smiled, mouthing a thank-you as the young policewoman left.

As she drove them both home, they discussed the break-in and the keys. He reassured her that it was just unlucky and was probably kids, just like Esther had said. What he didn't tell her was that he had found a reel of fishing line down the side of the property at the back of the garage. They did not own a fishing rod. Ed thought the break-in had been done professionally, by hooking his keys through the letter box from the hall table to let themselves in. It was an empty house without curtains. Although there were newspaper pages taped onto most of the front windows, one could still see into the property from up close. Any fool could see there was nothing to steal. It was obviously an old, empty, derelict house being done up. Even the gardens were a shamble of weeds and overgrown, unkempt shrubs and trees. There had been no posh or expensive cars on the drive and therefore no executive-type keys left in the hallway to catch. There was no damage to the windows or doors; neither was there any sign of someone sleeping rough. There were signs of a clumsy intruder knocking some things over, but that was about it. They could have been disturbed and, in a rush, simply put the keys back and closed the door to make it all look natural before getting a chance to tidy up the paintbrushes and broken glass. He had already refused the offer of fingerprint dusting before Esther had arrived. He knew there would be no fingerprints, but he didn't know why.

It bothered him for the rest of the week because he just couldn't work it out, but after several reassurances from Esther that it was all okay, he agreed to make one call to the cops to see if there was any update, and then he would drop the issue. He decided to put it aside and enjoy the excitement of going into town to book their eagerly awaited holiday. The break-in had disturbed them both, enough to shake Esther up a bit, so they were keen to get away for a few weeks.

~

They gave the young girl behind the desk their brief and their budget, asking for a four-star hotel anywhere hot next week.

The young redhead showed off her keyboard skills and travel knowledge, typing like a woman possessed. She rattled from one provider to another, stopping only to flick her hair and occasionally adjust her aqua-blue corporate necktie. She flicked the computer swiftly from one travel supplier website to another, back and forth with numerous options. Ed sat and watched her and Esther becoming engrossed in their project. He enjoyed their enthusiasm and gusto. Admiring the view of the women busily discussing all the options, he leaned back in the office chair, wishing he had found this redhead weeks ago, back in Portsmouth, and thereby saved himself and Dinger Bell endless wasted evenings fumbling with his old, clumsy laptop.

Over an hour and two coffees later, the holiday was booked. The nice young lady had worked diligently and earned her commission by finding them a fabulous package on Lake Beyşehir in Turkey. It was settled. After several discussions they had all agreed, including the redhead, although personally Ed wasn't too sure at first. He had passed through Turkey many times, usually via Ankara military airbase. His scepticism told him Turkey was a heavily Muslim country and although a long-time member of NATO, still not eligible to join the European Union, neither was it in the euro. He was thinking about cultural, travel and currency issues. However, the resort looked great. It had lots of positive TripAdvisor reviews, and the travel agent had recommended it and had even been there. *But then, they always have. How does that one work?* he thought cynically.

The brochure read:

> *More beach and surf, more casual and less rigorous, Beyşehir is very different in spirit from the rest of western Turkey. Young couples walk hand in hand on the main thoroughfares*

*and live bands ring out modern pop music in the pubs.
Sparkly beaches and serene coves…*

The marketing guys had made their point. Ed was pleased. Esther was excited too: it was a few years since they had taken a proper holiday together, and this was her treat to Ed. He felt a bit like a teenager cut loose from his parents for the first time. It would be a great, relaxing treat for them both.

# II

# BEN GURION AIRPORT, TEL AVIV, ISRAEL

The two agents sat quietly, several yards apart, in the arrivals lounge, blending in with the casual, calm ambience of the cavernous, circular central hub. The lounge area and food hall were not exceptionally busy and the six arched malls were free of obstructions. Advertising boards blinked and flashed from every pillar including the huge, long, curved overhead panels above the second-storey restaurants and shops. Amongst them, in identical size, were the arrivals and departures boards, displaying gates and times in red and green fonts. The agents watched as the central water fountain shot back into life and the noise of falling water and working pumps disrupted the quiet. They were waiting for the passengers of the Turkish Airlines Flight TA811 from Georgia to disembark. On the arrivals board, the red font changed to green, informing them of the flight's arrival and disembarkation. Agent Rabis sat pretending to read the news on his phone and Agent Jacob was sipping a strong coffee with his head buried deep in the *Jerusalem Post* broadsheet. Both men were dressed casually in worn clothes and blended in with all the other everyday individuals waiting to collect friends or family. Rabis was dressed more like a scruffy sports-obsessed adolescent and Jacob like an '80s geography teacher, complete with tweed jacket and leather elbow patches. Both men sat quietly and patiently, waiting for their respective 'friends' to come through passport control.

After a short walk from the baggage carousel, the hordes of passengers once again herded together as the queues bottlenecked at the final barriers. Staff in smart uniforms methodically and meticulously cross-checked passport photos against faces. The queue moved slowly, intermittently one by one, halting at the red markings on the tiled floor.

'Step forward, please,' demanded the border control officer.

Obediently, the passenger moved forward to the officers kiosk and presented his passport as instructed. Expressionless, the guard stared at him and then back at the passport. The man stood perfectly still without the slightest look of worry or concern.

'Look up to the camera, please, sir,' the guard instructed.

Smiling with his eyes, the man looked at the officer and then up at the camera.

'What is the nature of your trip here, sir?' asked the young border guard.

'Strictly business,' the passenger replied in an Eastern German accent. 'You know – gas, fuel, energy, for all your country's needs,' he added without prompting.

The guard was about to question him some more when a message transmitted through his twisted plastic earpiece. 'It's okay. He's ours. No more chat. Let him go,' came the order from a CCTV room high up in the airport's structure. The guard knew the drill and, without any change of expression, blankly gave a dismissive wave, beckoned the man on and called for the next passenger to step forward.

As though well-rehearsed, both Israeli agents met their people as the passengers meandered through into the now-busy arrivals lounge. Without any fuss, at timed intervals one folded his paper, the other put away his mobile phone and they moved to greet their respective passengers.

Jacob found his passenger. Their eyes met approvingly, acknowledging each other with hidden messages. They kissed intimately, and then he whispered in her ear, 'Is it him?'

'Yes,' she replied, kissing his neck affectionately and handing him her bag.

Rabis first waved, then walked toward his passenger, then slapped a very tall young man on the back and gave him a huge man hug. As they embraced, Rabis asked if the target was marked.

'Yes,' replied the tall young man, as he threw a sports bag over his shoulder. 'It's him. Grey jacket, cream shirt, loose tie, blue jeans, forty paces. It's him.'

~

FSB agent Pytor Stepanov walked straight ahead, looking for directions and bearings, then, looking around, dropped his gaze to the floor occasionally, trying to look casual. As he walked, he unzipped his bag's outer pocket and put away his passport, all the while following a family group, staying very close to them but without seeming to be part of them. He knew there was a strong chance he was being watched. He was always careful. He had trained for years on such missions.

This one, though, was a rushed job and he did not feel that he'd been given time to prepare. He had received his orders only a few days ago when he had been called to Moscow by the Chairman. Then, leaving hurriedly for his offices, he and other field agents had been briefed, then sent off in various directions around the globe. Pytor had flown down from Ryazan in Russia to Georgia before taking a connecting flight to Tel Aviv under the guise of a Russian energy salesman.

He carried one brown leather suit bag and a matching flight bag, both over his right shoulder. He only needed the flight bag but border patrols found that suspicious on international flights, so he always took the suit bag too. Leaving the air-conditioned complex and exiting through the automatic doors into the blistering heat of the day, he swung left sharply and headed to the end of the taxi queue rather than the front. He got into the latest cab to arrive and, before the driver could explain about the formalities of queueing, he pushed a 200-shekel note into his waving hand. In the mid-morning rush, no one noticed, and the driver drove quietly away and off into the highway traffic.

~

'Where's the mark?' Jacob asked Aretha, the female agent.

'No rush,' she said calmly. 'It's in his luggage. I flirted with him as I reached feebly for my bag in the overhead locker after touchdown. A certain very tall young man slipped it in his flight bag's zip pocket. He'll be headed into town.'

All four agents moved outside and, in their inconspicuous pairs, melted into the crowd as they passed the hustle and bustle of the buses, delivery vans, cars and taxis. A silver executive minibus with black-tinted windows slowly rolled by them. Without stopping and as if choreographed, the agents smoothly boarded the slow-moving vehicle unnoticed via its sliding side door. Within seconds they were all seated and chatting to each other as the minibus headed down the off-ramp and into the traffic.

Agent Rabis stretched out in his plush black leather seat and wiped his brow. He took a device resembling a cell phone from his jacket pocket and switched it on. All the agents quietened and waited. The screen flickered into life and, like a satnav, a street map of the city appeared. Then, after several more seconds, as icons flashed and vanished, a red dot settled itself on the screen and moved as slowly as they were.

Happy with the tracker, Rabis looked up at the staring faces. 'Great work, guys, well done. We're on the money. Let's get to work and flush him out. Remember, no contact and no heroics. Just watch him.'

~

Pytor sat quietly, not wishing to engage with the driver as his taxi trundled along in the simmering heat. His rear passenger window was open, and hot air blew across his face. He dabbed his brow with his neatly folded handkerchief, then pushed his sunglasses higher up on his nose and looked out at the landscape. He could not help but reflect on the obvious history, and of course the problems, that came with this country. The temperature was nearing thirty with a wind speed of ten. Initially, the scenery and highway looked as if they belonged to any other Middle Eastern country, until they entered the city. Approaching the Hatikva Quarter, Pytor noticed an ambience of calm and order, and the aroma of capitalism. The streets bustled with businesses. There was a distinct lack of boarded-up and bombed-out buildings. The streets were clean and free of litter. Even the pedestrians looked and behaved in an orderly manner. The Mercedes taxi swung off highway Route 1, over the Kibbutz Galuyot interchange, and picked its way through the narrow, tightly packed streets. It was a twenty-five-minute ride from the airport to the Jaffa district where Pytor's hotel was located. The agency staff had selected the accommodation to suit his cover, providing him with a mid-price, mediocre establishment suitable for an above-averagely successful salesman.

The taxi dropped him off at the hotel on the corner of Yefet and Ami'ad Streets and he gave the driver another 200 shekels. *More than enough*, he thought. After making his way to the room, he unpacked and took a shower. He was relaxed. This was not a high-level mission, but a Level 3. Level 1s were dangerous and could get him killed. A Level 3 was usually a fact-finding mission. The worst-case scenario was getting caught, arrested, possibly imprisoned and or deported. That only meant humiliation and possibly dismissal thereafter, depending on how the Kremlin felt at the time. The FSB had stopped shooting careless agents years ago, when they were known as the KGB, as the Kremlin realised too many were defecting to the West. In the Cold War days, if you were caught, it was better to defect and live out your days in Berkshire or Miami than face a firing squad, although Pytor recalled that the Israelis were not quite so accommodating with FSB spies.

After a leisurely shower, he lay on the bed and watched some TV. Later, he dressed for dinner and left the hotel, taking a short walk through the city to the plaza centre and eateries. Finding the required restaurant, he ordered a meal and a bottle of the house wine. Tomorrow, he had work to do and would be up early to begin his surveillance and fact-finding. He wasn't on edge and had no need for firearms. Initially, this would be an easy job: just find out who and what the Israelis knew and, if possible, the sources of the computer virus. As he finished his meal, he sipped his wine and watched diners come and go. Taking another drink, he looked up and saw a tall, slim man arrive wearing a coat and a flat cap.

The restaurant was dimly lit, but up three steps and along a short hallway he saw the man give his hat and coat to a waiter, who then led him through to Pytor's table. He was slender and about six feet two inches in height, with light brown hair brushed back and slightly receding. His face was weathered and wrinkled, with a pointed nose and thick, bushy eyebrows.

'Brandy, my Russian friend?' the tall man asked.

'But of course,' replied Pytor, standing up to shake hands.

The tall man ushered the waiter away, calling for two brandies as he sat down. 'My friend, my dear, good friend – how are you? How's the family? How is the energy business?' His voice feigned empathy but the words were hollow.

'And how are you, Dutch?' asked Pytor. 'Why haven't you retired, you old dog?'

Both men laughed and shook hands firmly again. The tall man really was called Dutch, although he too had been born and raised in East Berlin. His nickname came from his old KGB days as he was based in Holland and had once married a Dutchwoman. As the FSB's number-one European agent, and under instructions to divorce, he had been moved to Belgium in order to spy on the great Western European Union that was forever creeping closer and closer to Mother Russia's doorstep, swallowing up all the old Eastern bloc countries with promises of liberal freedom, capitalism and democracy. After the fall of the Berlin Wall, and under the present leadership at the Kremlin, Russia had to push back and regain lost ground. The likes of Dutch and Pytor were old defenders of the gate.

Once settled, and after the waiter had promptly delivered their drinks, their voices dropped lower. Happy that it was safe to do so, they talked about the good old days and then got down to business. Dutch explained that, although the news of a possible computer virus attacking the Iranian enrichment programme was out, no one would take ownership of it. It had been debated over and over, and the IT world agreed that it was too clever and too big to be the work of a lone operator. It was definitely of government origin, but no one could agree which government. The agents knew it was not Russian, as finding out more about it was their reason for being in Israel right now. Both men knew that their government applauded the viral assault for its technical genius and cunning and believed it to be the work of the Americans, even though sources suggested Israel or possibly a joint venture involving the Europeans. As the virus only affected the American software giant Microsoft and Germany's Siemens hardware empire, the Russian government were close to finalising several deals to replace all of Iran's nuclear computers with their own Russian products, convincing Iran that only Russia could truly help them achieve their end goal of becoming the only nuclear power in the Middle East. Russia always leaned heavily on its history as the only developed country and ally to continue commerce and trading, mainly in arms and machinery, with Iran over the past twenty years. Russia had, however, dropped the ball in the past decade when it came to cutting-edge technology. Now, with an Israeli, American or perhaps European virus sabotaging Iran's nuclear affairs, it was an ideal opportunity for Russia to regain some lost ground for the motherland. Once the contracts were signed, Pytor and Dutch's work would intensify, learning from the virus and discovering its originators to then use it against the West, and of course once all the Russian hardware and software was installed in the Iranian nuclear system, Russia would also control how the Iranians could proceed. The men discussed their tasks and directives at length to establish a game plan. Whoever was behind this problem could continue to wreak havoc until the contracts were agreed and signed off by both governments. Their question was, could it be managed and encouraged until the deals were complete?

Dutch explained about a deviation in plans. His task now was to brief Pytor on developing news. He spoke quietly but clearly. 'The Iranians are definitely on to something. They have recently dispatched agents into Turkey, France and Britain, but as yet we do not know why. What we do know is that any change in plans could result in disaster for our team. Damage at the Iranian nuclear plant is getting worse, but their investigations and the halting of the problem will completely change the dynamics of the multimillion-dollar deals with our government if this situation is allowed to improve. New orders from Moscow instruct us to not allow that to happen. The virus must continue to do its damage for now.' Whatever the Iranian SAVAK security and Intelligence Service were up to, and whatever leads they had, the status quo had to be maintained. Dutch was to cover Pytor's surveillance work in Israel and then return to Brussels. He was instructed to reassign Pytor to investigate the Iranian agents and leave immediately for Turkey.

The two men concluded their business and left the restaurant together. Once out of the door and into the night, they checked around carefully, then walked slowly and casually for a few minutes before splitting to the left and right. The streets were noisy and busy with evening commuters, revellers and tourists going about their business. Pytor went left and crossed the street, staying in full view and under the bright street lights. A tall young man casually lifted his burger in a wrapper and took a bite, then at the right moment threw it all in the bin and followed him.

Rabis watched from a fast-food takeaway window.

Dutch headed right and moved into a darkened side street, passing only a few kids throwing sticks and a couple locked in a passionate embrace, the man trying to push his tongue down the woman's throat. Happy that he wasn't being followed, Dutch pulled down his cap and increased his pace.

The couple fell back against the wall and the woman slapped the man hard but playfully on the neck. 'You bastard. You love that bit, don't you?' she whispered with a slight grin.

'No, I love *your* bits,' the man sniggered quietly as he buried his head in her neck once more.

'Get off me, you pervert,' she whispered, giggling. 'We've got work to do.' Grabbing Jacob's jaw, Aretha kissed him on the lips, grinned and then pushed him away. 'Now go.'

He twisted away from her, and she pulled down on his lapels as he did so. She helped him turn his beige leather jacket inside out to become a black bomber jacket, then handed him a black skullcap from her pocket. Jacob left her and set off to follow Dutch. Aretha reached into her shoulder bag and took out a pair of flat, black slip-on plimsolls. Changing out of her beige heels, she threw her bag over the wall and headed off in the opposite direction. She and Jacob knew the streets well and knew exactly where the Russian spy would exit, but she had to be quick to head him off as she'd more ground to cover. Breaking into a run, she hitched her skirt a little to help her with speed and tucked her right arm in to keep her pistol in check as her chest lifted and fell during the sprint. Within seconds she had vanished into the night.

Dutch slowly became aware of a young man following him and set about pre-empting his next moves. The street was long and narrow, with intermittent lights casting long shadows. He would go exactly the way he'd come and finding his mark on the wall, he dug his left foot into the sidewalk, transferred all his weight onto it and sprang up the six-foot wall. His hands grabbed the brickwork and he hauled his weight upwards with his biceps, whilst his right foot came up under his chest and levered him higher to level the wall copings. In seconds, he was over and into a yard.

Jacob called to Aretha through his earpiece. 'He's spotted me,' he whispered urgently as he broke into a run.

'I'll be there in five,' replied Aretha, panting and speeding up her sprint.

In the pitch-black backyard, Dutch was clearing the wall down the other side. As he fell, he stretched to dodge some trash bins, but miscalculated and, in his haste, caught his foot on the lids. Dogs barked and metal lids clattered as rubbish spewed onto the ground.

Aretha was sweating, her arms and legs pumping hard like pistons. Her chest heaved as she gulped in air, her body demanding more oxygen. Her light and agile frame flew around a corner and into the backstreet like an Olympic runner, her plimsolls landing softly and quietly as she galloped along. Jacob was heaving and panting and did not hear her as she rounded the bend into the dark street, surprising him with the speed of her arrival. He put a finger to his lips and gestured that he was about to jump the wall in pursuit. Aretha mouthed, 'Okay,' and gestured her reverse as she backed up and started to run back the way she had come to head off the Russian. As she hastened away, with her right hand she unzipped her jacket, reached in under her left arm, and unclipped the leather strap on her Beretta holster. With her right thumb, she flicked off the safety catch.

She ran to her left and then ducked right into an alley between the yards and scruffy apartment buildings. Halfway down she stopped and listened. Squinting in the dark, she heard Jacob approaching to her right. She was sure she had been fast enough to head off the tall Russian. Fighting to quieten her breathing, she pulled out her government-issue weapon from under her left arm.

A clatter of trash bins fell silent and the barking of dogs subsided. Her eyes struggled to adjust to the blackness and, panting as quietly as she could, she lifted her weapon in front of her face with both hands, dropping down low into a squat. With the alleyway wall in front of her, blinking hard, she scanned the alley up and down, left and right, and then quietly moved to her left, keeping as wide a field of vision as possible on the wall. Moving back into darker shadows, she watched as two hands appeared on top of the wall and, sure enough, she heard the scraping of shoes pushing up on the clay bricks. She lifted her pistol to eye level, pulling back on its hammer to cock the weapon in readiness. She needed the Russian spy on her side of the wall, for if she challenged him whilst he was climbing, he would simply drop back down, and although Jacob would be able to deal with him, she wanted him out of the backyards and into the alleyway.

As if unaware of her presence, the figure continued to climb and drop down over the wall. In the dim light she could see the tall frame of a man as his feet landed on the cobbled street. She stepped forward to confront him, keeping a safe distance to allow her to take control, arms outstretched, as her training had taught her. Applying light pressure to the trigger, her fingers tightened as she held her defensive stance.

'Stop!' she shouted as she brought her pistol up to align with the man's face. 'Stop right there.'

The man stood up, steadying himself after his drop. Before he could make a sound, she felt a warm, firm pressure against her back. She smelt body odour mixed with cologne, brandy and bad breath, and tightened her trigger finger. Within a split second, her weapon fired off a round. Jacob's eyes bulged. He stood there silently, staring vacantly at her as blood dripped from the bridge of his nose. Black and crimson gore shot from the back of his head and splattered on the wall behind him. Aretha looked in horror at the size of the hole in her partner's face, but before she could speak, she felt a sharp jab between her ribs as a blade slid into her heart. As if petrified, she stood perfectly still, unable to move. Her hands, still holding her pistol, were pushed down to her belly as her assailant's strong hand squeezed her trigger finger again, forcing her to shoot herself in the groin. The bullet blasted through her pelvis and shattered her pubic bone. She fell limply into his arms as the Russian released his hold on her hands. Withdrawing the short blade from her chest with his left hand and leaning to his right, he felt her petite body relax, her head rolling to the right.

The whole incident took no more than a minute. Although gunfire was not an uncommon sound in this part of Israel, Dutch knew that these agents would not be operating alone and every second he wasted brought the Security Services nearer to him. Releasing his grip on the dead agent, he let her roll out of his arms and onto the pavement. In a split second he had cleared the opposite wall and was again making his way through the backyards, this time exercising greater care to avoid more noise. Soon, he had vanished into the night.

Pytor heard the pop, pop of gunshots and the bark of a dog but kept walking to his hotel.

# 12

# BEYŞEHIR BEACH RESORT, TURKEY

The flight was uneventful and the air hostesses were doing their typical 'happy to help' thing, but Ed knew they were tut-tutting under their breath, cursing their demanding captive audience, groaning to each other that they should be at home with their kids. For him, it didn't matter. He had little family and the one woman he wanted was sitting right next to him. He could do the tourist bit no problem, and soon he would be taking his first holiday in years with the woman he loved. His requested window seat never disappointed. He loved looking out, and always marvelled at how insignificant everything became when viewed from such a height. At times he wished he could have been an astronaut, to be able to look down and see the curvature of the earth and the true colour of the blue planet. He loved flying, and back in the day had jumped at any chance he got to fly in the choppers. That was how he'd got into the squad: by jumping out of them as a search-and-rescue diver. He always thought flying was a contradiction. It fascinated him when he thought about how it took masses of clever, almost superhuman technology to get you up into the atmosphere, only to realise once there how humble and insignificant humans really are. The ground below lay in darkness, with islands of dusty, dark yellow street lighting marking out the built-up areas like a Polaroid map. Huge clusters of lights grouped together like land masses. The unlit areas looked like pitch tar; black oceans, lakes and rivers. This helped him to get his bearings, and he applied his mental geography of the city to the giant black-and-orange street map laid out before him.

After what seemed like several minutes spent staring in wonder, his neck was the first part of his body to remind him to sit back and relax. Then came the pain in his back, probably from his awkward sitting position over the past hour. He turned, unplugged his headphones from the armrest socket, pressed firmly on the 'recline' button, and allowed the seat to spring back into its upright position before he was instructed to do so by a member of the cabin crew. He looked at Esther, who was still sleeping. He loved to just watch her, especially when she was asleep. She was beautiful.

He pushed back against the seat and stretched out, whispering to her. 'Nearly there, darling. We're coming in to land.'

As he looked back out of the window, she opened her eyes, smiled and started to stretch.

After passport control, and with nothing to declare, they pushed through into the arrivals lounge. They retrieved their luggage and soon spotted their transport. A taxi driver had her name on a piece of card and waved it slowly to and fro, seemingly to fan himself. He greeted them in English, welcomed them to Turkey, and enthusiastically took their luggage trolley. The transfer drive was pleasant and the hotel just an hour and ten minutes away. It was already dark and getting late, and Ed just wanted a beer and a shower, in that order. Once checked in, they headed straight to the bar and lounge area. Shattered, they slumped into two dark leather tub chairs, and after downing half of his cold beer in one go, Ed called over a concierge and asked him to take up their luggage, pushing a ten-lira note into his hand. Esther drank a tall gin and tonic filled with ice. They looked at each other and smiled.

'Well, here we are,' they said, almost in stereo. Then they laughed and had some more drinks, then, even more tired, took their last drinks up with them to their room. In the lift Esther giggled as an older couple looked down their noses at them, as if they were teenagers sneaking drinks into their room. Their tipsiness made them laugh all the more.

The hotel was a four-star affair on the south-east edge of the lake. Built on the beach, facing out and to the north, it prided itself on being the top hotel in the resort, attracting the more financially comfortable tourists from all around Europe but, to Ed's surprise, mainly Russians and Icelanders. The resort was a bit off the British tourist radar due to extended flight times to the east and fewer amenities and services. The town, however, was an up-and-coming location, mainly because of the beautiful and unspoiled lake, which had given rise to many small independent water-sport companies and the obligatory restaurants and bars, which were making the most of Turkey's tourist boom. The hotel was perfectly positioned, the main building a convex curve overlooking the lake. This made the approach and entrance to the hotel concaved, as if to welcome as it wrapped itself around you. The building was a grand affair, clad in beige stone and marble, positioned perfectly just yards from the lake and on the main road to town. From the sandy shoreline ran a long jetty with a cream canopy and awning as a central focal and activity point. Between the hotel and shoreline lay beautifully gardened terraces and of course the pool, where they immediately made themselves at home. The holiday was a well-earned ten-day break, and after the break-in at their new home, Ed felt it was good that they were away from it all. This was, after all, their new start. He still puzzled over why their empty house had been broken into but had promised Esther he would not go on about it. They could sort out anything to do with that on their return home, but for now they would just enjoy their stay uninterrupted and unspoilt.

Their first evening was calm and laid-back. Slowly, they showered and dressed for dinner. After a leisurely and rewarding meal, they sat in the bar, drinking and chatting, interspersed with some quiet moments and some people-watching. After a few more drinks they took a bottle of wine up to their room. They fell on to the apartment-room couch, spreading out into a cosy cuddling position. They kissed, softly at first as they both wanted the moment to last, pretending they were in control of their actions and feelings. Despite the alcohol, Ed's manhood grew hard. Esther felt it through her dressing gown. Her soft jewel wept as she ached for him, dampening her underwear. She felt him standing tall and firm and couldn't wait any longer. He smelt her and pushed himself closer. She pulled at his trousers, forcing the waistband down, exposing him. Their kissing became more aggressive and they pulled harder at each other's clothes. His excitement grew as he felt the warmth of her body and the delicate lace of her pants against his erection. She felt her jewel weep more. Pulling her knickers to one side with one hand, she grabbed him with the other and guided him deep into her. He felt her warmth welcome him. She pulled him closer as he drove deep inside, their pubic bones thumping together as they writhed and twisted. Lying on top of her with his arms wrapped around her back, he whispered into her ear how he loved to be deep inside her. She gently bit his neck and whispered back, 'Fuck me.' He obliged, and their bodies heaved and sighed on the couch until they exploded, moaning in pleasure and ecstasy. Releasing themselves from their tight body lock, they collapsed into a deep, contented slumber.

~

They had enjoyed four hot, uneventful days, mainly by the pool. Each day they had lain there, sipping drinks and watching the world go by. Ed loved the sun but, being fair, always struggled for a deep tan and had to be content with a brown-red effect instead. On one six-month tour out in the Gulf he had come back lobster red. He also had to regulate his body temperature by alternating an hour of sunbathing with at least a good half-hour in the pool. With his short hair and high brow, he had also taken to wearing a bandana to prevent sunburn. Esther was more fortunate and her olive skin just seemed to get darker and darker. She joined him in the water only a few times a day as she had pushed her nose deep into a romantic novel and only glanced up periodically to discuss an odd chapter or just break the silence. They could easily go a good hour without talking. But the silence and tranquillity were welcome, and he did not mind. He often looked over and watched her, thinking how good she looked. She really did look great in her bikini and shades. She looked and acted the part of a celebrity on holiday, and they were getting into a routine, with the hotel staff beginning to notice them and get more familiar with 'the nice English couple.' Ed was now very familiar with the hotel, its grounds and layout, and the surrounding area. He always did this. It was a professional part of him; always being in control and fully aware of his environment was a number-one priority. After years of service, it was part of his own make-up.

Lying on his sun lounger, he tried to read and do some crosswords, but it was too sunny and too hot for him. He sat up and, facing her lounger, asked her what she wanted to drink.

Without moving a muscle, she softly replied, 'Something long and fruity. You decide.'

He leaned on his elbow, looked at her with a cheeky grin, and raised his eyebrows.

She read his mind instantly and laughed. 'Not that, darling; you do have a one-track mind. Besides, it's far too hot.'

They both laughed.

'You decide,' she said.

Brushing off the refusal, he went to the bar. As he ordered two long cocktails, his phone buzzed in his shorts pocket. Without looking at its screen for caller ID he answered it. 'Hello?'

It was Esther. Giggling, she said in a sultry tone, 'And don't forget lots of ice, big guy.'

He returned with two tall 'Sex on the Beach' cocktails and teased her back with the drink's name. They settled back into tanning mode, but he only lasted another half-hour. From boredom and the sheer heat, he sat up and checked his BlackBerry. Nothing. No mail, no notifications, just Esther's last call. At midday, it was a strong twenty-eight to thirty degrees, and the sweat just dripped off him onto his book. He tried another crossword puzzle but eventually gave up and lay there watching other tourists do tourist things. Paragliders came and went; boats left the long jetty. To him, this was 'empty-head time,' and he was enjoying it. He watched the steady stream of tourists trying their hand at various water sports, and locals working vigorously to attract clients. He had done all the activities on offer as part of his job and wasn't too interested. Skiing, windsurfing, jet-skiing, paragliding – they just did not appeal to him like they did to other tourists. He had also done parachuting, and loved it, but doing it as a tourist just didn't appeal. What did appeal, though, was the cool breeze that would be up there, and he would get to have a good look around too with aerial views.

# 13

## KASPERSKY LABS, MINSK, BELARUS

The lights in his office were the only ones on, and his desk light shone brighter than the overhead strip lights. Through the glass partition, all the other workstations and desks were abandoned and in darkness. An odd flashing red light of an answering machine blinked, and one PC screen bounced its logo around its monitor in screensaver mode as its operative had failed to switch it off properly. Documents, papers, pens, pencils and personal belongings lay where they had fallen in their owners' rush to beat the busy Friday traffic home. It was the end of a long day. In fact, it had been a long week.

He loosened his tie and unbuttoned his collar. He was tired and wanted to call it a day, but knew he had an even bigger day tomorrow. Looking at his desk, he had decided to stay behind for a clear-out in order to get more organised for the forthcoming day. At least then he would feel better. He hated being disorganised but, like most managers, struggled with time management on most days. He tugged his tie looser and scratched vigorously at the growing stubble on his chin, then kicked one leg up onto his desk and pushed back in his chair, clasping his fingers together at the back of his head. Looking up, he stared at the ceiling. Should he stay or go home? He looked down at his untidy desk and sprang into action. Lurching forward, he reached for his desk's bottom filing drawer. Pulling out a small bottle of whisky, he poured the remaining water from a paper cup into his cold coffee mug. Filling the paper cup with whisky, he took a swig and smacked his lips. Banging the paper cup down purposefully, he rolled up his sleeves and tidied the desktop, file by file, document by document. After a good hour or so and another large whisky, his desk was clear, clean and tidy. He looked down at his PC monitor, gave a sigh, took another swig from the paper cup, prepared himself for a second wave of proactive enthusiasm, and clicked into his emails. Next, he would remove hundreds of files and messages from his inbox. Then he could go home. Grabbing the whisky bottle, he poured again, took two more swigs, and slowly and methodically started wading through hundreds of emails. Deleting mercilessly as he went, sifting and scanning in a determined attempt to delete everything and anything, but wary of clearing out something really important, he slowed. Suddenly, a report caught his eye. He stopped and read. A computer belonging to a customer in Iran was caught in a reboot loop, shutting down and restarting repeatedly, despite attempts by operators to take control of it. It appeared the machine was infected with a virus.

Stephan headed up the antivirus division of a computer security firm based in Minsk. An offshoot of a well-known firm, the company had grown with the multibillion-dollar industry over the past decade, keeping pace with an explosion in sophisticated attacks, evolving viruses, Trojan horses and spyware programs. The firm was well known in Belarus but had until recently been unheard of across Europe or in the States. The best security specialists like Symantec and McAfee were rock stars among their peers, household names protecting everything from grandmothers' laptops to sensitive military networks. His firm, however, was neither a rock star nor a household name. His was an obscure company that few in the security industry had ever heard of. He did not know it, but that was soon to change. He read through the report a few more times and made a note for his team to have a look at it in the morning. Weary, he finally gave in and slowly switched everything off and locked up, all the while thinking about the Iranian customer's laptop problem.

~

The following morning, fresher than yesterday after some sleep, he burst into his office wanting to get on with things urgently. He dumped his attaché case and coat on his chair and headed straight for the canteen to grab a coffee. Other colleagues were in before him and the kettle was hot. The room was filled with office and clerical workers and the table stuffed with their handbags, sports bags and cycle helmets. Stephan was making himself a drink when Olef, his head researcher, arrived, also in search of a strong coffee. Stephan greeted him and spoke eagerly of his email report from last night, asking Olef to come to his office once he had got himself organised.

After a short meeting, Olef called the rest of the team into his office and explained what his boss had found the night before. Eager to exploit some good fortune, Stephan had instructed his team to bottom out this particular problem. He was extremely curious now and it had been on his mind all night. He didn't know why, but he wanted some answers. Computer cables snaked across the floor. Cryptic flow charts were scrawled across various whiteboards adorning the walls. A life-size Batman figure stood in the corner under a kids' toy basketball net which was fixed to the wall. The office might have seemed no different than any other geeky, high-tech workplace, but this one was in fact the front line of a new war: a cyber war. Unlike traditional battles played out in remote jungles or deserts, this one was being waged from a suburban office space just across the road from a kids' play park. Olef, the firm's most senior researcher, spent his days and many nights at the Eastern European branch, battling to keep the lid on a Pandora's box of the most insidious digital weapons ever to exist; ones capable of crippling water supplies, power plants, banks, and the very infrastructure that had once seemed invulnerable to attack.

After studying the virus and conferring with his peers, Olef reported back to Stephan. He had been able to work out that the worm was using a zero-day exploit to spread. Zero-days are the hacking world's most potent weapons: they exploit vulnerabilities in software that are still unknown to the program's manufacturer and antivirus vendors. They're also exceedingly rare. It takes considerable skill and persistence to find such vulnerabilities and exploit them. Of more than twelve million pieces of malware discovered by antivirus researchers each year, fewer than a dozen use a zero-day exploit. The discovery at this time was attributed to the virus accidentally spreading beyond its intended target due to a programming error introduced in an update. This led to the worm spreading to an engineer's laptop following a thumb-drive upgrade, and further when the engineer returned home and connected his computer to the internet. In Stephan's office over coffee, Olef explained all his findings. Steph was quiet for a while, thinking what to do. The virus had shown itself at over 38,000 locations but way over 20,000 of them were in Iran. Taiwan came in at a poor second place. Over 100,000 individual computers had been infected, again mostly in Iran.

Steph stared at Olef. 'Shit!' he exclaimed. 'Are you thinking what I'm thinking?'

Olef nodded back a very slow yes. In intercepting the virus data, the researchers risked tampering with a possible covert government operation against Iran.

'What do we know of its origin?' asked Steph, looking more worried.

'Nothing yet,' replied Olef.

Steph thought for a moment. 'Okay then. Let's home in on the Iran problem some more,' he said.

'Already done it. It's nuclear and it's Iran's uranium enrichment plant at Natanz for sure. Make no mistake,' urged Olef. 'Oh, and the malware was huge: 500 kilobytes.'

'Shit. Shit, shit, shit,' repeated Stephan angrily. His one big chance to break through into the big time of computer virus protection scuppered by the risk of it being a possible US government sting. 'Is it American?' he pleaded, sounding hopeful that it wasn't.

Olef paused. 'For the longest time I was thinking, well, maybe it just spread in Iran because they don't have up-to-date security software, and if it gets over to the States, some water treatment plant or some system or anything could be affected. I cannot say.'

Steph had confusion all over his face as he struggled with the gravity of the find. 'This discovery of a *500-kilobyte*,' he laboured heavily over the words, 'worm that has infected at least fourteen industrial sites in Iran including a uranium enrichment plant, and dozens of other countries, has been made...' he paused, 'by us, Olef. We have found this.' He laughed out loud, amazed. 'This is espionage at the highest, highest level.'

Olef nodded slowly. 'Although normally a virus relies on an unwitting victim to install it, this worm spreads on its own, over a network.'

'Yes, it's quite huge, isn't it? It's complicated too, and very professional. It's definitely government level at least.' Steph stared wide-eyed at Olef, excited like a child with a new toy. 'This discovery is potentially massive. Some very high-up and clever people are writing malicious codes that infect systems and cause collateral damage to thousands of computer-controlled systems around the world.'

Steph thought hard about his options. He wanted the fame and glory of the discovery for the good of his business, but did not want some CIA-led SWAT team crashing through his offices making his life hell. What could he do? The two men discussed the dilemma some more, then Steph came up with a plan. 'We go public!' he proclaimed. 'As the virus operates only through Windows and Step 7, we'll report our findings to both companies using the usual protocol.' Feigning ignorance would allow his small firm to put out feelers and get feedback from the two giants, as it was possible that they too had a hand in this cunning scheme. Meanwhile, they would put out some geeky posts on social media and in chat rooms, again to advertise their findings but also to attract any other information in return.

~

When Microsoft received the vulnerability report they sent some info back to Steph. After further decoding of the virus, and for ease of reference, they'd dubbed it 'Stuxnet,' combining the file names 'Stub' and 'MrXnet' found in the code. As the software giant prepared a patch to address the problem, Steph went public with the discovery in a post to a security forum. Three days later, security bloggers took up the story, and antivirus companies around the world scrambled to grab samples of the malware. The whole industry went into a frenzy. It turned out that the code had been launched into the wild as early as a year before and its mysterious creator had updated and refined it over time, releasing three different versions.

Steph sat alone at his desk and looked at his watch. He was both worried and excited by the discovery – more worried, really – and had begun to look over his shoulder, waiting for government officials to crash in and rip apart his business with arrest warrants from Europe's highest secret service agencies. He looked through his glass partition. Staff had begun to filter home and the office was slowly emptying. He lifted his desk phone and called his PA. 'Natasa?'

'Yes, Stephan,' she said curiously. 'Of course, it's me.'

'Err, yeah, yeah, I know, I know,' he said. 'Can you and Olef come back into the office, please?'

'Of course,' she said again. 'I will go get Olef before he leaves. Give me five minutes.' She put the phone down.

With both of them present, Stephan instructed Natasa – a middle-aged, dark-haired woman wearing thick-rimmed glasses and a smart but casual navy-blue trouser suit – to take some notes. 'It's Friday evening,' he said, 'and I'm going home. If I turn up dead and you're told I committed suicide over the weekend or on Monday, I just want to tell you guys, I am absolutely, categorically, definitely *not* suicidal.'

# 14

# BEYŞEHİR BEACH RESORT, TURKEY

It was nearing noon. They had been at the poolside for over two hours. It was hot. Too hot, and Ed was bored. Dripping sweat stung his eyes. He rubbed them, adjusted his bandana and pushed his Ray-Bans back up on his nose. He swung his legs around to his right, sat up on his lounger and looked at Esther. She was fast asleep, her big sun hat covering most of her face. He tilted it up a little to see more of her face, and again thought how beautiful she was and how much he loved her. He looked around as if to check where he was, then made his way to the pool but changed direction due to the cool breeze coming up from the shoreline, instead deciding on a dip in the lake. The sand was hot beneath his feet and he sped up, almost running to get into the water. He dived into the lake and rejoiced as the cool water soothed his pink, brown and red skin. It felt good, and it refreshed him. He swam further out and relaxed.

~

Two men walked nonchalantly and confidently across the hotel reception floor as if they themselves were residents of the hotel. They did not look at each other. One guy, in chinos and polo shirt, passed the long marble reception desk and stepped out onto the bar terrace. He pulled out one of the brown leather bar stools and made himself comfortable. Without rushing or demanding eye contact, he casually waited for the bartender to come to him and then quietly, but in perfect English, asked for a vodka and Coke on the rocks. The other man, dressed in smart brown shoes, trousers, a pale-yellow shirt and a lightweight jacket, wandered toward the toilets behind the reception area. Crossing the marbled floor to a foyer, he viewed the long corridor down to the men's and ladies' bathrooms. With a genuine need, he continued toward the men's room. Approaching the bathroom foyer, he moved to his right and looked into the unattended ladies.' It too had a reception area, and from the doorway he saw a row of vanity basins cut neatly into the grey marble worktops and complemented by mirrors, glass shelves and two pretty mirrored towel dispensers. Two wall-mounted hand dryers adorned the opposite wall, and below them an abstract print of a beach scene. Beyond the basins was a row of five cubicles. The man pulled his trousers up a little on each leg then crouched down to retie the lace of his shiny leather shoe, in the process covertly checking the occupancy of the cubicles. All were empty. Beyond them, another open door led through into three shower compartments. Confident that he was alone, he stepped further into the ladies' toilets and checked the shower cubicles. All were empty. He returned to the gents, finished his own personal business and then went back to the hotel terrace and ordered a coffee.

~

After approximately half an hour of bobbing and floating on his back, Ed swam back to shore and waded out onto the sandy beach.

A local guy working a speedboat parasailing activity walked past and tried to hand him a ticket. 'Want a go, my friend?' he said in a friendly manner.

'No, not today, thanks, mate,' Ed replied. Dripping wet, he felt compelled to take the voucher as he did not want to offend the local guy too much.

'Oh, my friend. Very good trip. You English? We love English. Look, you see my boat? Bayliner. Very British, yes. Very new, very fast. Beautiful boat and beautiful day for a man with a beautiful wife.' The man never stopped for breath. 'Look, voucher discount, gives you half price. Look at views of lake. Three hundred feet. Very beautiful, scenic, yes? You like to go, yes?'

Ed knew the that the Bayliner was American and that touts say anything for a sale. He paused, looked at the voucher and then up the beach to the poolside as if seeking Esther's approval. He thought for a moment. He *was* bored, and Esther *was* deep into her book or asleep. It *was* red hot and he wanted to keep cool. He looked at his watch: 12.30. 'How much?' he asked the vendor.

'Twenty euros, sir; you have voucher also, my friend,' the young Turk replied.

'For how long?' Ed asked.

'Twenty minutes, boss, but it quiet now. You tourists love siesta time.'

Ed thought for a moment. 'Okay,' he said, 'I will go get my wallet.'

'No, no, no! No problem, boss – we charge to reception. Your room can pay.'

'Okay.' Ed looked up toward the pool. He was thinking of telling Esther what he was doing before embarking on the activity, or leaving her a note or something, but the guy pulled persistently at his arm. He gave in. 'Okay, okay,' he said. 'Show me the lake and some beautiful views, then.'

The young Turk, too, looked up toward the hotel and pool bar, as if looking for approval, then whistled down the jetty to someone, snatched back the voucher and whistled again. He shouted to the man in the boat 'Malik! Start her up!'

Ed followed him to a very impressive, shiny and powerful Bayliner Bowrider speedboat. The driver powered up the two huge outboard Evinrude 300hp engines. Leaving the jetty, the boat took up position in the lake and built up speed, paying out its cargo of parachuted tourist on an electric winch. The parasail filled and took up the strain, and slowly Ed rose up off the back of the speedboat. As he lifted off, he looked over his shoulder to see if he could attract Esther's attention. He could maybe whistle to her or wave, he thought, just to let her know where he was and what he was up to, but he could see she was still slumbering on her lounger, and he was climbing rapidly. The boat headed out into the vast lake in a north-westerly direction, and Esther and the hotel soon shrank into the distance. He guessed he was at around 200 feet or so. The views were amazing, and his enthusiasm and interest grew as he shifted his body weight in the harness to get more comfortable. He slipped into tourist mode, telling himself to relax more, be less serious and have some fun. The warm breeze felt wonderful against his skin. The sun beat down and he could feel its strong rays on his forehead, arms and shoulders. He should have put more cream on before setting off, or a T-shirt. At least he had his bandana. His nylon beach shorts were drying out and the harness was becoming more comfortable. He soaked up the stunning, panoramic view and, adjusting his sunglasses, he maintained his bearings.

After a good ten minutes, the boat made a gentle U-turn and headed back toward the resort. As the resort grew bigger in Ed's view, he automatically started to look for Esther. First, he saw the distinct outline of the long jetty with its canopy leading to the hotel. At the end of it, the sand and straw parasols of the beach came into view, and then he could see the whole of the hotel. Behind the beach lay the pool area, then the terraces and balcony of the hotel bar and restaurant. He could now make out the apartments, reception, car park and delivery areas.

~

Esther, half dozing, half sweltering, lazily lifted her left arm to view her watch. She cupped her right hand over the top edge of her sunglasses. It was lunchtime. She also needed to powder her nose. The cocktails she had had that morning had helped her to doze off in the hot sun, but were now forcing her to take decisive action. She really did need the bathroom. Looking at Ed's empty lounger, she wondered if he too had needed the bathroom, or was perhaps at the bar again. She sat up and pushed her little feet into her turquoise-and-black flip-flops. Standing, she adjusted her bikini bottoms, pulled a matching sarong around her waist and threw a small matching sequinned bag over her arm. She looked around for Ed but saw only a couple of men drinking at the bar and a few people on loungers.

As Esther slipped past the reception lobby, the man in chinos downed his drink and left the bar. The man with the shiny shoes put down his coffee. As Esther breezed down the corridor to the ladies,' Chinos Man stealthily stalked her to within a few yards. Shiny Shoes Guy hung back until Esther and Chino Man turned into the toilet foyer area. Chinos Man now sped up to follow and stepped right into the bathroom foyer also. As he followed his colleague into the ladies,' he pulled at the damaged silver handle of a closed door, to his left, between the ladies and the gents. The cleaners' cupboard opened, revealing another door that opened into the car park. The outer door lay conveniently ajar.

From behind, before she could react to his reflection's presence in the row of mirrors, Chinos Man had Esther in a forearm lock with his left hand pushed firmly against her mouth. As if rehearsed, Shiny Shoes Guy pulled her face toward him and placed a dampened handkerchief over her nose and mouth. In shock and terror, she spat and hissed like a cat, kicking Chinos Man hard on his shins as he lifted her slight body off the ground. With her arms pinned down by her sides, she kicked and tried desperately to bite her assailants. The cloth was smelly and tasted like the dentists. She closed her eyes to protect them from the vapours she was involuntarily inhaling. *Don't breathe it in*, she told herself, but it was too late. Already the substance was having its effect, and she felt helpless against it and the pressure exerted by the big guy with the shiny shoes. She felt dizzy and light-headed. Her beach bag fell and spilled its guts across the bathroom floor. Toiletries and lipsticks clattered. Shiny Shoes Guy hit the hand dryer buttons to mask the noise. Chinos Man leaned back against the basins, knowing it would take time to complete the task, and after four minutes, Esther's kicking weakened as he held her frame with his right arm around her waist. Her feet hung off the floor, her delicate little red-varnished toes just touching the cool marbled tiles.

A voice called out in Turkish. A male janitor had entered the cleaners' room from the car park area to deposit his mop and bucket. He brandished the mop handle like a lance in some feeble attempt to ward off the attackers.

Shiny Shoes Guy spun around and pulled out an unusually rounded black Vektor CP1 pistol from under his jacket. The cleaner backed off in terror. Esther passed out and fell limp in Chinos Man's arms. The cleaner's eyes widened in panic and he backed away into the cleaners' room. The two assailants followed him, dragging Esther with them. In blind panic, the cleaner wanted to run, but as he went to drop the mop to flee back to the car park, Shiny Shoes Guy lifted the revolver and struck the janitor hard in the head with the heel of the gun handle. The employee fell to the floor and the hand dryer stopped blowing. Tyres screeched outside from the car park. Shiny Shoes Guy hissed into his radio and quickly returned to the ladies to gather up all the spilt items from Esther's beach bag. Then the two men hurriedly hauled the woman through the cleaners' cupboard, sending the mop bucket and its contents of dirty water flying into the car park. As they dragged Esther into the bright sunlight, outside, their getaway car revved its engine and squealed its tyres on the baking concrete of the hotel delivery area as it screamed into view, but then came a loud thump, followed by the sound of breaking glass and plastic. Unexpectedly, a white delivery van was blocking the car's path. The driver pushed the car hard, past the laundry van's front bumper and, with a shudder and a groan, more of the van's plastic gave way. The car pushed past and sped to the cleaner's door, screaming to a halt under a small canopy. The driver jumped out and flung open the boot lid. Within seconds, the two men bundled an unconscious Esther into the boot of the four-door saloon and Shiny Shoes threw her little bag onto the car's back seat. Again, there was a squeal of rubber as the engine revved high and the car pulled away from the parking lot with rear doors still open. Spinning the car around, the driver floored the accelerator and the manual transmission drove the engine to maximum revs, propelling the car forward past the damaged van, then out of the car park, across the highway and onto a dirt track opposite. Passing vehicles braked, skidded, and blasted their horns in disgust at the reckless manoeuvres. Suddenly, the car stopped for only a moment, allowing the driver to regain control, then, after checking the confusion of vehicles blocking the highway, he sped off down the dirt track in a south-easterly direction, toward the mountains.

# 15

## CIA HEADQUARTERS, LANGLEY, VIRGINIA, USA

It was 7.33am. Just an hour ago he had been walking and chatting on the lawn in the Jacqueline Kennedy Garden of the White House and drinking coffee with the President. Now he was on to the next leg of his assigned project. His shoes were still wet with morning dew and grass cuttings still clung to the polished black leather. Passing Sycamore Island in the Potomac River to his right, Defence Secretary Jack Harris sat back in his car seat as the chauffeur gently and effortlessly pushed the big black Lincoln's steering wheel with the palm of his right hand. Jack Harris's right elbow was anchored firmly into the grey leather armrest, and he held what was left of his paper-cup coffee, half full and lukewarm. The Lincoln hummed, almost silently but effortlessly, off the George Washington Memorial Parkway, along the river and up the off-ramp. The huge car veered left as it nosed around the long, lazy left-hand bend, up and over the highway. In seconds they were crossing the flyover. Harris looked out and down at the road he had just left, and then, turning left once more, they were on the final approach.

'Nearly there, sir!' said his aide.

Huge, established old oak and sycamore trees avenued the way in. Yellow 'no stop' lines flanked the black tarmac. The grass verges were dotted with yellow-and-black diamond-shaped 'slow' signs, but also signs warning drivers to keep their vehicle moving. A sizeable obvious sign, white letters on a red background, warned against photography, whilst another prohibited tourists; although a national park, this was not a picnic area. The avenue was beautiful, with verges and kerbs maintained to the highest standard. The sun shone early, low and bright across the asphalt, casting long shadows onto the manicured lawns behind the parallel rows of trees. The road led to a more important place. As the sign stated, after a thirty-minute commute, Harris had arrived at Langley, Fairfax, the United States Central Intelligence Agency's global headquarters. Ahead, he saw the familiar grey-and-yellow-painted automatic barriers and sentry boxes, staffed by perfectly iron-pressed, uniformed military guards. He groped across the seat for his ID card and lanyard and returned his coffee cup to the factory-fitted cup holder.

'I got that, sir,' said his aide, holding up the ID card in readiness.

~

Already seated around the huge, polished-glass conference table, the Vice President, the Secretary of State, the Principal Director for Homeland Security, the Director of Central Intelligence, the Head of Counterterrorism, the Intelligence Inspector General and the Director of National Intelligence greeted each other with combinations of 'Hi', 'Good morning' and warm handshakes.

Replenished with fresh coffee from an enthusiastic young female member of staff, Harris's aide handed out seven black faux-leather A4 attaché folders to all delegates and placed the eighth one in front of his boss. Each contained several copies of letters (one from the former President), information, instructions, and a copy of a letter Harris had brought with him from the current President. Every folder's cover bore a sticker on which, stamped in red ink, was the word 'Classified.' Harris tugged a little at his collar and pulled down on his tie knot to invite each member of the meeting to relax more. None of them needed his approval to adopt an informal stance, as they were all equal political giants in their own sphere of influence and power. They just afforded the Vice President and Secretary of State a little politeness before taking Harris's lead, as it was he who was heading up the meeting. Once satisfied with protocol, all members began to slump and relax a little around the table, pushing chairs back and flipping off the lids of their coffees.

Harris nodded to the Vice President and acknowledged his presence and superiority. 'Mr Vice President, ladies, gentlemen,' he started, undoing his top shirt button. 'Thanks for coming. Breakfast will be at ten; until then, let's knuckle down.'

The delegates looked at each other and scanned the table. No one wanted to leave for the bathroom and, after a momentary pause, Harris continued.

'We all know why we are here. Please open your dossiers at page one. You should be up to speed with our problem in Iran; however, for clarity and to ensure we're all singing from the same hymn sheet, our briefing begins with a short summary to explain why we are where we are currently.'

Heads dropped and pages rustled and turned.

Harris continued. 'The history to this is important, so please bear with me. In March 1957, research into the peaceful uses of atomic energy commenced under Eisenhower's Atoms for Peace programme. In 1967, under the Western-leaning rule of Shah Mohammad Reza Pahlavi, the Tehran Nuclear Research Centre was established and equipped with a US-supplied reactor, fuelled by US-supplied, highly enriched uranium. Iran signed the Nuclear Non-Proliferation Treaty in 1968 and ratified it in 1970 with a desire to electrify its barren country and lift its people out of poverty. During the 1970s, the Shah planned twenty-three nuclear power stations and a plutonium reprocessing facility.

'In 1975, a Pakistani metallurgist known as Guru Makhan was working at the European Uranium Consortium – Urenco – in the Netherlands. He stole design patterns for aluminium centrifuges, which are the backbone of the nuclear enrichment process. Then he vanished, but later showed up back in Pakistan as head of their nuclear programme, which of course later led to Pakistan obtaining the atomic bomb. Unknown to the Pakistani government, and using his research labs as cover, Makhan started a side business, selling his knowledge, technology and hardware to the highest bidder, including North Korea, Iran and Libya. Intel told us that, way back in 1978, he'd begun selling his technology to Iran, but Iran lacked precision engineering skills and so undertook to buying from Libya, in the form of centrifuge tubes. Later, after years of intel gathering, and under the Bush–Blair era, the CIA and MI6 compromised this supply chain with bogus parts. Makhan's trafficking system was shut down and the Libyan operation had to dismantle its nuclear ambitions.'

Harris checked his audience. They were enthralled and listening intently. Happy with his delivery, he moved on.

'Obviously, after the Iranian Islamic Revolution of 1979, with the last monarch of Persia in exile in Egypt, the Bushehr nuclear project was halted, with one power station fifty per cent complete and another at eighty-five per cent. In 1980, after the revolution, the US of course stopped supplying highly enriched uranium to Tehran.'

He looked around the table. Everyone was fully engaged and keen to know more.

'In the 1990s, the Russians and Chinese provided the Islamic regime with nuclear technical experts, assistance and materials, and in 2002, Iran began to build the enrichment plant at Natanz, 200 miles from Tehran. In 2002, the UK's MI6, our CIA and the French intelligence agencies corroborated evidence to prove that the Iranian Revolutionary Guard had established an anti-aircraft missile battery at the base of a mountain near Natanz. The site was deemed to be heavily protected. Unable to deny its presence any longer, in 2003 Iran admitted the Natanz project's existence and entered into negotiations with the UK, France and Germany, known at the time as the EU Three. We took a firmer stance and demanded Iran halt all nuclear ambition. From 2002 to 2006, International Atomic Energy Agency observers reported several breaches of the Non-Proliferation Treaty, and that they were being prevented from gaining access to many areas of the Iranian nuclear programme. As we are all aware, in 2005, a new hardliner, Mahmoud Ahmadinejad, was elected President on the platform of defiantly resuming the nuclear programme and, just for good measure, publicly announced that he would wipe Israel off the map.'

Harris looked across the table. Not a coffee cup was lifted, nor a document turned. All was silent. All the board attendees knew much of this, but were now learning more, in detail. On track, but knowing he had some way to go, Harris paused and took a drink, allowing them to digest what he had said, then picked up his story.

'Negotiations continued in Geneva, but finally in 2006 Iran announced that it had successfully enriched uranium, leading to more extensive negotiations with the IAEA and the EU. Satellite imagery of Natanz and Isfahan showed photos of the plant and its buildings slowly disappearing, but new, huge, heavy power lines running into new underground facilities were appearing. Ahmadinejad proudly pronounced the Fordow Fuel Enrichment Plant open. From 2006 to 2010, the UN Security Council issued eight resolutions and implemented tighter sanctions whilst condemning the regime for its violation of the treaty. As we all know, Iran's Parliament has recently seen angry clashes between protesters and police, for which we have of course taken the blame for stoking up anti-government sentiment, as it is about to approve a deal on its nuclear programme, to be agreed with the P5+1 world nuclear powers. The deal will be passed with an overwhelming majority. The official Islamic Republic News Agency is also expected to confirm this soon after, thereby cementing Iran as a nuclear power. Some of the more conservative Iranian Parliament members have criticised their President for being too aggressive toward the UN, the EU, the US and Israel, suggesting he was deliberately trying to delay the deal due to an upcoming election. We all know what an anti-Westerner he is. His cronies, the fanatics and his allies of course support him and will push this atomic issue during the election run-up. After his threat to exterminate the Jewish state, Ahmadinejad now wants to strike fast and get in the first punch.

'Nevertheless, the deal between Iran and the P5+1 – the US, the UK, France, China and Russia, plus Germany – would end twenty years of negotiations and, more importantly, twenty years of Iran not having atomic weapons. In May, Republicans in the US Congress tried to sink the deal by voting on a motion of disapproval. Democrats, however, gathered enough votes to block the motion and handed our President a public political policy victory. Inside sources confirm Iran's Parliament has seen angry clashes over the agreement. The UN Security Council passed seven resolutions back in 2006 requiring Iran to stop producing enriched uranium, which can be used for civilian purposes but also to build nuclear bombs. Four of the resolutions imposed tough sanctions in an effort to persuade Iran to comply.'

Beginning to find some rhythm, Harris interlocked his fingers and placed his elbows evenly on the table. 'Now Iran can operate 5,060 first-generation centrifuges, configured to enrich uranium to 3.67 per cent – well below the level needed to make an atomic weapon. It can also operate up to 1,000 centrifuges at its mountain facility at Fordow, but those cannot be used to enrich uranium. Iran has agreed to reconfigure its heavy water reactor at Arak so that it will only produce a small amount of plutonium as a by-product of power generation, and will not move heavy water reactors for at least fifteen years. International monitors already in the country are being given access and should be able to carry out comprehensive programmes of inspection of Iran's nuclear facilities, as we speak. Iran has promised to allow foreign inspectors to investigate the so-called 'possible military dimensions' to its programme. This should determine whether the country ever harboured military ambitions for its nuclear programme; a claim it has always strenuously denied. All this sounds great however,' he paused and, without raising his head too much, rolled his eyes high to look around at the delegates' body language, 'the Iranian Parliament insists that inspectors can only have very limited access to its military sites and, of course, not with exception, the Natanz plant. This is the plant we believe has the most potential to develop military-grade enriched uranium. Iran still insists that its nuclear programme is entirely peaceful and that it has the right to pursue alternative civilian and industrial energy. Let me be clear, folks!' He raised his voice and spoke slowly and firmly. 'For eighteen years, Iran ran and hid from the whole goddamned world a clandestine uranium enrichment programme, in absolute defiance and breach of the Nuclear Non-Proliferation Treaty. As most of you may know, the site in question was none other than the plant at Natanz.'

He paused and took a swig of his coffee, then stood up, loosened his tie some more, pushed his glasses up his nose and, placing his hands in his pockets, began to pace the floor as if he were a lecturer presenting to his students. 'All EU and US energy and economic sanctions, and most UN sanctions, will be lifted on the day Iran shows it has complied with the main parts of the deal. Iran will reduce its stockpile of enriched uranium by ninety-eight per cent, down to 660 pounds or 300 kilograms. It will also have to reduce by two-thirds – to 5,060 – the number of centrifuges installed to enrich the uranium. Sanctions will have to be lifted as Iran's compliance is verified by the IAEA inspectors and,' he paused again and rolled his eyes up and around the room for reactions, 'more than one hundred billion dollars' worth in assets frozen overseas will be...' He leaned on the back of his seat. 'Ladies,' he said, looking at the Secretary of State. 'Gentlemen. I fucking kid you not.' He paused again. 'Will be released,' he went on with a definite tone to his voice. 'Should this agreement be struck, it will authorise the lifting of those sanctions in return for Iran curbing sensitive nuclear activities, which we know ain't gonna happen. Therefore,' he checked again for reactions from his captive audience, 'please turn to page eleven in your dossiers. Folks, we too have an election coming up.'

Heads lifted immediately as if in salute.

'To that end, before you, you will see a letter from the President to me, agreeing that this deal ain't ever gonna happen. Privately, the President and all Defence and Security departments,' he looked over the top of his reading glasses at his colleagues, 'agree that this deal cannot ever go ahead. However, publicly and politically we must do all we can to secure and support the deal but,' he lifted and pointed his finger, 'privately, we absolutely cannot allow this agreement to come to fruition and we *most certainly* cannot allow these raving lunatic Islamist fanatics to get their grubby little hands on an extra hundred billion dollars of bomb-making money! Absolutely no way,' he stated, scanning the room.

Now he had the upper hand and the political clout and authority. He stared around the table, defying anyone to comment or to challenge him. The room was silent.

'Good, then we all agree?' Content that there was no doubt or lack of confidence, he continued quietly. 'Luckily, we have some options, a contingency plan, and if you turn to page thirteen, for those who are unaware, I will bring you up to date and brief you on the current operation.'

Page thirteen was headed 'Operation Olympic Games' in bold. He allowed his colleagues some time to read, then spoke again. 'When Gaddafi was driven to surrender his nuclear ambitions, we commenced dismantling his plants. We – or, I should say, the International Atomic Energy Agency – were able to warehouse and inspect over one thousand uranium enrichment centrifuges known as P1s. These aluminium tubes were found to be of poor quality as Libya also lacked the engineering and manufacturing skills needed to produce high-quality centrifuges. Working together with our secret service allies, over time, we slowly re-established the old Pakistani black-market supply chain and ensured the Iranians received all one thousand or more substandard P1 centrifuges.'

Harris pushed a button on a remote that lay nearby on the desk. A large, flat screen TV dropped down from its unconcealed resting place in the ceiling and flipped itself into a viewing position. He pressed some more buttons, and slowly, low-quality images flickered onto the screen. The filming was poor and the camera unsteady but the footage showed a scene of disruption, as many long metal cylinders were carried out of a factory-type environment. The pictures were poor but the event unfolding could be seen. A clean-up operation of many centrifuge tubes was being recorded covertly.

The Defence Secretary pressed the pause button on the remote and leaned forward into the conference table. 'Folks,' he said, more quietly, 'the incident you are witnessing was filmed secretly and very recently by an IAEA inspector, and the location of this incident was none other than Control Room 4 at the Natanz uranium enrichment plant.'

All the delegates sat quietly, watching the frozen, grainy image of tangled metal tubes being loaded onto long airport-baggage-type trucks.

Harris spoke again. 'The tubes being removed are indeed Gaddafi's old P1 centrifuge tubes. This brings us to page fourteen of your dossiers: more details of the contingency. If I could ask you all to take a look…'

# 16

# BEYŞEHIR BEACH RESORT, TURKEY

The Bayliner had turned and was now on approach back to its jetty. Still at a good altitude, Ed surveyed the patchwork quilt of fields, gardens and properties below. He watched as a beige coach pulled up at the main entrance of his hotel and lots of little ants disembarked. *Must be changeover day*, he thought. He saw a delivery van arrive at the rear delivery area, then a black car pushing its way past the van. An arm waved out of the van driver's window, but the car kept pushing through. Above the rush of wind in the chute he could hear the faint sound of car horns. The car careered through the arriving pedestrians in the hotel forecourt and then out of the car park, across the main road and over the central reservation. Clouds of dust billowed up as its wheels spun on the dry, baked earth between the tarmac routes. The car seemed to race off faster as it tore down a dirt road, away from the hotel. Ed tried to make out more of the incident but was now dropping faster and faster. It all looked a little odd, but then he remembered that this was Turkey. Maybe it wasn't too unusual after all, he thought, and his being unable to judge the car's speed and the amount of dust from the dry road probably made it look faster than it actually was.

He was still pondering when the boat guy shouted up at him to pay attention. He was fast approaching the landing platform on the stern of the powerboat. Shaking him out of his reverie, he heard the young guy shout, 'Boss! English! Look now!'

This bit came as second nature to Ed as he had landed on moving boats thousands of times whilst simultaneously performing other tasks without thought or blinking an eye. As he landed, his attention returned to being the tourist and doing as he was told. It was now gone 1pm and he had indeed been given a few minutes extra as promised. Thanking the boat driver and its crew, he walked up the jetty and across the beach, hopping over the hot sand. On reflection, he decided that, overall, he had enjoyed his little jaunt, and might invite Esther to do a tandem parasail later on. He was soon walking toward the pool. The lounger area was almost deserted. Only a few diehard sun worshippers remained at their stations: a trendy-looking young couple who couldn't leave each other alone; two newly arrived, pink-skinned women; a fat, hairy, dark-skinned old man snoring with an old beach hat over his face; and an older woman on her own across the pool. Anyone with any sense was in the restaurant, the bar or their air-conditioned rooms as the temperature was now climbing to thirty degrees plus.

Esther's lounger was empty. Everything was neatly in place. Her towel was laid across it as it had been when they'd arrived that morning. Her book was face down, open, resting on top of a rolled-up beach mat covered with her sun hat. Ed looked over at the bar. There was no sign of her. He screwed up his eyes as he replaced his Ray-Bans. He looked in the pool. It was empty. Maybe she had gone to lunch, he thought. No, she would have waited for him. He grabbed his flip-flops and headed to the reception area, passing a couple of staff who were shouting in Turkish. They seemed most flustered and confused. There had been some sort of commotion. After calling their room to no avail, he checked with the young lady behind the counter, who was also looking very agitated. She was on the phone, talking rapidly. Looking up from the desk, she saw him. Before he could ask the question, he spotted a male janitor sitting in an office room behind reception having some first-aid treatment administered to his head, and a number of staff congregating around him. The young receptionist put her hand over the mouthpiece and gestured to the ladies across the hallway near the elevators. Looking at the young girl's face, Ed too panicked. Esther had preferred those toilets rather than the poolside facilities, as she had said that they were cleaner. The entrance to the toilets was down a short corridor from reception, with smart wood-and-marble-effect walls. He walked down the hallway, attempting to knock discreetly on the ladies' door to see if Esther was okay. To his left was a cleaning cupboard with its broken door open. He looked in as he passed and stopped, noticing its contents. It was a typical cleaning cupboard with the usual brooms, trolleys, mop buckets, bottles of detergent, and shelves stuffed with cloths. Through an open exterior fire-exit door leading to the car park lay a yellow mop bucket on castors, tipped on its side with its long, tubular aluminium mop handle lying outside on the tarmac. Soapy water had been spilt from the receptacle and was drying in the midday sun, temporarily staining the black asphalt. Other cleaning items were strewn around the open doorway. Someone had left in a hurry. In an instant, Ed's mind flashed back to his parasailing session and the commotion between the black car and the van in the car park. He could see now that a scuffle had played out and that people had pushed someone into the black car. *That's why it sped off so fast.*

In a blind panic he burst into the ladies,' calling Esther's name. He slammed open and checked all the cubicles. Nothing. There was no sign of her. His eyes scoured the bare interior of the bathroom but found nothing. Then, as he moved out to the hallway, he caught a glint of metal in his peripheral vision. Not sure what he had seen, he looked again, carefully and slowly scanning the floor. Then he saw it. Half jammed in the skirting board almost behind the wedged-open door was a chromed nail file lying on the grey marble tiles. Only its hooked, shiny silver tip glinted in the light. He bent and retrieved the tool, examining it closely. It was definitely from Esther's travel kit. He had used it the day before. The break-in back at home came flooding into his mind and a real feeling of dread fell upon him. This was crazy, he thought. What the fuck was happening here? What was going on?

He stepped out through the open emergency exit, clearing the toppled cleaning equipment, and scanned the car park. The damaged Iveco delivery van was still there, its left-wing mirror bashed and the corresponding headlight broken. He could see thick gouge marks in its plastic bumper, and traces of black paintwork etched into its paint. He looked around to see the van driver standing in a doorway talking to a guy in a suit. The latter held a mobile to his ear, talking to someone else at the same time. The overweight, middle-aged van driver was in shock and nervous. The manager shouted into the phone, 'Please hurry, her husband is here now.'

The young receptionist had caught up to Ed and was standing behind him in the cleaners' doorway. Ed ran at the man on the phone. 'What's happened? What the hell's going on? What the fuck has happened here?' he yelled at the two men.

With panic in his voice, the manager pushed out both hands, fingers spread in a gesture for Ed to stop. 'Police are on way, sir.

We have called the police immediately. The driver saw it all. He was threatened with a gun. They took your lady wife, sir. We are so sorry – we haven't a clue what's going on or why. We are so sorry, sir.' With a tremble in his voice, he added, 'Sir, please come with me through to my office.'

Shaking and bemused, Ed racked his brains. What the hell was all this about? He pushed the manager away from him and, turning on his heels, ran out of the car park and across the road, then jumped the barrier of its central reservation. He ran up and down, looking for the gap where the car had passed through. Scouring the barriers and looking down at the dirt, he found what he was looking for. Tyre tracks. The black car was definitely a Mercedes. He knew his cars. It was a four-door sedan; an '80s style. Everyone knew that style of car; here there were thousands of them, many of them taxis, and they featured in many a movie. But it was the tyre tread marks he was after. Once the vehicle's location could be established, he could get the police to take a pattern and measurements for a match. That would help.

He ran back across the road, dodging traffic to interrogate the van driver. Soon, the police arrived and took charge, assuring him that this sort of occurrence was highly irregular. In his office, the manager calmed Ed down and gave him a whisky as the two police officers interviewed him, encouraging him to rack his brains for any information that could help them. He said nothing about the break-in back at home; he wasn't yet ready to pour fuel onto that fire. Besides, he wasn't confident the Turkish police were capable of solving such a crime. For now, he would just keep quiet.

After what seemed like hours with the police in the office, he returned to his room, exhausted. Lying on his back on the bed, he thought harder as he struggled to put together some sort of plan. Inside, he was raging; the anger burned deep. He felt so helpless and guilty but didn't know why. The rage kept him from thinking straight as he wrestled to calm himself and think rationally. Slowly, after a couple of whiskies from the minibar, he started to calm down. Fixing this problem would be more difficult unless he could detach a little. He still felt a lump in his throat and a pain in his gut as he took another swig. His mind returned to the break-in and those recent BBC news reports. Was there anything he was overlooking?

A knock at the door snapped him out of his thoughts. It was their holiday rep; a fresh-faced, dark-haired young man in his mid-twenties, dressed in shorts and a red polo shirt. Sheepish and apologetic, he asked if there was anything he could do to help, admitting that this situation was way outside his comfort zone and therefore his boss was coming over from another resort. Ed quizzed him for information on the area and then asked about the staff, the cleaners and any local tribal problems. All drew blanks. Then it came to him. No bag at the poolside. Esther had had her beach bag, and therefore her mobile, with her. *What lady goes to powder her nose without her handbag?* Still asking the young rep about the area, he hurriedly pulled on his jeans and changed his top from a sweaty polo to a navy-blue long-sleeved casual shirt. Stopping only to check the battery level on his mobile, he pulled on some socks and suede ankle boots. Rolling up his shirtsleeves, he thanked the young man and ushered him out before marching off to reception. It was getting on for three o'clock in Beyşehir, and that meant one back home. He took the stairs, clearing four steps at a time and swinging himself around the sharp turns using the wrought-iron banister as he bounded down the stairwell and headed straight for the poolside. He was right: there was no bag. *She must have had it with her*, he thought, *and that means she had her mobile too.* He desperately wanted to call her, but held back, thinking of the potential consequences. He couldn't jeopardise Esther's safety for the sake of a call. Not yet, anyway. *Think, man, think*, he told himself as he slapped his own forehead in anger. Maybe a text message? That would mean a shorter, softer and quieter alert. Her white BlackBerry Bold was quite small and discreet. *Maybe they're amateurs and haven't frisked her yet. Maybe she gave them hell and caused them problems*, he thought. *Yeah, that's it.* She wouldn't have gone quietly; he had told the police that. She wasn't the meek, timid type. And she had her mobile phone with her. He remembered her using it that morning: she'd received a couple of messages from work and, not wanting to disturb people around her, turned the phone's volume down. He decided not to do anything with the phone just yet. If nothing else it would help preserve the battery life for now. Maybe she would get a chance to call him, and he felt a little better knowing he had some sort of link to her.

He dashed to reception and made some calls back to the UK. The first was to his bank, to transfer several thousand pounds to his main card. On checking with the credit-card administrator, it seemed he was still okay for his agreed four-grand credit limit. *Good*, he thought. That gave him ten grand total in pounds sterling, which would be more than enough. The second call was to his mobile phone provider. Telling them of his predicament, he requested full roaming facilities regardless of tariffs and for any network bars to be removed. The third call was to his old boss back in Poole. He refused to leave a message and asked for him to call him back urgently. He then requested that reception get him a taxi and asked to be driven back to the police station.

# 17

## CIA HEADQUARTERS, LANGLEY, VIRGINIA, USA

Geoff Hackman rushed up the long, carpeted hallway, fixing his tie and trying to carry his briefcase and sort his folder all at the same time. He wished he'd had more time to stop for a coffee on the way up but, as always, he was running late. The only time he was ever close to being on time was when he had nothing to report or little preparation to do. That still didn't prevent him from always being the last one to enter the meeting room. It was common knowledge that he was more of a computer nerd than an agent, and that was exactly why he was where he was, and why it was exactly where he wanted to be: deputy head of the information technology department. This week he had something to say and they would see that he was still in tune with proper CIA business. He pulled his earphones from his ears as he struggled to adjust his tie.

It looked as if the meeting had already started. He rushed past the meeting room's glass panels until he arrived at the doorway. A feeling of mild dread came over him as he thought to himself,

*Here we go again.* He hated the modern glass partitions and walls. They were supposed to promote openness and honesty. To him, they promoted exposure and nakedness, allowed everyone to watch him arrive late, and then he would feel obliged to discuss his poor time management. Sitting in their black leather chairs with their chrome swivel castors, they all saw him coming and, before he could push open the polished teak door, chattered and poked fun at him once more.

'Sorry I'm late,' one colleague shouted.

'Yeah, sorry, but the coffee machine jammed up,' another cut in.

'I'm just disorganised,' a third quipped, followed by chortles and laughter.

'Okay, okay, knock it off, you guys,' said a fourth voice. 'What is it this week, Geoff?'

Acting Deputy CIA Director Ken Brendan headed up the meeting. From down the table, half stooped, Geoff looked over his glasses at his eleven seated colleagues. They were all seniors in their own right – some long-serving secretaries to departments, some understudies to statesmen, some senior clerks, some deputy heads of departments; all there to take his information back to their relevant enclaves of power, to discuss with their bosses and decide what to do with the intel. Trying to maintain some dignity and pride, Geoff apologised to Ken and allowed the strap of his briefcase to slip off his shoulder, intending for the bag to casually, but slickly, fall to the floor and land upright next to his chair. In the event, the strap caught on his jacket sleeve and, feeling even more awkward, he was left to fumble and place his folders, papers and bag into their intended positions.

'Well, you'll all be interested to know that we may have a new project this week,' he said, trying to compose himself.

The room went back into chatter mode as someone offered to get him a coffee, relieving some of the harmless tension in the air. Once all twelve of them were seated and papers and coffee had been passed around, the chit-chat quietened and Ken commenced to chair the meeting. Each head of department took their turn to brief their colleagues on where they were up to with various projects, intel reports, research, technology advancements and trials, intelligence supplies, and the perpetual court cases and countersuits. The focus of all present slowly worked its way clockwise toward Geoff, and after a leg stretch and a natural break, the meeting continued.

The secretary to the Deputy for Foreign Affairs for the Middle East spoke next, covering off and updating her colleagues on developments since their previous meeting. She spoke firmly and precisely, discussing various items from a pile of A4 papers, moving each sheet in turn from her right to her left, creating a fresh pile as she went. Twenty minutes in, after referring to a staffing issue at an Embassy in Yemen, she finished by saying, 'And slightly nearer to home – Europe, I mean – our Turkish Embassy reports a kidnapping of a female Brit. Apparently, she is some nuclear computer buff. She went missing from a hotel in Turkey whilst on vacation. We will put out the usual 'wanted' alerts, and we have promised the Brits that we'll share anything we have. It was reported as a kidnapping. Could be something or nothing, but with her background, we and the Brits think it's serious enough to take notice of. Any intel would be welcome. We have, of course, emailed all the details to each department. If you could all have a look that'd be great.' She paused and scoured her notes, then, after a few seconds of silence, looked around the table and confessed, 'And that's it from me. Thanks, guys.'

Slightly nervous, Geoff had subconsciously stopped listening to his colleague on his right and begun reading over his notes again, preparing for his briefing to somehow link in smoothly on handover.

'Okay,' his boss said slowly. 'Got any meat for the bone this week, Geoff?'

Geoff jumped in with his opening headline. His colleagues always switched off when his turn came. The very fact that his was the IT slot was enough to put them all to sleep, especially after a two-hour meeting. Being last always contributed to the disinterest, he believed. He had had this feeling before. He had a good story but, being on the nerdy side and not the best presenter, he had always found that his stories appealed more to him than to his colleagues. Still, his hopes were high that this one would get their attention. With an air of slight smugness, he launched it loud and clear in a single sentence. 'Staying in the East,' he segued smugly, 'Stuxnet.'

All eyes were on him, but only because of his assertiveness and volume.

He repeated the word. 'Stuxnet. A virus that allows machinery and computer programs to be sabotaged and or matrixes altered without a single boot being put on the ground or a single shot being fired.'

The room was silent. He knew he had their attention. He leaned back in his chair. Knowledge was power, and he savoured the moment. Questions were fired back at him. He explained how they had been monitoring emails and communications from Russia involving requests to replace Microsoft software and Siemens hardware for several companies in twelve countries. However, the country making the most enquiries was Iran. Since all major manufacturing in Iran was nationalised, all the requests came from one source: the Iranian government. The agency had logged 125 enquiries to replace Western computer equipment and machinery with Russian equivalents. Of these, over one hundred were from the nuclear enrichment and processing plant at Natanz. The remainder were from Iran's nuclear research and development departments, water and municipals, and hydroelectric. Obviously, Iran was having some problems.

Geoff was on a roll. The room was silent and all eyes remained fixed on him. He physically felt all the attention. He had not prepared for that. His top lip trembled slightly and he could feel the sweat in his armpits. He gulped discreetly, acknowledging the interest, and continued. 'There has been a hell of a lot of chatter over the internet referring to this virus. Someone in Belarus has identified it, flagged it and reported it to Microsoft. Now it's on every fuckin' computer forum going. Every man and his dog are discussing it.'

A defence colleague leaned in and asked innocently, 'Is that a problem?'

Geoff looked straight back at her. 'Hell yeah,' he said. 'Damned right it is.'

Spotting her embarrassment in thinking she had asked a stupid question, another delegate joined in. 'And why's that, Geoff? You obviously know something we don't.'

Geoff leaned back in his chair again. He knew he would have to say those fatal words. He'd rehearsed it. Throughout his career he had longed to say them, and now was his chance. He licked his lips and swigged his coffee. 'That, my friend,' he said slowly, savouring the moment, 'is at this time still classified.'

The whole room chattered indignantly, colleagues asking each other why they were not in the loop. Geoff looked down the long smoked-glass table at his boss and thought, *Yes, knowledge is indeed power.*

Ken Brendan obviously knew about the virus and did not look surprised. He spoke loudly over the ruckus. 'Geoff, can we have a brief history lesson please, to explain what all that has to do with the Russians?'

Geoff was primed; he had spent days compiling as much intel as possible. He coughed to clear his throat. 'Err, well, sir, as you know, the Russians are members of the International Nuclear Alliance opposed to Iran's nuclear development plans.'

He handed out a glossy eighty-four-page dossier prepared by the Institute for National Strategic Studies explaining where it thought Russia was currently with Iran. The delegates looked over it and passed it around.

Geoff continued. 'However, as you will all be aware, due to constantly being dismissed by us and Europe as a pain in the neck, to exert its strength and sphere of influence, Russia has needed to look to the Middle East and has dabbled extensively in this region against the West's wishes. They now have strong and supportive alliances with Iran and Syria. Both countries host Russian forces, including air and naval bases. Much to our annoyance, Russia has found ways to circumnavigate many sanction agreements in order to continue to supply Iran with just about anything. As a member of the Nuclear Alliance, and under much protest, Russia was cornered to publicly condemn Iran's threats to wipe Israel off the face of the earth. Israel is, of course, absolutely opposed to any further lifting of sanctions or nuclear development. But Russia sees Iran's current nuclear power problems as a huge opportunity to push a stick into the West's wheel spokes. All these requests and enquiries have been acknowledged as received by Russian agencies but, as yet, no action has been taken. We know that the Russians are sitting on them for some reason; we're just not sure why right now. As we all know, the Russian President enjoys playing these cat-and-mouse games with the West and keeping us guessing.'

Another head of department, Liz McKeowan, asked, 'Okay, so what about the virus? How good is it? It's obviously good enough to be classified. Is it ours? Does it work? Is it accurate? C'mon, Geoff.'

Geoff held up both his hands in a halting gesture. 'All I can tell you is that at the moment, the White House, Langley, Whitehall in London, and their GCHQ are all denying ownership. The Israelis, as usual, are saying nothing.'

He continued his briefing and explained that they were monitoring the Belarus malware security firm and all its correspondence, that all chatter and communications were being stored, and that his staff were, at this very minute, trawling through thousands of cell net and phone calls and millions of emails, and running thousands of algorithms' keywords. What was important right now was that the virus had indeed infected Iran's nuclear enrichment plant and had been assisting in disturbing the process for quite some time. What the agency didn't want was for the virus to be interrupted in any way. Therefore, all departments were to work with and inform Geoff first of anything that might be linked in any way at all to Stuxnet.

Another colleague piped up, 'Why Stuxnet?'

Geoff shot him down without hesitation. 'That's not us! It's Microsoft's name for it. It's nothing to do with us. We didn't name it.'

The same guy came back at him. 'Hell, is it ours?'

Again, Geoff fired back. 'Sorry, classified. What you can know is that it's been busy for quite some time, and very effective. We know that it is damaging the nuclear enrichment process and that the Iranians are pulling their hairy little beards out trying to fix it. Our intelligence from the IAEA tells us that they are struggling to make enough enriched uranium-252, which is what they badly need. We of course want this disruption to continue unhindered, so it really is imperative that I have full cooperation on this. Please brief *all* your teams.' He laboured the word for emphasis. 'And absolutely no leaks, guys. No one talks to the press on this at all. This is international espionage at its highest level.'

The room went quieter and some heads dropped slightly as the word 'leaks' was mentioned. Then chatter resumed as the staff discussed the subject between themselves.

~

Back in his office, Geoff leaned back in his chair and reflected on how the presentation had gone. He was pleased, and rewarded himself with a mental pat on the back.

His deputy, Tony, tapped on the door and poked his head into the room without waiting to be invited. 'How'd it go?' he asked, knowing that Geoff's presentation skills were somewhat lacking.

Geoff lifted his left foot onto his desk, emulating some old detective movie. 'Oh, pretty good,' he said. 'That one gave them all plenty of interest, and they sat up and listened for a change.'

Tony smiled and then, hearing some chatter back in the main open office area behind him, looked over his shoulder to see Geoff's boss and Liz McKeowan walking through the department. 'Uh-oh,' he said. 'Looks like you got company. You really did rattle some cages.'

Geoff peered past his colleague and out through his office window. 'Oh shit,' he muttered, and pulled his foot down off the desk. With his left hand he snowploughed a heap of papers, cups and rubbish off the desktop straight into the wastepaper bin beside it, regardless of each item's importance, in a vain attempt to remove the clutter for his uninvited guests.

'Hi, Geoff,' said his boss. 'Great presentation today, I heard. Well done.'

'Hi, Sam,' Geoff replied, slightly embarrassed. He shouted for someone to get coffee and, standing up, invited his guests to come in and have a seat as he cleared more files and rubbish off two chairs.

Sam sat down and crossed his legs. Liz copied his body language.

Sam asked, 'You know Liz, don't you, Geoff?'

Geoff checked his desktop for anything that could be embarrassing, then looked up. 'Err, well, only through coffee breaks and meetings, really.'

'Okay.' Sam paused. 'You know how this goes. Wheels start to turn and, well, I've had a phone call regarding your new friendly Project Stuxnet Virus, and I have been instructed to get Liz here involved and up to speed with all you have. You see, other interested departments are keen for this virus to keep on doing what it's doing without interruption. The President is due to attend a summit meeting soon on all things nuclear and he doesn't want any embarrassments, but obviously he also needs to be fully briefed on this Stuxnet thing should it come up. So, the plan is for you to work with Liz here, with all you got. How are you with that?'

Geoff looked at Liz. How could he not? They were instructions from the top. She was very attractive and knew how to flirt – and how to get what she wanted. Liz McKeowan was a slick and ambitious individual who had climbed the ladder the hard way. From a New York beat cop, she had earned promotion and recruitment to the CIA, and was now Assistant Deputy Adviser to the Secretary of Defence's office. After acquiring fame and glory for assisting in the capture of Osama bin Laden, she too now had a new project to propel her to the top if she got it right. Her brief was to protect the virus and its work at all costs. She too had no idea who was responsible for the virus yet, but that wasn't her brief. Her mission was crystal clear: protect the virus. She knew that if she got it right and was successful, her career would climb steeply to a possible directorate position. Head of European Operations, she hoped, and within hours she would be on a flight to London to work on that promotion.

# 18

## BEYŞEHIR POLICE STATION, TURKEY

The station was grubby and reeked of cigarette smoke. The walls were yellowed and stained from years of nicotine. The furniture was dark and worn, upholstered in grubby, unwashed fabrics stuck in the '90s. in the reception area there were four desks, each with a computer. Two of the four computer monitors were old, huge, bulbous, cream-beige affairs. The other two were black, slimmer and more modern.

At first glance the place seemed empty except for the policeman who'd interviewed Ed earlier, and who greeted him now. Anticipating the question before it was asked, the officer said, 'No news yet, sir.'

Ed looked at him, then around the reception area. The only apparent sign of habitation was the untidy desks. "No news yet"?' he repeated sarcastically. 'I bet you haven't even filed the report yet. Who's the officer in charge? What's his name? This isn't a missing person's report, this is a kidnap in broad daylight, in one of your main resorts,' he shouted.

The officer tried to calm him, explaining that he knew it must be a difficult time, but to no avail. The more Ed discussed it, the more he felt the anger, rage and helplessness boil up inside him. That was when the guilt hit him.

During his outburst, a short, round man dressed in a cream shirt, a brown nylon suit and brown slip-on shoes walked into the station. He looked at Ed and stated, 'You must be Mr Bennett?' Without waiting for a reply, he continued. 'I am Detective Ramoud. I have been looking for you. I have just come from your hotel, sir.'

Staring at the detective, Ed then heard a female voice from behind him. He looked around and, to the left of the main door, he saw a woman sat back, tucked away in the corner. 'Hi,' she said in an American accent. 'You're the Brit, right? I'm Tess.' She looked up from her chair, which was almost hidden behind the open door, and nodded to the detective.

'Tess,' repeated Ramoud acknowledging her presence, and nodded back.

The detective beckoned Ed to sit down at a desk and proceeded to interview him. He told him that the car had been spotted heading south. He didn't seem too concerned about retrieving Esther, but kept questioning Ed as to why she had been kidnapped. Ed repeated himself, consistently stating that he did not know why, and was more alarmed than anyone by the incident. This was supposed to be a holiday. Ed also lied to the detective's questions, stating he did not know if Esther had a phone with her, how she was dressed and would she have personal belongings with her.

Ramoud was not convinced, and showed his hand. 'Mr Bennett, what are you doing here in Beyşehir? Your incident form says your partner is a computer scientist, and now I learn in nuclear engineering, yes? And you are just here on vacation?'

Ed stood up, angered by the insinuation. 'What the fuck are you suggesting?' he said, forcing his chair away.

'Well, perhaps you know that the Turkish Parliament are in the final stages of completing a deal with the Russians to build our first nuclear power station in Akkuyu?'

Ed was furious. Before he could speak, Tess jumped up, grabbed at Ed's left arm and pulled him back to the station door. Calming a little in front of the woman, he stereotyped her immediately. She was mid-forties, he thought. Weathered, but not unattractive; perhaps a tomboy in her youth and now more of an independent feminist, the type who would refuse help whenever she could. Once she spoke to the detective, in what he thought was good Turkish, Ed instantly realised that she could be useful. Dressed in pale blue jeans, a beige blouse, and beige suede trekking shoes, she had black hair held back by an Alice band, brown eyes, and tiny, very modest stud earrings. She wore no make-up. As Ed retreated from Ramoud, Tess spun him around half a turn. He looked at her and was about to go on the defensive, guessing she was a reporter after a juicy scoop, but then resisted, realising he needed all the help he could get.

'And you would be the press, right?' he said.

'Yep,' she said, then continued in a sincere tone, 'I'm sorry to hear what happened. Really, it's shocking. You must be devastated.'

He said nothing and thought for a moment. Then he asked, 'You a resident here?'

'Yeah,' she said, 'been here five years. Nothing like this ever happens. It's usually dross and trivia. I'm really surprised.'

'You'll be wanting a story, then?' Ed said suspiciously.

She nodded. 'Do you want to trade?' She smiled, seeming sincere enough.

He knew he would have to trade with her. A kidnap story in

exchange for her help with local knowledge, information, chatter and the language.

'If I can help?' she asked, quizzically. 'I have a friend on it right now,' she said. 'He's finding out what he can. Do you have anything for me?' She held out her hand.

Ed looked her up and down again. He looked straight into her eyes, then reached out and shook her hand. 'I'm Ed. Ed Bennett.'

'I know,' she said. 'And I'm Tess Anders.' She looked at Ramoud, took two bottles of drinking water off the junior policeman's desk, and then ushered Ed out of the police station. Speaking over her shoulder to the policemen, she asked, 'Would you excuse us for a few minutes, please?'

Outside, she sat Ed down on the steps and handed him a bottle of water. In the hot afternoon sun, she asked him more and more questions, and he quizzed her for more local information. During their conversation, his mobile vibrated in his rear pocket and then began to ring. He looked at the screen. It was his old boss. *Thank God for that*, he thought, excusing himself as he took the call.

'Chief,' Ed answered, 'Bloody hell, I'm right in the shit here.' The line wasn't brilliant but they could talk.

'Hey, fella, what going on? Didn't think I'd be hearing from you till the wedding invites were ready. You wouldn't leave a message – what's all the mystery?'

Ed dived in. 'There won't be a bloody wedding if I can't sort this out. It's Esther,' he said anxiously. 'She's been kidnapped. Kidnapped, for fuck's sake. I saw it! Can you believe that?'

After a moment's silence, his old boss, Terry Foster, a Chief Warrant Officer, first class, of twenty-plus years replied, 'Bloody hell, Ed, you've only been gone ten minutes.'

The Chief Warrant Officer calmed him down and took as much information as he could. Ed felt much better knowing that the Navy's intelligence and expertise could help, and that he wasn't alone. Calmly, the Chief told him that he was now recording the call, so he should babble away. Babbling was a trick they had used for years; they also called it 'verbal brainstorming.' A witness could just rant, rave and scream out all they thought, or thought they thought, about the problem. The eyes see things that the brain may not initially log or remember, especially concerning peripheral vision. The brain half remembers and needs stimuli. Verbal brainstorming lets the subconscious out of the box. Any info was good info, though some of Ed's recollections would be better than others. The specialists could pick out the most important and relevant bits later.

'Is there more to it than a kidnap, d'ya think?' the Chief asked.

Ed explained his worries about the break-in back home and why it was unusual.

'Who at work knew about the holiday?' the Chief came back.

'Just colleagues in chit-chat, I guess,' said Ed. 'I don't know her work mates, and she worked at such a high level.'

'We'll make some enquiries and speak to her work,' said the Chief quietly, before beckoning through his open office door to Caroline, his civilian secretary.

As she moved into his office, the Chief put the conversation onto speaker. Caroline quickly got the gist of the situation and pushed her boss to one side, allowing her access to his PC monitor. Immediately, she pulled at his keyboard and mouse and called up Google Maps with the satellite viewing option, clicking the mouse to drill down into the Beyşehir resort and locate the police station and Ed's hotel.

The Chief's brain had already started to swing into action. He explained to Ed that things would be awkward initially for him and his section until government departments such as Embassy staff could be involved. It wasn't an official problem just yet, but he could make enough noise to change that within a few hours. He spoke firmly. 'I'll call you back with Embassy names and numbers. We've got all the details and your hotel. You okay for money, Ed? We'll get you trusted police contact, too. Scotland Yard and Interpol need to know, but let the normal channels sort that. Have you done all the forms? Make sure the Turks fax over all the reports to the Embassy, then we can sort a press release of some sort and let the cops think they're handling it. We'll need protocol on our side for now. The nearest Embassy to you is 200 miles away in Ankara.'

Ed had guessed that, and also doubted that the missing person's report had even been faxed over to them yet. Tess could sort that.

The Chief told him to stay put and he would get back to him. 'What resources have you on site, and what's your next move, Ed?' he asked.

'Just one reporter so far,' Ed admitted. 'I need a car next. I've got tyre tracks and Esther has her BlackBerry with her, I'm sure of it. Can we use BBM where we can? I think it's safer.'

'No probs,' said the Chief. 'That's fine. Leave all that to me, Ed. Go and chase those tyre tracks before you lose them. Save your battery life, and yes, use BBM as much as possible. It's safer, too. Go buy a cheap new phone and SIM card in case you're a target too.'

~

Throughout the conversation, Tess remained seated on the steps. She took a drink from her bottle, then made a call. 'Ged? Hi, it's Tess!' she shouted, cupping her hand a little over the mouthpiece to shield it from traffic noise, and as if to compensate for the distance of the call to Ankara.

'Yeah, I know. Yer number comes up on screen. Hiya, gorgeous. How ya doin'?' Ged asked.

'Yeah, I'm good, thanks,' she replied. 'You keepin' busy?'

'Oh, ya know, always looking for the big retirement one,' he laughed.

She didn't respond to that. 'Listen, Ged, here's one for you. I got a Brit tourist here. His girlfriend's gone missing.'

'Yeah, I know all about it,' Ged replied, rather smugly knowing he was one step ahead of her. 'Seen the faxes that came through from your end. Ankara is all over it already. American and British suits in and out of the building like crazy. Something big is going on and Tim ain't talking.'

She looked puzzled. 'Why all the fuss, then?'

''Cause she's got four keywords on her missing person's form: "British", "nuclear", "computer" and "kidnap", baby!' he replied. 'Come on, girl, you know how it goes! That's gonna cause a stir. Besides, Turkey is desperate to join the EU and don't want this shit on their desk.'

Tess looked at Ed, who was walking around in a circle, talking to someone on his mobile. She tried to catch some of his conversation. 'What's the update?' she asked her former colleague.

'Well, the BBC guy has a hold on it but only knows what I've told him, and France Vingt-Quatre have asked me to prepare a report ready to edit within the hour.'

'Hmm,' she replied. 'Can you give me anymore? Her partner's here with me now.'

'I'll try,' Ged said. 'Got an old chum over in Manchester; he's working for a small local paper up north. He's already trying to dig deeper for me. Do what I can, babe.'

'Oh, you're such a sweetie, Ged. You are such a babe and I love you. Keep me posted. You know I will reward you as soon as I can,' she purred, sultry and promising.

She was just about to hang up when Ged asked, 'Who's your guy?'

'The boyfriend? Oh, just another regular tourist missing his girl.'

'Come on, now *you* give *me* something. Give me an angle,' he pressed her. He was about to say he would do his best, when two men in suits brushed past him on the Embassy steps as if he wasn't there. 'Gotta go, babe!' he said abruptly. Hanging up, he scurried back into the Embassy to find out some more and follow the two guys.

~

Slipping his mobile back into his pocket, Ed looked at Tess. She sat quietly on the steps, looking up at him. Although he had moved away to take his old boss's call, he realised that he hadn't moved away far enough – not that it really mattered, but she had probably overheard a good chunk of his conversation.

She looked puzzled. 'Sorry,' she said, 'but who did you say you were?' Suspicious now, she was more than just interested in a mundane tabloid story. She was intrigued.

'I need a car,' he said. 'Got any wheels?'

She nodded. 'Behind you.' She pointed with her eyes to the car park. 'Why, where're we going?'

'*We* aren't,' he told her firmly. 'I am. I'll rent it from you. I'm going back to the scene and you're going back in there,' he gestured with his head toward the police station doors, 'to make sure all those forms get faxed off to Ankara for me. No one will move on it until it's official at the Embassy.'

'They've already been sent. Won't they have to wait twenty-four hours anyway before moving?' she asked.

He stared at her. 'But this isn't just missing persons. It's a daylight kidnapping of a British citizen!' he snarled. Gritting his teeth, he felt the anger rush through his body again. Rage was building and he knew he had to keep focused to stop his emotions overspilling into what was now a 'special job'.

Tess declined his request for her to be the admin girl. She had called her fixer back to the police station, and set him about sorting the paperwork. She then offered to drive Ed back to the hotel, explaining that her fixer was experienced in these administrative matters and, on her instructions, would talk to his contact at the Ankara Embassy and have them collect all the faxed documents and hand them over personally to the Ambassador. The missing persons forms Ed had filled in were already causing a massive storm up in Ankara. This was now an international incident, and an embarrassing situation for both Turkey and Britain. Embassy staff would have to give it their immediate attention, she explained.

As they continued their conversation, Ed watched a Renault Clio hire car as it pulled up in the car park. A fresh-faced young man in a smart-casual suit and sunglasses got out and made his way over to the steps. He looked at them and asked for Detective Ramoud. They both pointed up the steps into the building.

'Who are you?' asked Tess.

The young man just smiled, said, 'Thanks,' and continued to walk into the police station.

Ed looked disapprovingly at Tess.

'What?' she asked. 'What I say?'

'Where's your car?' he asked.

~

Tess parked her black Chrysler Jeep in the hotel car park. Ed crossed the road to the central reservation and walked to the gap in the barriers. Tess followed like a curious puppy. Finding the tyre marks, he photographed them over and over with the camera on his phone. He also photographed the landscape and the direction in which the car had gone. He guessed the sun's position at the time and photographed some more. He needed a road map.

'Where does that lead?' he asked Tess.

'Err, south-ish,' she said. 'The main road leads to Seydişehir, and then on to Alanya. Then the Med coast, I guess?'

'And that one?'

She nodded in the direction of the tyre marks, replying, 'Konya, Adana, and eventually the border.'

He looked up from his phone. He now had a compass app on its screen and was saving the coordinates. Pushing his sunglasses up onto his forehead, he stared her in the eye. 'And then where?' he asked.

She could see in his face and eyes that he really loved this woman, and that deep underneath that façade, he was panicking and very worried. She genuinely wanted to help him. It would make a great story with a healthy financial reward, but she was sure there was more to this than a random kidnapping. 'Gaziantep,' she said.

'Then where?'

'Then on to, err, Syria, Iran, Iraq, I guess.' Throwing up her hands, she allowed them to slap down on her hips as they fell. 'Tell me what you know. Level with me,' she almost pleaded. 'Tell me what's missing here and I promise to help you all I can.'

He thought for a moment. 'I don't know yet,' he said. 'I just don't know.' He pressed a button on his phone, sending the images of the tyre tracks across the airwaves.

Crossing the road, they walked back to the hotel. The damaged laundry van was still in the staff area of the car park, but parked out of the way. Ed learnt that the hotel manager had surrendered its keys to the police as the vehicle's damage had to be more closely examined. He was pleasantly surprised and reassured by this action, and said as much to the manager.

The manager looked a little disappointed. 'I understand you are distressed, sir, but we are not stuck in the Dark Ages here. We are almost a member of Europe, and way ahead of some other Union members in certain areas.'

Ed apologised, explaining that he hadn't meant to offend. On walking outside to check the van, their conversation triggered a thought in his head. How would the papers report it? Esther was a computer engineer kidnapped in a non-EU country. He envisaged the headlines back home. He photographed the van, paying particular attention to the black paint etched into its bumper. He told Tess about the break-in back home, and that he was trying to put two and two together but couldn't get things to add up. He was sure there was a connection but didn't know what it was. He refrained from divulging any more information about himself and Esther and pressed Tess for more local knowledge and more about herself, her fixer, and why she was in Beyşehir. He was no tyre expert but knew a little of some tread patterns, mainly military and 4x4 patterns. You had to be an expert, however, to check a tread on a certain type of car. The guys back at HQ had the resources to match things up better, but at least he had some images to help him find the car. He had sent them via SMS and the Chief would have someone working on them in no time.

# 19

## SECRET INTELLIGENCE SERVICE HEADQUARTERS, LONDON, ENGLAND

Foreign Secretary Katherine Dacre stood up, stretched, pushed her skirt down her thighs, and looked out of the office window, over the Albert Embankment and down to the river. Her back was turned to Clive Pemberton, a colleague of fifteen years or more who was now the Head of the Secret Intelligence Service. Looking out through the triple-glazed, bomb-proof window, she watched as little dinghies, river-tour barges and boats bobbed gently as they went about their business. Below her, spanned the visually nondescript, grade-two-listed, steel Vauxhall Bridge, only really impressive from the waterline, its rustic red-and-gold-painted barriers, pavements and roads soaking up the volume of hectic London traffic and commuters. In the sunshine, the bridge was awash with glinting metal, colours, and the vaguest of sounds. Taxis beeped at scooters and scooters beeped at pedestrians as they stepped off the pavements to overtake fellow commuters. She continued looking down at the Thames from the twelfth-floor, bay-windowed office, across the SIS building's castle-like terraces and moats, watching the workers scurry around the city. She thought to herself for a moment, took a swig of her brandy and lemonade, then commented to Clive with her metaphor of how oblivious the worker ants were to the soldier ants. As if in deep thought, she muttered, 'It's us and our soldier ants that protect the colony, Clive.' She paused. '*And* a real bloody Queen!' she mused. 'The PM's not impressed, and especially so with Six.' She continued, referring to MI6. 'I need to give him something pronto.'

Clive looked up at the silhouette of the Minister at his window as she drank from her glass. He too took a large swig of his whisky. *God, Ministers are annoying*, he thought. *They don't have a bloody clue until it all goes wrong, then they bravely take the 'buck stops here' stance and cause more chaos.* But for this Minister he made exceptions. 'Oh, come on, Katherine. Give him the basics of what we know,' he said. 'That one of our tourists was kidnapped in Turkey and we're dealing with it. It's that simple. But how does the PM know so soon?'

She turned and looked at him. 'Oh, well, that's easy,' she scoffed. 'Because I told him. I had to. The bloody Yanks were gobbing off and crying into their Starbucks coffees at the GCHQ meeting this morning, complaining that our newly adopted Australian Wiki whistle-blower and the good old British press are exposing every fucking detail of our listening programme. So, they used today's kidnapping as an example of how accurate and up to the minute their intelligence is, as long as they're left alone unencumbered. The PM was cornered and embarrassed, so I couldn't deny it.'

Clive stared into his glass for a second. 'I didn't know the PM was going to that meeting.'

Katherine replied. 'No, none of us did, but you should have seen the looks on the Yanks' faces when they saw him enter. They bloody shit themselves at first. But then their faces lit up like Christmas trees. God, they were lobbying him for everything and anything. So, I had to get in there quick to save us some face. But now I have egg on it!' she finished, swigging her drink.

In his defence, Clive replied crossly, 'And I have some very bored and pissed-off SBS staff and a field agent sat on their arses at Ankara airport, still waiting for a bloody lift.'

She stared at him. 'You've activated Special Forces? You haven't mentioned it, and I haven't authorised *anything* yet.'

'No, no,' retorted Clive. 'They're on leave and offered their services, and would be assisting my field agents. Trouble is the lift I arranged. Their transport was a US private charter which left without them for… guess where?'

He paused and waited for the Foreign Secretary to guess, but her eyes widened with impatience.

'Adana airport, southern Turkey. How come the Yanks are so hot on the heels of this and know so bloody much?' asked Clive.

Katherine knew the flak she was about to get following her next statement. 'They had boots on the ground in Ankara and found out from our Consulate when we asked their Embassy to keep an eye out and pass over any intel.'

Then came the expected return volley. Clive crossed his legs. 'Boots on the ground? Christ, I can't even get bums on fuckin' seats because of all the cutbacks.'

She cut him off and, as if they were lovers bickering, chirped, 'Not now, Clive. I've had a shitty enough day as it is. Apart from another large whisky, what's your plan?'

Clive lowered his voice and leaned back in his leather chair, preparing himself and getting comfortable for his opportunity to show who was managing whom. 'Well,' he said, pleased to be able to take the lead and discuss his plans, 'we know the CIA are trying to get to her and why, but no one wants to discuss that or to take ownership of the main problem. We'll see who the true perpetrators really are in due course. Then once we have that information it will be our Joker to use any time, as we like.' He smiled. 'The Israelis are now on the move and, after a very nasty incident with a Russian salesman, the hunt is very much on, but we expect they will push it all back onto the Yanks. They think that we are still very much in the dark, and they want to keep us that way. We will, of course, oblige as usual for now and let them think that we are just the clumsy Brits, only good for fumbling about before the negotiation stages. The Americans already deny not waiting at Ankara for our guys, but we know the private plane was a Learjet 35, tail number N221SG. After Iraq and Kuwait, it left Ankara and, after being used for extraordinary renditions, was then redirected from Istanbul. The plane is registered to a private company in Delaware which we know is a front for the CIA. We also know that the same Delaware company chartered an AgustaWestland chopper today and flew out from Adana in Turkey. Another perfect aircraft for extraction work, so we're betting they're ready to make an attempted snatch for her.'

He stopped and checked the Foreign Secretary's facial expression. *So far, so good*, he thought. *These Ministers get really pissy when they've got nothing to give their bosses.* His colleague stood listening intently. She seemed pleased so far with his accurate intel and report. Although they had been friends for years, careers, livelihoods and pensions all had to be protected first. It was dog eat dog most of the time, but more for her, over the river in Whitehall.

'Go on,' Katherine encouraged, pouring them both another drink. Casually tossing some ice cubes into their glasses and then unbuttoning her jacket, she added, 'But I want her back safe and unharmed. I don't want her used as political bait to draw out our friends. That isn't our way.'

'No, no, not at all,' Clive lied. 'We both need her back immediately to prevent a huge international and political embarrassment.'

The Foreign Secretary looked at him with a steely eye. 'She is also one of our top nuclear engineering scientists. Her loss alone could cause us years of setbacks. And at such a delicate moment in time, what with the Iran, UN and US negotiations, we cannot afford for this to go public. Where is the boyfriend now?' she asked.

'Oh, err, he was last seen ranting and raving at the local police station, threatening them with every European law he could think of,' Clive lied again. 'And of course, it will show the PM just how capable we both are when we work together.'

Curious, she immediately asked, 'And how will you do that with your best men stuck several hundred miles away at Ankara airport?'

'You leave that to me. I have a guy on the ground as we speak.'

The Foreign Secretary looked pleasantly surprised and a little impressed by his swift intervention. 'Hmm,' she purred. 'Oh, very well done, Clive. Are we ahead of the Americans now, then?'

With an air of confidence, he smiled back at her. 'Oh yes, Foreign Secretary, I do believe we are,' he said, undoing his top button and loosening his tie. 'That's what you pay me for.'

She smiled, and they clinked glasses before drinking. 'So, tell me again where we are and where our computer engineer girl is?'

Clive motioned her to sit. 'Are you aware of the story of Ishtar from the Book of Esther?' he asked.

Katherine paused. 'No, not really.' She felt quite embarrassed.

'Well!' Clive began smugly. 'Let me enlighten you on the dark arts of religion, history, intelligence and espionage.' Again, refilling her glass, he was pleased to be able to further show off his prowess at intelligence-gathering. Leaning forward in his seat, he continued.

'We believe the virus to be Israeli at source, but a collaboration between the Americans and Israelis, initiated quite some time ago; developed by our American cousins and tested in Israel before being launched into Iran under the Bush administration. We've been following this one for bloody ages. Encrypted into the virus are several clues alluding to Jewish history. Firstly, the virus avoids anything with a registration number beginning 19790509. That is the date when the head of the Iranian Jews and Western-leaning multimillionaire businessman Habib Hadassah and his wife were hanged for alleged treason against the newly formed Iranian revolutionary government: the 9$^{th}$ of May 1979. So, as if to tease, the virus is designed to pass by anything with this number, as did the plague with the red crosses marked on Jewish doors in the Bible's Exodus story. Secondly, to confirm this suggestion, our code breakers conclude "Hadassah" suggests "had a sash." "Sash" in Hebrew means "rope, strop, hoop or noose", confirming the hanging theory. Thirdly, there are the letters, in capitals, M-Y-R-T-U-S.'

He checked to confirm that Katherine was taking all the information on board.

'Now, RTUs are what the virus hijacks. Remote Terminal Units control machinery, pumps, motors and so on. That is how the damage was caused at the nuclear plant: the malware buggers about with and speeds up centrifuge motors, causing all sorts of damage. The virus adopts these RTUs as its own, thereafter calling them "My RTUs." My RTU's spells Myrtus. However,' he took a breath and then another drink, '*Myrtus* is a Hebrew reference to the myrtle tree, and the scientific genus name for the plant. Also, "Hadassah" comes from the Hebrew word meaning "myrtle", as in the tree. So, there it is again. The myrtle tree keeps coming up.'

Clive paused and took a swig from his glass whilst Katherine sat silently, amazed by the intrigue. She could feel the espionage unravelling and couldn't help but get excited.

Clive continued. 'The Tree of Life, or the myrtle tree, you will recall from your Sunday school lessons, was said to have stood in the Garden of Eden. It was said to be the tree from which the serpent appeared to Adam and Eve, and from its branches came the Rod of Aaron and the famous cane that Moses used to part the seas. The assumption here is that the virus is also acting as a metaphorical Rod of Aaron, to strike at the heart of the enemy. Again, all biblical references to Jewish history.'

'And where does our girl fit in with all this?' the Foreign Secretary interjected, amazed.

'Well, here it comes again,' continued Clive, enjoying his moment. 'The story goes that a Hebrew girl, from the Benjamite tribe, named Hadassah, the feminine form of the Hebrew word *hadas, meaning* Myrtle, after the flowering tree, was in fact Esther, or rather Esther was Hadassah, but renamed Ishtar or Esther when she married the Persian King. And guess what?' he teased. 'Our girl just happens to be Esther Hadassah, daughter of Habib Hadassah, not Esther Hassadah as she believes. In the Book of Esther, Hadassah had a cousin called Mordecai who refuses to bow to some prince. And now, as an eminent nuclear computer engineer, just like the book says, she will save all the Iranian Jews. At least, that's what the fanatics think. She even has a cousin called Mord. You couldn't make this stuff up. Oh! And the final numbers of the code, we believe to be an inception date: the 24$^{th}$ of September 2007. And finally,' he paused again, feeling like he'd just finished a conference speech, 'if you are of the religious persuasion and a bit fanatical, it is suggested that it all ends where it all started: in the Garden of Eden. What goes around comes around. They say

World War III will start in the Middle East. Iran has already called for Israel to be wiped off the face of the earth. If they get nuclear warheads, it may well happen. And where is the Garden of Eden?'

The Foreign Secretary chipped in, keen to redeem herself following her earlier lack of biblical knowledge. 'Somewhere between Iraq and Iran,' she said, still quite excited.

'Exactly,' confirmed Clive. 'Exactly. If this all kicks off, the Russians will get further involved, as will the Yanks, and *boom*! Game over! The nuclear annihilation of all humanity. Armageddon, if Iran gets its way with the Jews.'

# 20

## BUCAK, DANA PROVINCE, TURKEY, 390 MILES FROM THE SYRIAN BORDER

Esther woke to find her head pressed against the roof of what she thought was a steel box. As her head and nostrils cleared, she soon realised that she was in the boot of a car. It stank of old rags, oil and grease, and she was lying on what she thought were potato sacks. Someone had tried to wrap her up. Her head hurt from constantly banging on the boot lid as the car had crossed the rough, unsurfaced desert and dirt tracks. Through some screw holes formerly used to secure licence plates, and around the edges of the trunk lid, which moved slightly as the vehicle drove, she saw slivers of daylight.

She felt okay and didn't think she had any injuries. Slowly realising her predicament, she lay perfectly still and then, with her mind focused, flexed her muscles one by one from head to toe, checking that she was indeed physically all right. She then told her brain to retrace her steps prior to her blackout in an attempt to recall just what had happened. She remembered her fight with the two men in the bathroom. She tried to remember their clothing and what they'd looked like, but could only recall the smell of their body odour, bland beige clothing, and dark hair.

Lying diagonally across the vehicle on her right side, she was curled up from wheel arch to wheel arch. Steadying herself with her free left arm, she gagged as dust and sand found their way into her throat and mixed with the old, dry smell of workshop rags and potato sacks. It was very dark and hot, and the beams of light she could see were fine as needles. In her poolside attire she felt naked and vulnerable. Her legs and hips ached from being trapped in position, and her neck throbbed. She could feel pins and needles in her right arm, but more importantly she felt vulnerable again as her left breast was falling out of her bikini top. As the car hit some smoother roadway, she squirmed about in order to address the problem, pushing the sacks off her shoulders and feeling for her sarong. She checked that it was still tied in position around her waist, then flicked it over her leg in an attempt to feel more secure. *Thank God*, she thought. At least she still had it on and they hadn't raped or hurt her. At least, she didn't think they had.

With her eyes adjusted to the dark light and conscious now of the situation, she was determined to remain perfectly still and quiet. Her brain flashed through the events of her abduction. She wanted to panic. Fight or flight had set in. She fought back tears. She was terrified and, for now, helpless. She focused her brain to fix on the present. What would Ed tell her to do? How would he react? He always said the brain worked better when it was calm. She knew that, of course.

She heard the car radio playing what sounded like the call to prayer, and the men speaking in Arabic. She could smell the smoke from their cigarettes and the odd whiff of petrol from the fuel tank beneath her. She blinked to adjust her eyes to the darkness, then shivered from the shock. She was dazed and confused and could not think straight. Had they simply confused her for someone else? Surely this was all just a big mistake.

After covering her legs, she adjusted her bikini straps. As she did so, she felt a tug on her left hand. Something was catching her fingers as she pulled. It was the shoulder strap of her small beach bag. Pushing out her right arm, she rolled left toward the strap, which had worked its way through between the car's rear seat base and its centre arm rest. She gently pulled at the thin white strap for what seemed like ages and pulled the bag as close to her as the seat would allow. The top of the bag butted up against the foam of the seat and, pushing her fingers through the small gap in the seat's cushions, she slowly felt for its zip. Bouncing around in the dark, trying carefully, and hoping not to arouse any suspicion, she slowly unzipped the small bag and carefully opened it. The car rocked and swayed. Nauseous and light-headed, she continued to unzip the bag, cautious not to spill any of its contents. Her index and middle finger worked like chopsticks to find her mobile as she dug deeper into the bag. Finally, they found the edge of the phone's tactile rubber and after a few attempts, they got a grip. Esther slowly retrieved the mobile phone and gently zipped the bag up. Her first instinct was to use her phone as a torch to help her see better. Clutching the white BlackBerry, she pushed the tracker ball and activated the main screen. In the palm of her right hand, through her pins and needles, she felt the phone give a short and very quiet buzz, vibrating as it responded to her command. Its screen gave off a bluish glow, illuminating the interior of the boot. She blinked again to adjust to the reassuring light. In a stupid way, she thought, that little act of obedience made her love her phone even more, and she sighed, taking some comfort from the fact that it was still working. She moved the light around. She already knew that she was in the boot of a vehicle but she needed to see if there was anything there that might help her. Dirty hessian sackcloth covered her calves and draped loosely over her shoulder. She saw the dark paintwork of the metal interior, and black carpet of the sort typically found in cars. By her feet lay bits of hay and straw, and a plastic bag containing a car jack and tools. She also saw some broken pieces of a red-and-orange plastic tail-light lens. *The car must have been involved in other collisions*, she thought.

Reaching behind her, she felt a long, cold piece of metal in her back, jabbing her in her shoulder blades. Holding her phone in her squashed right hand, she groped behind her with her free arm. Pulling and tugging in the cramped, tight space, she realised that the steel rod she had been lying on was in fact a rifle. It too had been wrapped in potato sacks for concealment, no doubt by her captors. In a moment of dread, she let go of the weapon and sobbed uncontrollably.

As she clutched at the BlackBerry in her hand, the screen flickered as the phone obeyed another command. Her thumb had inadvertently hit the 'last call' icon. Looking to see what she had done, she remembered that Ed was the last person she had called when she was teasing him at the bar only hours ago. She watched as the tiny screen brought up her partner's number. Her eyes widened and she froze as the SIM card gave the instruction to search for a network. She could only gaze for what seemed like an age as the numbers finished stacking up. Then the connection icon flashed, and then came the dial tone.

Ed's voice spat into life. 'Babe? I'm coming for you.'

At the sound of his voice, she began to cry. Right there and then, it was the sweetest thing she had ever heard. 'Ed?' she sobbed in a whisper. 'Ed?'

She heard a long 'Shhhh' as he tried to calm her. 'Honest, darling, I am coming to get you.' Then his voice tightened and became stern as he took control. 'Sit tight; I'm going to find you. Let this call go on for a couple of minutes, then I'm going to hang up, but don't you, do you hear? Do not finish this call. Leave it open. We're going to get a fix on your phone, so whatever you do, do not hang up.'

He asked Tess to log the time of the call to the second, and she made a note.

'Christ,' he said, returning his attention to Esther. 'Are you okay, baby?'

With a tremble in her voice she whispered, 'I'm stuck in the boot of a car.'

'What can you tell me?' he interrupted.

She paused. 'They're Arabic, I think. One stinks of sweat, the other cigars. They look the same.'

Ed spoke again. 'Okay, I'm gonna have to hang up soon, baby. Switch off all your phone's notification functions without hanging up, is that clear?'

She heard herself mumble a weak 'Yes' as tears rolled down her cheeks onto her lips. She tasted the salt.

'Baby, I am already on my way for you. I promise, those fuckers won't know what's hit them. Are you hurt?'

Again, she muttered a soft 'No.'

'When we've finished talking,' Ed continued, 'make sure your phone is on silent and remove the vibrate function. From now on, use only the BBM Blackberry messaging service. I'm gonna hang up in a minute. I will message you to tell you when you can hang up. Do you understand, darling? Use BBM only and conserve battery power. We can track your phone. I love you, babe.' He checked his watch. *A good three-minute call*, he thought, and without a goodbye, he hung up.

The line went silent. Esther sobbed some more and cried into her handset. 'I love you, Ed.' She could have sworn he was still talking to her, but he had gone. His words replayed over and over in her head. She knew he would come and get her. She knew he would be burning with rage and nothing would stop him. It made her feel much better and, following his instructions, she switched off the phone's functions and immediately sent him a BBM:

*Locked in boot of car.*

Curiously, Tess asked Ed about his instruction for Esther not to hang up. As they drove back toward the police station, he explained that it was a technique that, back in the old analogue days, had been known as triangulation. Now it was known as pinging and worked via digital frequencies. Ed explained that BlackBerry phones were the latest smartphones with two advantages. They used a special server technology that sat between phone and email systems to offer better performance and were Triple Data Encrypted, giving them a higher security level for calls and messaging. Also, because of this, they could share real time location on a digital map and were set up so that the phone knew where it was at all times unless face down or switched off. This was mainly for street mapping and route planning, and therefore the handset sent out a GPS signal of longitude and latitude via the SMS system that all phones use for texting. BlackBerrys, however, were the only mobile phones to operate on a double-signal system. Their little lights flashed blue on receipt of an email or message, or maintained a steady green when the phone was in touch with its nominated satellites. Taking a photograph with the phone would also tag the image with its location. They were the only phones on the market that worked in real time with the internet and Gmail, so they could duplicate their signal by default, allowing the phone to be pinged and located to within several feet. Even conversations in areas of poor coverage could be easily detected. Government Communications Headquarters in Cheltenham and the CIA in Langley had been doing it for years with the Taliban. They called it 'chatter'. Ed knew they would have been listening to his call with Esther. All he needed to do was to get access to the tracking system via his boss. He just had to call it in. They would need Home Office approval for the coordinates, but under the circumstances that should be doable. He told Tess to message Esther back, instructing her to check her phone was on silent without vibrate, and to darken down the display. From now on she was only to communicate via BBM and only to call as a last resort if she felt threatened. He then told Tess to instruct Esther to hang up.

Pressing the red 'finish call' button, Esther willed herself off the line and immediately felt alone again.

Without hesitation, Ed snatched the phone and scrolled through his contacts for the number of his boss back in Poole.

The call was answered with an abrupt 'Hello!'

'Is that you, boss?' Ed shouted. 'Did you get it?'

Tess could hear the Chief's voice. 'Yep, we got it, lad. We're on it now. I'm with Commander Reynolds and Brigadier Chapman-Hall in Admiralty Office as we speak. Give me the precise time of the call.'

Tess recited the time and Ed relayed it to the Chief, who nodded to the brigadier. The brigadier nodded back and made the call.

# 21

## FOREIGN OFFICE, WHITEHALL, LONDON, ENGLAND

Several blocks away from the dark, old wood-panelled rooms of Parliament in the City of Westminster, to the rear of Horseferry Road and one block from the River Thames, was a spartan but smart office, perched high up on the top floor of a new office block, way above the visa, passport and immigration departments. Kitted out in a mix of cream leather lounge furniture and teak-legged desks, the office was used by the Foreign Secretary, and since her appointment she had given it a minimalist look to reflect the modern, des-res building in which it was located. It was occupied by David Hamilton, the department executive whose job it was to manage the agency's day-to-day affairs and Charlotte, his personal secretary.

They were enjoying a quiet moment with a coffee when the phone rang. The caller's number and a code came up on the base-set screen. Instinctively reading the code number, Charlotte pressed the orange button to scramble the forthcoming conversation. She knew it was the Royal Marine garrison in Poole, and said so out loud before answering. 'Hello, Poole,' the experienced secretary answered. 'How can I help?'

The caller identified himself. 'Hi, Charlotte; Jeremy Chapman-Hall. Are we good to talk right now?'

'Yes, all good. How can I help?' she replied.

'I need to speak to your boss. I've left her a voicemail but can't really wait. Is she there at all?'

Charlotte looked at her boss, who motioned for her to find out more and mouthed that the Foreign Secretary was in a meeting. 'She's in a meeting right now over at Vauxhall, can she call you back?' she asked the brigadier.

'I'm afraid not. This one's a bit of a red light. She might know a bit about it already. Tell her it's urgent, please, and I need protocol clearance.'

Charlotte put her hand over the mouthpiece and looked at her boss with apologetic raised eyebrows.

Realising the urgency, the head of department put down his coffee and rolled out his left arm, flexing and curling the fingers of his outstretched hand, beckoning the call to be transferred to his desk. Catching Charlotte's eye, he mouthed, *I got it; put him through.* Lifting the handset, the senior civil servant introduced himself. 'Brigadier? Hi, it's David Hamilton, department exec, here.' There would definitely be something massively wrong for the brigadier to call personally. 'Sorry, but she really is in a meeting with the Head of SIS. How can I help?'

'Hi, David,' came the reply in a matter-of-fact, military fashion. 'Listen, you'll be getting this one later through the usual channels but it involves one of our own guys. Wondered if I could get a couple of green lights and plenty of heads-up? Your man in Ankara should be on the phone any time now if he hasn't been already. One of ours has gone on a jolly with his lady friend to Turkey and she's been kidnapped. She's dual nationality – British-American – and the cherry on top: she's one of our computer boffs working for British Nuclear Fuels.'

David listened, then replied, 'Yes, I saw an email about that about fifteen minutes ago. Let me look. Hold on.'

Charlotte mouthed, *Is it the missing girl in Turkey?*

David nodded and she twisted around her monitor to display an email inbox.

'Yep, aha, here it is. We've had an email from the Embassy. It was grinding its way through the system until some American admin guy flagged it up. All reported by the boyfriend, a guy named Bennett. The Turks in Ankara crapped themselves when they saw it, and the Yanks are flapping too for some reason. Dumped the whole lot on our Embassy desk, trying to wash their hands of it. It's here ready for the Secretary after her meeting.'

'That's great,' said the brigadier. 'Bennett's our man; just retired and on his first civvy holiday with his girl, but I don't want anything advertised yet. We're the SBS, not the bloody SAS. I don't want media hype or Ministry of Defence donations flooding in just now; it could all be something or nothing. We don't want half the British Army running around trampling their desert welly boots all over it. Just need some green lights to get on with things. Can you deal? Who gets it: Five or Six?'

That last question meant who should deal with the problem and who could he lean on for assistance: MI5 or MI6? Since it was an overseas issue, but not a proven threat to UK intelligence, nor at this stage a link to terrorism from abroad, it was not cut and dried who should deal with it. It would be decided whether the Security Service (MI5) or the Secret Intelligence Service (MI6) should attend to it. Protocol was to inform the Home Secretary first, which he had already done, who would only brief the Prime Minister, the Chief of the Defence Staff and relevant members of a COBRA committee once a squadron required activation. The Home Secretary would discuss the case with the Foreign Secretary through departmental discussions with their secretaries, and then the Directors General of GCHQ and the Security Services would allocate it, coining the phrase 'Whitehall is dealing with it.' Until then, the Captain General (usually an Admiral) would call the shots. Only when a squadron was called up for active service would he be obliged to inform Whitehall. At this point, Royal Marine Brigadier Chapman-Hall didn't need to involve the Admiral. He just needed some intelligence, protocol and Embassy-level assistance.

'You will require mandates to operate overseas, but they will probably come from the Home Office. What do you need?' David asked.

The brigadier paused. *This means the Home Office, MI5 and a missing persons route*, he thought to himself. That was not what he'd hoped for. 'Err, not too much right now,' he said, 'but I need clarity on which resources I can fall back on. Protocol dictates that I pass it by you anyway, so we're all good on that one, but can I now push for Six, David, given that this is a kidnapping and not a missing person, close to the Syrian–Turkish border? I need Six for the intel and field operative assistance, old boy.'

The line went quiet.

'I'm not bothered who at this stage,' the brigadier continued, 'but I need to make a start on it immediately and I need to request warrants for telecom chatter info from UK and Turkish phone service providers.'

A slight intake of breath, then the department executive okayed the requests. 'Yes, I will swing it past the boss on her return;

you can have what you need for now until I can discuss it with her. No promises, but I'll push for Six to assist.'

'Great news,' said the brigadier. 'We've just had a mobile call from the girl, so I need chatter intel pretty damned quick, please.'

Another pause. 'Oh, that's tricky right now,' came David's reply. 'I can't sign that off. It has to be the boss, and as I said, she is in with the Head of SIS.'

'Good – that'll save you briefing them individually. Look, my friend, I need to be quite precise. I haven't got time for GCHQ and Langley to wade through hours of al-Qaeda chatter. I have her call locked in a ping hold and I need a location. We know she is still on the move and we are certain it's a kidnap.' Growing bored with the conversation, and conscious of time, the brigadier growled down the phone.

'I'll make some calls and come back to you.' David understood the request, and thought about how much abuse he could take from a Royal Marine brigadier spitting his dummy out, and of course the need to preserve intelligence on the case. 'I'll call you back,' he said, handing the phone back to Charlotte.

The brigadier thanked the civil servant. Putting the phone down and looking across at the Chief, he muttered, 'Swing it past the bloody boss? Are these people for real? They want to try living outside their bloody Whitehall bubbles.'

The two men looked at each other, then pushed back their chairs and said, almost in unison, 'Fuckin' Whitehall.' Then, leaning back in toward the coffee table, they discussed the problem further whilst waiting for the return call to confirm the telecommunication intercept warrants, and started scribbling notes, preparing forms and putting a plan into action.

# 22

## BEYŞEHIR BEACH RESORT, TURKEY

Unable to think straight, in sheer frustration and lost for a plan, Ed spun the Jeep around and headed back to the hotel, parked the vehicle and surrendered the keys back to Tess. He walked aimlessly around the hotel car park, his hands behind his head with fingers interlocked. Tess watched helplessly as the man seemed so lost.

Suddenly, out of the silence, Ed said abruptly, 'We go now. No messing. I mean right now!'

Tess paused and thought. She really wanted to go, but she also wanted time to go back to her place and grab some gear. Her heart jumped. Not since covering the Iraq War had she felt the buzz of just grabbing a bag and going off into the unknown to chase a great story. But she also felt a pang of panic and a sense of fear and dread as she considered what might lie ahead. She had a feeling this story would not end well. She also realised that Ed was not kidding; he really meant to go right there and then. On impulse, she agreed, and within seconds tossed him back the keys to her Jeep.

He didn't wait for her. He strode out of the car park like a man possessed, across the tarmac to the dusty roadside where they had parked earlier to check the kidnappers' tyre marks. Driven by desperation, helplessness and fear for his girlfriend, he jumped into the driver's seat, his right foot hitting the brake pedal as he started the ignition. Squeezing the button on its handle, he pulled the gear shift back from park and into drive, releasing pressure from the brake pedal and tapping the accelerator with his right foot. The Jeep jolted forward, but before releasing the brake pedal fully he offered Tess a get-out. 'You don't have to come,' he said. 'I can deal with this on my own and it might get messy.'

She now knew he could handle himself, having seen his steely behaviour, the way he carried himself, the logging of the times of his mobile calls, the photographing and sending images of the tyre marks. She had overheard some of his call to the UK and had seen his cool determination to head off into the unknown. He wasn't just a regular tourist. There was something different about him. She didn't know what yet, but she wanted to find out more and, without another thought, hurried over to the car.

He reached across and flung open the passenger door. 'Last chance,' he said. 'I'm not messing about. Make your mind up now.' He was deadly serious. Secretly, he wanted her with him. She knew the area, the language and the protocols. She would be a great asset. Besides, he liked her and thought she could handle herself, in a reporter sort of way, and could be a strong ally.

She threw her old canvas shoulder bag into the back and jumped into the front passenger seat. Before her legs were fully inside, he released the brake pedal and pushed down on the accelerator. He steered the hefty four-by-four off the sandy verge and onto the track in the direction of the tyre marks. The powerful V6 roared, throwing up a huge cloud of dust. He drove it forward, allowing the gearbox to stretch its engine revs to maximum before kicking up into its next gear. The velocity pushed Tess back into her seat as she stretched round to pull her seat belt across her chest. She was a good-looking woman; maybe a fitness type. He liked what he saw, and quietly admired his new acquaintance.

She pulled her sunglasses down off her head, sat back in the seat, then spoke. 'Do we have a plan, Mr Mystery Guy?'

He didn't reply.

They stopped at a fuel station He topped up the Jeep's tank to the brim as well as purchasing three five-gallon jerrycans, which he also filled. Climbing back into the driver's seat, he threw her four bottles of water and said, 'Last chance! Now or never. I mean it! The Turks will take days to start an investigation. I'm following that car right now!'

She looked directly into his eyes, smiled and replied, 'I'm in, scoop or no scoop.'

He nodded and they set off again, following the road southeast. He settled down into a comfortable driving position and found a suitable place for his phone in the centre console. She rummaged through her bag, pulled out a charger, plugged it in, then produced two more bottles of water. She placed hers in the holder set in the door, then held his by the neck and swung it over the central armrest, allowing it to fall onto his lap. He gave her a look of thanks. She felt a warmth for this guy but could see he was deep in thought.

'What's the plan?' she repeated.

'Dunno yet; just get Esther,' he replied. 'Waiting for work to get back to me first.'

'And what work would that be?' she enquired, knowing this part of the conversation would be slow due to his reluctance to divulge. 'You're not an engineer, a shopkeeper or a sales rep, so what type of work analyses tyre prints and calls Embassies to track phone calls?'

He'd known she would start to investigate him at the earliest opportunity, and had prepared some blunt, straightforward answers. 'I might work for an IT firm.'

'Yeah, you might,' she retorted, 'but come on, for Christ's sake; you've gotta level with me. I've just handed over my car and am heading off into the desert with a complete stranger who's had his girlfriend kidnapped.' She was frustrated now. 'Aw, come on, fella. This is not the deal. You tell me what's going on and I help you find your girl.'

With both hands on top of the steering wheel, he stared at the road ahead, still in deep thought. He squeezed the wheel and his knuckles whitened. The Jeep purred on. He glanced down at the fuel gauge: full. That was good, at least for now.

'Well?' she said.

Reluctantly, he decided. 'I'm ex-forces. I just retired. Literally, just weeks ago. This is our first proper holiday together in years. We've had weekends and minibreaks, but this was our first real trip due to work commitments.'

'I knew it,' she said. 'I knew it. You're ex-forces.' As a reporter covering war zones, she had seen it so many times in so many soldiers. They couldn't hide it. It was in their DNA. She had seen that matter-of-fact, disciplined swagger about him. They all had it. 'Come on then, what unit? Where were you based?'

Slowly, he replied. 'Royal Navy, Boat Squad.'

'Special forces, eh?' she interrupted. 'That's all SAS shit, isn't it?'

'No, it isn't,' he retorted sarcastically. 'It's Boat Squad shit actually!'

His snarl took her aback. Now she was puzzled. Although its title was self-explanatory, as a veteran American war reporter, she knew of, but still wasn't too familiar with, this branch. 'What's that, then?' she asked.

With his eyes still fixed on the dusty road ahead, he had anticipated her ignorance, and reluctantly growled, 'It's SBS. Special Boat Service.'

'Oh, all that Navy SEAL stuff?'

'Nope, *not* all that Hollywood SEAL stuff, or all that SAS shit either,' he snapped again, defensively. 'We don't do all that "hope and glory", Purple Heart crap. We work quietly.' His mood switched from disgruntled to proud as he began to explain the work his unit did. '"By Strength and Guile" is our motto, and that's exactly how the unit goes about its business.'

Eager to learn more, she asked, 'We hardly ever hear of them; which is the most secret of the two, then?'

He grinned to himself; he saw every question coming. 'Which one do you know more about?' he asked.

'Well, the SAS I guess…' She stopped, realising he had trapped her into answering her own question.

He scoffed, explaining that the SBS mockingly called the SAS their marketing arm, bringing in revenue from Hollywood and the big publishers. 'You won't read or hear about us, or see us in glossy shoot-'em-up movies. Unlike some well-known glorified units, the subject of book after book from enthusiastic writers and publishers, the Boat Squad, as we used to be called years ago, is a stealthy operator. Always there, working away quietly on covert and tactical operations, doing the legwork and the donkey work with reconnaissance, or backing up SAS regiments or pulling them out of the shit with helicopter and boat extractions. Just as the Home Office makes the decision whether to use MI5 or MI6, so too it decides whether to use the SAS or the SBS, depending on the job and the skill set required. Anything aquatic is our first discipline and strength. We're a tight unit of about 200 SCs – that's swimmer canoeists – split into four squadrons.'

She was fascinated and prodded him for more of his life story, wanting to know how he'd ended up here. She also suggested that it could be him the kidnappers really wanted. He'd thought of that too, but had dismissed it. After several minutes of interrogation, he was running out of answers and patience, so switched roles and asked for her backstory. She told him she used to work for CNN and then Reuters. She and her French partner had picked Beyşehir as a strategic camp for their work. They'd liked the place. It was safe, and its border location allowed them to cross back and forth easily when good Middle East stories came up. They'd had a nice condo there, and while reporting on the lengthy Iraq invasion and war, had retreated to it weekly to regroup and relax. He'd been a TV cameraman for France Vingt-Quatre; he was killed in a roadside ambush whilst they were travelling in separate vehicles in a press convoy to Baghdad. It had been covered extensively back home, and Ed remembered hearing about it on the BBC. Aameen, Tess's driver and fixer, had been driving her vehicle. Shot and wounded, he'd managed to save her. She told Ed that Aameen meant 'trustworthy and faithful' in Arabic, and that they had worked together ever since. Emotionally lost after losing her partner of fifteen years, she'd returned to Beyşehir with her fixer to pack up, but loved the place so much they'd stayed a bit longer. In that time, Aameen had met and married a local girl, so Tess had ended up staying, working as a freelancer with less ambition to enter dangerous conflict zones. Being American, it was too dangerous for her near the borders, so she'd decided to keep Beyşehir as her base.

'I just send Aameen and my spies in, then good old Nokia and Samsung do the rest. It's beautiful here by the lake so I decided to stay awhile. It's a stop-off for travellers from the borders, so I get the odd snippet of info here and there as well. I just ended up stuck here,' she explained. 'Then, as it's a growing resort, the Embassy asked if I'd stay longer to help out with more local stuff like this, so I got stuck here some more. I do pretty boring tourist reports and every now and then put in a bill for little jobs like this, and they decide if they'll pay it or not.' With her experience and knowledge of the area, she made a modest living and was on a small financial retainer doing minor work for expats and the US Embassy back in Ankara.

The Jeep heaved and bounced up the dirt tracks toward the mountains until they came to the main road that would take them to Seydişehir. Ed skidded the four-by-four to a halt in the arid gravel before hitting the asphalt. He looked left and right and pondered. All around was desert landscape. 'What's up that way?' he said, nodding ahead.

'Just little villages and the mountains,' she replied, puzzled. 'Why that way?'

'Well, these guys were pros,' he said, 'and Esther's kidnap was no accident. It was supposed to look like a missing tourist, not a kidnap. But that laundry van bungled it for them and nearly got them caught. Why didn't they shoot the janitor? Because they don't want a murder case raising the profile and all of Turkey chasing them. They know police will follow with road blocks and checks eventually, so now they won't want to be seen on the main highways. Through some bad luck, they've slowed their escape but they still have a couple of hours' head start. Still, they didn't reckon on old hubby jumping straight on their case. That car of theirs is a tough old bus, so for now, hang on!'

He pushed on the accelerator, driving the heavy SUV across the highway onto more dirt tracks and on toward the mountains. He pushed the vehicle across the rugged mountain tracks but never needed to stop to engage the four-wheel drive mechanism.

If a Merc sedan could handle it, then so could a two-tonne Jeep with bigger tyres to soak up the undulations of the terrain. He was driving as fast as he dared but was cautious of damaging the drive system. If he was right and this was the kidnappers' Plan B route, he could close the gap significantly within a few hours, if he could maintain the pace. Quiet and concentrating on the drive, Ed thought about Esther. Tess had her private phone, but for her work she used two others for the best mobile coverage in the mountainous region and all using different networks. At his request, Tess had already accessed Google Maps and jotted down main routes, trunk roads and any other tracks available, knowing that they would probably lose internet connectivity sooner or later. She'd also sketched him a rough map of southern Turkey.

Telling Esther to hang up the phone had been the hardest thing ever and had saddened him greatly, but he knew it was the right thing to do at the time. He did not know her full situation and her life could be in danger if she was caught contacting anyone. Rage boiled up inside him again and the skin over his knuckles tightened as he gripped the SUV's steering wheel.

# 23

# BRITISH EMBASSY, ANKARA, TURKEY

Over 200 miles away in the British Embassy at Ankara, the ancient ceiling fan spun slowly in the centre of the room, which was yellow from years of nicotine, dust and grime. But still it spun, faithful and obedient to the end. All the doors and windows were wide open, and even if you shut them, they'd only be opened again by uneducated staff. It was nearly two o'clock and getting to the hottest part of the day.

'Shut the fucking door,' a man shouted in a light Scottish accent, followed by 'for Christ's sake,' and then an almighty slam of his office door. 'Let's keep the fucking cold out, shall we?' he called to the Turkish administration assistant as she wandered off down the corridor, oblivious to his temperature requirements. 'Don't you know how air conditioning works?' he muttered to himself, realising his outburst and not wanting the woman to hear him, or to cause any more offence.

Turning from the door, he lifted and released one of his braces and let it slap back onto his shirt, then adjusted his trousers as he moved back to his desk with a missing person's report in his right hand. Sitting back down on the grubby, stained chair, he tugged at his pink shirt collar and dark red paisley bow tie, then pushed his tortoiseshell-effect round-rimmed glasses back up his nose and focused.

Timothy Blake-Leigh was a sweaty, fattish, ginger-haired, freckled sort of guy who had piled on the pounds since taking the office role in Ankara a couple of years ago. The cocktail and dinner parties, not to mention the desk job and a lack of good exercise, had all played their part. It was a cushy number which mostly involved collating information, political or otherwise, filtering out the crap from Embassy staff and reporters in the field and on the ground, finding the juicy bits, editing it all and sending it off to Paris. This meant he sat idle and typed a lot. More recently, he'd been Facebooking and tweeting his bosses back in Paris. He was a nine-till-five type of guy, wearing dark brown calf-length cargo shorts with braces over his pale pink cotton shirt. His sports socks were pulled up high on his calves above his dark brown Trekker trainers.

Gulping down another huge swig of bottled water, he turned the front page to read and digest the contents of a fax-copied four-page missing persons file which had been sneaked in to him by an admin assistant. He scanned it whilst mopping his brow with a dirty handkerchief. This was usually the reason why he wanted doors closed: so that others couldn't see what information he had sneaked before sending it off to other third parties. He had worked for Reuters, Al Jazeera and Fox over the years, on and off, and in his younger days had covered many Middle Eastern stories, mainly the Palestine–Israel struggles and, more recently, Iraq. Working from one of the hundreds of offices in the huge Consulate building which his firm rented from the Embassy, he enjoyed a few more creature comforts than he had in the past. Mainly, staff thought he was more important than he actually was, and he played the 'British gent' role often and well. Using his years of experience, he also managed to slip easily between Embassies, including the Turkish, Israeli and American.

This juicy little snippet about a missing holidaymaker had caught his eye, though. Initially, he didn't think it was too newsworthy, not just yet, but he wanted to read the report to be up to speed if things got more interesting. Besides, it was a little too early for emails to Paris. The missing girl could be lying pissed on a beach with another boyfriend for all he knew. Better to wait at least a good forty-eight hours or so and see what developed.

There was a rap on his door. 'Yeah,' he called, as if expecting it, and turned the photocopy blank side up.

It was an English reporter colleague. Ged was a freelancer whom Tim had met while working for France Vingt-Quatre. The French cable news firm was now selling itself as a truly European reporting service with boots on the ground in the Middle East and an enviable base camp in the Embassy of the British Consulate. The bulk of Ged's work had been following the Iraq troubles and sucking up to the US military to get the best scoops. He and Tim worked well as a team and between them managed to please their French paymasters. However, Iraq was coming to a close and as troops were pulled back, so too were the scoops. To Ged, Ankara seemed like a decent place to retreat to; safe in a more European way, but still close enough to the Syrian, Iraqi and Iranian borders, and he was well versed in nipping in and out across those borders.

'Hey!' said Ged, pushing his head around the door frame. 'Will you speak to Tess's fixer? He's been calling you for hours. He's on the line now. Wanna word with him? You've heard, right? About the Brit girl being kidnapped?' He pointed to a front office phone somewhere on hold.

'Ged, that was about three fucking questions in one sentence. Yeah, I'll speak to him,' said Tim, not giving much away until he'd had a chance to fully read the report on his desk.

'Then we'll have coffee?' said Ged. 'And discuss the report?'

'Ah, yeah, it's that time, I guess,' replied Tim, looking at his watch and rising to his feet. 'Discuss what report?'

'This one, of course,' said Ged. 'This missing Brit girl. Now her boyfriend's gone missing too. Vanished from the hotel, but I think Tess is with him.'

'Oh,' replied Tim, hanging on to this new snippet of information. Ged had the jump on him and knew far more about this issue than he did. He did not like that one bit and, trying to regain some lost ground, asked, 'And do the Turk police know this?'

'Not sure,' said Ged. 'But those guys in suits are in a right flap over something and I'm betting it's losing two tourists within the same day. One of the suits is a Yank. Dunno what he's poking his nose in for, though.'

*Hmm*, Tim thought. Years of experience in snooping, assuming and digging gave him a hunch. He wiped his brow. His interest had just notched up a few more levels. 'And how do you know all this?' he asked finally and reluctantly, embarrassed that Ged knew more than he did.

"Cause I spoke to Tess's fucking fixer on the phone when he kept calling, dum-dum!'

Tim could have kicked himself. He'd been far too busy dealing with admin and trivia to take the four attempted calls. 'Right, tell her to put him through to me. I will talk to him; see what he knows. Where did you say Tess was?'

'Dunno,' said Ged. 'Shot off somewhere with the boyfriend. Near Konya, I think.'

Tim stared at him. 'Think she's with him now?' he shouted. 'Fucking hell, Ged!' He grinned excitedly as the phone on his desk rang; he rubbed his hands, picked up the phone with his right hand and flapped his left at Ged, gesturing for him to fetch some coffees.

He gleaned a lot of information from the fixer's phone call, reassuring Aameen that he had the report in his hand as they spoke and would ensure the Ambassador got the information immediately; he would hand it to him personally.

Afterwards, Tim and Ged sat at Tim's desk. They pooled some ideas, deciding that there was more to this kidnapping than they had first thought.

Tim sat back in his chair. Grinning at Ged and slapping his hands together, he said, 'I think we got a story!'

They began making calls and asking all their contacts to busy themselves for fresh information on the British couple. They even called the fixer back and asked him to film the kidnap scene, the hotel and the surrounding area on his phone and forward the footage to them. Tim also asked for some photos of the couple to help launch their editing and presentation plans.

# 24

## BOTSA CREEK, KONYA PROVINCE, TURKEY, 370 MILES FROM THE SYRIAN BORDER

The CIA agent had followed slowly but methodically, keeping a safe distance as instructed. His dark blue Renault Clio struggled to keep up along the dirt tracks in parts. However, he picked his way cautiously across the terrain, out of the suburbs and up into the mountains in his shiny new hire car. His problem now was remaining inconspicuous. He needed to change vehicles to something even less noticeable. With his binoculars he could still maintain contact with his target, and stopped intermittently to watch the four-by-four vanish around bends or into dips. This was the only track for at least forty miles, so the big black Jeep was his easiest tail job ever.

He had been sent down from Ankara in a hurry. Earlier in the day, the American Ambassador had been involved in a conversation with the British Consulate about a missing person, and after a couple of phone calls Langley had offered to make some enquiries. He was told to wait casually to be asked by the British Embassy if he could help until they could 'get one of their own chaps on the ground'. On the back of that request, and as a consequence of the latest meetings at Langley, the young agent had received his instructions to fly direct to Beyşehir and assist the Brits with the missing woman and give whatever help was needed until they had their game plan sorted. It was meant to be an easy task: just sit around some hotel, liaise with and assist the local police, babysit and give tea and sympathy to the victim's partner; hold his hand and offer him a shoulder to cry on until HQ or the Brits solved the puzzle. It should have been a mundane job for the thirty-year-old with only two years' field experience; another of those low-key, safe jobs that he could even discuss details of with his girlfriend over email if he wanted.

Strangely, however, it had not panned out like that. He had only been in Beyşehir for thirty minutes or so when, as per protocol, he had reported back to his boss in Ankara and called Virginia with an update, only to be told, quite bluntly by his boss, back in the safety of the city in her nice, comfy, air-conditioned office, 'Well, fucking follow him then and see what he's up to!' It was thirty-something up in the mountains and there was no shade. For now, he would have to keep his engine-assisted car fan on full blast and tolerate the warm, sandy air blowing on him from the dashboard vents, or suffer greater heat with his windows down. He had two one litre bottles of water and was gagging to down the lot, but dared not until he could work out how long he would be following the Brit in the Jeep.

The dirt track climbed higher into the barren mountains. He was feeling the heat even at altitude, and praying for a stop of some sort. A village or a town, perhaps, where he could buy more water and cool down under a tap. The sweat ran down his brow into his eyes and he used his shirtsleeves to wipe his face. The more they climbed, the hotter it got, and it felt as if even his hire car was struggling for air. Working the little Renault harder, he strained to maintain visual contact with the Jeep, and he worried about losing it altogether. There was no way he was going to call that one in, so he sped up more, creating dust clouds beneath his spinning wheels, crashing and thumping the little chassis and dragging the French axles over the arid terrain, forcing the car over gullies and trenches where flash floods had previously carved out their paths.

The dust clouds did not go unnoticed.

~

Ahead of Ed and Tess, down in the Botsa Deresi valley, was a dam. The reservoir was empty and the place looked deserted. Tess informed Ed that, although the dam was unused due to lack of rain, just beyond it there was a village called Güneydere where they could get a good phone signal and more bottled water. The Jeep had worked well and been reliable. Even its air conditioning was still bathing them in cool air. A couple of times Ed had stopped and looked back at the tiny dust cloud, miles behind on the meandering dirt track. Now he stopped again and thought for a few seconds. He told Tess to buckle up, and pulled over his seat belt, locking it into position. Pressing hard on the brake pedal, holding the vehicle still, he selected 'full-time four-wheel drive – low gear' on the secondary, smaller gear stick. Then he selected 'drive – first gear' once more and eased the pressure off the brakes. Steering sharp right, he allowed the big machine to turn away from the track and make its way over the steep drop at the side of the road, down the hillside and into the next sharp hairpin bend.

Tess let out a gasp and muttered, 'Oh my God.'

Using the massive torque of the 3.7-litre engine, the low gear ratios, and at times some firm braking, he nudged the Jeep's bonnet down over the next drop and again lowered her onto the returning track, cutting off two long pieces of trail. He did this several more times, dropping the four-by-four down the mountain, off road, cutting out the huge chunks of track, much to Tess's annoyance.

She looked on in shock as the car once again tackled a fifty-degree incline over rocks, shale and gravel. 'What the hell was wrong with the goddamned road?' she said, banging her head on the roof lining for the umpteenth time and grabbing on to anything she could.

Ed did not reply. He just focused on the steep hill descents and steering the front wheels with his head stuck out the window.

'Hello?' she shouted, demanding an answer. 'Is there any need for this when there's a perfectly good, crappy, shitty dirt trail we can use?'

He stopped the car on the next level as they crossed yet another horizontal part of the road. Staring at Tess with a look of seriousness, he replied, 'See that dust cloud up behind us?' He thumbed over his shoulder in the direction of the Renault. 'We seem to have a tail. Someone from town is very interested in us as he's followed us all the way up here from Beyşehir. The driver was at my hotel, fussing around in reception, and we saw him at the police station when filing the missing person's report. Now, call me cynical, but I don't think that's a coincidence. It's definitely not normal customer service from your local holiday rep.'

Tess looked back up the mountainside and could just make out the little car and a faint amount of dust to its rear. 'Oh yeah, right,' she said, sounding a little nervous. 'I never noticed. Is it the guy that was asking for the detective at the police station?'

'Yep, I think so,' replied Ed. 'The guy in the suit with the sunglasses on his head.'

'Oh yeah,' she repeated. 'The guy with the dark skin. What are we gonna do?' She sounded more nervous now, her eyes wide and curious.

Ed turned and looked at her. 'You, my friend, are gonna play dead.' And with that, he booted the accelerator hard, causing the big engine to make an enormous roar, which reverberated and echoed up and across the valley like thunder.

Their tail must have heard the noise. Ed relaxed his foot off the big brake pedal again and the SUV lurched forward across the track, and once again Tess's view went from bright blue sky and clouds to dirty beige gravel as the Jeep's hood dipped violently and the car bashed its way down another great incline, creating lots of noise and dust. Ed even beeped the horn to attract attention as they hurtled down another two crossings and levelled out onto a smooth concreted stretch of road adjacent to the entrance to the dam's maintenance works. Just as Tess gave a sigh of relief, Ed braked and veered left, throwing his right arm across her chest and forcing her back into her seat. The SUV slammed into the concrete wall of the entrance gate, scattering plastic pieces from its fender and grille.

In shock yet again at the abrupt and violent force, Tess screamed, 'What are you doing, you crazy English bastard?'

Slamming the car to a stop, Ed put it in park but kept the engine running. He told her to slide over into the driver's seat whilst he got out and lifted the bonnet. Grabbing a bottle of spring water from the seat, he moved around to the other side of the vehicle. Lifting the hood just enough, he poured a full two litres over the red-hot engine. The steam spewed up in a thick cloud. Leaving the hood open and off its catch, he told her to beep the horn sharply once more and then lean over the steering wheel.

Tess started to protest, saying how ridiculous it was, and that the driver might just be on his way to a village.

Impatient, Ed looked her straight in the eye and snapped, 'Just friggin' do it. You wanted to be part of this shitty mess for your big story, so here you are and here's your chance of an equity card, so get on with it and act. Do as I say and we'll both be okay. Now play dead!'

He opened the passenger door and crouched down to see what he could see from under it. Without a good viewpoint, he pushed himself backward down a slope until he could see the road behind and the approach, then he lay down in the gravel and watched patiently.

Eventually, the Clio came to a squeaky stop. The driver got out and looked down into the valley at their fake car crash. With an air of urgency, he jumped back into his car and sped down the track, zigzagging every sharp turn and hairpin that Ed had avoided. After what seemed an eternity, they heard the car's tyres slowly crunch the gravel as it arrived in their vicinity. Tess's heart thumped hard. She was scared now; really scared. *Oh shit*, she thought. What the hell had she gotten herself into? Her reality was becoming a nightmare.

Just before real panic set in, as if on cue she heard Ed's deep but comforting voice from the open passenger door. 'Shhh,' he whispered. 'Take a deep breath and relax. Don't worry; we're just having a cheeky look. That's all. We're just looking to see who's interested in us. Worst-case scenario is he'll want to give you mouth-to-mouth!'

'Oh, very funny,' she whispered back.

He interrupted her. 'Shhh!'

They heard the driver's footsteps on the gravel, and Ed's eyes scanned for every bit of information he could get from under the belly of the SUV. The hem of the Clio man's dishdasha was grubby and he was wearing beige suede desert boots and dark socks, confirming Ed's suspicions that he wasn't a local. Petrified of moving, Tess felt the man standing over her. She thought she was going to pee herself.

Her door opened very slowly and she heard a Virginian accent. 'Hello there, lady, are you all right? Are you okay?'

Relieved to hear an American voice, she relaxed a little and groaned theatrically, then let out a sigh. She was about to lift her head as the Clio guy turned off the Jeep's engine and put his hand on her shoulder.

As he lifted his hand, the agent felt a thick, numbing pain on his left cheekbone from his ear to his nose. His head jerked violently to his right and hit the metal of the Jeep's pillar and door frame. Then again, and more pain flowed across his forehead and down into his face. Impulsively, he lashed out with his left fist and caught Ed in the lower ribs, causing him to exhale involuntarily. Ed went to bang the agent's head against the door frame again, but he'd gone into defensive mode and dropped down low, this time coming up with a fist into Ed's abdomen before he could inhale again after the first punch. Ed sucked it up, acknowledging that the guy was a pro. As he gulped for air, the Clio guy spun round low, attempting to sweep his legs away with a foot. Shin bone hit shin bone and the pain was sharp, but it didn't last long and there wasn't enough inertia in the attack to bring Ed down. He was much lower now, and the Clio guy grabbed his shirt and pulled him down into the dirt. The two men tumbled away from the car and Tess hovered over them, trying to decide whether she should kick at the stranger, wait to see what happened, or hit him with a rock or something. Instead, she froze, gazing at them, unable to come to a decision. Ed pulled the guy's robe over his head, hoping to regain some advantage. The dishdasha ripped a little and came up and over easily. This allowed Ed to swing around a little and get a knee up into the guy's chin. *Crack!* He felt the pain as it made contact. An 'Ugh' confirmed a direct hit, and he thought the guy had bitten his tongue too, but couldn't tell as there was no sign of blood yet. The guy was roughly the same build and weight as Ed and so, unfortunately, they were fairly evenly matched. Ed thought he looked like a toned and physically fit young man, and that he was on someone's payroll. They tumbled and fell, each trying to gain the advantage. Banging his head on rocks as they tumbled, the agent thought that this was the worst day of his short career. *How the fuck had he managed to get into this situation?*

Ed felt his hair being pulled and reluctantly lifted his head to negate the tugging pain in his scalp. This allowed the Clio guy to get his arm in under his throat. Ed saw it coming and tried to wriggle away, but too late. The guy was behind him, his right arm closing in on his Adam's apple. Knowing how this could end, Ed started pumping his arms as if skiing, rowing back and forth with imaginary ski poles, elbowing the guy in the ribs over and over. It didn't matter if each blow had lots of pressure or not; as long as there was decent contact, the guy's ribs would eventually start to hurt, hopefully long before Ed choked to death. After several blows, Ed lifted his left arm to prevent the guy using his own left arm to apply more choking pressure; then with both hands he pulled down on the guy's left thumb, wrist and forearm. Feeling the pressure build and knowing his face would soon turn blue, he salivated involuntarily, almost foaming as he slowly suffocated. Fearing the worst, and with all his strength, Ed pulled down and twisted the Clio guy's left forearm and wrist outward. As he did so, he curled into a ball, then got his left knee up and between the ever-tightening arm and his own chest. Forcing the man's arm away at a peculiar angle, and pulling down sharply on his wrist, it finally came. The snap was loud and clear. The American gave a huge scream as the burning pain rocketed deep into his radial bone and the surrounding flesh, extending from the lateral side of his elbow down to his thumb. His radius no longer ran parallel to his ulna. It was a massive fracture. The American released his stranglehold, sliding on his backside across the desert ground, back toward the Jeep as if to find some refuge.

'Aw, Ed. You broke his fucking arm!' screamed Tess. 'You friggin' baboon.'

Ed stood up straight, wiped his brow and began tucking his shirt in.

'Yeah, you shit!' the American added. 'You broke my goddamned arm, you son of a bitch.' He cursed as he scrambled to gather his composure and tried in vain to take charge of the two civilians and the deteriorating situation. His arm was already massively swollen and banana-shaped. He cradled it with his good arm. There was no flesh wound or jutting bone; just a fracture.

'I'll break your fucking neck in a minute,' replied Ed angrily, stepping closer.

'Back off, big guy,' Tess said. 'I think he's had enough.'

'Who are you and why are you tailing us?' Ed demanded.

'Go fuck yourself,' said the Clio guy. 'What the fucking hell d'ya think you're doing assaulting an…' He stopped himself.

'… an American citizen, or an American agent?' Ed finished the sentence for him. 'You're too far from home and way out of jurisdiction to be FBI, and American Embassy staff don't wear fancy watches or Beretta Storm sidearms with clip-on holsters. Oh, or zip-off shorts underneath. That means I've got the interest of the CIA. Now why would that be, I wonder?' asked Ed sarcastically.

'Are you gonna tell me, or do I have to beat the crap outta you, then crack on and leave here?'

'Fuck you,' replied the agent. 'I'm just a messenger boy. The Embassy told me to keep an eye on you. That's all.'

Ed moved over to the little Clio. On the passenger seat lay a black Motorola two-way radio and a Nokia mobile phone. He clicked the Motorola's speak button twice. The frequency knob indicated that it was on Channel 4. All he got was crackle. They were too far up in the mountains for the device to be usable, but back in Beyşehir it would work well when communicating with another operative within a couple of miles' radius. 'Who's with ya?' he asked, throwing the radio down onto the rocks. It shattered into pieces. 'Walkie-talkies only work in pairs.'

He checked the last dialled number on the Clio guy's phone. It started 001. Ed read out the digits. 'Zero-zero-one, eh? You weren't calling the UK; that starts four-four.' He looked at Tess. 'Where's zero-zero-one?' he asked sarcastically, knowing the answer.

'It's the States,' she replied without hesitating.

'That's right,' said Ed. 'And I'm betting the next digit along is for Langley, Virginia. Who's with ya, mate?' he repeated.

'No one,' whimpered the agent. 'I was just sent down from Ankara by my Embassy at the request of your Embassy because of the missing persons tag on your girlfriend, because your guys had no one available. That's all.' The more he spoke, the angrier he got, but he still managed to lay it on thick and play the innocent. 'And this is the thanks we get; you know, friends across the pond and all that bullshit. Lend the Brits a hand! Wish we'd never bothered!' he shouted wildly whilst nursing his fractured arm.

Ed stood over and watched him as he let off steam. 'A valiant attempt at being pathetic, but you're far too early. The ink on the missing persons form is barely dry, yet here you are' he said.

'Hmm, but very plausible,' said Tess quietly, worried now about landing herself in trouble with the authorities.

'Yep. And a good cover story too.' Ed slammed the Jeep's bonnet shut. 'But Embassy staff do not and cannot just authorise CIA agents out into the field. And who's at the other end of that two-way radio?' Moving around the Jeep, he continued, 'You may look like an *A-rab*, but from where I'm stood, you look more like an *a-hole*, my friend. Come on, Tess, get in. We're leaving.'

Tess was still in a mild state of shock. 'What? We're leaving? Just like that? We can't just leave him here like this!'

'Yep, yep and yep,' said Ed. 'Are you getting in?' He fired up the Jeep and leaned out toward her. 'He ain't talking. He won't, 'cause he's trained and he's a pro.'

Tess dithered. She looked at Ed and then at the agent on the ground. Deciding, she held out her hands with open palms to the injured agent and made an apologetic pushing-down gesture. 'Dude, I'm so, so sorry,' she said, genuinely upset. 'I'm sorry about your arm and all, but this guy's on a mission and I gotta go. You've got a cell phone, right? You can call it in, can't you?' She turned, threw the downed agent a bottle of water and then jumped back into the Jeep.

The injured agent leaned away from the SUV as it reversed, kicking up dust and grit into his face. He was angry and embarrassed, and had already begun to work on his story for when he had to phone it in. His day had just got a whole lot worse.

Ed reversed the Jeep away from the concrete wall, then jumped out and inspected the damage from the manufactured collision. Just as he'd intended, it was purely superficial, with damaged plastic only. The last thing he needed right now was a bust radiator. Happy with the vehicle, he looked at Tess and shoved the auto box out of low gears and into high-drive, pushing onward down the valley, continuing their pursuit of the kidnappers' Mercedes sedan.

Tess seized the grab handle above her head and gripped it tightly, knowing that this trip was going to get a whole lot bumpier. She looked at Ed with much more respect now. 'He's CIA, then?' she asked.

'Almost definitely,' said Ed. 'I'd put money on it.'

Tess stared, and before she could say any more, he beat her to it.

'Yep, I know. Why are the CIA so interested in a missing tourist? Because it's all about Esther. It's always been about Esther.'

Still puzzling for clues and some better answers, he explained Esther's role as a nuclear engineer and computer whizz-kid, along with the break-in back home and a bit about her background, hoping Tess could find something for him to work on. As he steered the SUV down the dirt track towards Adana, she busied herself with telephoning reporter colleagues she thought might be able to help.

# 25

## US EMBASSY, LONDON, ENGLAND

Less than three miles from Her Majesty's Secret Intelligence Service building on the River Thames, two blocks back from Park Lane and flanked by bronze statues of Reagan and Eisenhower, stood the largest United States Embassy in Europe. It was watched over from its roof by a huge, gilded bald eagle, and a facade of angular stone framed the windows that overlooked the pristinely manicured Grosvenor Square Garden. Four floors up and to the western end of the building, way down the corridor, away from humdrum activities concerning matters such as passports, tourists and visas, were Rooms A402 to A404. These had been knocked through into one, making a very spacious operation room with small temporary booths and workstations, all facing inwards toward the centre where one grand round table and numerous conference chairs were positioned, giving the field officers and workstation operators one focal area into which to feed information. At the far end, against the wall, was an array of huge TV screens, monitors and pull-down movie screens. To the far right were thick glass panels with blinds, which acted as dividing walls for three offices which looked out over the park.

Liz McKeowan dropped her handbag and attaché case. Jet-lagged but enthusiastic, she walked around her new desk. 'Let's get down to business, gentlemen, please,' she said, as two head-of-office agents walked into her office carrying documents. 'Please, have a seat.' She gestured with one hand as she undid the middle button of her grey tweed jacket with the other, allowing it to fall open for comfort. She then flicked back her auburn hair and sat in her chair.

Both men leaned in and slipped their respective documents onto her desk. She pulled them toward her and straightened them up, allowing her to read their front covers before opening the top file marked 'Classified Level 5'. One officer pulled up a chair to sit.

'Err, coffee, boss, before we start?' asked her deputy.

'No thanks,' came her reply, her face blank and expressionless. 'This is urgent,' she said grimly, 'and we've no time for coffee. What I need are some answers and some results. When I was put in charge of this operation, we all agreed to work this one together. So, what the hell is going on?'

Both men looked around, up and down in embarrassment. The senior case handler regretted asking the coffee question and tried to defuse the tension that was already building.

'Who's the case officer for the two agents on the ground?' she asked. Before her deputy could answer, she stared at him and, with a sigh of disapproval, continued, 'Go get him. He should be here.'

Her deputy nodded to his colleague and then at the open door, indicating to him to leave, as he sat on Liz's desk. 'We'll sort it today, boss, don't you worry. Calm down,' he said, trying in vain to show some solidarity. 'We can pull this off by close of play.'

Her head lifted from the reports on her desk. She grabbed a bottle of spring water, twisted off the blue cap in a vicious motion, and drank. Slamming the bottle down, she stared at him and blasted, 'Oh, really? You think so, huh? By the numbers,' she leaned forward, her right index finger jabbing her desktop, 'I've got a Russian spy on the run, an Israeli Mossad skewered good 'n' kosher, a rookie field agent licking a broken arm, a cleaner nearly clubbed to death and some fuckin' computer buff kidnapped, God knows where. Oh! And I forgot – one pain-in-the-ass British tourist boyfriend on the loose, screwing up my career.' Rising to her feet, she continued, 'Not to mention European Ambassadors, one US Security Senator, and probably the British Prime Minister beating my goddamn door down and chewing my ass too. So don't you tell me to calm down! Now, who the fuck is this guy and what's his MO?'

With anger and frustration in her eyes, and before her deputy could answer, she continued her rant.

'This is now an international incident and we need to get a grip and stick a lid on it pretty damned quick. Find out who this boyfriend clown is and get me someone out there who is professional and capable enough to remove him. This comes from the top. The very top. The top with a capital T, and Capitol as in DC. Capiche?'

Her deputy looked shocked. He knew she was a stress-head and had seen her temper many times, but he had never seen her like this. On this occasion she was worried. *Worried for her career*, he thought. *If this goes pear-shaped, she'll be back on the beat in the Bronx in no time.* He looked at his boss.

'That woman must not get into Iran. Have I made myself perfectly clear?'

Her deputy nodded.

'I now have to report on this project every four hours to our Ambassador and the Head of MI6 and prepare a brief for the UK Foreign Minister's secretary, who will probably brief the Prime

Minister and then the National fucking Security Council and oh, and probably a COBRA meeting too.'

He wondered how red her face could get.

'And get your fat ass off my freaking desk,' she finally finished.

Wes Casey had watched Liz climb the ranks over the years thanks to her temerity and dogged persistence, but this behaviour was out of the ordinary. He got up from her desk and left her office feeling shitty. Pulling down his tie, he crossed the open-plan room, knowing that everyone had heard the conversation. He looked back at the staring staff. In a sarcastic, disappointed tone, he said softly, 'Well? Back to work – you heard the lady!' before scanning the operation room for his colleague whom he had sent to look for the case officer she had requested.

A good ten minutes later they returned with the missing case officer, who had just come back to the office from across town, and pushed him forward as a sort of peace offering.

Looking up from her desk, Liz encouraged them into her office. 'I hope you have something decent for me?'

Wes spoke up. 'Yep. We have. We've only just got it. It took some doing but we have it.' Luckily, he did have something for her.

The case officer was out of breath after receiving panicked phone calls from his line manager, then rushing around Whitehall, calling in favours and jumping in and out of taxis, to return swiftly to the office. He had just blown his month's budget in dollars to a contact at GCHQ over in Cheltenham for the required information. From his inside pocket he drew a folded brown A4 envelope. Removing his coat, he opened the envelope, revealing pages of email printouts and reports. 'The info's been difficult to obtain as he's only just been released from the service. His files were about to be buried for the next thirty years,' he said, unfolding the paper. 'My meeting with my informant made him late for another meeting, so it's hot off the press.'

He looked at her for approval. Her face was blank. Disappointed, he looked down at his notes. Wary of antagonising his new boss, he started reading.

'Okay,' he said, dragging out the word. 'So…' He reeled off the info in bullet points. 'This guy's ex-forces. Boat Squad. Special Boat Service. An instructor for the last five years in Poole, Dorset. That's where the Boat Service are holed up. He's been sitting it out, waiting for early retirement. He's literally just finished; released from duties a few weeks ago. A busy boy. Joined and completed his apprenticeship as a Navy marine engineer, then re-categorised to the diving branch. Moved from the diving branch to the Royal Navy Commandos early '80s before they merged with the Royal Marines. Invited to SBS "selection process" by an officer whose life he saved during the Falklands War. Completed with flying colours and was offered a four-year secondment. Never returned to normal duties. Plenty of active service: Falklands; Northern Ireland; the first Gulf War with Iraq and Iran.'

He glanced up for reactions. There were none, so he continued to read from the folded sheets, which he had previously used to rehearse this roll call in the taxi on his way back to the Embassy.

'In '84, did twenty-eight days "over the wall". That's DQs, Detention Quarters, Portsmouth. Naval prison equivalent. He put some French Legionnaire officer in hospital whilst in Mogadishu and was busted down from Chief to Petty Officer. Refused promotion ever since. In '85, Northern Ireland again; '86, Somalia again and Djibouti.' In '86 he even did a six-month exchange with the US Navy. He paused for breath and composure, then continued. 'Yemen '87, then Egypt, oh and Karachi, Pakistan. This guy's no tourist. Core skills are marine engineering, clearance diving and suchlike. Err, boat craft, search and rescue, extractions, reconnaissance and sabotage… oh, and killing people. Apparently, he doesn't mind pulling a trigger. He's been investigated several times by the MOD Board of Inquiries for fatal shootings, but all legit. Left the service in '89, married, own business, one kid, divorced, rejoined the service with a stint in UK Forces Internal Security, no info on that I'm afraid, that's treble classified… and then he reappears back at the Boat Service circa'98.'

Wes looked up at his boss. She looked slightly relieved that they had something worthwhile, but not happy with what she'd heard. He slapped the case officer on the shoulder. 'Well done, buddy. Good work. I didn't know the Brits were so damned busy all those years.'

The tension in the office relaxed a little, and then Liz spoke with the slightest of smiles. 'Good work. I've just spoken to the Israelis. They've agreed to cooperate with us. They will focus on the FSB agent if we want. They have some unfinished business with him. So, they will take care of him, leaving us to focus on the girl, her boyfriend and her kidnappers. Take the boyfriend out if you have to. Carry on digging; I want to know everything we can about this guy. How many fillings he has! MI6 are playing it dumb. Not sure how much they know but they've asked us twice for our assistance. Any more suggestions?' she asked.

No? 'Good,' she said. 'I'll prepare my four-hourly report for the Brits.' She sat back into her chair, then looked up at the three men still standing. 'Well?' she said. 'Let's go, go, go, gents! And slam the door on your way out!'

# 26

## KONYA MOUNTAINS, TURKEY, 340 MILES FROM THE SYRIAN BORDER

Ed and Tess's conversation was interrupted by his BlackBerry jumping around in the driver's cup holder. He grabbed it immediately. It was the Chief. 'Boss! Hi! What you got?' he said impatiently.

'Okay, Ed. Brace yourself pal,' came the reply. 'Don't be mad at your girl 'cause we don't believe she knows. I have here, from Whitehall, a copy of an MI5 dossier on Esther's parents, obtained by the brigadier. As I say, we don't think Esther knows about this, so don't flip out on her. The dossier originates from activities back in the seventies.'

Ed slowed the Jeep to a crawl and turned off the air conditioning to hear better. Tess could hear too; not everything, but she was getting snippets of the conversation.

'Where to start?' said the Chief. 'You know she was orphaned and adopted and believes her parents to have been killed in a road traffic accident in Israel when she was five?'

'Yeah, that's right,' said Ed.

'And she was then looked after by her older cousin?' Again, the Chief phrased the statement as a question.

Ed agreed and finished off the statement. 'And later sent to friends of her mother's in New Jersey, and then on to Britain, where she was brought up in a nunnery up on the north-west coast.'

'That's mainly correct,' said his boss. 'But it was all paid for by a US Zionist women's charity set up by none other than her great-grandmother and aided by the Israeli government. That all seems to be true. But…' he paused, 'here comes the rub. She was actually an only child, born into a very wealthy Jewish family in Iran. Her parents were Iranian Jews living in Tehran. Her grandmother founded a women's Zionist movement over in New York, which financed Esther's future. Ed, your Esther's real surname is Hadassah, not Hassadah.' Again, he paused for a while.

'Her father was Habib Hadassah, a multimillionaire businessman and philanthropist who made his money from manufacturing based in Tehran. For a while he was the symbolic head of Iran's Jewish community. Notice that her surname is different? The letters have been exactly reversed. An anadrome was used in a bid to protect her.'

'Yeah?' said Ed quietly and thoughtfully as he pulled the Jeep to a stop. 'What happened to them?'

'Well…' the Chief hesitated. 'The Iranian Islamic Revolution happened. It brought about the overthrow of the last Persian King and the Pahlavi dynasty, which had been heavily supported by the UK and the Americans. Just before the revolution, Esther's parents were sent to the US for diplomatic reasons along with other dignitaries and eminent citizens, but they later returned to Tehran. In '79, they were arrested and executed on the same day due to their strong ties to the West, Israel and Zionism. Both of them were accused of spying against the state. Your Esther's parents were the first two Jews to be executed under the new Islamic state of Iran. There was no car crash. Their only crime was being Jewish, metaphorically speaking.'

Tess had caught most of what had been said. Ed had got it all and just sat at the wheel, thinking and staring out of the window. All he could see was Esther tied and curled up somewhere, all alone and held hostage.

The Chief continued. 'Ed, son, we've had some green lights from Whitehall but no magic wands, I'm afraid. As you probably know, we have two squads working with the Yanks there and two on standby in Iraq. They can't deploy or come off station without the Foreign Office or the PM's approval, and we ain't got that yet. We haven't climbed the priority tree 'cause it's too early. There'll be no boots on the ground yet, but the good news: I do have some guys on standby. They're about to take their leave back to the UK any day now. Don't know who exactly just yet, but they're ready for some R&R in southern Turkey. I've signed off on travel warrants to fly Turkish Airlines on Wednesday if needed.'

A wave of relief flowed over Ed and he felt, for a moment at least, a little lighter. The thought of some of the team coming out to give him a helping hand was a huge boost to his morale. Those lads would give up anything to help a squad mate; even a well-earned early night in bed with their wives. 'So, what about Esther then, boss? What's all this got to do with her?'

The Chief had no answer. 'Standby on that one. We're researching like mad here and no one's going home till we sort this, so don't worry, we'll have something positive for you soon. It's only been a few hours. We're working on the phone call so we'll have a fix on that pretty soon. I'm signing off to chase it now. Stay safe and stay legal. Don't do anything to compromise yourself with the authorities. You are our only man on the ground, remember.'

'Yeah, yeah. Roger that. Cheers,' replied Ed sadly, and the line fell silent.

Tess grabbed her own phone and dialled a number. He went to stop her but she pulled away. Seeing the dread in his face, she spoke quietly. 'Let reporters do what we do best: sniff around and find stuff out. I can help you. That's why I'm here, isn't it?'

He let go of her arm and drove on, back up to their previous speed.

She phoned Ged, back in Ankara. It rang a number of times with no immediate answer. She bounced her leg up and down impatiently. 'Come on, pick up,' she muttered.

Her caller ID showed up on Ged's screen. 'Tess, how's it going? Where you at? Are you with the boyfriend?'

She cut him short. 'Aw, Jesus, Ged, that's three questions before we even say hello! How do you do that? Now listen carefully and make some notes.' She told him everything she had heard and been told.

'Whoa, for Christ's sake!' exclaimed another voice. Tim, sitting next to Ged, had snatched the phone out of his hand. 'So, we're saying she's dual nationality, an Iranian-British Jew with a hidden past, a computer buff working for British Nuclear Fuels, and she's been kidnapped in Turkey by two guys, possibly Arabs? Is that what we've got?'

'Yep, that's about the size of it,' replied Tess. 'Apparently, their home and her workplace were broken into before they left the UK too. Someone seems pretty keen to get hold of her. And if the kidnappers aren't Arabs after all, but Iranian, then it doesn't look that good.'

Ed was focused on driving but immediately shouted over, 'Why, though? What's with the Iranian thing now?'

She gave him a worried smile to say she did not know. She told

Tim, 'I'll call you back,' and immediately hung up.

Tim thought this was looking like a damned good story after all, and Ged couldn't help but get even more excited. Picking up the landline on Tim's desk, he feverishly started chasing down old colleagues and anyone he could think of who could get him some information, calling in as many favours as he could.

Ed and Tess looked at each other. Each could see the fresh worry in the other's eyes.

'Where next on this damned shitty road?' asked Ed.

Tess sat in silence, staring through the windshield. She felt more apprehensive than ever. Truth be told, she was beginning to panic a little, wondering what she had got herself into.

'Tess?' shouted Ed. 'Where next? Come on, girl, stay focused.' He threw the SUV around another rutted, rocky bend.

'Oh, err, yeah, sorry,' she mumbled as she came back to the present and rummaged through her bag for her notepad. 'Err, Karaman, if we continue east, then toward Adana.'

Ed thought for a moment, keeping his eyes on the road. Then he spoke. 'If they take her on to Adana or beyond, then they must be heading for one of the borders, and that, I reckon, would confirm an Iranian connection.' He paused, gulped, then continued. 'And that means a whole world of shit that we're not prepared for. We have to get to her before they leave Turkey.'

Tess said nothing and they drove on in silence, staring ahead, their bodies swaying side to side in their seats and their heads nodding to and fro in unison as the Jeep climbed and descended the dirt roads toward the next town.

Again, Ed's phone broke the silence. The Chief was back. 'Go, boss,' said Ed. 'Hope it's good?'

'Yeah. It's good; at least *some* good news,' came the reply on a faint, crackling and distant line.

Ed slowed the vehicle to a silent crawl once more, allowing the huge engine's idle tick-over speed and the low gear of the auto gearbox to do the work. All that could be heard now was the gentle crunch of the tyres on rugged gravel and a quiet burble from the exhaust. Instinctively, he turned off the dashboard blowers once more so he could hear much better.

The Chief proclaimed, 'We're starting to move some treacle; we're swimming now. The brigadier is pulling strings up at Whitehall and we got a special warrant approved for all of Esther's and your phone calls. I'm pleased to tell you, Ed, that she is now officially being tracked. GCHQ recorded some pings and the triangulation of her mobile to within two metres at 1634 hours. I've literally just had them send me the coordinates via SMS, and I've forwarded them to you. It's a village called Kavak, approximately twenty miles east of the town, on a road called Köyü İç Yolu. Google Earth confirms it. It goes from metalled road to dirt track. Follow the Boylakkurasi creek. Take the dirt track, follow it south-east, down and pass the May Baraji reservoir on your right, then take a left to pick up the D705 to Karaman. That's a two-lane freeway so you'll be able to pick up the pace once you're on it.'

Ed listened intently. 'Yeah, and so will they,' he said.

'Yeah, I know,' said the Chief. 'But you must be gaining on them if you're keeping to your pace in that Jeep. From what you say, those tracks will be pretty tough on a normal saloon. Also, it's not black.'

'What's not?' enquired Ed.

'It's not black,' the chief repeated. 'The car isn't black. Had the guys go over the images you sent. We cannot get a match from the Merc boffs over in Stuttgart. It's too old. The tyres are re-treads. It's an unknown dark navy-blue spray job, From the images you sent of the van, its original colour was a bronze-gold used by Mercedes from 2000 to 2004 on limited-edition vehicles. You're looking for a dark navy resprayed Merc E200L four-door. It could have been resprayed for this very job. We still don't know for sure if it's you or Esther they're after, but it's pointing to Esther. Looks like it was all carefully planned. And we reckon you're spoiling their planned exit route. They're definitely headed east, and probably onward to at least the Syrian border. But we still don't know why.'

Ed didn't get the chance to hang up. The signal was poor and the line went dead as the vehicle crept round a sharp S-bend, revealing a huge cliff face and below them a massive drop as they approached a steep section of the valley wall. The single track made their way forward slow, and he dumped the phone back in its cup holder.

Suddenly, almost making him jump, Tess cried out. 'Stop, stop! There, look, down there!' Pointing, she wound down her window. 'Just there on the valley floor, to the east. Is that them? That's them, isn't it?' she said with excitement that threatened to turn to panic.

Ed pulled the Jeep to a halt to focus his view. He leaned over, stretching across Tess's chest without realising. With the vehicle now stationary, he stared out. It seemed like miles away, but sure enough, parked in what looked like a passing place, there was indeed a dark saloon. He slammed the SUV into reverse, blipped the throttle gently, reversed out of sight and turned off the engine. He jumped out and stood by the roadside. In a rush of panic, he called back to Tess. 'Got any binoculars?'

'Err, no,' she replied apologetically as she too climbed out of the Jeep. Aware of their unintentional moment, she wondered what might have been, had the present situation been different and not as urgent and dramatic. Embarrassed, she told herself off for being so silly. Besides, they were chasing after Ed's girlfriend – how wrong to start feeling like a teenage girl again at a time like this. She now also felt silly for being all the way out here up in the mountains without basic equipment such as binoculars. 'I've never bothered with them.'

Ed was disappointed too, remembering that he was now just a simple tourist. He could do with some useful kit right now; in the past, jobs like this had been easy because they'd always had whatever kit they needed, and of course permission to act. He crouched and shielded his eyes to improve his view.

In an attempt to regain some dignity and prowess, Tess scurried to the back of the car. 'I've never bothered with them,' she repeated more confidently, 'because I always have my zoom-lens cameras!' She made the statement with an air of confidence and suddenly felt more adequate. She heaved at the big rear swing door with its mounted spare wheel and from the cavernous trunk pulled out a beaten-up black nylon bag. In haste, she unloaded its contents onto the trunk floor, unclipping and clipping, removing caps and screwing pieces of cameras together.

'Hurry!' shouted Ed.

Frantically, Tess rummaged and fiddled with the equipment and then, like a true professional, in one swift motion, she stepped back, spun around and squatted down discreetly. Leaning forward, as steady as a rock, she pointed the powerful lens down to the valley floor and began shooting. In old-school style, she avoided the modern, three-inch digital screen on the camera's back, instead pressing her eye up against the rubber sock that protected the viewfinder. Slowly and purposefully, she adjusted the powerful tele-lens as she moved forward to the cliff edge, crouching and stooping as she shifted her body weight onto her hips and knees, steadying herself as she fired the Nikon, shot after shot. Ed heard the familiar electronic whirring and whizzing and the *click-click* repeating noise, machine-gun style, as if the paparazzi had just arrived. The camera recorded hundreds of still digital images to its memory card. Staring through the lens, Tess twisted and pulled at the telescopic eye. Using the immense technology and all the zooming power of the digital machine, she swooped in, shot after shot, until she could not only see all the images but identify plate numbers and markings. Ed could only see little black ants moving about, but Tess, like a rookie journalist out for her first big scoop, got excited about her clear shots.

It was indeed a parked Mercedes, and there were three men visible. They all looked the same to her: short black hair and black moustaches. One, in a beige shirt, sat at the wheel smoking a cigarette. Another, in blue chinos, was out of the car on the roadside, taking a pee. The third was in the rear seat, messing with what looked like a pistol. The one with the pistol was shouting and throwing his hands about. The one taking a pee was obviously arguing with him, and he too was waving his hands after zipping up his flies. The driver threw his cigarette out of the window and started the engine.

There was no sign of Esther, Ed thought. The bastards still had her in the trunk after all this time and in this heat. A veil of rage passed over him as he stood on the mountaintop, looking down at the car. His skin tightened over his knuckles. He would kill every one of them, he thought, as he and Tess watched the sedan pull off and gradually move away until it was a black speck in the distance.

Tess released the button, halting the camera's Gatling-gun action, and the air fell silent. They looked at each other, and a gentle breeze swept around the car and over them.

'I got the lot,' she said proudly, feeling worthy and useful again, but a wave of guilt and sadness came over Ed, and she saw it. Immediately, she walked over to him, opened her arms and gave him a huge hug. He responded similarly. 'Come on,' she said. 'Now we're onto them. They don't know how close we are.'

She felt his thick, confident bulk against her and felt safe. She now knew for sure that this guy would deliver. Her feelings of anxiety faded as she felt this guy give her a certain confidence. She could see what Esther saw in him. Realising what she had just done, she pulled away, fumbling for the camera strapped around her neck, lifting it over her head. She became embarrassed, clutching for the camera to defuse whatever might have just happened. She was particularly embarrassed about it given their current circumstances, and lifted the camera so they could both view the digital screen and analyse the images.

Ed did not even realise what had happened and moved his gaze down to the small screen. 'Yep, let's get those bastards,' he said quietly. He told Tess to jump back into the car to shade the images for a better look.

They returned to the vehicle and scanned through the photos, Ed telling Tess to flick forward or back so he could build a mental picture of who he was up against. As the crow flies, they were probably only a couple of miles away, but on these mountain roads, it could be treble that distance before they could close the gap. Satisfied for now, they drove off. Ed felt better. Now they were in pursuit and he felt he had an edge on them. He gave Tess his mobile and asked her to text his old boss and, using the images, give him as much info as possible on the target. The Merc's plates were probably fake, but at least it was marked and they had made visual contact. As he drove, he had to discipline himself to slow down a little and curb his enthusiasm. Damage to the Jeep now would be his worst nightmare.

# 27

## MAY BARAJI RESERVOIR, TURKEY, 140 MILES FROM THE SYRIAN BORDER

'Where are you now?' Liz McKeowan demanded abruptly through his earpiece as the rotor blades whined into life.

The senior agent pushed his sunglasses up his nose and replied through his mouthpiece, 'We're just leaving Adana airport now, ma'am. We're in the chopper.'

'Good,' she said in a more relaxed tone. 'You know what needs to be done. This really is a matter of national security from the highest level. I cannot emphasise enough how important this is. The ramifications could be colossal. Save and salvage at all costs, but you know your task.'

The operative pushed the headphones closer over his ear and clicked a button. He looked over at his colleague, who was unzipping a long black sports bag. The two veteran field operatives opened their eyes wider, acknowledging the severity of their project. They nodded to each other.

'Roger that; understood, ma'am,' replied the agent. 'We'll be in touch when we are in position at the forward observation post. Out.'

Buckled in and headsets on, they had already been briefed by their commanding officer and the specially hired pilot had been given coordinates for their point of interest. Their brief was to head for the May Baraji reservoir and dam, about thirty miles south of Kavak in the Botsa Deresi province. There they were to apprehend the kidnappers, retrieve the girl, and publicly hand over the incident to the local police as a tourist robbery. They were to stay in the vicinity until national police and UK officials were involved and then quietly slip away and report back to their commanding officer. Not the toughest assignment and no more than an afternoon's work, they thought. Both men were dressed casually in beige chinos, polo shirts, and the seemingly obligatory standard-issue shades and bomber jackets. Their only outward signs of real discipline and efficiency (although not too obvious) were that one had highly polished brown leather Doc Marten boots and the other, razor-sharp creases down his trousers.

With a twirl of his wrist and fingers, the Doc Marten agent gesticulated onward. A final hand motion, and the old, privately chartered AW109 helicopter lifted a little above the yellow-painted tarmac. The wind whirled around the two men as both slide doors were still wide open. The men were nonchalant and busy, as they had done this many times. The pilot nodded, twisted the throttle and fiddled the pedals. The chopper dumped fuel and thumped louder and louder as it lifted higher. As they rose, both agents pulled their respective doors shut, dulling the turbulence and noise. Agent One unbuckled and leaned forward, reaching above the back of the pilot's head, he tapped the pilot's shoulder to tell him he was unclipping a rolled-up privacy screen. The pilot looked over his shoulder and gave his 'concrete dam engineering specialist' clients a cheery thumbs-up to indicate that he wasn't offended. The silver-coloured blanket slowly unfurled from the bulkhead and ceiling, giving the two agents some privacy.

The agents unplugged the pilot from their communications headsets and settled down to work. Flying at a comfortable cruise speed of one hundred miles per hour, they would be on target within the hour. That gave them time to go over their plan, which they had agreed and signed off with their station commander. If they had to deviate from it, then that was their prerogative, but only if they had to. The agency always insisted on a Plan B and they never objected. However, as veterans, they always objected to the growing levels of form-filling, health and safety, and risk-assessment documents, which even the agency itself seemed powerless to ward off. They also had to follow protocol and 'zero off', or minimise any political fuss. After forty minutes in the air and revisiting Plans A and B, they discussed the 'protocol and political' section of their brief with less enthusiasm. Happy with their project, they pushed aside bogus drawings and plans of the dam, purposely and conspicuously leaving a smaller one, covered in scribbled builders' notes, on the floor of the chopper. With less than ten minutes to go, they opened the sports bag and checked their personal 'risk assessment' kit: boxes of ammunition and rounds, binoculars, hunting knives, a bundle of black plastic zip ties, even a matt black-and-silver thermos flask and ration packs. Almost falling out of the bag were two black Colt M4 carbine automatic rifles complete with scopes and foregrip handles, and one very powerful green Barrett M8 sniper rifle zipped up in its bespoke canvas-and-nylon bag. This came complete with various scopes and all manner of accessories and cleaning equipment, and was capable of excellent accuracy over a distance of a mile. Also in the sports bag were two reddish-brown soft leather pistol cases, each containing a nine-millimetre

Browning High-Power pistol and two fully loaded magazines of thirteen rounds apiece. With just over five minutes before landing, the men calmly removed their chest-strap holsters from the bag and donned them along with lightweight nylon golf jackets. They then unzipped the pistol cases and loaded their sidearms. Zipping up the holdall and happy with their brief, they sat back in their seats like proper civilians and waited patiently with folded arms for the pilot's instructions on landing.

The bird whined and nosed up. It rattled somewhat under its own strain, and then came the familiar thud as its skids bumped on the ground. After the nose levelled off, the pilot eased off the throttle and allowed the weight of the aircraft to land naturally without fuss. Pulling back the blanket divider, he shouted through in broken English, 'Here. We here, safe now, eh?'

Thanking him, the two agents jumped out. The pilot had already been told to return to Adana on drop-off, as his passengers would be some time at the dam, measuring and assessing the site, and it was quite possible that another pilot or firm would be collecting them later on. And so, without any suspicion, he waved his goodbyes and the two men ducked down into the air wash and, as they walked away from the whining beast, put their thumbs up to signal an 'okay'. The rotors spun wildly again to form a solid disc and the chopper lifted off and swung away.

With the chopper gone, the valley fell silent and the reservoir and construction area were deserted.

The agents walked casually and nonchalantly toward the unfinished dam and immediately set to work, assessing vantage points, flat and comfortable viewing areas, high ground, low ground, firm terrain, and concealed areas for surprise approaches. Agent one with the Doc Martens, the senior agent, signalled with his right arm and pointed out a large, flat concrete pad higher up toward the dam. The other nodded to suggest that he'd already spotted it, then pulled out a radio phone and called in their location to confirm their arrival. Agent One walked off down the dirt track several hundred yards away from the dam construction area. The sun was lower now and casting longer shadows. The light would be more important and preparation would be key to their success. He walked on further to assess the only access track and the surrounding area, constantly scanning the hillside above him to his left and right.

The ambush would be a relatively simple and straightforward textbook affair. The agency had a military chopper already on standby to pick them up. The extraction of the girl would be slick and swift. What happened to the three kidnappers would be entirely down to the agents and depend on how well they cooperated. All were certainly expendable and any shootings would be put down to the three unknowns: either a tourist kidnap gone wrong or, worse, a terrorist plot thwarted by the Turkish authorities and not really part of any plan. Either way, the men would be arrested, extradited, jailed or shot. The agents did not care. All that mattered was the girl's extraction; a swift, quiet affair executed by two of the agency's finest. She would be handed over to the Brits, who'd be left with egg on their faces and still wiping their backsides, whilst the agents threw the Turk intelligence agency a bone in the shape of three terrorists and would be back at their command base in their comfy offices in Baghdad with a Jack Daniel's before dusk.

Agent Two finished his call, slung the sports bag over his shoulder and climbed the incline up a smooth concrete footpath to a sizeable section of the concrete slab that led off to the construction area. Here, he decided, looking straight down the valley entrance, would be a good position, and he parked the bag. Using a scope, he looked down the valley, took some measurements and calculated distances. Assessing the terrain and the forecast time of sunset, he decided that conditions were perfect, and then used his main telescope to focus on his colleague. Content, he proceeded to set up his observation post. Rolling out a soft nylon mat, he lay flat and tested out an ammo bag as a pillow under the left side of his head. This was where he would lie, waiting, relaxed and supported, neck and eye muscles resting but ready. Agent One would give him all the required signals and radio clicks once he too was in position. Looking through his powerful scope, ahead and to his left, he spied Agent One scrambling up a short climb of approximately a hundred metres and eventually finding a thin natural ledge to the left of the valley floor.

Agent One could see for miles in one direction and so cleared some stones, then lay down on his belly and looked at where he thought the target would emerge and where the sun would be at the time. Using the dirt track as a datum line, he pointed his weapon and, aiming, sketched out imaginary lines on the valley floor where he would direct his gunfire if required, for best effect. How he laid down the suppressing fire was very important; it would immediately demonstrate superior firepower and give the targets the impression of more than just two shooters, thereby forcing a quicker surrender. Their brief suggested that the hijackers would only have handguns, and with their powerful semi-automatic assault rifles, he could snipe accurately in tandem with Agent Two, from this position, as he was several hundred yards nearer and picking off any of the three targets at any time would be easy. Agent Two's primary task was to place one or two high-powered rounds straight through the grille and into the engine block of the oncoming car, rendering the Merc 'dead in the water'. The hijackers would not realise their predicament initially, so once the vehicle rolled to a halt, he would direct a short burst of fire around the car, allowing the kidnappers a second or so to form an idea of their situation. His job then was to keep them in the car. The girl was the priority. He rehearsed his role and scenarios a couple of times to train his brain. After pushing some bigger rocks into place to obstruct any onlookers' vision, he was happy with his forward observation post. A quiet whistle to his colleague, and soon they were walking the road together, westward, away from the unfinished dam and toward where the sun was soon to set.

Marching out the distance, Agent Two checked his calculations, then Agent One checked the numbers and concurred. The two men debated a while and then, once happy with their distances and therefore their measurements and timings, walked back to the concrete slab to split their kit. Agent One made a final situation report to command via a radio phone, confirming their extraction point and that the required chopper and staff, including a female officer trained to deal with hostage situations and a medic experienced in field traumas, were on standby only several minutes away. Happy with their plan, backup and logistics, he switched off the radio, checked through a first-aid trauma bag and made it more accessible. Agent Two took some more rifle accessories out of the bag, including a bipod. Two Motorola walkie-talkies were switched on and set to Channel 6. From now on there would be no talking at all; no names, references, accents or even dialects. Once powered on they would be using a series of clicks via these radios until the job was complete. Sharing out the ammo, zip ties, black cotton hoods, field first-aid kits, flasks and military hardware, the two agents were now organised and right on script. The men nodded to each other as if in agreement and double-clicked their walkie-talkies to check communications. They then took up their respective positions and began the wait.

# 28

## MAY BARAJI RESERVOIR, TURKEY, 320 MILES FROM THE SYRIAN BORDER

Ed's driving had closed the gap between the Jeep and the kidnappers' Mercedes but he was still frustrated about not getting closer to the car. He swung the Jeep to the left, bringing it to a stop as they looked down the valley once again.

'Should be a dam further ahead,' said Tess as she climbed out, dragging the telephoto-lens camera with her. Crouching and lifting her leg onto a mound to steady herself, she flicked on the power button and a panoramic view of the valley and a dam appeared on the back screen. She scanned the vista, looking for the track. Sure enough, below was a black car meandering its way toward the dam. 'Got them,' she said. 'There, look. I think we've gained a fair bit on them. Have a look for yourself. Must be a mile or so from the dam.'

She passed the huge camera to Ed. He peered through the viewfinder and focused his eye. He saw the car and, twisting the long lens, zoomed in on it some more.

Tess was rummaging in her reporter's bag. 'Here, let me change the lens. This one is even better; didn't get a chance before in all the panic,' she said.

After changing to a superior lens, Ed could see the car and its surroundings much more magnified. The dark Mercedes still carried the three men, and ahead of them was the unfinished dam. Ed was amazed that he could zoom in still further, and began scanning the dam area for a much-needed plan. He couldn't find one; heading them off was all he could come up with. After that he would just bluff it. After the dam came civilisation, which meant better roads, and that meant traffic and possibly losing them. He had to do something now and head them off before they left the empty mountains. He scanned the dam again and again, looking for inspiration.

'Well?' Tess asked. 'What are you thinking?'

Ed stopped dead in his tracks and fell silent for a while. Then he dropped to the ground and replied, with a quiver in his voice, 'Oh no. For God's sake, get down.'

Tess closed in behind him, almost cowering. His urgent call had scared her. 'What is it?' she asked with a tremble.

'Look there. Over to our left, high up on the dam.'

On a bright white slab of concrete lay a small, square patch of khaki-beige and black. She stopped and focused, pushed harder on the zoom and spied some more. Initially, she was shocked by her findings; then dread came over her and she could only mutter, 'Oh my God. What the hell's going on?' Staring hard, she realised there was a guy lying flat on the ground in a sniper position.

'I told you this was bigger than we thought. This is getting very dangerous now,' whispered Ed.

'What can we do? Are they waiting for the car?' asked Tess.

'I reckon,' replied Ed.

'What can we do?' repeated Tess.

'We sort this mess right now,' said Ed. 'I'm sick of all this. Come on, get in.' And he pulled her back toward the Jeep.

Not far back they had passed a service road, a tiny track that now, after seeing the lie of the land, Ed was sure led down to the dam. Taking a calculated guess, he reversed the car. Trying not to make a dust cloud or noise, he turned the vehicle around, slammed the Jeep into low-gear, full-time four-wheel drive again and set off down the track, back to the service road. His priority was to head the Mercedes off at the dam and expose the sniper.

'There'll be others?' asked Tess as she bounced around in her seat, clutching at her grab handle.

'Hang on,' said Ed. 'Yep, there'll be more. This is gonna get shitty, Tess.'

He pushed the SUV bonnet down a steeper incline. The vehicle thumped and banged its way down. The tyres tried in vain to maintain traction but they just snowploughed into the sand and rocks. When the descent slowed, Ed pushed the accelerator pedal again, forcing the wheels forward to the next, even steeper incline. The Jeep tilted violently but kept its approach angle and dipped its front deeper. Ed pushed it harder and onward at some speed. Clinging on, Tess felt sick. The Jeep crashed down on its suspension and springs. Axles twisted and tyres bellied out under the strain. Now they were almost flying, as all four wheels left the terrain at the next lip and they hurtled down a natural ravine in the valley which led to a huge storm gully channel. Ed hoped they hadn't been seen. They were using a super-powerful telescopic lens to spot the sniper miles away, from far higher up, so the chances were that they hadn't been. They were also positioned on the west side next mountain so the sound of their approach shouldn't be a problem either. He just wanted to get nearer now without being heard or seen. The element of surprise was absolutely key.

Sure enough, the Jeep bulldozed down the mountain toward the dam. As the four-by-four system scrabbled and pulled them across a wide section of boulders and rock, the dam came into sight and Ed stopped the SUV, jumped out, and groped around in the trunk for the wheel brace.

'What should I do?' asked Tess.

Ed grunted. 'What you are trained to do: report from a safe distance.' Pausing, he looked at her with more benevolence. 'Stay here, Tess, this isn't your fight. Get on my phone and message Esther. Tell her I'm coming for her and to stay curled up tight behind those back seats. Then, last number redial and tell my boss what's happening and where we are.' Then he was gone, scrabbling down the steep shale slope using the wheel brace as a rudder.

~

Sweat ran down Agent Two's temple. His eyes were still focused down the rifle's telescope. He lay flat, still and unflinching on the nylon mat with his legs spread wide and the toes of his polished shoes digging into the gravel. The valley was almost silent; only a gentle breeze could be heard as the warm afternoon air was pushed up between the mountains. A distant bird called to its mate, and the sun beat down hard. His head was leaning slightly to the left against the rucksack, his eyes blinking only on command after years of discipline, and his sunglasses sat on his forehead. His hearing, however, was slightly impaired by the strain of prioritising looking through his scope.

The last bead of sweat should have rolled down his face, but something had intervened. A cold, thick object that he believed to be the barrel of a gun jabbed into his right temple. Instinctively he froze, his brain ordering him to remain static and assess. He felt a body close in on him from behind, and warm air across his face. His hearing burst into life as his brain switched senses in order to survive. A warmer breath of air brushed over his exposed ear as the barrel pressed harder into his temple. Knowing he was compromised, Agent Two slowly stretched out his left hand for his radio. It was not there.

'Click-click, arsehole,' a voice whispered.

Agent Two heard the radio's 'talk now' button being pressed twice, creating two clicks.

Then he heard the stranger's voice again. 'Knock-knock.'

Suddenly, the full weight of the Jeep's wheel brace made contact with his skull, causing his brain to shake violently inside its shell, sending his head vibrating to the left. His right eye just caught a glimpse of a fair-haired guy before he blacked out.

~

The walkie-talkie clicked twice, once, then twice again. Ed lay still and silent on the ground. He did not know what code they were using. He retrieved his boots from several metres away and put them back on. Then he lay low, avoiding detection by Agent One from across the valley. It had taken him ages to sneak up on Agent Two but his patience and his boots-off strategy had paid off. As he'd suspected, the radio confirmed that the sniper had backup and he was about to enter a world of pain. Spreading out on top of the concussed sniper to conceal him, he looked down the unconscious man's rifle. The navy-blue sedan was closing in on them, heading into the ambush on the valley floor. After his violent spurt of energy, Ed disciplined himself to now relax and calm his breathing.

He took deep breaths and crammed the air into his lungs to get his heart rate down. He was no sniper, but with years of experience he could put a target into a set of crosshairs. Besides, the sniper had it all set up, ready to go. He would certainly try.

Composing himself, he stared down the scope with his right eye. Adjusting his focus, he watched the dust cloud as he saw the Merc coming toward him. He tried to decide what to do. His best option was to stop the car. Deciding where to shoot, his right index finger felt the cold steel of the trigger. He started to squeeze, tightening and hooking his finger into the curved metal. His knuckles turned white and his knuckle skin tightened. He told himself not to blink. Exhaling one last time, he prepared for the shot and the recoil. His heart thumped within his ribcage and he felt himself moving to its every beat. His throat dried and he tried to swallow. He felt the sweat appearing on his brow and, waiting for that microsecond between heart beats, make his final decision, and went for the shot.

*Bang!* The valley echoed and birds scattered. Ed stared at his target. He had missed. From out of the following silence there came a loud crack and, still using the weapons telescope, Ed watched as the car driver's head was flung to his right, exploding over the front-seat passenger. The driver slumped at the wheel, and the car swerved violently off its path. *Shit, more snipers*, thought Ed, scanning the terrain with wide eyes. He knew there would be others but had not expected more snipers. This was very serious shit, and he was neck deep in it. He'd never expected that.

Almost immediately, another shot rang out toward the car from the left of the valley. Then from the radio came three clicks, then one click, then three more. There was no reply.

Agent One's voice fired into life from the set. 'Break cover! Break cover! What the hell's going on?'

Ed was confused. The voice was American. *Was it the CIA again*, he thought? But why was the guy complaining? It was an excellent sniper shot and had halted the Mercedes. Surely that was their plan?

Another loud crack came and a dull noise as a second shot rang out through the valley. This one seemed to miss and bury itself in the boulders. Then more radio cries of 'Back off. Back off.'

Flat on his belly, and panicking now, Ed rummaged through the sniper's black nylon bag. It was as he'd thought. These guys were professionals, but he hadn't worked out who they were yet. From the bag he grabbed a rifle and a pistol, along with several magazines. Rolling on his back for deeper cover, he tried to get a look at the crashed car. The two surviving men had climbed out and were firing their handguns up the valley walls toward the second sniper.

Agent One had already squeezed his trigger and followed through on his own brief of pinning down the kidnappers close to the car. A hail of bullets rained down on the hijackers as they cowered close to their car, trying to figure out what was happening. The radio sounded again. 'Break cover!' Agent One shouted. 'Compromised, I repeat, Myrtle Tree compromised. Activate support. Need extraction immediately.' He unleashed another wave of terror on the desert floor, pinning the two guys down as they cowered under his superior firepower.

*Boom!* Another shot sounded from up the slope. Ed struggled to locate it precisely, but Agent One had spotted it. Lifting his semi-automatic, he blasted a number of rounds into the cliff wall. Even more confused, Ed followed the bullets and zoomed in with the scope. He could just see what he thought was a wheel of a motorcycle lying on its side, but the rest was heavily camouflaged. Another rattle of rounds burst up the hillside toward the sniper's hideout from Agent One. Then, through the powerful scope, Ed spotted it. Dug in and well hidden in a mountainside hole, secreted behind draped sackcloth, a second sniper and a motorbike. Ed composed himself and tried to think. This sniper was intent on shooting at the car. Was he trying to shoot Esther or the kidnappers, or both? He wasn't part of the planned ambush. He must be a third party, but who?

A hail of rounds flailed up the hill, throwing rocks and dirt everywhere. Ed joined in, firing round after round up at the sniper. Splinters and shards of stone flew as bullets ricocheted around. Ed's finger pulled and squeezed. Dust and rocks pelted him, and he realised that the last burst of fire was aimed at him. Looking down, he could see Agent One firing up at him. The noise was deafening, and stones peppered Ed's face and hands as he returned fire. With his left arm, he grabbed Agent Two's collar and hauled the concussed body over himself for protection. 'Every man for himself,' he muttered.

His right hand squeezed the grip of the rifle. His index finger held down the trigger for two tap cycles, and the acrid bite of ammunition propellant hovered around his face as he pushed his cheek flat up to the rear sight drum. The smell lingered as the ejection port spat out empty shell after empty shell. The three-way firefight was in full swing, leaving the two hijackers down by the Mercedes bewildered and silent. Ed jumped up and, grabbing a pistol from Agent Two's belt, raced across the concrete slab and into the construction area for a closer shot at Agent One. Chips of concrete flew and puffs of dust danced around his feet as the sniper and the agent tried to take him down. Running hard, he leapt across the building site and took cover behind a huge mixer. Climbing into it for extra protection, he threw out several random suppression shots, allowing him time to assess his situation.

'What the hell is happening?!' he shouted. This was surreal. 'It was just a fucking holiday!'

It had to be terrorists, he concluded, and that meant it was now a no-holds-barred, all-out war. His head was spinning. All he could think about was Esther in the boot, trussed up and scared. He would kill every one of these bastards and wouldn't stop until he had.

# 29

## MAY BARAJI RESERVOIR, TURKEY, 320 MILES FROM THE SYRIAN BORDER

The sniper fire had stopped. Ed heard the distinct sound of a motorcycle engine starting, then revving hard. The sniper was on the move. Ed rolled out of the mixer and thumped onto the ground. Bullets spat at the metal drum and rang out loud as they ricocheted around him. Rolling over, he caught a glimpse of Agent One leaving his position.

Then out of nowhere came the rolling thunder of a CIA-adapted Mi-17 heavy-duty Russian helicopter, thumping the air and scooping up loose gravel and dust. Agent One scrambled away, perhaps to get to the chopper, and in doing so lowered his guard. Rolling onto his back, Ed exhaled and blinked twice. Then he brought up the semi-automatic and gave two taps of the trigger. He missed the agent, and the bullets thudded into the rocks behind him. More composed now, Ed exhaled again and let off two more taps, watching as the agent was flung left by the impact. Falling to the ground, Agent One let out a guttural scream, involuntarily lifting his right arm to grab at the pain.

Ed was happy that he had scored a major shoulder wound. Adjusting his focus down the ravine, he saw that the hijackers had taken advantage of the confusion. Throwing back a couple more shots, they dragged the dead driver from the car, climbed back in and started the engine. Ed repositioned himself, bending low on one knee to get in a first shot. Lining up his sights, he fired off two taps, but the car only swerved and veered. Jumping down off scaffolding and ladders, he tried to get nearer as they drove toward him through the construction site. He fired more shots. The replacement driver spun the steering wheel left and right, throwing the rear end of the car to drift, cornering the track and sliding in the gravel in a bid to escape down the access road. Ed ran down huge concrete steps, along more scaffolding, past idle machinery and tools. Leaping over a tarped pile of sand, he could now see the damage to the Merc's front bumper from its collision in the hotel car park. Jumping down another level, he aimed and fired at the front tyres, but it was going too fast.

From overhead and seemingly out of nowhere came the roar of the chopper again as it whooshed past him with its nose down. Ed flailed his arms and legs to control his fall. Before landing, and in desperation, he let go a full burst of fire at the chopper, then bit his lip as he hit the hard, dry gravel. Instinctively, he ducked down and scrambled back under the scaffold as the helicopter thumped its way across the building works in pursuit of the car.

Deflated by his failure, Ed climbed out from his cover and spat blood. Then he heard the distinct roar of the Jeep's huge V6 engine. Tess had watched the firefight unfold from the safety of the mountainside, and had followed down the track to the building site. Steering the SUV into a broadside halt, she screamed, 'Get in!'

Ed threw himself into the Jeep, Tess thumped the pedal, and they sped off. The Mercedes bounced down the track, clanking and crashing in protest at its imminent demise. Its suspension, steering and chassis slammed, groaned and banged with every steering and throttle adjustment. The driver gritted his teeth as he attempted to drive like an ace rally driver. Overhead, the helicopter circled for another pass, still tilting forward, but now also rocking from port to starboard as it banked left and right in close pursuit.

Over the horizon, from between two hills came the sniper on a khaki-green motocross scramble bike. His face was obscured by a black helmet and a dark scarf. As he entered the fray, he pulled himself up to sit forward and clenched the seat and fuel tank with his thighs and knees. With his left hand he groped at the small of his back and pulled around his weapon on its shoulder strap. Picking his moment in between steering and aiming, crossing his left arm over himself and resting it on top of his right forearm, he opened the throttle some more and, with a steady left hand, let out a frightening burst of automatic fire from his Uzi nine-millimetre machine gun.

Ed flinched away for a moment. Then, reloading with a fresh magazine, he leaned back out of the Jeep's window with his stolen assault rifle. 'Get me closer,' he growled.

Tess raced as fast as she dared, closing the gap between them and the escaping car. Ed's back thumped against the door frame as he tried to aim at the motorcyclist. Shots rained down from the helicopter at the Jeep and the bike as the entourage bounced down the valley, all shooting at each other. Ed knew he was no match for the helicopter and its well-armed crew, so began jabbing at the motorcyclist with a volley of two-round bursts. The downwash from the chopper created a massive sand ball and played havoc with his visibility so Ed had to estimate his shots, firing them in an arc ahead of the bike. As the valley floor widened and opened out toward civilisation, the outflanked and outgunned motorcyclist veered off and away, choosing a different track. The automatic rifle fire now focused on Ed and Tess as the SUV took bullets in its roof. As its windows shattered one by one, throwing glass in their wake, Ed managed to ward off the attack with several shots to the giant bird's belly. The chopper pilot shouted a request into his headpiece to abort the chase.

On the ground, Agent One crawled over the rocks and groped for his radio. He pushed the translucent plastic audio tube back closer into his ear and pressed the talk button. 'That's a negative, that's a negative. Get the car, get the car at all costs,' he shouted to the pilot. 'Follow the car.'

But it was soon too late. The dirt track became asphalt and the Mercedes sped past civilians on pedal bikes and women with carts. Farmers crossed the road, and several hundred yards ahead was a T-junction with more traffic. Here, the dirt tracks led out onto a metalled road. To the left, the new road headed north-east to the town of Alibeyhüyüğü. To the right it led south, first to a quarry, then onto a major artery road leading to the city of Karmaran. The pilot had twice questioned Agent One's last instruction and was now ordered by an agent inside the chopper to peel off and pull away, leaving Ed and Tess to continue their chase into the early evening traffic.

The Mercedes hit the ramp where the dirt track met the road, and the driver swerved many times to correct himself before accelerating off and joining the traffic. Ed slipped back through the window of the battered Jeep and Tess veered as she guided the vehicle up onto the metalled road. The bonnet was steaming and there was glass everywhere.

'You okay?' Ed shouted over the noise of the wind and the departing helicopter.

'Oh yeah,' replied Tess sarcastically, totally aghast at the events of the past few minutes. 'Just fine.'

Ed looked at her. She was shaking and very pale. Her knuckles were white from gripping the steering wheel. She was frightened, but at the same time swept up in the euphoria and heat of the chase. As the engine coughed and hissed steam, he asked, 'Really?'

'Jesus!' shouted Tess. 'No! I'm not okay. Look at me.' She held out her hand to show Ed how much she was shaking.

'Calm down,' he replied reassuringly. 'Deep breaths. Get some oxygen inside you. You did great. Honestly, you were amazing. I can't believe what just happened either.'

'Did you see what we've just done?' she screamed. 'Have you seen the whole world of shit we're in now?'

Ed could see she was hyperventilating a little and let her continue to scream and rant as she drove. Looking behind their seats amongst the broken glass and scattered pieces of seating foam, he reached over, grabbed a scrunched-up fast-food bag off the floor and offered it to her. 'Here, take some deep breaths.'

She snatched it from his hand and threw it to the floor, realising that she was indeed stressing out massively.

Ed watched as her chest rose and fell. He really did like Tess. She was a great girl. Realising she was going into shock, he focused her mind. 'Deep breaths. Keep driving,' he said. 'You're bloody good at it and doing a superb job. I can't believe you got us through all that. Well done. Don't let's lose them after all that.'

Tess's terror turned to anger. 'Don't you patronise me,' she spat over the noise of the cars hissing. 'I didn't realise we would be killing people. I don't want to be involved in murders and shootings.' She bent down to retrieve the paper bag and began to breathe into it rapidly.

'Stay on it,' Ed repeated. He was sweating and his shirt was soaking. His face was full of cuts from glass and gravel. Dirt and sand clung to his lips. 'Can you get us closer?' As he asked, he checked his weapons and reloaded.

Taking control of herself, Tess wiped her mouth and concentrated hard on overtaking and speeding up southbound along the highway. Ed kept watching the car ahead as it weaved dangerously in and out of the evening rush-hour traffic. Horns blared and headlights flashed as the damaged Mercedes swerved to and fro, struggling to increase its speed. Smoke started to pour from under the hood and grille, causing it to veer even more amid the decreased visibility. Then without warning the driver threw it left off the tarmac, back onto farm tracks and across a plateau of lush green fields.

Several hundred yards behind, Tess shouted, 'Hold on! Here we go again.' She timed her speed and jumped into a gap between a lorry stacked high with hay and a local school bus. She pushed the accelerator down and the Jeep threw a heavy left across the cooling tarmac, its tyres scrabbling for traction as she pulled the steering wheel left and then corrected to the right. Feeling the tyres bite, she again leaned on the throttle. The Jeep responded and threw its nose into the dirt lane. Within seconds they were back on gravel tracks and chasing across the fields, but the saloon was gone, way ahead in a plume of sand, dust and thick mechanical smoke. Ed was squinting to follow the car through the hissing steam escaping from the SUV's hood. Then they came to a sudden halt as Tess slammed on the brakes and switched off the engine. They both jumped out and Ed flipped the bonnet to assess the damage, cursing the broken-down vehicle and wondering why the escaping Merc was still running as he had scored several direct hits on it during the firefight. Tess handed him a cloth from the boot, and Ed set about repairing the damage as best he could to get the engine running again.

# 30

## AYDOGMUS VILLAGE, TURKEY, 305 MILES FROM THE SYRIAN BORDER

Esther was tired and bruised. She ached all over and felt filthy, like she had been sitting in a manure heap. The smaller guy had pulled her from the trunk and she had stood for a few minutes at the corner of an alley, blinking madly, rubbing her eyes and coughing whilst the other, taller man spoke to a mechanic. The smaller guy had given her a bottle of water and she had pushed and pulled as he held her upper arm tight. After they had dragged her on a short walk to a hotel, she had been allowed to wash and was given some old, baggy jeans, a new T-shirt still in its cellophane wrapper, a new toothbrush and a bottle of mouthwash. During the walk to the hotel and since entering the room, she had twice been threatened with a pistol. She had also been told politely to behave and that, if she cooperated, she would not be hurt. After a hot drink of tea and some food, she was allowed to sit on a sofa to rest, then later she was told to go and sit back at a table. As she moved back to the table the taller man pushed her down, forcing her onto a chair.

Once seated, the other man unzipped a soft nylon attaché case, brought out a silver laptop and passed it to the taller man, who placed it on the tabletop. He stared at Esther, then grabbed her shoulders and turned her toward the laptop. Pulling a pistol from his chest holster, he banged it down loudly on the bare wood and gestured to the now open screen. Then, like a surgeon who had just been handed a surgical instrument, he held up a pen drive in front of her eyes, pushed it into a side port and clicked on a number of icons.

After a few seconds of loading, she was forced to watch CCTV footage of an explosion in a nuclear enrichment plant. She knew immediately who, what, where and when, but she did not know why or how. She watched as the tall uranium centrifugal separator tubes wobbled and writhed out of control and their electrical motors ignited and exploded, causing mass carnage within the processing hall. As she was about to ask one of the men a question, the screen flickered and jumped to another grainy CCTV clip. It was of the image of a man lying on a stone floor, apparently covered in sweat and blood. She had not seen this man in the flesh for several years; she had spoken to him only a couple of weeks ago via Skype, but she had not heard from him since. It was her cousin Mord. Esther stared at the monitor and then, in absolute shock, lifted her hand to her mouth and began to cry. He looked awful and in great pain. The filming was of low quality and the sound was poor but she could hear her cousin shouting about a laptop and that it was nothing to do with him. She listened in horror as he almost chanted the words 'Myrtus had a sash: 09 05 97. We are all Esther's children. By the Staff of Moses under the Tree of Life I will die!'

Esther screamed and cried more. The tall man stood over her shoulder, leaned down to her ear and asked quietly what Mord meant by 'We are all Esther's children', and what the words 'Myrtus had a sash' and the numbers meant. He said that she could save her cousin and thousands more Jewish Iranians if she could just neutralise or reverse the virus plaguing her cousin's laptop and spreading to the enrichment plant at Natanz. As he spoke, the laptop's home screen returned, showing an old photo of Esther and Mord when they were younger. Realising that the device could indeed be Mord's, she lifted her arms away from it in shock.

Sobbing, she looked up at the man and asked, 'Why me? What does all this have to do with me?'

The Iranian secret police agent pulled over a chair and, straddling it to lean on the backrest, sat down. He stared at her again before saying, 'We not so stupid, you know? Persia was once centre of all civilisation, and we, a greatest country, feared by your West. Once we have the enrichment process mastered, we will be an equal with your country and your beloved America. We will be most powerful nation in the Middle East. You Westerners will rightfully show us respect and courtesy once more. You think you can sabotage our efforts to process the uranium? Never! And you, my dear? We have had you under surveillance for months. We too have expert IT engineers and, whilst trying to unhook the virus, they kept finding you and your details on the hard drive and search history of this very laptop. You can thank all your Western capitalist technology methods for handing you over to us so easily. Some call it spying, but I think we just call it Skype,' he finished sarcastically.

Esther looked at him, amazed and shocked as she finally understood why she had been kidnapped. She decided to feign ignorance. 'But why me?'

'Come, come now, my dear,' he said patronisingly, having expected this. He spoke quietly at first. 'My dear girl. Please forgive me, but you know well why it is you. You, a well-respected nuclear engineer, excelling in computer science engineering and specialising in mathematical algorithms and viral infections. Whose name is Esther and who has a brother – or is it cousin? – named Mord. You are a Jew, are you not?'

Esther nodded slowly, unsure whether to answer.

'Did you sleep with your brother, as it is written? Did you fuck your cousin? Was he a good fuck? He tells me you were amazing and everything he wished for.' The man leaned in and reached out his hand to stroke her cheek.

Esther jerked back her head and screamed, 'How dare you, you disgusting pig? Go to hell!'

He grabbed at her shirt and pulled, but only to frighten her. He continued, with more passion and hatred, spitting as he spoke. 'Then, as it is written in the Scriptures, you, my little shining star, are a miracle sent to save the Jews.'

Esther rolled her head back away from him and cried, 'What are you talking about? You are crazy. I don't know anything.'

The captain smiled at her and lowered his voice. She leaned back in her chair as his eyes bulged and his face came close to hers. She could smell his nicotine-tainted breath and his body odour.

'If this virus proves to be of Israeli origin...' He paused a moment to let that thought sink in. 'Have you any idea how many Jews will suffer in Iran because of this treachery and your unwillingness to cooperate? Could you live with that on your conscience? You *will* undo this treachery and save our great nation from this Western espionage.'

His breath lingered in her nostrils as she tried to remember her last conversation with her poor cousin.

'And with this machine,' he pushed the laptop closer to her, 'and the information we have so far on this pen drive, we will not only reverse this sabotage, but we will expose the instigators of this attack and show the world what lying traitors they really are.'

~

The lush green valley floor was extremely flat and open. As the sun began to set, Ed and Tess could see ahead for miles. They had lost some hours as Ed tried desperately to repair the Jeep. With some paid help from a local motorist, who gave them raw eggs to block up the holes, some plasters, electrician's tape and some dirty water, he had repaired, albeit temporarily, the SUV's shot-up cooling system. The huge engine had fortunately been spared the rain of bullets, although the car's bonnet, windshield, roof and interior suggested otherwise. As they continued their drive, Ed told Tess to ease off and drop back a little; he needed time to think. What the hell had happened that afternoon, and what was going on? What was it all about? He slammed his knee with his fist. Checking his phone, he found he had missed three calls and a BBM message from his boss during the gunfight and chase. He clicked on the balloon icon and read the text.

*Ed, I've been told to hand over to Whitehall. The Foreign Office are on the job now and will contact you soon. Whitehall have all the numbers and our intel, so we'll find her. Go get the bastards and get Esther, son.*

Ed slammed buttons with his thumb and dialled his voicemail. Two messages from his boss reiterating the content of the BBM message, and one from a guy called Tom. He replayed the latter on speaker for Tess to hear.

'Ed? My name is Tom Creighton. I've been assigned by the

Foreign Office to give you some support at this difficult time. I'm not too far away and will pop over soon to see if I can help. Message ends.'

Tess looked at Ed. 'Oh? That's good, isn't it?' she asked, wondering if she had said the right thing.

'No, it's not good!' replied Ed sternly.

She seemed confused, and her eyes searched for his as she guided the vehicle along the field tracks.

'That's my boss's way of telling me that he has to stand down, reminding me that phones are being monitored, and alerting me that MI6 will be in touch. That means Whitehall, MI6 and GCHQ are all involved, and this right royal plum Tom Creighton is actually an MI6 field agent, who I suspect will be paying us a visit very shortly, given what's just happened.'

They went over and over everything they knew and had seen, trying to fathom why Esther had been kidnapped by some very professional people. Then they discussed what their next move would be once they got to her. The plan wasn't much more than a simple armed hold-up, thought Ed, but it was all he had. With his eyes fixed like a tank commander's on the town ahead, he instructed Tess to speed up, then slow down, then go left, then back off. Darkness soon descended, and as they entered the isolated farming town, the traffic began to build a little. Cars, mopeds and bikes weaved in and about; even a dark-coloured motocross bike shot past in a rush. Ed thought he recognised it but it became difficult to follow all the red tail lights, and he panicked again at the thought of losing Esther for good.

'Hurry up, speed up, forward, quickly,' he shouted to Tess as she negotiated the small-town rush-hour traffic.

On entering the town centre, they both knew they had lost the trail.

'Shit! That's it, then,' said Ed, thumping the dashboard.

'Our shot-up car is also getting a lot of attention,' said Tess quietly, feeling as down as Ed.

Ed agreed with her as another local motorist stared out through his passenger window at them. 'Need a fresh car,' he muttered.

'Yeah,' she replied, 'but we don't want the local gendarmerie sniffing around us.'

Ed agreed but was busy scanning up and down every street for a sign of the Mercedes. Tess commented that the town looked dilapidated. Offices and shops were closed and most of the buildings' lights were out. The buildings were faded and whitewashed, and earthen clay walls peeled from lack of maintenance. They noticed a lack of pedestrians. The main street was dimly lit with ancient lamps that flickered as if choking or gagging for some electricity. The town was run-down and seemed empty, its main road running typically straight and long right through the centre, and was just big enough to get lost once, which they did. After that, they circled around another couple of times, searching hard. Only one supermarket, a phone shop, a few farm shops, and some empty market stalls on the pavements. They noticed only a few parked vehicles dotted about. The offices and buildings showed no sign of occupation as the town had emptied for the night.

'They could have stolen another car or repaired the one they have,' said Tess.

'Yeah,' agreed Ed. 'Could've, but my guess is they won't want their car found, nor will they chance a theft in a small town where it might raise the local police's suspicions. They won't fly her out of the country as there's no chance of getting through airport security. Esther would make a scene. Nor could they drug her. She wouldn't be allowed on the plane.'

'What about a helicopter?' Tess asked.

'Hmm,' said Ed. 'Possibly, but only if they're government. Civilian choppers need the same clearance as planes, especially to cross borders, and they leave trails unless they're using the diplomatic services. Nah.' He paused. 'Car is the best option, and border staff out here can be bribed easily, as you know.'

Tess slowed the vehicle and looked at him. 'They're obviously professionals. Surely they must have backup, or some support?'

'Yeah,' he agreed.

Quietly, Tess swung the battered Jeep down yet another dark side road, both of them scanning the street and the back alleys.

'Stop!' said Ed. 'Back up. No, no. Keep going! Keep moving. Slowly. There, in that garage, back there. Just under some roller shutter doors, up on ramps.'

Tess faltered a little on the throttle, then pressed harder, moving the purring black SUV along the street. 'Where? Where?' she asked excitedly.

'Just back there,' repeated Ed. 'Pull over there and switch off.' He pointed to an unlit part of the street. 'Take your foot off the brake to extinguish the tail lights, and switch the ignition back on, ready to go,' he demanded.

Tess drove on a little then, following Ed's instructions carefully, parked up, switched off and turned out all the lights.

'Stay here,' instructed Ed. 'Let me just do a recce on the joint first. I could be wrong.'

Slipping out of the car, he walked along the street, then, after crossing the road, turned into a dim alley. Quietly and slowly, he walked along the cobbled lane back to the street they had driven down minutes earlier. Ahead of him was the garage with its shutter door still only half closed. Ed stopped and scanned around him, then he moved as far as he could into the workshop yard. Not a sound from his immediate vicinity. He could hear dog barks further up the street, and a car drove past somewhere near where they had parked. He crouched down and moved in for a better look. Sneaking along the side of the yard, using the light from the workshop, he got close enough to establish that it was indeed the kidnappers' car, complete with bullet holes, collision scuffs and damage to its front fender. Then he heard the distinct metallic rattle of a toolbox and a car door slam. Backing away, he retraced his steps to the car, his brain in overdrive. Was Esther in the boot still? He could snatch her right now. But without any assistance? What if she wasn't there? Where would she be? The mechanic would have been paid well to keep quiet.

~

The man had spoken perfect Turkish and had paid the mechanic handsomely. His 'brother' and 'sister' stood and waited at the end of the alley. Their dilemma was half convincing. Their journey was long, from Ankara via Konya, where they had collected their sister, who lectured at one of its universities, on their way to Adana before their father passed away. Terrible student riots and shootings had caused the vehicle damage. Student riots were unheard of in Konya, but with its three universities and half a million residents, it was a possibility, and of course with lots of fifty-euro notes pushed into his hand, the mechanic didn't ask any more questions. It was his best job in years and would not be turned away. The man had asked politely for an approximate timescale on the job, and for the location of the nearest hotel so they could get some food and freshen up. The young mechanic had obliged, pointing them back to the main street. There was a traditional tea room next to a shut-down filling station and a twelve-roomed motel which they should have passed on their way in. The man had thanked him and said they would telephone later to check on the state of their father's car.

~

Ed snuck back into the Jeep and confirmed to Tess that it was the kidnappers' car and that he had a plan of a sort. He figured the men must be hanging around waiting somewhere and, much to his relief, they wouldn't have risked leaving Esther in the boot. His sweetheart would be out in the fresh air, given water and maybe allowed to freshen up. The bastards were still going to get it, though. He would soon exact revenge on the two remaining perpetrators. With her dark hair, skin and eyes, Tess could pass as a Turk or at least a Middle Easterner, especially if she wore a headscarf. She could speak Turkish too. Ed explained his plan. She was to act as an accomplice of the kidnappers and casually explain to the mechanic that they had called her to come and collect them as their car had broken down, and did the mechanic know where they were?

The plan worked. The greedy mechanic, after taking more euros off Tess, said he thought they had gone to the motel. She and Ed left the Jeep where it was, a couple of blocks from the filling station; just a five-minute sprint if needed. He told her to leave it in the side alley out of sight, unlocked, with the keys in the side pocket of the driver's door. He threw the rifle and all the magazines into the trunk and, pushing the Browning Hi-Power nine-millimetre semi-automatic pistol into Tess's hands, told her not to look at it. Instead, she was to close her eyes and 'feel' the weapon, to familiarise her brain and fingers with the safety catch, hammer, magazine release button, and trigger. As she gripped the gun tight with both hands, he pushed it down, pointing it at the floor, and told her to keep it down at all times. He showed her how to rest her trigger finger on the slide-stop flank, away from the trigger guard until she felt she actually needed to use it.

As they slowly moved out of the alley, they saw an old woman locking up the tea room for the night. Ed told Tess to stay put. He had identified a safe area for her and told her to remain there as a lookout only. Any sign of trouble and she was to go back to the car. Sternly, he told her to avoid contact with the guys at all costs, and that she would be more use to him calling the local police if he got into the shit. 'If it all goes belly up,' he warned her, 'you're to drive away and call the cops. No heroics.'

# 31

## AYDOGMUS MOTEL, TURKEY

Ahead of them, just two blocks away, set back from the main road behind the disused and boarded-up filling station, was the motel. It was an early '80s single-storey building with apartments lined up, with the one at the end of the block being the reception and office. The rest were rooms for rent. There were a few cars parked out front. Only one clean one looked as if it did not belong. A hire car, Ed assumed. The rest looked as if they had been parked there a while. The motel's brickwork was the same as the filling station's and they shared the same car park and forecourt areas, but with separate exits. All of the apartments were connected by a long corridor leading from a pair of entrance doors in front of reception, and at the far end two pairs of doors led out to the car park and a fire exit. Peering in, Ed could just make out each apartment comprised a lounge diner to the front with a square window overlooking the corridor and car park, and a double bedroom to the rear, with a bathroom containing an over-bath shower sandwiched in the middle. Each bedroom had a square window and French doors leading out onto patios. Some of the patios had derelict fencing, while others had none. Once upon a time they would have led out onto pretty gardens that overlooked a lush green paddock or field, but now an arid wasteland led to some smallholdings, with pig and goat pens and chicken coops. Ed reckoned that back in the day the site had been built by some small-time property developer who'd run out of money. Ed counted twelve chalets but only two showed signs of life; one was giving off a dim yellow glow and the other a brighter, more modern blue-whitish light.

Under the cover of darkness, he stalked around the hotel perimeter, avoiding the few flickering street lights. Sneaking around the back of the block of chalets, he slowly and patiently, one by one, got as close as he dared to each bedroom window and listened carefully. When he heard nothing, he then looked as hard as he could into the apartment. The wide-open backyards offered him no protection but also meant that no one could sneak up and surprise him. He made it to the ninth apartment, sure that the previous three were definitely empty. Then he went back to number three. Checking around to make sure he was not being watched, he peered through the window which gave off the dim yellow light. Through a tattered net curtain, he could make out a tall, pot-bellied man with a piece of pizza in his mouth and a bottle of beer in his left hand. He was dressed only in his socks and vest, and his beer belly hung over the elastic waistband of his shorts. He was struggling to hang his shirt on a hanger with his right hand. *Too many pizzas, mate*, Ed thought to himself, and wrote the guy off as a genuine hotel guest before moving on to chalet number eight, where the whiter light had been showing. Perhaps the differing light was down to a TV, or newer lamp bulbs, or maybe a computer screen.

Suddenly, he crouched lower, jumping back from the French doors as some instinct told him to move. Initially, he was adamant that he was alone, but now he got that weird feeling that someone was behind him. He dived out of the way, rolling onto his back away from the wall – and from the butt of a weapon as it caught him in the back. It didn't hurt him but he felt it as he tried to stand and face his assailant. Then came the second blow. This time it hurt, dropping him back to the ground. Lifting his arms to defend himself, he pulled at the attacker's legs and wrapped both arms around them as if in a rugby tackle, trying to bring the man down. Pushing up and pulling in, Ed tried desperately to unbalance the guy as he took more thumps to the head and neck from the heel and butt of a nine-millimetre Uzi. Finally bringing the man to the ground, Ed got in several punches as payback. They scuffled in the dirt for a couple of minutes until the attacker pulled the trigger. Ed felt the swish of the bullets pass his leg as they both fell to the ground. He backed off and kicked the intruder away. As he did so, the man lurched to his feet and started running. Ed gave chase across the motel backyards, over a low fence and through some wasteland. Goat bells jangled; they had reached a goat pen. Ed ran round the pen as the assailant jumped the fence and vanished into the dark. Rounding the other side, Ed stopped and listened. Over his panting he heard another's gulps of air and the rustle of clothing on the goat shed roof. Then, calming his breathing more, Ed heard repeating, low-volume clicks by the goat shed wall. It was the fence manufacturer's way of warning that the metre-high nylon-mesh fence was electrified. Looking around to check the shed and fencing, Ed crept to the power box and silently pulled at the plug, slowly rocking it left to right until the plug pins were released from its power source, rendering the fence safe to touch. The low-volume clicks ceased. The assailant flattened himself more on the goat shed roof but with one foot still slightly overhanging to the sloping rear.

Sneaking around, Ed swung up wildly and caught the man's trouser leg, dragging him back down on top of him. Leaning back and pulling with his right arm around the man's neck, Ed punched the guy in the left cheek from behind. The man struggled to turn, and only managed to grab Ed's shirt collar. They both hit the ground and the melee continued as each man tried to gain the advantage. Ed punched and punched while taking reverse headbutts to his nose and chin. They rolled in the dirt, straw and goat crap. The other man pulled out a short knife and was trying to jab behind him with his left hand whilst keeping hold of Ed's shirt collar with his right. Ed improved his headlock and wrapped his legs around the stranger's waist, squeezing with all his might to hold him still while he went for the stranglehold. As the men rolled across the ground, and in sheer desperation, Ed reached for the hanging cable running from the exterior plug on the shed wall and, in a split second, decided to strangle the man with it, but he could not find enough length for the job. Then, as they rolled and scuffled toward the fencing itself, Ed realised the cable's true purpose and changed tack. Releasing his legs from the man's waist, he kicked away to fend him off, pushing him away into the fence. The man's feet soon became entwined in the black-and-yellow wire and nylon mesh. Slashing out with his knife, he caught Ed around the waist, tearing his shirt as the blade scratched his skin. Ed groaned and kicked again, cursing and swearing, but releasing his grip on the man. The man jabbed more with the knife. Ed kicked harder whilst the thin, plastic fence poles collapsed under the weight of the two men. Lurching to his left a little, Ed then kicked right, deliberately forcing the man to roll further into the netting, who was now becoming ensnared in the mesh. Leaning forward, Ed punched his assailant in the mouth and nose, and blood and snot flew out as his head reeled back and hit the ground with force. Again, Ed rolled the man violently to his right, and this time his flailing arms became ensnared. Rising to his knees, Ed hit him again in the dead centre of his face. Once more the attacker's head jolted back, and he let out a low bellow. Ed leaned over him and grabbed more of the fencing net, but the short knife came up from the elbow of the assailant, between the gaps in the mesh and caught him in the stomach again. This time there was blood as the dagger ripped into his abdominal muscles. Falling on his backside, Ed rolled to his left and, stretching hard, grabbed hold of the electric cable, which was still dangling from the shed wall. He stretched and stretched with his fingertips to get a good grip on it, all the while kicking at his assailant who was still wielding the knife. Ed eventually caught a firm hold of the plug and, lying on his back, he looked up to find the fence's electric supply box and socket. With a huge effort, he stretched one more time, connecting the male plug with the female socket. He continued kicking and punching as the assailant tried to untangle himself. Ed then threw himself to the side to break free, knowing he had to be totally clear of the tangled mesh. Clawing at the fence posts, he gave one final kick as he twisted away and then thumped the plug fully into its aperture.

There was a click and a buzz, and then came the screams. The man fitted and jolted as the electrified fence became a lethal blanket which shocked him time and time again. Ed rolled over onto his front and leaned up on his elbows as 220 volts of current pulsated through the man's body. The man rolled onto his side as his body flipped like a netted fish out of water. His eyes bulged wide and bright in his bloody, snotty face. He screamed in terror as he convulsed. Fury ran through Ed's mind as he stared for a few moments, watching his foe go into shock, his body jumping in sequence with the electric pulses. Gasping for air himself, wiping his bloody mouth, Ed leaned in. 'Who are you working for? What do you want with Esther?' he said, reaching for the plug.

The man pleaded with his eyes for help, staring back at Ed, gasping for air as his heart jumped out of sync and then stopped beating altogether. The bare skin on his hands, face and neck began to burn.

The man did not reply. His eyes widened and bubbles of snotty mucus blew from his broken nose. He could only gargle on his own spittle. His heart had stopped pumping and his brain was already being starved of oxygen.

'Who are you with?' repeated Ed, falling backward as he gulped in air, reaching to unplug the wired fence.

The man's head dropped to the ground. Agent Rabis was stone-cold dead.

Ed stretched up and unplugged the electric fence and took another gulp of air. Then he heard shots, lots of them, and ran fast back to the hotel.

~

The whole incident had lasted only a few minutes, but the goats had bleated and jangled their bells more than enough in the quiet of the evening and the noise of the scuffle had travelled across the quiet little town. To a local it may have sounded like nothing, but Tess thought that Ed was probably 'in the shit.' She trembled and looked around nervously. A shadow ran across the empty fuel station forecourt from her right and into the small motel car park, then around the back of the building. She froze, uncertain of what to do. Then she saw the shadow move again; this time from the left of the building, from the tea room next door. Her brain tried to compute the speed and timing. She could not tally the two events.

There was no way the first shadow could have got to the other side so quickly, and with a gulp, the penny dropped. There was more than one of them.

She moved forward for a better look. Defying Ed's instructions, she hastened closer by two blocks to see if this really was the time to call the cops. The second shadow had stopped dead in its tracks and dropped out of sight behind the parked cars on the motel forecourt. Tess stopped too and crouched in terror, not knowing if she had been seen or not. A dog barked, a scooter hummed somewhere across town, and a goat's bell jangled again. Then there was silence once more. Tess could feel her pulse thumping in her chest and throat. She ran through Ed's instructions again, and felt the controls of the still-lowered pistol. She felt nauseous. She was cold, but at the same time clammy with sweat. *What should I do?* Calming herself, she kept her eyes on the second shadow. Her heart slowed. Then, in the silence, she heard a deep *putt-putt* sound and then noises from chalet number eight.

~

A black watch glinted for a split second as his pistol silencer met the glass of the motel room's lounge window. Through the gap in the faded, tatty curtains he saw the girl being pushed under a table. A man sat reaching for a laptop with his left hand whilst his right gripped a pistol. The other, taller guy was loading an AK-9 Kalashnikov assault rifle.

Just as the assassin took his first shot through the glass, the man with the pistol stood up. Taking the hit in his lower back, he fell to the floor. Esther screamed and instinctively dropped lower, huddling under the table as another shot zipped past her head into the wall behind her. Staring at the smashed window, she tried to decide her next move, but then froze again. Within seconds of the first shot she heard several very loud bangs as debris flew around the front door. Bullets slammed through the wood and out into the corridor, sending shards, splinters and plaster flying. The tatty curtains danced like puppets as the missiles tore through them. The taller agent walked past the bathroom toward the front room. He had emptied his rifle's ammunition at the door and window, reloaded and continued to shoot toward the front room's exterior wall and door.

The assassin had dropped to the floor for cover and backed away up the corridor as the debris flew. Looking through the dust and the smoke, he now had another problem. Down the hall, in the shadows of the motel reception, he could just make out a man in black beginning to rise from his crouched position. Sure of his, the man unleashed a reign of terror from his Uzi, hosing the corridor with hundreds of rounds. In the confined space, the noise was deafening and the damage unimaginable as plaster, wood, glass and concrete exploded everywhere. The assassin shot back in controlled one-two taps, covering himself in a hasty retreat. In the melee of shooting, and under cover of the smoke, the assassin ducked down and slipped out of the fire exit at the far end of the corridor. Stooped, head low, but with his pistol held high, like a bolt of lightning he darted back up the length of the exterior corridor and car park to the reception. Catching glimpses of his new quarry through the broken windows, he dropped and rolled into the corridor behind the man in black, firing off three more double-tap rounds. Jacob, the second Mossad agent, fell to the floor in agony.

~

Tess had decided to make a move before the gunshots had started. She had followed the first shadowy figure to the hotel. Hiding in the dark, her nerves had only allowed her to go as far as the cylindrical wheelie bins parked by the corner of the building. There, she had frozen and heard the firefight unravel. The assassin had not seen her in his haste to survive the hail of bullets. She had tried several times to move but, hearing the thuds of the silenced shots, had frozen again, a blanket of fear and dread falling over her once more.

After what felt like several minutes of silence, she found herself creeping down the motel hallway. She was scared and alone, but moved on impulse, looking for Ed and a girl she had never met. It was dark and her eyes strained to see what was going on. Clutching the pistol that Ed had given her close to her chest, she quietly and slowly pushed her head around the door frame and into the eighth apartment. A desktop lamp had survived the blizzard of bullets and the room was still dimly lit, although the lamp had been knocked over. A laptop lay on the floor amid cups, glasses, pizza boxes and beer bottles. Tess choked on the gun smoke and rubble dust. The room was a mess, with debris all over. She looked down at the floor, wary of standing on anything or anyone, or making a noise. Trembling, she moved around the door frame for a closer look. Tess's eyes adjusted to the light. A dead man was slumped on a sofa and an upside-down table lay broken with bullet holes and ripped wood; the door to the hallway was hanging open with its top hinge shot off. She could see through to the bedroom and the open French doors leading out to the back, and felt a slight breeze as cold, fresh air flowed into the destroyed front room. Looking down, her eyes fixed onto the dead guy. Noticing a small key-fob like piece of black-and-silver plastic in his left hand, she went to pull it free.

As she leaned forward, she felt a sharp stabbing pain in her right side and exhaled involuntarily as her lung was punctured with precise skill. She groaned, but a hand covered her mouth, jolting her head backward and gagging her before she could cry out. She fought back and struggled, and felt a metal watch strap scratch her lips as the hand repositioned itself over her mouth. She tried biting, but the hand raised her chin higher and she felt another stabbing pain, this time sharper as the blade slipped into her neck just above her hyoid bone and through her mouth and tongue muscles. Tess gagged. The air from her right lung had rushed from the slit between her ribs, and she began to sink toward the floor. As the knife was pulled from her neck, she felt cold air rush in through the gaping wound. The hand held her mouth shut and only released her when she had suffocated. She fell on top of the dead man.

~

Ed was running hard, back to the hotel room where the carnage had unravelled. Out of breath from his fight, he drew several heavy breaths as he came across Tess slumped on top of the dead man on the sofa. Stooping, he pulled her toward him, holding her as if she were just asleep. Her blouse and jeans were covered in blood. He put his hand over her weeping neck wound but knew he was far too late. He fell back onto the arm of the sofa, pulling her with him. Her body was still warm but lifeless as he squeezed and cuddled her, quietly screaming between his gritted teeth, 'Fuck, fuck, fuck. I am so sorry, Tess. I am so fuckin' sorry. They will all pay for this, I swear.'

Her arms slowly fell down to her sides. Her left hand came to rest, palm up, on his knee, and her fingers relaxed open, revealing a small black-and-silver PNY pen drive. Trying not to fill up, Ed pocketed the pen drive.

Behind him, out in the corridor, Ed heard someone walking very slowly on the broken glass and rubble. The footsteps were deliberate; this was someone who did not want to be heard. He carefully slipped from under Tess's body and let her fall gently back onto the sofa. Laying her head down, he backed out through the bedroom doorway.

In seconds, he was on the run and heard the footsteps behind him match his speed. With the *putt-putt* of a silenced pistol, he felt bullets fly past him. He ran into the blackness of the night, into the backyards and through the goat pen where the dead guy still lay entangled in the fencing. He jumped the fence and doubled back on himself, off the wasteland and into a cobbled side alley toward the main street. As he ran, bullets hit the street wall and the cobbled road. Running for his life, Ed cleared the three blocks back to where they had left the Jeep. Within seconds, he had the engine running and shifted the car into reverse. Before he could shift back into drive, another bullet pinged off the rear quarter panel. Finding drive gear, Ed hit the accelerator and floored the pedal. The tyres screeched on the dry ground and propelled the machine forward as more bullets rained down on him. He headed down the main road and up toward the mountains.

~

The assassin ran after the SUV and fired his last volley of shots, knowing now that its driver was far more capable than he had imagined. Sirens wailed and voices pierced the night air. The assassin spun round as another shot rang out and ricocheted off the clay wall just behind him, mortar and dust hitting him in the face. He ducked low, fired back twice, and then melted back into the shadows.

# 32

## KARASINIR MOUNTAIN AREA, 290 MILES FROM THE SYRIAN BORDER

Driving well clear of the town and several miles back up into the mountains, Ed found a quiet place out of sight to park and tried to pull himself together. His head was in pieces and he felt sick and stressed. He climbed out of the Jeep and walked around with his hands on his head, trying to piece the puzzle together. Swearing and cursing, he downed a full bottle of water from Tess's bag. Emotionally, he felt like shit, but the sickness subsided as rage took over. He kicked the Jeep's wheel and screamed, then grabbed hold of one of the vehicle's roof bars and shook the Jeep violently. 'It was just supposed to be a fucking holiday!'

Grabbing his mobile from the car's console, he checked for calls and messages. There were several. One was an earlier garbled BBM message from Esther. He scrabbled to the next SMS message.

*ID unknown: You have a new voicemail.*

He looked at the voicemail icon, which was flashing the number two. The next text message was the same. He called his BlackBerry voicemail service. The automated voice read from a script. 'You have two new messages. Press one to play.'

He pressed number one on the keypad.

'Your first message is four minutes long.'

It was from his old boss. 'Ed, this call is probably being traced so I won't say much. There's a lot of shit going on here and I've been ordered to stand down, but before I do, I know you're confused and really pissed off, son, but stay calm and level-headed for us. We'll get her back. Esther doesn't really know who she is. She was born an Iranian and they're using her as bait. There's a guy called Creighton gonna get in touch. I've been assured he's safe. He knows more and can fill you in.'

Ed grabbed Tess's phone and looked at her screen. She also had several missed calls, all from the same number. *It must be her reporter friends in Ankara*, he assumed, and pressed last number redial. He listened patiently as the dial tones clicked and connected. He was keen to know what they'd found out.

'Hi, Tess!' said a Scottish accent. 'Thank God for that; I've been trying to call you for ages.'

'This isn't Tess,' replied Ed.

'Oh well, pass her on, pal, if you don't mind?'

Ed thought for a second, not wanting to waste time with explanations. 'Err, she's busy, tied up. I'm Ed, the missing girl's boyfriend. Tess is talking to some Turks and asked me to call you back. You've got some info for us?'

Tim Blake-Leigh's tone was excited. 'Absolutely, my friend. Abso-fucking-lutely. You'll need to pull up a chair, I think. Firstly, your hotel and the local police station are becoming a media frenzy. They're swarming with reporters so I wouldn't go back yet. Secondly, the police are looking for you both; they say you've jumped bail or something like that, and there is a warrant out for you.' He continued to explain but the signal became poor. Eventually, the line went dead.

Ed used his own phone again and redialled his voicemail. The second message was from Tom Creighton asking him to call urgently and saying that he could meet Ed in a village outside Adana and that, unless her kidnappers were stopped, Esther's destination was more than likely to be Iran. It was imperative that Ed cooperated to avoid any more trouble. 'Whitehall have asked your boss to step aside for a while and let us handle it from here. He's left you a voicemail.'

*Fucking hell!* Ed thought. *They even know that my boss has left me a voicemail?* He rang the number Creighton had left.

'Hello,' said a smooth southern English accent.

'Who's this?' asked Ed abruptly, trying to check out the situation.

'Is that you, Ed? It's Tom here – Tom Creighton. Are you okay?' Tom asked in a seemingly genuine tone.

Ed was in no mood to be pleasant. He was fed up with everyone else knowing what was really happening. 'Where have you been while we were getting shot at?' he demanded.

'Don't worry, they don't want you—'

Before the MI6 agent could get another word out, Ed interrupted. 'Don't worry? Don't bloody worry?!' he repeated. 'My girlfriend gets kidnapped and my reporter friend is dead, you arsehole. She's dead, you hear me? Assassinated by one of your lot.'

The line went quiet. 'Oh shit,' replied Tom. 'Then this whole thing really is going tits up. I'm so sorry, Ed, but you shouldn't have got involved. You should have left this to us. You know it's Esther they want, don't you? We've been busy following a car from Syria. Because you got involved, it's gone tits up for them too, so the Iranians have sent a new vehicle with fresh men to rendezvous with Esther's kidnappers. They're at a farmhouse in Bandarak.'

Ed was silent and thought for a while. 'Is that so?' he said sarcastically.

Unmoved, Tom continued. 'Yes, it is. And that's where I want you to head for. Now, drop down onto the main highway 715 east, to Karaman, then the E90 past Adana. Then the D410 east until you pass the village of Kazikli. Follow the long left sweeping bend, then a mile down the straight you'll see a road sign saying Deliosman and a cattle-crossing sign. Turn right there and follow the metalled road to a T-junction, but then go straight on and up a dirt track. Keep climbing. Directly ahead, over those mountains, is where I need you to be. Get to the summit where there's a tourist info board. You're headed for the village of Bandarak down in the valley. No lights. Your Jeep will cope with it. Do you have a map? It's about five miles east of Maydan Akbis. Pick up the well-used track and when it meets the tarmac, dump your car in the trees there. Do not drive through the village. Walk down the south hillside. Stay off the road. Pass a shepherd's dwelling and then on the left, up to the farmhouse. In the courtyard you'll see a battered silver Ford and a red Citroën. I'll be here waiting. I'll call you back and leave these directions on your voicemail, so don't pick up.'

Ed hung up and weighed up his options. His best bet was to hook up with this Creighton guy and find out what else he knew and if they could work together to get Esther back. Tess had been killed by the CIA, he thought. If the Iranians were involved and it was all about nuclear stuff, then the CIA would definitely be involved, and possibly, if they were collaborating as they usually did, MI6 as well. So, who were the others? Who were the sniper on the motorcycle and the other guys back at the motel? Tom had said, 'I'll be here,' not 'I'll be there.' *That means he's already there, so he must be ahead of the game.* But Ed's boss had said, 'They're using Esther as bait.' Bait for what? He didn't know. Tom also said, 'Drop down onto the 715.' *That meant that he also knew where he was.* That thought enraged Ed. He decided the best thing now was to have a face-off with Creighton and see what could be done. His mind flashed to Esther in the boot of the car, or being beaten by the kidnappers. His blood boiled and he began to shake with anger once more. *Calm down, Ed*, he told himself. *Calm down. Let's go get her.* He turned out the car's interior light, switched the external lights to side lights only, slammed the Jeep into drive and sped back down the other side of the mountain toward Adana.

Using Tess's scribbled map and Tom's directions, he made his way onto the main road and drove through the night toward Kazikli. Then, as instructed, he turned off the highway and onto the dirt track which led up the mountain. Focused on the terrain and staying on the track, without headlights and in almost complete darkness, he drove up the hills and over barren scrubland. Slowly, he reached the ridge and the Jeep levelled. He stopped momentarily to see a scattering of village lights down in the next valley. Continuing and without any notice, he crossed the border into Syria. He was now driving through olive groves on steep terraces. Crawling on down the steep inclines, the four-by-four's tyres picked their way over the rugged terrain and eventually lowered him onto a main track. Finally, sure enough, that track met asphalt. As instructed, he dumped the Jeep out of sight in the vegetation. Before he abandoned it, he reversed it, facing outward, ready to go, with the keys hidden. Then he removed Tess's camera and collected all the remaining ammunition and firearms from the trunk. He stuffed everything into the agent's holdall, including the automatic rifle, which protruded at the unzipped end. Throwing the bag over his shoulder, he walked, careful not to be observed.

He made progress and was soon in the vicinity of the farmhouse. Lying on his belly, he used Tess's camera to scan the area. Zooming in on the farmhouse with the telephoto lens, he saw the courtyard and the two cars, just as Tom had described. So far so good, but if 'they' were using Esther as bait, Ed smelt a rat and he couldn't trust this Tom guy either. He would have to use great caution and get an accurate measure on the situation.

After forty minutes of sneaking around and a full recce on the farmhouse, he decided it was time to enter. He called the number, which was duly answered by Tom Creighton. He assured Ed it was safe. During the call, Tom put on an outside light and came to the door. He showed himself to Ed and beckoned him in. Ed came down from his vantage point and eventually accepted the hospitality of the Syrian farmer and his wife. Tom told Ed to relax as the farmers could not speak English and were on the payroll, and MI6 also had another villager on the payroll to keep check on the farmer's loyalty. Then he took Ed to a window at the back of the farmhouse and pointed out a dimly lit building across the valley. He explained that this was the safe house the Iranians had chosen to use and that the handover team was already there, but they wouldn't move Esther just yet. Ed asked why this was, and how Tom knew all this. They would set Esther to work at the earliest opportunity, said Tom. Her task was purely computer program functions and she could do what they wanted her to do here at the safe house. She may even stay in that safe house for some time but if compromised they will move her deeper into Syria or even take her back to Iran. She would not be harmed, as she was a vital piece of the puzzle and the whole kidnap mission would be worthless without her, and therefore, neither would MI6 be crashing in on the safe house. Sitting at the farmhouse table, Ed began to interrogate Tom, pumping him for details on the full story and who the other guys were. Tom passed him a beer. They both took thirsty gulps from their bottles.

Tom began to explain his position. 'This Stuxnet operation has been ongoing for several months, and we have a sleeper cell in Iran whose only job is to uncover its source and then report back.' He leaned on his elbows and looked right at Ed. 'There are elections all over the place, you know?' he said, half asking, half telling. 'US, Germany, Iran, and even us back home.' He paused and took a long swig.

Ed still wasn't feeling the love from the agent yet and remained on the defensive, half listening, but thinking about where Esther was. Using his peripheral vision, he tried to keep an eye on what the farmer couple were doing. Then, staring back at Tom, he quietly said, 'Go on…'

In his polished Oxford accent, Tom continued. 'Along with the Yanks, our leader is very keen to correct a lot of negative press over invading Iraq. The people need some rather more positive news from the Middle East. The Iranian Prime Minister, a well-publicised Israel-hating fanatic and Muslim hardliner, has sacked, imprisoned and even tortured hundreds of staff, many of them Jews, from the Bushehr and Natanz nuclear plants, because of their so-called incompetence in the face of the problems this Stuxnet virus has caused. Setback after setback has made it impossible for the PM to deliver on his electoral promise of nuclear power to the nation and, by extension, making Iran the strongest, most powerful and most feared state in the Middle East, and to hell with the infidel West and Israel. You know all this, though, right?'

Ed played along and agreed, though in truth he knew nothing of the Stuxnet virus.

Tom continued. 'It was, therefore, crucial that this didn't happen, and Whitehall wants to know why we've been left out of the loop. It was either the Yanks or the Israelis or both, and it is my job to find out who planted it and how, then report back.' He swigged again. 'Unbeknown to the Iranians, on Whitehall's instructions it was our Intelligence Service and our sleeper cells that steered them toward the virus and a possible solution.'

Ed had decided to keep his latest information from Tess's reporter friends, and so maintained his air of ignorance, testing the MI6 agent to the full. 'Why?' he asked. 'What for?'

'Well, because we were left out in the cold on it, without any say or control, but Britain is being blamed and we have elections happening too. We have to know who is behind it,' replied Tom, casually unbuttoning his shirt cuffs and rolling up his sleeves. 'We agree one hundred per cent with the deployment of the virus. Very clever, causing uranium centrifuges to blow up, thereby prohibiting the enrichment, thereby holding the Iranians back by at least fifteen years or so, giving us plenty of time to flush out the perpetrators and get an edge over them. It was my team that pointed the Iranians in the right direction and offered them a solution. MI6 has even provided the safe house across the valley. We've led them like lambs and put it all on a plate for the Iranians. Well, actually, a dish. A satellite dish. We've even been sending bogus TV broadcasts to them. We've installed internet and Sky TV in the safe house.'

Ed was becoming impressed. Pennies were dropping all over the place. Trying to look innocent and in need of Tom's help, he finished his beer and looked down at the table. Putting on a pathetic, meek tremble in his voice, he asked, 'So what's the plan now, then?'

Tom stared back. 'Well.' He paused a moment. 'The first problem in this saga is Russia. They have seen a massive drop in their fuel revenues as European leaders look for cheaper and safer oil and gas. So...' he looked over and beyond Ed's head, 'to bolster their national income they want the American Microsoft and German Siemens systems to suffer heavily and for the virus to go on causing more damage, so they can slide in and sign up the Iranians for a multimillion-dollar deal using their own computer systems and hardware. The second problem is...' he paused again, '... you getting involved.'

As Tom said the word 'you', and as Ed's eyebrows raised, the Syrian farmer, acting on a silent cue from Tom, thumped Ed across the back of his upper neck with a thick wooden stick. Ed heard a loud bang inside his head and what felt like an electric shock shuddered up from his shoulders. It was like an instant brain freeze from too much ice cream. Then he felt sick and dizzy. His nose spattered blood as his head fell onto the wooden table, bounced once, then came to rest on his right cheek. Tom was on his feet instantly, pulling out a pair of handcuffs. The Syrian farmer hauled Ed upright and shouted for his wife to come through from the kitchen. Within seconds, Tom had Ed's hands cuffed behind his back. The two men grunted and groaned as they carried Ed's huge dead weight across the rear courtyard and into a stable, Tom telling the farmer to be careful with him. The farmer's wife dutifully followed with a saucepan of cold water. As they dumped Ed on the stable floor, she pulled a grubby tea towel from her dirty apron and began to wipe his bloody and snotty nose.

The farmer gestured to a metal ring on the stable door, and agreeing, Tom secured the cuffs to a metal hay-net ring fixed to the wooden wall. Putting on an exaggerated Etonian accent, he told Ed, 'Sorry, old chap, but it's for your own good.'

Both men left, leaving the old lady to bathe Ed's broken nose.

~

Ed hadn't totally passed out and was still conscious when they carried him into the stable, but, fighting the massive headache, he felt himself dozing for minutes at a time. He did not know how long he had been there but guessed it was a couple of hours. A lack of sleep, high emotions and stress, the sheer dread of losing his beautiful Esther, and now being clubbed on the back of the neck had totally exhausted him. He wanted to sleep but dared not, and so he continued to drift in and out of consciousness, hearing and seeing Esther. He also saw Tess lying dead in his arms, and the torrent of bullets, glass and debris at the hotel.

Struggling to breathe, with his hands cuffed above his head, Ed woke with a start. He was shivering, and through a window he could see that the night sky was crystal clear, where the heat of the day had dissipated high into the atmosphere and dawn was now on its way. Shaking his arm, he realised he was handcuffed to a metal ring. He used it to pull himself up and look around. On one side of the stable were piles of hay bales, all neatly stacked. He had been lying on concrete against one of the wooden doors, to which the metal ring was attached. To his left was a wooden wheelbarrow, and inside it a yellow plastic storage box. In the box, filthy and covered in straw and dirt, were several items for animal care: horse brushes, scissors, disposable rubber gloves, bottles of mosquito repellent, sprays, olive oil, and cloths. Ed scanned the wheelbarrow for anything that might be of use. All he saw was an old metal hand shovel, a dustpan and brush, and an empty plastic bottle. He looked up at his handcuffs. They were military-issue cuffs and he should know, he had worn a few in his time, and apparently, they weren't too difficult to open if you had the knack. But he didn't have the knack. He remembered that a guy had once shown him how to release them in seconds, but he'd never been convinced, knowing he was being fleeced. *It was just like the movies,* he thought. A load of shit, and he was deep in it. Forcing himself to think hard, he hauled himself up on the metal ring and dug his feet into the ground. With some grunts, like a contortionist, he twisted his body, crossed his arms and stood. The ring's fixing plate had moved under his weight, as had the ancient wooden door. Wrapping his fingers around the ring, Ed suddenly dropped his weight down and felt the cuffs dig in. The ring moved again and its fixing screws were pulled a little out of the wood. Ed repeated this process over and over, until eventually, tired and out of breath, he was free of the door and free to move around. He rubbed and nursed his wrists whilst he rummaged in the yellow box. There were brushes, plasters, some tools and an old, plain, brown box containing several syringes. With one hand, he grabbed the brown box and read the instructions.

*Acepromazine maleate: For use on horses and similar large animals. This medication has a depressing effect on the central nervous system, causing sedation and muscle relaxation, and reducing spontaneous activity.*

Ed heard a door close and someone coming toward the stable. Behind him, to his right, was the other door. The one they had dragged him through. Ed grabbed four syringes from the box and fell to the floor. Aware of someone approaching, he lifted his cuffed hands, to mimic the metal ring back in its normal fixed position, then feigning unconsciousness, lay silent, facing away from the opening door. The farmer entered carrying a tray of food including a generous piece of loaf, a jug of water, a metal cup, and a box of headache tablets. Just as he stooped to place the tray, Ed rolled around, swinging his cuffed hands and the metal ring, lifting his arms high and swinging them upward to the man. The farmer let out a cry as Ed slashed the fixing plate across the man's lower jaw, dragging skin and blood from his face. The tray fell and clattered and Ed pushed up and over, forcing the man to fall onto his back. Within seconds, Ed straddled the man and drove a syringe down into the farmer's shoulder and, with his left thumb, injected the horse sedative into his bloodstream, not knowing if the dose would kill or sedate the man. Ed released the syringe and covered the farmer's mouth, muffling his cries as he lay on the floor.

Ed began searching him for the handcuffs key. Releasing himself, he ducked low in the darkened stable as the farmer's wife approached. She had heard her husband's cry and was crossing the farmyard as if she was on a mission. Ed looked around again. He could find nothing to assist him. As the small woman entered the barn, he grabbed her mouth and picked her up by the waist. He shushed her and told her to be good. After a few minutes wrestling with her, he finally cuffed them both to a more secure wall bracket and checked his watch. It was nearly dawn. He pushed the four headache tablets and all the bread into his mouth and gulped down the whole jug of water, then went back into the house. The Citroën had gone from the courtyard. *Perfect*, thought Ed. The farmer's beaten-up Ford suited him fine.

# 33

## MI6 SAFE HOUSE, BANDARAK, 5 MILES INSIDE THE SYRIAN BORDER

He jumped the farm's back wall and ran up the elevation, then crept into the bushes from where he had observed the farm earlier and retrieved the black bag still containing the camera, ammunition and firearms. When Ed had used Tess's powerful zoom lens to scan the farmhouse earlier, he had mapped out in his head a simple overview of the village and its roads. Ed returned to the farmhouse and stole the beaten-up Ford, driving it out onto the main dirt track. As he breached the first crest, he turned off the engine but left the ignition on. The car rolled quietly down the track toward the west side of the village. After a few hundred yards, using only the handbrake, he quietly stopped the car way below his last recce point and breathed in big gulps of air. From the farmhouse it was all downhill; first to a junction, then a left turn, taking him down to the south junction, from where he could loop back on himself to the safe house. The village, of possibly no more than thirty dwellings, ran east to west and was flanked by two main tracks. One ran east to west across the north of the village. The other ran parallel across the south, with both roads meeting up at the forks, approximately two miles to either side of the village. High up, above the north road, hidden, was where Ed had left the Jeep. At least he still had one get-out-of-jail ticket hidden in the shrubs. If he approached the safe house from the west, the Iranians and anyone else would be suspicious, but coming in from the east, as if from the Syrian interior, would give him more credibility. Listening and on full alert for any compromise, he slowly released the handbrake, rolling the small car along, downhill. He heaved and pulled at the steering wheel as, without its engine running, the little car had no power-assisted steering. Using the handbrake and what pressure was left in the brake servo, he guided the car down the winding track with surprisingly little sound. Only the crunch of gravel on the rubber treads gave him away, and Ed steered out of the well-used ruts onto softer verges to minimise noise. He arrived at the junction. Without stopping, he checked both ways and, using what inertia he had, pulled on the wheel, forcing the vehicle sharp right and on, down toward the main junction.

As the car descended, he checked continually for a view of the safe house. He found a good spot and pulled up, steering the car off the track into a gap in the bushes to maintain his covert approach. This was one of Ed's specialities. Patience. Sitting and watching. Making notes, he fixed on the exact location, taking bearings from all around, then he listened for several minutes. A cockerel sounded across the sleepy valley. Happy that he was alone, he moved quietly from his location a number of times to fully recce the target. Using the powerful camera, he zoomed in and scanned left to right, constantly adjusting the focus. To the rear he saw cars parked out of sight in the courtyard and some stables and outhouses attached to the house. Completing the courtyard enclosure was a barn furthest to the rear, with a one-metre boundary wall, leading away, on the far left of the property, back to the front and forming a driveway out to the road. He zoomed in closer on the windows. The curtains were drawn in all rooms but in one window they were not closed enough, revealing a glimpse of a table where Ed could see a female figure working at a laptop under a dim yellow light. A man walked past the window, busy talking to someone who was not in view. Ed saw only one guy on lookout. That made at least three, but he guessed there were more. There he sat for another thirty minutes, completing his study. Ed kept moving back to the woman at the table. The light was poor but he was sure it was Esther. He felt emotions rush through his brain as his thoughts intensified from anger to rage, from hatred to violence, then back to controlled calm. Slowly, he began to plan his kills. His new count told him there was four men, but he also scanned for observers and snipers outside the house. His mind flashed back to the sniper at the dam. *Could that have been another one of the Arabs?* he thought. *Where are they now?* Satisfied with his covert operation, he psyched himself up for his next task. He focused on formulating a detailed plan with backup deviations and scenarios. Several ideas swirled in his head but, worried he would bog himself down with more problems, he decided to make his move.

He placed the camera in its bag and checked the semi-automatic rifle. He patted his pockets for anything that jingled, removing his watch and any loose change. He reached behind into the waistband of his trousers and pulled out a pistol. Pulling its barrel slide back, he cocked the hammer, inspected the ejection port, then removed the safety catch. He checked that the automatic had a live round in the chamber ready to go. Happy, he returned the gun to his waistband, loosening his belt two notches to allow its easier removal, then pushed his socks down out of sight into his suede boots, rolled up his trouser cuffs and tightened his shoelaces so they were snug. Not comfortable, he retightened his belt one notch and pushed the pistol's muzzle down behind it, against his back. He was already sweating. He put on the *shemagh* headwear that he had taken from the farmhouse along with the Syrian farmer's dishdasha, adjusting it in the rear-view mirror to ensure that he didn't look like some Marvel Comic Arabian knight. He stooped under the car for some dark, greasy exhaust dirt, mixed it with grit and gravel, then rubbed it into his hands and face to cover his European skin tone. Knowing his blue eyes were a giveaway, he searched the car for sunglasses. Finding a pair tucked into the sun visor, he slipped them on. Grabbing sand and dirt from the ground, he wiped his hands up and down his cream dishdasha, pulling the robe down to cover his trousers better. Bending low under the car once more, he carefully scraped some grease off the steering mechanism with a stick and spread it over the engine cylinder head, knowing that it would start to smell and burn when the engine was up to running temperature. He removed the carburettor cap and pushed in a sugar cube he'd taken from the farmhouse, checking that the sweet white lump dissolved fully into the liquid. Then he squashed a small plastic bottle, half full of water, down the side of the engine, jamming it between the engine block and the starter motor. He dirtied his hands, eyebrows and checked he had fully concealed his hair once more and got into the car. Composing himself, he allowed the engine to tick over for a few minutes and warm up, then slowly, the smell of burning grease intensified.

Finally, he set off. Convincingly, he was now driving west toward the village and the house on the main route, from the direction of Shengal and Aleppo. They wouldn't be expecting that. The car started to sputter as the sugar in the petrol took effect. Backfires flew from the exhaust, giving off the occasional blue-

and-yellow flame. Now they would definitely know he was coming. The backfires were as loud as gunshots, and the more backfires the better. He knew Tom would be somewhere close by, watching, but he was past caring. If they were using Esther then he was quite happy to be the spanner in their works. And with the secret agents on his tail, he needed to be fast enough, so he could be in and out in no time. Besides, at least he was fairly sure the CIA and MI6 wouldn't shoot them down in cold blood. Or would they? He did not dwell on the possibility and refocused on his plan to retrieve Esther. *It was just supposed to be a bloody holiday*, he thought again. *How the hell has it gone so wrong?*

The safe house grew nearer. He could feel himself sweating and ran through the series of events and how he was going to allow them to unfold. As he drove slowly toward the front of the house on his left, looking only at the dashboard and the road ahead, he dipped the clutch slightly and simultaneously jabbed at the brakes. The car appeared to falter. Intensifying these actions and following several more backfires as the little engine struggled to burn off the sweetened petrol, he timed it to stall approximately twenty yards or so past the house. It was important to have the car in the right position for a getaway. He knew Esther would be dazed and disorientated after the fight and he would have to lead her straight to the car. For this reason, and for speed, he would make sure both doors were wide open. Also, bypassing the house and not stopping at or before it made things look more convincing and kept him at a safer distance initially. Controlling his anger, he thought for a moment. He actually would not mind hanging around for a full-on firefight and killing every single one of them, but his real priority was getting Esther away from the house. Knowing he was being watched by the guard on the veranda, he stopped the car as loudly as he could, its partly deflated tyres crunching over the stones of the temporary track. Its nose and grille dipped and lifted as if choking for air as it sputtered. He slapped the steering wheel and cursed in muttered pretend Arabic. He'd stopped just before a gentle descent, in full view of the safe house. Smoke from the red-hot axle grease escaped from under the bonnet and the smell of burning grease filled the air. As if on cue, the plastic bottle trapped inside the engine split, spraying its boiling contents across the engine bay, hissing loudly and adding to the stench.

The guard could smell it too but suspected nothing. He just saw a local idiot driving a piece of junk. Inside the house, the Iranian agents were on their feet and on full alert. They had cocked their weapons and assumed their defensive positions immediately on hearing what sounded like gunfire. Ed counted one on the porch and two at the windows. *Right on cue*, he thought. He'd expected four, but guessed the driver was sleeping somewhere in the back rooms. The agent at the front window was mouthing and gesturing for the guard on the porch to get rid of the peasant and remove the car off the road. Thumping the steering wheel, Ed opened his door slowly, checking around him as he did so. Through his mirrors, he could see the guard having a good look at his seemingly failing car. After opening the front passenger door, he slipped out of the driver's seat, attempting to look like a tired and desperate man. He left his driver's door wide open and made a fuss of trying to open the bonnet, pretending to look for its release mechanism. Moving around to the passenger's door on the right, he pulled the release handle under the dashboard and made some complaining noises. He left the passenger door wide open also. He lifted the bonnet, looking in as if in disbelief, and feigned tinkering with the engine.

Looking up at the house through the gaps between the bonnet's hinges, he could see the front door. It was exactly as his reconnaissance had indicated: an old solid single-storey drystone farmhouse. Four wide steps ran up to the porch. From the front to the right and leading to the rear was a path flanked with a metre-high whitewashed wall. The veranda at the front led left to the farmhouse courtyard via a cobbled driveway. From his earlier recces, Ed had deduced where the kitchen was and decided there was a reception area behind the front door. After that, the rest was guesswork, although the kitchen had a door to a rear yard which led to the stables, with three mud-walled outhouses and barns all linked to the main building. The property was run-down and weather-beaten, with poor repairs visible, though it had evidently defied the elements for many a year. Outhouse doors were ajar, allowing hens and goats to wander in and out freely. Ed had last seen Esther working at a laptop on a dining table at the rear of the house about thirty minutes earlier. The question was, was she still there or had they moved her to one of the outbuildings? They must have moved her closer to the getaway car, surely?

He left the handbrake off and allowed the car to fall back slightly in first gear against its gearbox. He was sweating heavily. It was gravely important that what he was about to do was executed exactly according to the plan. If this went south, he would either be shot dead or end up in some godforsaken prison for the rest of his life without a chance of probation. By walking up to the building, he would be opening a massive can of worms and there'd be absolutely no going back. This time he did not have backup from his seasoned teammates or a well-oiled government machine that could kick in if things went bad. He was on his own. He could not believe he was in this predicament. 'It was just a bloody holiday,' he said to himself yet again, and, with a deep inhale, he stood up straight, looked ahead at the dwelling and thought through his two-minute plan again. As he moved away from the car, he threw his hands in the air, cursing his selfish nephew for not maintaining it, and asking Allah for patience. Pretending that he'd only just noticed the Iranian man who had been sitting on a white plastic chair on the veranda, he slowly approached him.

'*Arkadasim, arkadasim,*' ('My friend, my friend') Ed said in poor Turkish. '*Yardim luften?*' ('Can you help me?')

The man slowly moved toward him, holding his sidearm down behind his leg and below the wall out of view, but Ed knew he was armed. He indicated that Ed should head down into the village, but Ed was now in full flow.

'Ah! Praise to Allah, my friend. Can you help me? My car has broken down; it's my nephew's fault for not maintaining it and he will be punished, I swear, God willing.'

The Iranian agent looked cross. He was about to tell Ed to go away and that he could not help, when Ed's acting skills took hold as he moved into the farmhouse driveway, drawing the Iranian down the steps, off the veranda and away from the view of the windows. He would not let the man get a word in; he just repeated his plea for mechanical assistance. In seconds, he was within yards of the agent. Lifting his arms in the air one last time in a request for forgiveness, Ed brought them down and, through a slit in his robe, pulled the pistol out of his waistband with his right hand. The agent spoke no more. Ed fired off the round before the muzzle had a chance to touch the man's skin. The ballistic tip ripped through the agent's neck muscles below his ear and out of the top of his head. The man lifted off the ground a little and, with a push from Ed, fell backwards onto the gravel courtyard, eyes staring blindly up into the morning sky. The pool of blood only emerged once the body levelled out.

Ed continued his rant, as if nothing had happened and the last shot was just another backfire from the car, all the while drawing closer to the house. At the front door he looked through the windows. Continuing his one-sided conversation, he ducked under them and slipped around the veranda to the back door. He was pumped with energy, emotion and adrenaline. Taking deep breaths to steady his hands, like lightning, he swung open the back door. The dining room was empty as he'd expected, but in the front room the second guard was crouched as if peeping out through the window from behind the tatty old curtains. Rolling into the room, and before the agent could turn from the window to raise his weapon, Ed planted his first two shots in the wall behind him, causing the Iranian to duck instinctively, putting him off balance. Within a split second, Ed fired his second two shots, hitting the agent once in the shoulder. The final two shots came in rapid succession as Ed found his aim, deep in the agent's suprasternal notch, below his neck and the other into his upper chest, drilling through his lung and out his back, shattering and splintering the bone as the bullets exited, into the walls plaster. A yell on the first hit transformed into a gurgle on the second as the man grabbed at the curtain for support. The material held him for only a few seconds, then he slipped to the floor as the rail gave way.

Ed was already under the dining table, snatching a pen drive from an abandoned laptop. Then, scouring the room and hallway, he was on the move again, through the open door. Where were Agents Three and Four? He wanted to call out to Esther but dared not for fear of being compromised. He rolled over on his belly into the hall, then paused for a second. *Bedrooms or stables?* he thought. His goal was to rescue Esther, not to deal with the agents. They would have rushed her out the back to the stables and the cars, he decided, and quickly got to his feet, propelling himself out into the hallway behind the front door. He looked down the hall and counted three doors to its left. He had to clear them and be sure the rooms were empty before he could move on. Silently, stooping as low as he could, he quickly checked each room almost from ground level, prepared to shoot upward from the least expected position. The bedrooms had been used, each containing bags of clothes, food packets and water bottles. Satisfied there were no people present, he sprinted back to the kitchen and out into the rear yard. Crouching close to the stone wall, he listened. He took a deep breath and exhaled slowly, then sucked in another good gulp of air and released it quietly. All was still and silent. Between him and Esther were three outhouses and a stable, and then the barn. Ed weighed up his options. They had whisked her out more quickly than he'd expected, and he still had to find at least two guards.

Moving toward the barn, as low as he could for cover, he crept past the three outhouses and entered the darkness of the stable doorway. As he went to stand, something made him stop dead. Legs bent, thigh muscles taut, holding his body like a loaded spring, he froze. Beads of sweat ran from his forehead. Slowly, he leaned in toward the wall in a vain attempt to hide from it. The red dot passed over his left hand and moved along the wall, then down across the courtyard floor and hovered at the barn door. Ed froze and thought, *Tom or the CIA?* He couldn't possibly know, so inched along the outer wall to see if the dot followed him. If it did then he'd been spotted and was on target. The dot lingered on the doorway, then vanished, then reappeared by his foot. He stared at it, knowing that whoever controlled it could eradicate him there and then. The dot moved slowly back toward the barn doors across the courtyard. Ed's eyes followed, but he remained motionless. The dot came back to him, danced at his feet, then returned to the doors.

'Tom,' Ed whispered. 'Thank Christ.' He moved to open the lower half of the divided stable door.

Inside the stable he struggled to adjust his eyes to the deeper darkness. Slowly, he began to make out horse tack and blankets hanging from a beam. A chicken clucked outside, and somewhere he heard a goat bell. He crept silently through the building, into the adjoining barn and up to a parked car. A BMW four-door saloon, it looked very clean. *An improvement on the Merc*, he thought. Looking back at the doorway, he saw the laser beam drilling down onto the floor. Maybe Tom had him covered, or at least anyone trying to leave. That idea was comforting but he could not rely on it. As far as he was concerned, he was still on his own. With his pistol at the ready, close to his chest and its muzzle almost against his chin, he raised his head above the BMW's bonnet. He could just make out another car parked behind: a gold Nissan. Ed concluded that the kidnappers must have stolen it back in Aydogmus.

# 34

## MI6 SAFE HOUSE, BANDARAK, SYRIA

Ed was about to make a move around the rear of the BMW when he heard a noise very close to him. He froze in anticipation. Lowered on one knee, he felt in his back pocket and pulled out a four-inch Colt G10 pocket knife. He unfolded the blade and silently locked it into position. Gripping it tight in his left hand, he inched forward to the corner of the car. The noise grew louder but he struggled to identify it. Then he realised it was the sound of breathing. His heart thumped in his ears. The carotid artery in his neck beat like a drum. He took a huge breath and raised the knife high. As the breathing came closer, he prepared to strike. Poised ready, he heard a soft snort next to him, and felt warm breath on his face. Eyes glinted at him out of the darkness. Then a bell jangled gently. *Bloody goat bells!* Ed thought. They had become infamous due to the downfall of an SAS team, dropping them into a whole world of hurt during the Iraq invasion, and since then the practice was to take goats out. The military mantra was 'thousands of pounds sterling, men, kit, and years of training ruined and given away by the clang of a goat bell.' Grabbing the bell to silence it, he dragged the goat in toward him, twisting its collar tight to strangle it whilst, with his left hand, forcing his knife deep into its neck. Only when the hilt of the knife hit the goat's hide did he stop pushing. Then, with a flick of his wrist, he twisted the knife for good measure before extracting the blade. The goat dropped immediately, making no noise. Pulling back on its collar, he stabbed its neck again then dropped it as the blood gushed out. A chicken clucked and a goose honked somewhere in the distance but there was no other disturbance or sign of activity. Ed leaned back against the car, wiped the blood from his face and hands, and composed himself.

Out of the silence it came from behind, cold and swift. A loud metallic clang rang inside his skull. The shovel hit and made him feel sick. He fell forward onto all fours with his face in the goat's bleeding neck as he heard the attacker move around him. A shot rang out and Ed scrabbled to turn. The red beam of light jumped, and he instantly assumed that its operative must have night vision. The shot missed and the weapon fell silent. The attacker ducked and vanished around the far side of the car. Ed shook his head violently, trying to clear the shock and relieve some pain as quickly as he could. Then he got to his feet and moved forward. Another shot rang out and the BMW took a hit in its rear quarter. Ed ducked a little and found his attacker had returned. He grabbed his shirt and pulled him down, throwing his left fist up into his nose. He felt the cartilage make contact with his knuckles as the agent pushed his hand into Ed's face to push him away. Both men went into a spin as they grappled for a good hold on each other's clothing. Ed wanted the man face on for another punch, but the agent had other plans. A knee to Ed's groin stopped him momentarily and he groaned in pain, but clung on. They tumbled away from the car and into a pile of hay, empty food buckets and sacking. Ed tried to outmanoeuvre the man and force him into position for a stranglehold. The agent was strong and determined but Ed was far heavier, and used his weight as an advantage, grabbing the man's hair and pulling him backward. Ed felt for his knife but all he could find was the dead goat's hoofs. The blade was too far out of reach. A clump of the agent's hair came away as he elbowed Ed in the ribs, winding him. The agent wriggled free, pushing one knee into Ed's chest and trying to pull his gun from its holster at the same time. Ed felt another knee in his groin and the pain ran up through his stomach. He lunged and punched at the Iranian until he got a foot into his belly and kicked him away into the wall. As he went, the man pulled at Ed, inadvertently helping him to pull himself up. Ed's hand found the long, thick wooden handle of a pitchfork standing up in the hay to his left. He pushed it into the man's face, splitting his nose and lip, then stepped back and kicked him between his legs with all his might. The man dropped to his knees in excruciating pain, but put his hands out to save himself from the fall. As he knelt on all fours, Ed kicked him in the face, sending blood and teeth flying. The man struggled to get up, only making it back to his knees. Ed thumped him on the neck, forcing him down again, then lifted the pitchfork high and brought its tines down on the back of his neck, tearing skin and arteries as it impaled him face down on the hay and onto the pallet beneath. With a massive scream the man lifted his arms to his throat and fought to release himself. Ed fell backward onto the rear bumper of the Nissan. Within seconds, he found the knife under the dead goat, and his pistol, which had fallen from his belt in the skirmish. The man was grunting and groaning but Ed focused his attention on Agent Four, who was nowhere to be seen. Neither was Esther. Unless…

In the heat of the moment, he had seen the trunk end of the car moving. At once, he crouched and struggled for the lock button. He opened it and there, to his relief, lay Esther, bound and gagged, eyes wide and terrified. The Iranian secret police had been quicker than Ed had expected in getting her in the car ready for a getaway. He lifted her up and she kneeled to face him. He cut one of her zip-tie restraints, releasing her from her bonds. He pulled the rag and tape from her mouth and kissed her, then looked into her eyes. She was clearly frightened but otherwise seemed unhurt. He went to help her out of the car, when suddenly a bullet whizzed past his head. He ducked and pushed Esther back into the trunk, slamming the lid shut. Another shot rattled across the stable, sending splinters and years of dust flying into the air. Ed tried to make out where it was coming from, and wondered why Mr Laser Man hadn't taken Agent Four out. Another bullet slammed into the car, and Ed flattened himself on the cold barn floor. Rummaging under the car for his attacker, he caught his hand on the exhaust and yelped. The car had been running, ready to go. They must have known he was coming. *Tom again*, thought Ed. Then he saw the agent's feet sidling around the car toward him. Lying on his left side, he wriggled to hide as best he could under the car's rear. He tightened his grip on the knife and momentarily rested it on his right thigh. As the agent crept into his vicinity, Ed lunged, bringing the knife up into the man's left calf. The man screamed and stumbled away, and Ed slashed again, this time at the man's right Achilles tendon. The agent fell to the floor in agony. Ed rolled out from under the car, jumped up and kicked him in the face, then, deciding Esther was safer out of sight, he opened the trunk again and told her to stay where she was for a little longer.

Quickly, Ed moved to open the barn doors. They were still chained and padlocked shut. Ed's swift assault on the safe house meant the kidnappers had not had time to open them. He moved back to the stable door through which he'd entered. On his way in, he had passed an empty oil drum, which clearly had been used for burning garden waste. Hastily, he scoured the rear of the building and found some petrol in an old metal can and some cloths and paper. He dragged the drum across the courtyard cobbles to the barn doors. He stuffed a heaped pile of dead olive branches, twigs and wood from an adjacent wheelbarrow and soaked them with the fuel. He tore up and knotted some cloth, knotted the paper, soaked them in petrol and placed them in the centre of the drum. He had just created a combustion sandwich. To the top of the pile, he added more olive branches, which he doused in more petrol. Then he tipped the barrel to about fifty degrees against the doors, laid out some dry cloth on the top edge of the barrel, and with a cigarette lighter from the Nissan, he lit the dry cloth, but only enough to allow it to smoulder. Then he poured the remaining petrol across the doorway and splashed the old wooden doors and frame with it. That was all he wanted for now, and he rushed back through the stable to the car where Esther lay.

He jumped into the driver's seat and started the engine. Slamming the clutch down, he found reverse and held the car still on the brake pedal. He waited anxiously for what felt like ages. Finally, there was a boom and the barn doors bellowed inward as wood splinters rained onto the car's bonnet. The smouldering cloth had ignited the newspaper and then the fuel-soaked mass of leaves. The fireball shot out of the barrel and into the barn door, forcing it to buckle at its old hinges. Within seconds, the dry hay and old wood were alight. The whoosh of air needed to fuel the explosion was sucked into the barrel and sounded like a bomb. Ed slammed the Nissan into the stable doors, causing it to stall. Ed restarted the car, reversed and repeated his action. As the two injured agents recovered themselves, they cowered in fear at the noise and took cover as the flames blew in. With the accelerator flat to the floor and the rev-counter needle redlining inside the gauge, the Nissan engine screamed and shook violently. Ed dumped the clutch and the car crashed out through the burning doors into the courtyard, sending timber, embers, pallets and burning hay everywhere. Chickens flew, squawked and cackled. Splinters, smoke, muck and dust rained down on the car. Esther rolled in the trunk, thumping and banging as the car bounced through the yard and to a halt. The fourth Iranian agent, shocked and with ears bleeding, staggered to his feet and shot at the Nissan, but it was too late.

Ed also heard the distinct sound of a rifle and the metallic clang as several shots pierced the thin metal car panels. The rear window shattered. Ed slammed the car into first gear and again hit the accelerator as hard as he could. The Nissan's front wheels spun wildly on the dusty cobbled surface as they scrambled for some traction. Rubber burned and smoke rose. After what seemed an eternity, the car lurched forward, allowing Ed to get the revs on again and find second gear. The car shot out of the yard quicker than Ed expected, swinging left as he pulled on the steering wheel, trying to avoid a collision, but the car made contact and ripped off the open door of the abandoned Ford, forcing it to stall again.

Limping around the BMW, the mobile Iranian had attended to his colleague and gingerly pulled the pitchfork from the other's neck. Dripping with blood, the surviving agents crawled into the second motor. Wiping his face, Agent Three drove the BMW out through the gaping, burning hole in the barn and down onto the track, bashing into the Ford and Ed's stalled car. Ed turned the ignition key again to restart the Nissan. As he tried for reverse gear, Agent Four reloaded his weapon and fired at the fleeing vehicle, but was eventually made to duck back in and take cover as they too began to take bullets.

Ed shouted to Esther to hang on as he straightened the wheel for his last manoeuvre, only to be forced down for cover by more shots. He slumped low, and pushed on the accelerator, forcing the car to reverse into the BMW. Turning to his left, Ed now had a view of the second dwelling, set back to the left of the safe house. A hail of bullets was coming from there. He only needed five more minutes, and then they would be out of range and heading back toward the border, into Turkey and to the nearest police station. In first gear, he corrected the car one more time and accelerated before hearing another shot. This one was different: louder, and it gave out a heavy clang. This one sounded more like a missile. It had buried itself on target, deep inside the car's engine block. This shot was a sniper's shot. Ed stamped on the pedal but the machine refused to respond. The Nissan gradually came to a halt. They had only managed fifty yards or so from the safe house. Outflanked, outmanoeuvred, outgunned and outnumbered, Ed swore as he scrambled out of the driver's seat and, still under fire, crawled to the trunk to pull Esther out. They would have to continue their escape on foot. As he and Esther sheltered behind the car, Ed fired back in the direction of the second house and the BMW. From across the road came more shots, but these were not directed at him. They zipped overhead and slammed into the stonework of the second property.

Approximately one hundred yards behind, screaming down on their BMW, were rifle shots. It too took shots to its windshield and tyres. Under overwhelming firepower, both men jumped out and fired back, using their car doors as shields. Ed returned fire also. Both cars were outflanked: from the right, by the superior firepower of two CIA agents and from the left by the MI6 agent.

From ahead, they were also being pinned down by an anonymous sniper. Ed had opened all four doors of the Nissan for cover. Looking back toward the BMW, he spotted Toms red laser dot on the car metal over to his right, who had now moved into a kneeling stance behind a small electricity supply building, beckoning them. Ed told Esther to make a run for it and get to cover behind Tom. She cowered and huddled into Ed's crouched body. He grabbed her and squeezed her tight.

'Don't worry, babe,' he whispered. 'This is it now. I'm gonna get us out of all this. It's time to go home.'

In sheer terror, she nodded. Firing two shots, Ed tapped her shoulder, indicating to her to run whilst Tom covered her escape. She was up and moving. Her lungs sucked in large gulps of air.

'Go, go, go,' shouted Ed, and fired back at the Iranian hijackers.

A hail of CIA bullets rained down on the BMW whilst Tom's automatic rifle kept the sniper at bay. As she ran, Esther veered to her right, to avoid getting too close to the BMW and her kidnappers. Swerving, she heard more shots and felt gravel spit up from the ground. Something snapped in her leg, and she fell. The bullet had only clipped her but it was enough to take her down. She felt the searing pain. Then someone grabbed her and yanked her backward, almost pulling her arm out of its socket. She twisted around to see who it was. Agent Three had her by the wrist and was dragging her toward the car and his colleague, who was emptying his pistol at the CIA operatives. As Esther was pulled behind the car door, slowly, the gunfire petered out. The valley fell quiet as if in an interlude, allowing each team to weigh up their next move. Esther was now fully in the crossfire. All that could be heard was the reloading of weapons.

Then one of the Iranian agents shouted to Ed, 'Give up the girl. She will not be harmed.'

With his arms outstretched, keeping his gun trained on the man holding Esther, Ed leaned against the rear of the car, then slowly allowed himself to slide down onto his backside. He weighed up the situation. He would never give her up, but he was out of options.

Then Tom shouted, 'Ed, can you hear me?'

Ed looked down and saw the red laser dot on his chest. 'Yeah,' he replied desperately.

'Give Esther to me! Do a swap. We'll come get you. You can handle it better than she can. You're okay with this sort of stuff. We can negotiate a release for you.'

Ed thought a while and weighed up all his options. Short on ideas, this, he thought, was probably the only workable plan. He had the two pen drives containing all of Esther's work. They were what the Iranians needed. Exhausted, he conceded and relaxed his grip on the pistol, allowing it to swing loosely in his right hand, then slowly raised his arms in surrender. As he went to stand, a single shot was fired from behind him. He stooped again. Tom let off a double tap with his rifle to drive the sniper back into cover.

Ed dropped his weapon and held up the two pen drives in his left hand. 'I have the pen drives. I have them here,' he shouted to the kidnappers, waving them about slowly, as if to tease. 'This is what you need. Let her go. I know all about the virus. I know who, what, when and why. I know the whole plot and who's responsible. It's me for Esther. That's the deal. Let her go.'

Agent Four looked at Agent Three with eyes wide. Fixed firmly on Agent Three's shirt collar was a red laser dot. The Iranians looked at each other and, after what felt like an eternity, came to the same conclusion, as they too wished for a more favourable outcome. They agreed. Agent Three maintained his grip but pushed Esther an arm's length away from the car, and Ed stood to walk toward it. Another shot rang out, and more return shots volleyed back up the valley, this time from the CIA agents, who were now in communication with Tom.

Ed ran the rest of the way to the car, holding out the pen drives. 'Let her go,' he shouted, and the Iranian released his grip.

Limping badly, Esther ran as fast as she could and did not stop until she was a good ten yards or so behind Tom. As she ran, the sniper attacked again, flicking up grit and gravel at her heels. Tom and the CIA agents returned fire. Esther threw herself to the ground for cover, making herself as flat as she could, and Tom and the Americans let off yet another volley of automatic fire.

Ed dropped behind the BMW's driver's door and immediately felt the cold, bare steel of a sidearm pressing into his throat, then another in his lower back. Agent Four looked at him with hatred. Pressing his gun harder into Ed's neck, he said, 'Get in.'

Agent Three tugged at Ed's shirt and he was dragged into the back of the car. Within seconds, the BMW was reversing hard back toward the safe house. The driver flicked the steering wheel, forcing the huge saloon into a J-turn. Its nose swung around in a broadside sweep and the driver found first gear easily. Within seconds, Ed was on his way toward Aleppo.

# 35

## KASAN PROVINCE, SYRIA, 200 MILES FROM THE IRANIAN BORDER

The only sign of life was the sound of his heart beating in his chest; the air coming and going, in and out of his nostrils. Ed heaved to take in more oxygen in an attempt to slow his heart rate and compose himself. He wanted to listen. It was the only sense he could rely on just now. His knees hurt from kneeling on the hard, rocky desert ground. Adjusting his position, he found some softer sand. He sat back on his heels, his arms hanging at his sides with remnants of their plastic restraints still in place and red-raw marks around each wrist. But for now, he was free. The vehicle had long gone. The dust had settled and the sound of the engine had faded into silence. He heard the wind and felt the vast, desolate isolation. He pulled at the hessian cloth which had been his blindfold, tugging it away from his neck and over his head. Sucking in another massive gulp of fresh air and looking out over the plateau and the valley beyond, he rubbed his eyes to adjust to the bright sunshine. His head made a quick 180-degree sweep. Moving slowly, he rolled over to his right and fell back on his bent knee, spinning around to check behind him. He saw nothing but the barren, empty desert. The cold morning air intermittently created little whirlwinds, kicking up sand and grit. The horizon went on forever, only giving up its flat, level contours to the mountains in the distance. He was alone and miles from anywhere.

It was still early and there was plenty of time. He just had to sit and wait. He was exhausted and wanted to sleep, but knew that was impossible. To his right was a wadi, a deep, dry riverbed gully that would have been created years ago by flash floods. He noticed more wadis and gullies. He was parched and craved water. He thought of the dry riverbed. How old were the wadis, and why were there so many of them here? Surely that meant he was close to a water source. He felt he looked thin. The past few days had been mentally and physically draining and he hadn't eaten or slept. He fell back and sat on his backside to rest. Placing his arms over his knees and looking down, he saw a mixture of blood and urine on his trousers. The gunshot wound to his left calf was agonising and the tourniquet dug deep into his muscle, but was doing its job. His broken nose throbbed and his ear had stopped bleeding. To his left lay one of his Iranian kidnappers, stone-cold dead.

The fight had been vicious but the outcome favourable. The gunshot had been fatal and merciless as he'd intended. As his captors brought the car to its resting point, he had figured that after the long drive they would be momentarily preoccupied with stopping and stretching their legs. He had been right. The one driving had got out, walked a few yards toward the gully, adjusted the bandage on his neck and, with his back to the car, begun to relieve himself. Agent Four had been just as keen to free himself from the car's stinking hot and dusty interior for yet another smoke and to attend to his injured leg. When he'd told Ed to get out, he had made his move. Obeying the instruction but choosing which side of the car to climb out from, Ed had run at the guy who was peeing. His eyes had locked onto the pistol in the holder on the kidnapper's belt, and he lunged and grabbed at it, knowing he would have only moments before Agent Four was on him. If he could pull it off, he would fell one of his captors in seconds, matching him one to one with the other and giving him far better odds. It had not gone to plan. Still peeing in the dirt and caressing his neck wounds, Agent Three had heard his approach, turned to defend himself, and deflected Ed's attempt to take the pistol from him. In a frenzied scrabble, Ed had managed to twist around and push the man's own gun deep into his swollen and bloody neck. Grabbing him from behind and throttling him with his left arm, he should have pulled the trigger, but was already taking a battering from the second guy and also, being literally peed on caught him by surprise. Refusing to let go as Agent Four beat him around the head and neck with his gun, with sheer determination and a will to survive, Ed wrapped his legs around Agent Three's waist to pull him down to the ground, winding himself as they hit the gravel. Agent Three fought hard and pushed the gun down away from his neck, forcing the trigger to activate the hammer. Ed heard an explosion and then felt a piercing pain as the bullet shot through his left leg. In pain and shock, he screamed out loud, but then used the adrenaline rush to his advantage. With all his might, he tugged on the agent's neck, suffocating him more. As they rolled in the dirt, he managed to push the gun back into the Iranian's throat, squeezing his fingers against the trigger. A second round left the chamber and ripped through Agent Three's head, spitting blood and flesh everywhere. Ed jerked his head back and closed his eyes, but the detritus still spattered his face and neck. Sinking down onto his back, he felt Agent Three's body fall limp on top of him. Agent Four still followed, kicking Ed wherever he could, his face, his head and back, all whilst trying to level his gun at Ed for a clean shot. Fearing another blow to his head, Ed quickly lifted the dead guy's right hand and adjusted his position to defend himself. As Agent Four rained down more blows, Ed let off three more shots. Agent Four stumbled back and fell. Ed pushed Agent Three's corpse aside, freeing him to stand up, but the pain in his leg wouldn't allow it. He fell back, wincing. Agent Four had taken a hit but Ed could not tell where. Winded and in agony, his eyes had tried to follow his opponent around the car, intending to take him down with another shot, but it had all happened too fast. Ed had fired, but the agent was already driving the vehicle away from the scene.

Working back from his last known location, following an almost-constant drive of approximately eight hours and with little knowledge of the area, Ed guessed that he was still somewhere in Syria and, without any checkpoint border crossings, near the Turkish borders with Iraq. If so, then he would indeed be near a river. That would explain the presence of so many wadis. Using the early morning sun as a reference, he concluded that he was on a main road headed east. That meant northern Syria or northern Iran. But he could not be in Iran, as the Iranian cavalry would have emerged by now. He also deduced that the valley floor looked greener and more arable, which again indicated irrigation. If he was correct, then ahead of him, hidden below the horizon of what looked like flat desert ground, would be the river Tigris, but he needed to be cautious, as if it was the Tigris, then he was dangerously close to the Iranian border.

He decided he was right. He had a vague grasp of the layout of the Turkish and Syrian borders. Earlier in his career, serving as an operative in the Middle East, it had been necessary to memorise strategic border towns. Getting caught – or worse, being found with maps – was never an option, and the Turkish border via Syria or Jordan had been the get-out-of-jail card. Memorising towns and villages had been crucial to a safe escape. After World War II, where possible, the Turkish Ottoman and Persian borders had been geopolitically mapped out by the Western powers around natural water features, thus preventing one country having the upper hand of drinking or fishing rights over a neighbour. Lakes, rivers and coasts were divided up as part of the negotiations. It had been several years, but Ed's memory of his training was still good. Although he didn't know exactly where he was, he was working on it. He figured that if he was on the Tigris then he was somewhere in the Syrian province of Kasan and probably about one hundred clicks from Cizre, in NATO Turkey. He would have to take an educated guess. He asked himself if his captors had stopped the car simply to relieve themselves, or if a handover had been planned, involving a fresh team and a change of cars. He decided on the latter and therefore, could not relax. He had taken his chances with a fairly reasonable outcome, killing one and chasing off the other was good, but he still didn't know where he was. If this was the stop for a changeover then he could sit tight and wait for some transport. If it was just a natural break stopping point then he could not be too far from the border due to the travel time. He figured the exchange was intended to take place by vehicle and would require an isolated area away from goat herders and prying eyes. The less chatter the better, and these Iranian agents weren't fools. He had learnt that they were fairly good at their craft.

Stemming the bleeding and attending to his bullet wound, he considered his options. In his favour, he was naked: a term used when you were off duty and mixing with civilians, not carrying a weapon, maps or identity papers. He was under the radar and definitely off the grid. Not many knew about him or what was happening. Against him, he had blond hair and blue eyes and was obviously a Westerner. Without a yashmak or headscarf, he would be spotted instantly. Getting off the road was a definite option, but crossing the rough terrain would be difficult. Exhausted, dehydrated and with his newly acquired gunshot wound, traversing land would be a major problem and too slow a process. The gullies and wadis were deep and the terrain was rugged. He was miles from anywhere with no shade, and as a fair-haired European, his skin hated lengthy exposure to harsh sun. His bandana was now being used as a tourniquet. He didn't know if he was in the right position or not. He had to think. It was fifty-fifty. The drive in the Beemer may have been completed, in which case he was in the exchange location. The landscape was perfect for a covert handover. Ahead of him, slightly to the east, he could make out an elevated piece of land several hundred yards away. It was an outcrop of rock. Maybe he should head for that. It was certainly a better vantage point and he would be able to see anything coming for miles, but there would be no shelter from the sun and fewer places to hide. He decided to stay put; if any vehicles came, at least he would hear them early enough to climb down into the wadi out of sight. Losing blood, he forced his eyes to stay open, looking down at his wound. He decided to sit tight and sort out his dressing, rest a while, then reconsider his options. Falling back on his good leg, leaning against some boulders and mud, in a world of pain, he began to attend to his left calf.

~

Several hundred feet above, the helicopter shot up through the valley as if out of nowhere, startling the Iranian agent, who instinctively ducked down in his seat as he drove the only road east. The chopper was gone as quickly as it had arrived, but he knew its intentions. Braking hard and pushing down the clutch, he shifted from fifth gear into second. Bleeding from under his left arm, dropping a shirt he'd been holding to the wound with his right hand, he threw the steering wheel into a full right lock. The car obeyed and its tyres dug in, turning the vehicle on the asphalt road. He pushed the engine to the maximum before any gear change. The car accelerated and followed the helicopter back toward the changeover point.

~

From a distance, Ed could hear a dull, atmospheric thumping noise. He stopped fixing his dressing, panicking that his position would be compromised, but excited that maybe a handover was imminent and he was in a drop zone. He looked up and listened harder. The noise was definitely mechanical and getting louder. Cars and trucks engines did not reverberate in the air like that. As the aircraft neared, he knew from the *thump-thump* of its rotor blades, beating a downwash in the air, that it was a helicopter. Scrabbling to get up, he crawled from the roadside back into the desert dirt toward the wadi. Passing the agent's body, he pulled at its bloody shirt collar and dragged the dead man down with him into the deep natural trench. Moaning in agony as they hit the dry riverbed, and spitting out sand from his mouth, he made sure he and the corpse were covered in mud to camouflage them. The helicopter circled three times. Squinting as its fly-by raised more dust, Ed could make out its silhouette. It was a Westland Lynx, Combat Attack helicopter. He recognised it immediately. He had flown hundreds of missions in them. They were incredible machines, capable of speeds in excess of 240 miles per hour; the world's undisputed fastest combat chopper since its launch back in 1977. Even the Americans and their Apache Black Hawks couldn't keep up with it. He leaned back into the mud wall of the wadi to conceal himself and gather his thoughts. The primary users of these machines were friendlies: British, NATO or European. The nearest base it could have come from was Gaziantep. That was hours away, but within the chopper's remit, subject to fuel stops. The khaki-and-grey bird circled for the fourth time as the crew scoured the area for signs of life. The dust cloud thickened and Ed's visibility of the pilot and co-pilot diminished. Before losing them in the dust ball, he glimpsed the Royal Navy insignia and an RAF roundel toward the tail. *What a beautiful sight*, he thought. Certain it was safe to reveal himself, he pushed aside the dead guy and climbed out of the gully, trying to keep an eye on the chopper's whereabouts. Reaching the top of the wadi, he checked all around before leaving the relative safety of the trench. As with any extraction, and before the dust caused a complete white-out, it was imperative to remain vigilant before a last dash to board. Waving his arms, he began to signal to the door gunner.

Several hundred yards away to the north-east, the Iranian agent swerved his car off the tarmac and bounced it mercilessly up a short, inclined deserted track, spinning its wheels and scraping its underbelly. Approaching the summit of an elevated area, he screeched the vehicle to a halt, sending a cloud of dirt pluming up into the morning air. Jumping out, he rushed to open the trunk. Rummaging around, he found what he was looking for. Pushing his bloodied shirt against the wound under his arm, and reaching in with his left hand, he pulled out the rifle and snapped down the two short legs at the front of the long barrel.

~

Ed stopped in his tracks. He could see dust rising from a rocky outcrop, and just made out the silhouette of a car. The Lynx had landed and he could see at least four persons in the cargo hold. One was the gunner and winch man in his all-in-one khaki drybag jumpsuit and a white helmet with the black visor down. Two others wore civilian clothes under their camouflage jackets. Ed recognised one of these men as Tom Creighton and the other he did not know.

The fourth figure was smaller. A woman in a bright orange jumpsuit and a flight helmet with the visor up. It was Esther. She was alive, safe and well. Ed felt his body come alive. His heart thumped in his chest and he felt a surge of excitement. His adrenaline kicked in, rushing around his system, allowing him to move quicker. As soon as the metal skids of the helicopter had hit the ground, she had jumped down, and now she ran over to him. She came at him out of the swirling dust, running, stooped with her head down as per her brief from the crewman. The whirly bird's noise was deafening. Ed waved his arms frantically, dragging his left leg behind him as he limped toward the aircraft. He waved in vain as he tried to indicate to her to re-board the chopper, but she didn't understand. Hesitating, he tried to get the pilot's attention. It was useless. He wanted Esther back inside the dust cloud, out of sight. It was too late. She ran to him, throwing out her arms. His brain was fully engaged. As soon as he had her, he would push her to the ground and out of danger. She grabbed him tightly around his neck. He in turn grabbed her around the waist and, forcing his weight onto his good leg, prepared to knock them both over.

He never got the chance. Suddenly, a force beyond belief lifted them both toward the waiting helicopter. It was like a red-hot poker hitting Ed at one thousand miles an hour. Esther felt as if she had been snatched from Ed's arms, but then he was thrown into her as they were propelled to the ground by what seemed like a giant's hand. As they fell, Ed felt an agonising pain in his back and below his right shoulder. Esther's arms slipped from his neck, flailing. He fell on top of her with a dull thud, hitting her chest with his head and then rolling onto the gravel. Immediately, the two agents jumped from the chopper, aiming their automatic assault rifles. Following them from the back came another two men Ed hadn't seen. The gunner pulled back the hammer on the belt-fed L7 door gun, preparing his 'Gimpy', or GPMG (general-purpose machine gun). The pilot had already taken off. Within seconds, the agents on the ground laid down hundreds of covering rounds across the valley floor whilst the chopper rose high above its own downwash. The two soldiers were on top of Ed and Esther, shielding them with their protective vests and armour. Once the pilot had regained a clear view, he moved the bird forward and then strafed to port, flying quickly toward the rocky outcrop and then away to its port side again, allowing the gunner to unleash his mighty weapon from the open starboard door, accurately from a safe range and altitude. Within minutes of the first shot being fired, the gunner was spraying the car with hundreds of loaded rounds. It exploded in a fireball that could be seen for miles.

The agent's aim had been steady and true. The high-powered shot had ripped through Ed's lower right shoulder, shattering his scapula and puncturing his lung's upper lobe, then passing out through his chest and into Esther's. The wound was fatal, killing her instantly as it crashed through her ribcage and then her heart, out of her back and embedding in the chopper's fuselage. Lying on his back on the ground, Ed couldn't breathe. His blood flowed crimson and oozed into his lung as dust filled his nostrils. He was choking. Feeling paralysed down his side, convinced he had lost his arm, he reached out with his left hand, feeling for Esther. He groped for her hand and squeezed it, pulling her toward him. Looking up, dazed and winded like never before, he saw the metal bird return, with both its cargo doors slid back, open wide, moving up and away from him like the closing scene in a *M*A*S*H* episode. Over the roaring engine, the gunfire and men's voices shouting, he could hear the theme tune playing in his head:

*Suicide is painless.*
*It brings on many changes*
*And I can take or leave it if I please.*

His head fell to his left and he saw her. She lay there, eyes closed and looking peaceful and as beautiful as ever. Weeping, he gripped her hand. He tried to crawl over to her, to hold her, for one last time, but it was useless. He couldn't move. Haemorrhaging from at least one artery, he too was dying. He coughed, spitting blood. The pain in his back and chest increased, and as tears rolled down his dirty, blood-spattered face, a mist gently blurred his vision and he slowly lost consciousness.

~

Almost a half-mile away, on a dusty outcrop, the sniper remained still for some time, pleased with the conclusion of his operation. Then, checking the time on his Omega watch, he looked around and listened. Happy he had not been seen; he quietly dismantled his Dragunov sniper rifle. Sliding from under a camouflage canvas, he quickly gathered his equipment and packed away all evidence of his presence. Strapping the tarp to his Enduro motorcycle, which lay on its side, he lifted the bike up onto its stand. He strapped the rifle bag to the machine, threw a black rucksack onto his back, and straddled the bike. Pushing the start button, he clunked the gear lever down into first and squeezed the throttle. Gently, he released the clutch and the bike sped away, off into the desert.